THE SEER'S ASSASSIN

A CARTOGRAPHER'S WAR NOVEL

ALLISON ANDERSON

OLIVERHEBERBOOKS

For Gemma
Let's go to Disneyland soon, okay?

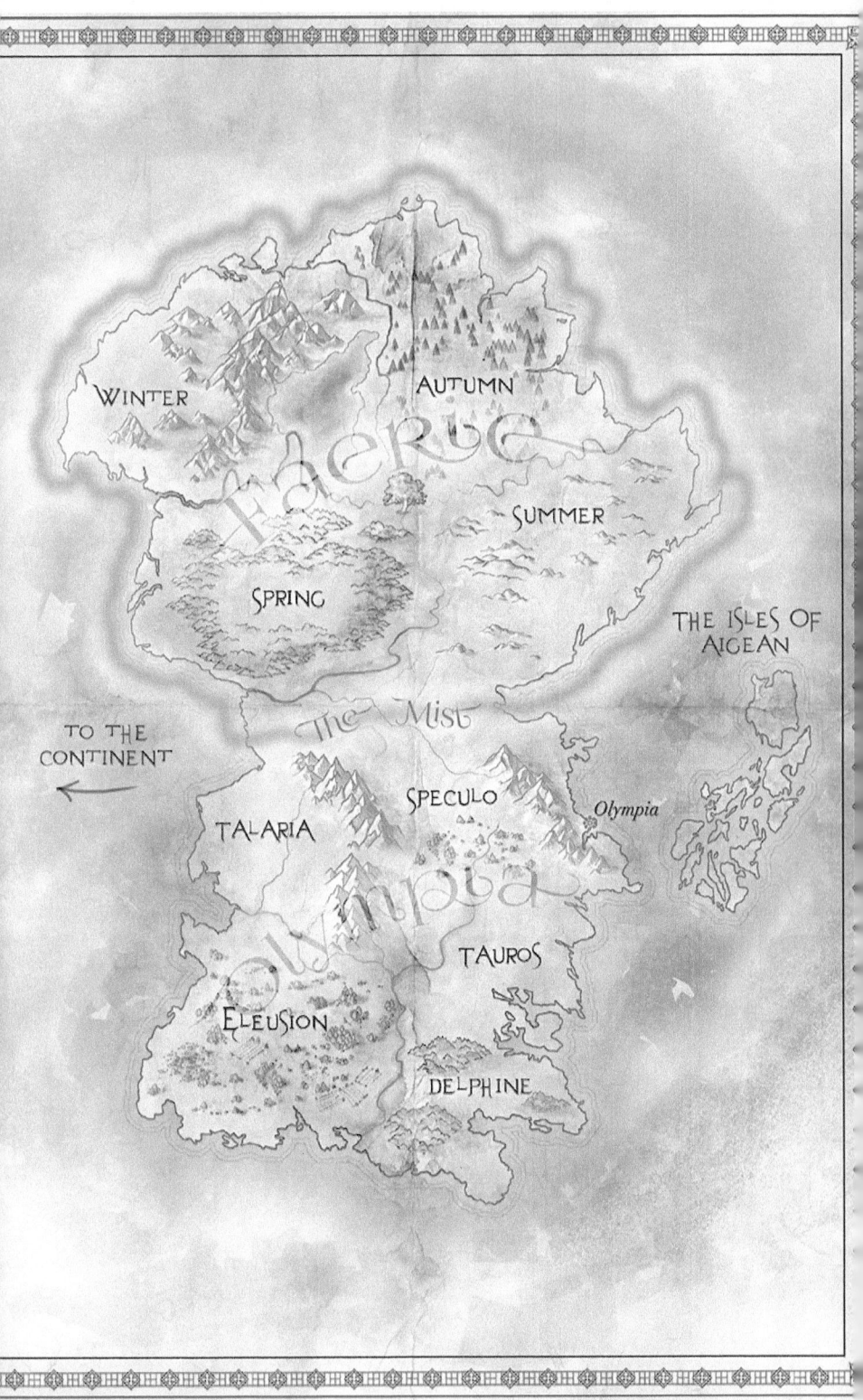

PROLOGUE: AN UNFORTUNATE LETTER

Every lie I've ever told I made to get me to this very moment.

PAULO MACGREGOR SET DOWN THE PEN AND RAN A HAND THROUGH his already unruly hair. The line was a bit melodramatic, even for him. He picked up the paper, ready to crumple it. Before he could toss it into the bin, he looked around him, finding dozens of balls of paper surrounding the bin. And his chair.

"Curses," he muttered. Of all the things not to receive visions about, this was what the Goddess chose? He set the paper down and smoothed out the crinkled edge. This was the single most important letter he had ever and would ever write, but he didn't know what words would help him. And he needed help.

With a sigh, he took up the pen once again.

I know this doesn't help my cause, but I pray our

friendship will overcome any animosity you feel toward me after you finish this letter.

His chest tightened and he pushed away from the writing desk to look out the window. The first light of dawn grayed the horizon. He could make out the still crumbled stone of the outer wall of Iatrus Castle. If anyone found out what he'd done to make this happen, he could be hanged. *Treason* wasn't the worst of his crimes. He'd allowed war to come to his kingdom. His lands. His home.

He returned to the desk.

There are so many things that would have made everyone else's lives easier. So many things I could have prevented.

Sometimes, when the moon rose high in the sky and only the stars danced outside, he could hear Diana cry in the room across from his. Mater still looked at him with those wise eyes of hers, but the lines around her mouth had transformed from the history of her smiles to the evidence of her hidden frowns. Even Iatrus Castle itself felt the weight of Paulo's decisions. His deceit.

But if I'd changed the future, this future would not be possible.

He reached a hand into his pocket and once again squeezed the gift he'd been given. His last chance.

With a deep breath, he pressed the tip of his pen to the page.

Let me start from the beginning.

1
THE BEGINNING

There will be blood dripping from Laurel's hand. Someone will call "First blood on Flumen!" and she will turn to them, her dark braid whipping as she does. Her brown eyes will widen slightly before her eyelids close once, twice, blinking the predatory light in her gaze away.

LAUREL DUCKED AS THE DAGGER SLICED RIGHT WHERE HER FACE HAD been a moment before. Her foot twisted on the rough dirt under her boots, but she kept the flow of her movement and came up behind her opponent. The sharp edge of her hand scythe swept down toward the girl's arm, but only met air.

I should have gone with the whip today.

Her opponent spun and brought the dagger up toward Laurel's ribs. Laurel jumped back and the dagger cut through the warm air in front of her nose.

The move opened up the right side of her opponent's body. Laurel flipped the scythe in her grip and pounced. The dulled edge thumped against her opponent's ribcage. An audible *"oof"* slipped between the girl's lips. There was no cut, but Laurel was sure there would be bruises later. Her opponent jumped back, but Laurel had been watching for it. She stuck the toe of her boot right under where the opponent stepped and watched their footing as they tried to stay on their toes. Dropping her scythe, Laurel grabbed her arm and used the heel of her other hand to smack her forearm. She plucked the dagger from the girl's grasp, careful to tuck the edges against the leather of her gloves and not the open tips where her fingers stuck out.

The opponent pushed her away, but not before Laurel could kick the scythe she'd dropped out of reach. It hit the ground in a spray of dust. The opponent pulled another dagger, but instead of taking another swipe at Laurel, she threw it.

Laurel's mouth twitched and she turned to dodge the blade. She watched its spin and caught it before it could hit the short wall behind her. She spun with its momentum, lifting it to her ear to throw back. The edge bit into the unprotected skin of her finger.

Blast it.

"First blood on Flumen!" she heard called.

Laurel blinked and real-life crashed in.

The sun beat down on the back of her neck and the tops of her shoulders where her tunic's sleeves were cut off to allow for more movement. Sweat dripped down her face and ribs and she could feel the dust from the outdoor sparring ring coat her arms. Her breaths came quickly as her blood pumped through her veins. She slowed her breathing and straightened from her stance.

Cheers went up around her. Two dozen of the Continent's best assassins stood around the ring, hollering taunts as the blood welled on Laurel's finger.

Their cheers meant nothing to Aspen though.

Aspen brushed small wisps of her ashy-blond hair from her cheeks. "I almost had you!" She reached for Laurel's hand and the dagger she'd caught. "How do you do that? My spin has only gotten faster, and you still manage to catch it."

With a small smile, Laurel passed the dagger back to her. "Because you keep getting faster, I have to keep getting better. I can't have my little sister getting the upper hand on me." Though, Aspen wasn't *littler* than her anymore. She stood three or four inches taller than Laurel now.

If they stood right next to one another, it was hard to tell they were siblings. Aspen had the height and build of a warrior woman. Even at seventeen, she had the beauty and curves to compete with the older women in the Order. In comparison, Laurel's lack of womanly assets made her look like some kind of spindly tree. Laurel's skin was also three shades darker thanks to Father's golden tan and she didn't have any of the freckles Aspen did. The only real commonality between them was the dark color of their eyes.

The crowd around them dispersed, except for Luc. He swept toward them. "You got first blood this time." He tucked Aspen close to his side and brushed the backs of his fingers against her upper arm.

Aspen frowned. "Cutting fingers isn't going to get the job done. Besides, she got my ribs pretty good with that scythe. If it had been a sword, I would be a bleeding mess on the floor over there."

Laurel picked up the scythe. "But hits weren't the rules of the match this time." The spars changed. First hit. First blood. First unconscious. The opponents chose depending on what their schedules could handle. Or what their trainers wanted.

Or how badly they wanted revenge against one of their comrades.

The Order of Stellatus wasn't known for being one of the most pleasant groups on the Continent. It was known for being the most ruthless. The most heartless. The most dangerous.

Laurel looked once again around the ring and the retreating forms of the other assassins. A few of them looked back at her with suspicion and what she could only label as envy— neither good in a society of assassins. By the Goddess, she couldn't wait to get out of this place. To take her sister far away from all these people.

Luc plucked the dagger from Aspen's fingers. "Don't be too hard on yourself, Aspen. You would have skewered anyone else, and it's not like you'll be facing off against Laurel in real life." He flipped the dagger in the air and caught it by the tip, not slicing *his* fingers.

Laurel headed out of the sparring ring and set her scythe on the weapons rack, next to all the other weapons the Order left out for practices. There were daggers, swords, whips, axes, spears, brass knuckles, and every kind of throwing blade the Order's resident blacksmith could come up with. There had been a sharpened boomerang once, but too many of the younger assassins had lost fingers before one of the masters had banned them from the practice rings. Laurel was pretty sure Aspen had stolen one and tucked it away somewhere.

"Are you going to join us for luncheon?" Aspen asked.

Laurel shook her head. "I think I'm going to go see if Master Serpens will give me some new drills." She needed to work on her climbing. Her last job had finished two weeks ago, but she had nearly met an early end scaling the wall of a guard tower. The paranoid merchant lord residing close to Fortitudo, the Continent's most populated city, had built some of the tallest walls she'd ever seen.

Luc swung an arm over Aspen's shoulder. "How much do I have to pay to talk you out of meeting up with Old Man Serpens so you can cook up some *souvlaki* in that frilly kitchen of yours?"

Aspen elbowed him in the gut. "Don't mock the kitchen, or you might find yourself with a nasty rash in the morning."

"Or at least some kind of venomous snake in your bed," Laurel teased. Luc had been on the receiving end of many a prank from both Aspen and Laurel. Both of them were known for their expertise with poisons. It wouldn't have been too hard to slip something into his food. Though, she couldn't blame him for thinking their kitchen frilly. Laurel had made sure it was. She'd had every detail copied from their childhood kitchen— from the lacy curtains to the yellow daisies painted on the corners of each cupboard. There was no point in having a memory like hers if she didn't use it.

"Not the snake!" Luc gave an exaggerated shiver.

Aspen giggled and tucked her hand into his. "What do you say, Laurel? Will you come with us?"

The sun high overhead glared down at them. If Laurel went to Master Serpens now, he'd have her scaling a wall in the heat of the day. If she didn't, she risked someone finding her after supper and distracting her from asking him. Teagan Obscuritas, the leader of their order, was set to return to Stellatus Hall that very day and would likely seek her out simply to annoy her. It would probably be best to track down the other master before Teagan returned.

Aspen clasped her hands together, Luc's hand getting trapped between them, and gave Laurel her most pitiful expression. "Please, Laurel?"

"Maybe tomorrow."

Aspen took a step forward, pulling Luc with her. "But I'm *so hungry*. We can count it as my prize for beating you today in the ring."

Laurel rolled her eyes. "Fine." Aspen could be a menace, but Laurel couldn't say "no" to her. Very often. "But you two have to do dishes."

"Deal!" they both agreed. As a single unit, the couple spun around and headed for the door leading back into the hall.

Nestled on top of the small mountain outside the coastal city of Vale, Laurel could see the ocean from the west side of the building and the open expanse of wilderness to the east. There were three floors of the sprawling villa above ground and three below. The building topside had been built in an open square with walls surrounding an open courtyard where many of the order's gatherings took place. Potted trees and raised gardens full of poisonous plants decorated the red tiled courtyard. When Laurel had first seen the tiles, she hadn't known if the clay had originally been that color or if it was so stained with blood the squares eventually adopted the rusty hue.

They passed by a group of younger assassins-in-training, ranging from age five to age twelve, working on their balancing techniques. When one of the younger boys wobbled, the master watching them wacked the backs of his legs with a reed. The boy didn't cry out but steadied himself, even as red stripes burned across his calves. One didn't make it long in the Order if they showed any signs of weakness.

The courtyard disappeared as Laurel followed Aspen and Luc to the staircase and down a floor. Their boots tread silently over the hard floor at the bottom. Their masters had drilled quiet steps into them from a very young age.

Halfway down one of the halls, a shadow peeled away from the wall. Laurel's heart sank and she took a deep breath.

"Laurel."

The sharp voice made Laurel's fists clench at her sides even as she opened her eyes and put on her flattest expression. She made eye contact with Aspen and nodded her chin to keep her and Luc moving toward their rooms. Aspen gave Teagan a wide smile but knew better than to stick around when he wished to talk to Laurel. Both she and Luc beat a hasty retreat as Laurel faced him.

Teagan Obscuritas stood not three feet away. His dark hair was slightly damp, likely having sought her out as soon as he'd cleaned up from whatever trip he'd just been on. The icy gray of his eyes flicked over her, looking for any weaknesses that might have sprung up while he was away.

Not that he'll find any.

Teagan had been back and forth from the isles across the sea several times over the last few months. Their order didn't often travel across the sea. Laurel hadn't ever been there, though there were a few of the older assassins that had. They'd told her about the land of magic and war. The Continent didn't have much magic. There were a few people that had seemed to do some unusual things, but it never went further than having a very prosperous garden or an uncanny ability with horses. The few Sireadh still traveling about spoke about the magic fading from the world, but Laurel didn't pay them much heed. If magic was leaving, it would make it that much easier to get her job done.

No one really knew what was going on with Teagan, but it wasn't like the masters went around sharing their plans with everyone and most of the assassins didn't care— so long as they got paid.

One of Teagan's dark eyebrows rose. "Well?"

Laurel withheld a sigh. "Well, what?"

"I heard about your little match with your sister." He

leaned against the wall. "Aspen's showing great promise at such a young age. She may even surpass you."

Laurel didn't let a flick of her eyebrow, or a twitch of her lips betray the annoyance she felt. Remaining silent was the best option. Teagan wielded words as well as he wielded a blade, gutting just as many people with both.

He picked at the velvet of his dark-blue waistcoat. "You really ought to rethink your career choice, child. Soon, not even your bright mind will be enough. You've taken on too much and that flash of ambition is going to fade. You'll be nothing."

Oh, Laurel didn't care one whit that Teagan didn't think she was worth anything. That fact had been ingrained in her from a very young age.

No, it was the fact that Teagan was so delusional when it came to Aspen and her talents. Not that there was anything to scoff at. Aspen was one of the best assassins on the Continent — as were most of the men and women in Stellatus Hall. Aspen had worked hard for her place among their ranks, but Teagan's near obsessive fascination with her could be danger- ous. Aspen was only seventeen. She didn't need to prove anything to anyone. She didn't need to do the things Laurel had done to get where they were now.

In fact, if Laurel had her way, she wouldn't need to do anything the Order said. Soon enough, they would leave this cursed place behind and everyone in it for good.

Teagan included.

His eyes narrowed slightly. "Are you going to say anything?"

Laurel tilted her head slightly. "I didn't realize your state- ment warranted a response."

Teagan stepped closer to her. "Don't forget your place, Laurel. You may hold some degree of respect in these halls, but I still own you."

The small tendril of patience Laurel had snapped. She stepped right up to Teagan until they were nearly nose to nose. "That threat is growing old."

The corner of his lips twitched. His only sign of agitation. "But it is still effective, is it not?" He took a step back, a sardonic smile stretching across his face as he walked away.

Great Goddess, she would kill that man if she ever got the chance, and she would smile as she did.

2

THE CARTOGRAPHER

LAUREL'S ARMS SHOOK AS SHE HELD HERSELF CLOSE TO THE CLIFF face. For three days, she had scaled this particular cliff up and down until her limbs wouldn't cooperate anymore. She didn't look down at the ground or she would fall. She knew she would. Instead, she stuck her right hand in the small pocket of chalk hanging from her waist and dusted her fingers. Sweat coated every inch of her, and she couldn't risk having a slippery grip. Not now.

The rumble of thunder sounded a way off. She repositioned herself and grabbed the next small crack on the smooth cliff. Praise the Goddess it wasn't raining yet. She could reach the top before the whole cliff was slick as death. Though, she wouldn't put it past Master Serpens to force her do another pass while it rained. The old man could be a bugger when wanted to be.

She continued up, the tremor in her arms radiating down to her core by the time she reached the last twenty feet. Pressing her cheek against the cold stone of the cliff, she reached her left hand down for more chalk.

"Hurry up, Flumen!" Master Serpens booming voice cracked with the thunder around them. "None of us want to be caught in this storm."

Laurel gritted her teeth and pulled herself up another ten feet as the first drop of rain hit her shoulder.

Curses.

"Laurel?"

She didn't look up, but recognized Conley's voice. She should have known he would come looking for her today. As second in command in her sect, the scholae, he liked to boss her around when he could.

"Teagan's asking for you."

Laurel held back a grimace. *Of course he is.* She took a couple of quick breaths, bouncing on the very tips of her toes tucked into the cliff face, then reached up for the edge of the cliff with her left hand.

Her fingers slipped on the sandy edge.

"*Blast!*" she hissed. Her foot dropped and she swung out from the cliff.

A shadow fell over her.

"He returned with his friend too," Conley added, not even a hint of worry for her in his voice.

Laurel pulled herself back in and regained her hold on the cliff. Her right hand ached from the strain of holding her body up, but she kept her grip.

"Did he say what he wanted?" she asked.

"Just said he had a job for you."

The cursed man had been foisting every job he could on her, trying to keep her from the Hall. From Aspen.

While assassinating people was easier when you didn't know the reasons why they were targeted, it ate at Laurel. When she'd been younger, she'd been fine doing whatever Teagan ordered. As long as there was food on the table in front of Aspen, Laurel would slide a knife between anyone's ribs. But Laurel had found success in this occupation. She realized she could give their family of two a good life without killing innocent people Teagan had deemed worthy of death simply because the coin was good.

The small lead ball around her neck sat heavy as she reached for the edge once more. They were so close to leaving the Order. Laurel estimated another year or two and she'd have enough money to pay for her and Aspen's contracts and get out of this place.

Conley dangled his legs over the edge next to her. "What do you think Teagan will have you do?"

If he wasn't such a good second, Laurel might have pulled him off the cliff right there and then.

"Are you here to take a pass at the cliff, Coulter?" Master Serpens said. "Or will you leave Flumen to figure out how to get up here without taking a plummet straight to the Goddess's realm?"

Bugger.

Laurel got a firm grip on the edge and lifted her foot to boost her torso up over the top. Her lungs deflated and she laid on the gritty ground, legs hanging over the side of the cliff. Another raindrop hit her cheek. With a groan, Laurel pulled the rest of her body away from the edge. The raindrops came a bit quicker, darkening the sand near her face.

A pair of thin leather shoes, made to form around each toe, stepped into view. Laurel looked up and found Master Serpens's lips turned down under his long mustache. He lifted a red umbrella over his head.

"What did you do wrong?"

Laurel flopped onto her back. "Should have used my foot to prop me rather than hanging. Wouldn't have slipped."

"And?"

She blew out a breath. "Let Conley distract me."

"Correct." Master Serpens walked off without another word. Such was his way.

Laurel gave herself a few seconds before she sat up. If she didn't get moving, her muscles would seize.

"When did Teagan want me at his office?"

Conley shrugged. "He just said, 'Fetch her, Coulter.'"

By the Goddess, she should have pulled Conley off the cliff. She shoved herself to her feet and raced up the path toward the hall.

Laurel clipped her hood into place and strode toward Teagan's office on the third floor. Well, the sixth floor, technically. She ignored everyone she passed, the mask concealing all of her face giving her some anonymity and garnering the respect of her peers. Their eyes flicked back and forth over her as she swept past them. The hiss of whispers bounced around her. She did her best to catch a piece of what passed by her ears, but it seemed everyone would quiet when she walked by. Not a good sign.

She stopped at the large door situated in the middle of the hall. Two men stood on either side, their faces concealed behind masks carved in the likeness of demons as they bowed to her. The masks were an ingenious design, crafted to fit the wearer's face exactly and used specialized clips to attach to the hood to hold it all together. It completely hid anything that could be used to identify one of them and kept everything in place. Laurel would know. It was the same mask she wore. Aspen didn't know Laurel had become a member of the scholae two years ago, just after she'd turned sixteen.

Laurel tapped the proper places on her mask, giving the secret signs of their sect. One on each corner of her eye, on each side of her nose, then her lips.

I am watchful. I am focused. I am silent.

The schola to the left gave an almost imperceptible nod and knocked on the door.

"Enter," Teagan's voice commanded from the other side.

The scholae bowed low to her again. Laurel twisted the gilded doorhandle and slid into the room.

Teagan's office may have been the largest, but it was the least decorated Laurel had seen in the order. He didn't flaunt his wealth as so many of the other masters did. There was a single fireplace that crackled with a pleasant heat. A crimson rug took up most of the hardwood floor, but the design wasn't elaborate by any means. The one thing the office did boast was a large collection of books. Teagan had always been the most scholarly of the Order, which made him the most dangerous in Laurel's opinion. One could only sharpen a blade so much, but a mind? The only constraint to one's knowledge was their limit to information and Teagan had never lacked in that.

Laurel kept her pace slow as she approached the desk against the far wall. The window behind it was draped in heavy, black curtains. She'd never seen those curtains open. Teagan may have been proud, but he wasn't stupid. The large window would have made him susceptible to attack from the outside. Laurel had looked in from the other side and had seen the full sheet of metal that blocked any sun from breaking into the room. Being the leader of an elite group of assassins put a target on his back, and he knew better than to pretend otherwise. Not that he ever acted paranoid. Only cautious. Conniving. Possessive.

Teagan sat in a leather chair on the other side of the desk, but his cold eyes never flicked in Laurel's direction. He was watching the woman who perused his shelves across the room.

Adira Durant— or as her growing rebellion liked to call her, The Cartographer. Unlike many in Stellatus Hall, Laurel knew about the woman and her mission to take over the isles across the sea. Adira had been to Stellatus Hall when Laurel had been a child, but she'd become a regular face when her king had died at the hands of his sons over four years ago. She and Teagan had been scheming a rebellion to take back her kingdom since she arrived, traveling around the Continent and sometimes even across the sea to recruit people to their cause.

The islander turned, her green eyes finding Laurel still standing in the doorway. "Ah, you must be the assassin I've heard so much about. What was your name again?"

Teagan's mouth curved up in feigned mirth. "As I've said in the past, we do not divulge the names of the scholae." He gestured to the two chairs across from him.

Laurel stalked toward a chair as Adira took the other. "Schola, then," Adira said. "I'm sure you're curious as to why we've called you here."

Saying that she really didn't care wouldn't endear Laurel to the rebel woman, so she kept that to herself. "What do you need me for?" she asked instead. The mask against her face muffled her voice slightly, giving it an echoing ring through the metal.

Adira grinned. "What I wouldn't give to have my men come to me with such an attitude. Where do you find such loyalty, Teagan?"

Teagan leaned back in his chair, fingers steepled in front of him. "She is one of few."

Laurel nodded her thanks but kept her thoughts to herself. He played his role of conscious leader well, but she could still read him. His eyes were bright with the power their situation afforded him. While she would rather cut off her right arm than work for him, he had her chained to him like a prized dog because of the contract her cursed mother had signed. When she'd abandoned them at the door to the assassin's hall for a handful of coin, never to be seen again.

Laurel braced herself for what was sure to be a new mission. It was about time she got away from this place. She'd been sitting around Stellatus Hall for two weeks. It wasn't unusual, but besides drilling with the scholae, she'd felt as if she were sitting on her hands. Staying at Stellatus Hall wouldn't get her any closer to escaping it for good.

"And I'm sure," Adira said, "her loyalty has much to do with why she's the perfect fit for our little *project*."

Laurel turned to Teagan. If this conversation was going to last past breakfast, she was going to pummel someone. "What do you need me to do?"

"The future king of Olympia needs taken care of." Teagan pushed a leather folder on his desk toward her. "We don't believe it will be long before he finally takes the crown. The Lord of the Underworld has done well with his network and situated Crown Prince Dion in a position to easily assume his throne."

Adira's fists curled on the arms of her chair, but Laurel kept most of her focus on the papers in front of her. A map of the palace. A list of supplies. A detailed accounting of Crown Prince Dion's life along with a sketch. Great Gaia the man's jaw could likely cut through stone.

"Security?" she asked.

"Tight," Teagan replied. "He has a retinue of guards and rarely leaves the palace. His brothers are his feet around the kingdom, the youngest specifically."

"Do you want me to take out the other princes as well?"

"No," Adira answered. "We have plans for the other two,

but Dion's death will do more for us than his life. In fact, I would steer clear of the youngest. He will sniff you out faster than a hound will find blood. The mer prince shouldn't pose any problems but keep your focus on the Crown Prince."

Laurel studied the papers. This mission could take months. She would have to infiltrate the palace, gain the trust of those within it before she could strike. It would also be best to go in with no contact for the first few weeks— or months if need be. Sacrificing herself wasn't an option. She was a mercenary, not a martyr. For a mission like this, she would have to do everything just right.

"How much?"

Teagan glanced at Adira before looking back at Laurel. "You do this, and I'll sign over your contract, free of charge."

Laurel's heart nearly stopped in her chest, and she had to strain not to react. "Is it negotiable?"

Teagan's eyes flashed, but not with malice. He knew she wanted out. He knew what this meant to her. When she'd finished a job six months ago and assassinated for a warlord heir in the southern region of the Continent, he'd realized that she was making plans to leave. Since then, he'd been trying to sink his claws into her and Aspen as deep as he could. Laurel had made sure she secured her fortune by putting it into the vault of the northern warlord after saving his daughter and killing off his rival's heir. It put Teagan in a tight position if he wanted to thwart her. They'd both been standing at an impasse for months now, but apparently it had come to a head.

The edges of Teagan's mouth quirked up. "Everything is negotiable."

"I want my sister's." It didn't matter which contract she earned from this job, but Aspen had more years to pay off. If Teagan signed over Aspen's contract, Laurel could simply buy hers off him after the job and they would have more money set aside to get their lives started.

"Done— so long as she agrees of course."

Aspen would agree. It's what they'd been working toward for the last five years. She narrowed her eyes. "Free of charge?"

"I'll even pay the legal fees."

Laurel almost couldn't believe it, but Teagan wasn't one to lie about something like this. He may have been a demon in man's skin, but he was a smart demon. If he was offering this to her, that meant this mission wasn't one to be taken lightly. She would be waltzing with death, and he knew it. Which was the only reason he would dangle something like this in front of her.

Laurel slipped the glove from her left hand and held it over the desk. The tips of her fingers had scabbed over, praise the Goddess.

Teagan unlocked the right drawer of his desk and drew out a blade. The hilt was a simple design, old brown leather wrapped around the handle and the pommel a tapered point. The blade, however, was riddled with charms, each one as black as the promises made on it.

A geas blade.

There were many enchanted objects Laurel had seen pass through Stellatus Hall, but this blade was the worst of them. While items enchanted to create the magical geases were rare, most of them were simple devices with simple promises. They were most often used for protection, the magic making those that promise with the geas unable to harm the other party. Generally used by domineering employers who wanted to have full control over their workforce or keep someone from betraying their seedy affairs. The magic could be enchanted into trinkets or jewelry. All anyone had to do was make a deal with the charm activated and the geas was set.

But this was different.

Teagan removed his own glove then turned to Adira. "You too."

Adira sighed and put out her hand.

Teagan marked each of their palms, wetting the tip of the blade with their blood, then spoke. "I, Teagan Obscuritas, swear to give Schola the contract of her sister upon completion of the assassination of one Dion of Olympian royal blood by her own hand in service to the rebellion and the agreed upon payment." He smeared the blood in his hand onto the blade, sealing his part of the geas.

Adira quirked a brow. "My turn?" At Teagan's nod, she said, "I, Adira Durant, swear to pay Teagan Obscuritas the agreed upon one hundred fae slaves upon completion of Dion's death." She followed Teagan's actions and smeared her blood.

Laurel bit her tongue. So that was what Teagan was getting out of all this? Magical slaves? She watched the blood pool in her hand. "I, Schola, swear to assassinate one Dion of Olympian royal blood in service to the rebellion and for the payment of my sister's contract of indentured servitude agreed upon by Teagan Obscuritas."

Her blood joined the others.

Now came the worst part.

Teagan cleared his throat. "Until Dion of Olympian royal blood is dead, I, Teagan Obscuritas will continue to aid Adira Durant in her quest to enslave fae-kind and bring magic to the world. Adira Durant will pay for services rendered and keep the secrets of the Stellataen Order she learns while within the bounds of this geas."

Adira bristled next to Laurel but said nothing. It probably rankled her that Teagan would limit her in any way, even if she'd already agreed to it. But that was why Teagan used a geas. It was his insurance policy.

Laurel braced herself for the blow.

Teagan smiled at her. An ugly thing. "Once she steps foot on Olympian soil, Schola will remain within the bounds of Olympia's borders until she assassinates Dion of Olympian royal blood, and if she leaves, will forfeit her life and die the moment she crosses the border."

Laurel tried not to move, but her fingers twitched slightly. That was how he would ensure her cooperation. She wouldn't be able to do anything until this job was done. She would be cut off from her sister, her savings, everything that mattered.

Well, Laurel wasn't known for not doing her job.

Teagan lifted the dagger. "I seal this geas with its parties, that none shall speak of what has been agreed upon with any who do not know the details of the geas until the geas has been satisfied."

"I seal this geas," Laurel and Adira echoed.

The blood on the blade disappeared, soaked up by the magic of the charms. Laurel looked down at her hand as that same magic healed the cut in her palm, sealing the magic under her skin.

She slipped her hand back into her glove. "When do I leave?"

3
AN UNFORTUNATE STRIKE

PAULO IGNORED THE ACHE BEHIND HIS EYES AS HE SIFTED THROUGH the tangles of strings in his mind. That was really the only way he could describe the lines of Fate. Each person had a string, a fate the Goddess had designed for each of Her children. People obviously didn't always follow the lines of fate, and so often there were splits in the strings. Sometimes, the lines returned to normal, sometimes they twisted into ugly things. Sometimes, they were stronger at the ends. Paulo couldn't imagine how the Goddess kept track of all of it, but it was a beautiful chaos he remained in awe of.

He flipped through flashes of what was yet to come. It was a good thing he couldn't see into the past. His mind would have turned to mush ages ago. The future, while full of possibilities, only went for so long before it began to loop. The decisions yet to be made, the tragedies yet to occur, kept people from making decisions in the present and that was what he saw. Every decision twisted and flipped around. If the youngest prince and Lord of the Underworld decided not to replace his boot laces before his sparring practice one of these nights, Penny Barclay, heiress to the Duchy of Eleusion, would smack him in the nose with a magic branch and make him bleed. If Lady Carnation wore the blue dress instead of the cream, she would be late to supper because her maid wouldn't be able to find the matching pins to put in her hair until Lady Carnation was already fifteen minutes late and offended the newly arrived Aigean delegation seated at the supper table.

Every person was met with a million choices and every choice had its consequence. Paulo could see all of them if he wanted to, but there were only a few fated lines he watched with care.

If he knew whose future he was looking for, he could sift through the strings of fate and find their cord. He waded through time, past the amber and green, the peacock blue and amethyst, the dark purple and sky blue— though he didn't brush against the segment of pure white on that line— until he found the lines of pearl and silver. He'd always thought that second color so interesting. It wasn't the silver of mirrors or diamonds, but the silver of steel. Of strength and determination. He found where the two lines met, ignoring where they separated later down the line. He pushed his awareness into the lines and found himself in a tumult of time.

The Mist.

A host of humans, led by a silver-haired woman walking through with a talisman made of forbidden magic. The talisman breaking when they made it to the other side.

Penny Barclay, heir to the duchy of Eleusion, walking alongside the Gray Man. Her screams as she is pulled through the portal into another place.

Moments later, the youngest prince of Olympia arriving, asking after Penny's screams. His fraught expression.

The Mist falling. The Gray Man standing on the open plains, disappearing in the night.

Paulo let go of the magic and opened his eyes.

Mater sat across from him, a teacup halfway to her lips. "Are you back?"

Paulo blinked and sat up in his chair, rubbing at his temples. The blasted price of his magic set his head to aching. "How long was I out for?"

"Thirty minutes or so," she answered, pointing up at the mantle. This particular sitting room in the palace had gilded accents, and the gold clock simply blended into the rest of the décor. "Anything exciting coming?"

Paulo reached over and poured himself a cup of peppermint tea. He took a long sip, scalding his mouth as he tried to get the tea to suppress the massive headache he felt coming on. It would take a gallon of the stuff to even touch the ache.

He reached out to Mater, and she grabbed his hand. As he'd gotten more adept at using his gifts, he had been able to project those visions into the minds of those closest to him. He had easily shared the visions with Father when he'd come into his gift, but after Father's passing... Well, he'd had to figure out another way, and luckily, he liked Mater and Diana enough that he could share it with them. First, it had only been impressions or feelings. As he'd grown into his powers more, he'd been able to incorporate smells and sometimes sound into what Mater or Diana saw. Now, he could share an entire moment, though they told him it was slightly blurred, leaving out finer details. But it was enough. He brought the magic back to the surface and pushed the most important visions he'd seen into her mind. He knew she couldn't see them as clearly as he could but sharing them with her lessened some of his own burden.

Mater released his hand after he'd finished. "Our Penny is about to embark on quite the adventure."

He nodded. "I'll need you to see to gather some items. I also need to give Diana a refresher on Faerie lore." Or more accurately, made-up Faerie lore. Penny couldn't allow anyone to know who she was in order for Faerie's soon-to-be High King to fully accept his new lot in life. Paulo would also have to get a book on old lore from the palace library into Lady Attina Alvis's office. That could be easily arranged.

Paulo grabbed his sketchbook and did a couple of rough sketches of what he'd seen. He tried to do it anytime he sought out a future or if he saw something important, not bothering to sketch out every tiny vision he saw in a day. The images always helped him remember better than words did. He did some dark shading on the portal then jotted down the date on the upper right-hand corner. His memory wasn't as good as he wished, so he always dated each sketch.

"Have you seen your sister this morning?" Mater asked.

Paulo poured another cup and slouched down in his chair, likely wrinkling his bright-yellow waistcoat. Jenkins would be muttering all evening, but Paulo couldn't find it in himself to really care. "I haven't seen her. She's probably taking another go at the shooting range before we have to leave."

They needed to be in Eleusia in six days. By the Goddess, it felt like only a snippet of time and also an eternity. He'd been waiting for this day to come for years. If they left day after tomorrow, they would have plenty of time to get home before heading toward Eleusion's main city. Plenty of time to for his nerves to fray and his patience to finally run out.

Mater stilled. "Did she say she was actually going to shoot? I know several of the young lords had planned on using the royal archery range this morning."

A flash of Diana swinging a fist added to Paulo's growing headache. He blinked the vision away.

"Curses," he hissed. His tea sloshed over the side of his cup and burned his hand as he leapt to his feet.

Mater jumped up and grabbed the cup from him. "Go."

He didn't need any more encouragement. Without another word, he bolted for the door and raced down the hall. Magic flared, and he pushed his magic into the future a few seconds ahead of him. Using his gift, he dodged a gaggle of young ladies turning a corner toward him, ducked down a servants' staircase to avoid Prince Dion and his retinue of sycophants, and raced out onto the palace grounds.

Turning the corner toward the archery range, he arrived just in time to watch Diana smash her fist right into Lord Dexter Finton's very stately nose.

He fell to the ground and the small crowd of gentlemen standing with wide eyes and gaping mouths rushed toward them.

"Stop!" Paulo shouted.

The men turned at the bark of his voice, all except Donnie, who had reached Diana first and was in the process of standing between her and Dexter. Wise man. His was the only face Diana would hesitate to hit.

Diana shoved him instead.

"Step away from her, Lord Abrams," another of the group, Mr. Hectors, grabbed Donnie's arm and attempted to pull him away.

"Do *not* put your hands on me," Donnie snapped as he stepped closer to Diana once again.

Paulo reached them, stepping over the groaning Dexter and looking Diana over. No injuries. Nothing indicating the man had laid his hands on her, but that didn't prove anything. However, she did look whole enough to go back to their rooms.

He nudged his chin in the direction of the palace. "Mater is waiting for you."

Diana's furious blue eyes— so much like his own— finally moved from Dexter to him. That look easily communicated what she'd like to do instead, but Paulo was her twin and knew her better than most. She had gotten spooked by what Dexter, blackguard that he was, had done.

"It was just a kiss!" Dexter finally groaned, spitting blood on the ground.

Diana's eyes shot back to the man, and she took a step forward.

Both Paulo and Donnie jumped to stop her.

"Go, Diana!" Paulo barked.

With a growl, she spun to grab her bow and stomped back toward the palace. Paulo would be facing quite the battle when he got up to their rooms.

He whirled on the men standing around him. "What on Gaia's blasted green earth happened?"

Mr. Hectors had crouched down and was now helping Dexter to his feet. "She attacked him."

Donnie folded his arms over his chest. "I believe he attacked her first."

Paulo took a step toward Dexter. "What did you do?"

Dexter met Paulo's gaze with an angry one of his own. "Stealing a kiss isn't the same as attacking someone. I couldn't help myself when I saw her shoot. Her attire—"

Paulo's fist smashed into the man's gut, stealing whatever refuse he was about to spew. When the men pulled him away, he laughed. "Whoops! I couldn't help myself." He yanked his arms free.

Donnie spat at Dexter's feet. "Paulo ought to call you out."

"You're one to talk, Abrams."

Donnie's face turned very serious. "I don't force myself on women, *Finton*."

Dexter pinched his nose as blood dripped on the dirt between his feet. "I wouldn't call Diana MacGregor a proper woman."

Paulo snapped. His magic flared behind his eyes, and he used his gift to see where the men would move a split second ahead and dodged every hand that reached for him. He slammed his fist into Dexter's jaw. The man went down like a sack of potatoes. With the magic still blazing through him, he slipped through every man that attempted to grab at his clothes and escaped the group before any of them realized what was happening. He stormed back in the direction of the palace, the men calling after him.

Donnie caught up to him and Paulo's jaw tightened. "What really happened?"

"I saw him approach her. Diana, as Diana does, didn't back down when he drew near. He caught her by surprise and grabbed her in a kiss. It lasted no longer than a second before Diana kneed him in the groin. I didn't hear what he said after that, but she slugged him in the gut, and you walked around the corner when she got him in the face."

How dare that man! Paulo's magic made his vision split. His sight could be a fickle thing when it wanted to. More often than not, the Goddess simply shoved the visions on him, thrusting him into the future and leaving him with a massive headache. However, he'd learned to keep his part of his mind in the present as the visions cascaded over him and could even keep up a conversation if needed.

He saw what Donnie would ask before he actually started shooting questions at Paulo.

"No, I'm not going to call him out. Diana would be furious at me for fighting her battles no matter how much I want to stick a sword in the man's gut. Yes, he is a blackguard. No, we can't stay any longer. I was planning on leaving in two days, but I'll have the carriages readied for tomorrow morning. Yes, it would be great for you to stay and mollify the gentlemen, thank you for offering."

Donnie laughed. "You're welcome?"

Mater tucked her arm into Diana's elbow as she led her through the palace's grand hall. "At least we'll be able to make it in plenty of time for Paulo's appointment in Eleusia. We certainly wouldn't want him to miss it." She was nearly as excited about the next several days as Paulo was. How he would manage not to pace the docks of Eleusia for days on end, he didn't know.

Paulo followed behind them, carrying a trunk full of sticks. Yes, sticks.

He readjusted his fingers on the handle. This was what he got for trying to save Diana from ridicule. Should he have snapped at her at the archery range the way he had? Probably not, but she was going to cause more problems if she'd stayed, and she knew it.

"How are you doing back there?" Diana asked.

Paulo glared at the braid hanging down between her shoulder blades. "I can't believe you collected this many sticks while we were here."

"One should never pass up a good stick. All the sticks in there will make excellent arrows once I fletch them."

Paulo cast his eyes heavenward.

They reached the carriage before the sun was truly up. Dinner the night before had been abysmal. Paulo and Donnie both had been the recipients of many pointed glares, the most from a black-eyed Dexter. Paulo had done his best not to wish the man to choke on his supper. He really did.

Mater paused. "Where's Jenkins?"

Paulo withheld a smile. "He's caught some kind of illness overnight, though the palace was kind enough to lend me a substitute valet in his absence. I'll make sure to send a carriage back for him once we get to Iatrus Castle."

Mater turned back to him with a confused look.

Poor Jenkins. Paulo turned his attention to the young man at the back of the carriage. Mr. Hart Carys met his gaze and gave him a congenial smile befitting a mild-mannered servant. Not at all what Paulo would have imagined from one of the spies working for the Lord of the Underworld. Though, there was a reason their spy network was the greatest in the kingdom. Paulo had seen Jenkins's poisoning last week. Luckily, with their travels being expedited, the valet wouldn't be experiencing a more prolonged exposure to the poison.

But bringing Mr. Carys close to Eleusion was nonnegotiable.

The man would leave them when they reached the Black River, taking a separate route to Eleusia and onto Barclay Manor. Paulo would have told him to wait and go with them in a few days, but then he would have to reveal what he knew, and that information would get back to the youngest prince.

And Paulo *really* didn't want that.

Paulo dropped the trunk at Mr. Carys's feet and gave him a grateful smile before heading to the side of the carriage. He swore to pack his trunks lighter in the future. He certainly wouldn't want to lug the massive things around.

Diana hopped into the carriage unassisted, but Paulo offered his hand to Mater.

"Thank you, dear." She took his hand and ascended the

short steps. Once she was settled, Paulo joined them, sitting beside Mater so he could face forward. Both he and Mater could get motion sick if they faced the other way, but Diana and Father could read a book and sit backward without so much as batting an eye, so they'd compromised years ago.

Now, Diana sat in the rear-facing seat alone.

There wasn't a day that passed in which Paulo didn't think about Father. His death six years ago had been a blow they still woke up facing every morning. Mater hadn't veered from her wardrobe of full mourning black in all that time. Paulo caught Diana using Father's bow every once in a while, even though it wasn't made for her height.

"Diana." Mater reached out and set her hand on Diana's knee. "If there's anything else you need, you can talk to us about it."

Diana rolled her eyes. "It really was only a stupid man who made an even stupider decision. Between Paulo and I, he certainly got his comeuppance, though it's another matter entirely if he learned his lesson."

Heat simmered in Paulo's gut. No, the man hadn't learned his lesson, though he would steer clear of Diana in the future, praise the Goddess. Paulo had seen that much.

"The offer still stands," Mater said. "For both of you. You can always talk to me, and I'll always be here to listen."

"Thank you, Mater," Paulo said.

"Don't thank me for being a good parent. While I fully believe children can outgrow the sins of their parents and that they need to fly from the nest, it doesn't mean I need to be an absentee mother to help raise good adults."

A vision flashed into Paulo's mind.

Morning light will break over the water, painting it gold. A black shadow will bob in the surface, the current slowly dragging it down then pushing it back up. A shout will ring out and a hooked staff will reach out, grabbing onto the form and pulling it onto the shore. Mr. Carys's face will be swollen with water, but the uniform is the same as what he wears leaving the capital. A large gash mars his hairline.

Paulo jumped up and slammed on the top of the carriage. "Change of plans. We're going to Barclay Manor."

4
AN UNFORTUNATE ARRIVAL

The harbor in Eleusia will be bustling with people when she goes to step off the small ship. She will walk down the streets of Eleusia's market, past a coral-colored building. A few strands of her dark hair will shine in the afternoon light as a street vendor will start yelling at someone who knocked over a crate of apples. She'll slow to watch the fight unfold. She won't notice the flowerpot fall from above before it hits her on the head.

PAULO'S BODY NEARLY BUZZED AS HE READIED HIMSELF IN THE MIRROR of Barclay Manor's guest room. He hadn't called Mr. Carys in to help him, seeing beforehand the long night the man had been in for. The sun hadn't even touched the horizon but the energy zipping through his blood was nearly as electric as when he and Diana had snuck some of Father's imported coffee when they were ten. They hadn't slept for a straight two days and crashed so hard afterward Mater thought they had come down with some kind of illness. When she'd found out, both Paulo and Diana had had to dust the entire library.

But Paulo hadn't had any coffee that morning. No, the future he'd been waiting for had nearly arrived.

Laurel was coming.

A quiet knock sounded on the door and Diana stuck her head in before he could respond. "It's not even dawn and you're already preening?" She stepped fully into the room, completely dressed and ready to go. Her hunting knife hung from her waist. She'd already been out that morning and had brought in three Wood Pigeons for Barclay Manor's cook. He'd seen her hunt them down two days ago, when they'd stopped at an inn for the night on their way here.

"I can preen any time of day, thank you." He straightened the lapels of his purple jacket. It was one of his more flamboyant pieces, the perfect ensemble to take a jaunt around Eleusia with his family and, hopefully, Lady Barclay.

And to drive Laurel absolutely mad.

Paulo grabbed his riding gloves and the silk top hat with a long peacock feather sticking out the side. "How do I look?"

Diana perused his outfit for a minute. "Like an idiot."

"Excellent," Paulo said with a grin. He grabbed his riding gloves, and they headed toward the dining room. While the sun barely hinted at waking, Barclay Manor was already bustling. Paulo led Diana into the dining room and found Lady Dominique Barclay seated at the head of the table, a newspaper in hand and a steaming cup of tea on the table in front of her. Whenever Paulo walked into a room with the duchess, he always felt his spine straightening and had to push himself to keep his ridiculous mask on his face. It often felt like she could see straight through it, her jade eyes measuring and always finding him lacking, but it didn't matter. The mask remained in place and the two of them never discussed it.

Though, today she raised one auburn eyebrow at his choice of ensemble.

"Good morning," Paulo greeted, grinning at the traveling gown the duchess wore. Mater had done her job splendidly, as he knew she would. Penny would be ecstatic her mother was coming with them.

"It should be," Lady Barclay said. She folded the paper and set it to the side. "The weather report states the mages will be sending another torrent down on Discordia, but the rains won't stretch farther than Tauros. Apparently, Crown Prince Dion has been stirring up more storms than normal and it's causing an imbalance in atmospheric pressure in the capital, and they need to relieve it."

Paulo kept a pleasant smile on his face even though all he wanted to do was grab the woman around the middle and throw her into the carriage so they could leave for Eleusia that instant. "Will that affect your harvests this year?" he asked instead. Always safe to talk business with Lady Barclay. The Barclay's thriving farming empire was the safest topic when speaking with, as many others referred to her as, the "Domineering Duchess."

"Not overly much." Lady Barclay gave a delicate shrug. "Our water mage has done a wonderful job making sure everything is in order."

Diana sagged back into the chair at Lady Barclay's left. The two of them had always had a special regard for one another. "Where is Penny?" she asked.

Lady Barclay frowned slightly. "She's been sleeping past sunup the last few days and comes to breakfast looking like the dead. She says she isn't ill, but I wonder if I've been pushing her too hard these last few weeks."

Paulo ladled a spoonful of honeyed eggs onto his plate. He tried not to grin as he thought about what he had seen would happen last night. If everything went according to the vision Paulo had had two weeks ago— as they usually did— Mr. Carys would have shot Penny Barclay with a dart and the youngest prince, wearing the glamour of a farmhand, would have given the lad the verbal lashing of a lifetime. Olympia's resident spymaster may have been one of the good guys, but he could be vicious when he felt threatened, and Penny's well-being meant everything to him. At least, it should by now. There would be a few other things that would really solidify that in the next few months, praise the Goddess.

"I'm sure there's nothing to worry about," Paulo said, grabbing two pieces of toast and a cup of peppermint tea then sliding into the chair next to Diana. He prayed the tea would help ease the headache that had taken root behind his eyes the night before. Flashes of visions had prodded at him all night, but he was glad for them. It helped prepare him for today, and he would gladly deal with the cost of his magic if it meant the events of the day went according to plan— both here at Barclay Manor and in Eleusia.

Mater joined them a few moments later, sweeping into the room with an excited smile on her face. She met Paulo's eye, and her grin widened. He'd shown Mater the vision he'd seen of today's events only minutes after he'd received it two months ago. They'd spent ages going over it, trying to figure out what day it would be and where he should meet her. He'd flicked through decision after decision, but how it all played out changed every time.

Mater was followed into the dining room by none other than Penny Barclay, sporting a rather lovely dart wound on her neck.

"Penny," Lady Barclay exclaimed, "what happened to your neck?"

Paulo nearly snorted.

Penny's emerald eyes widened, and her hand flew up to cover the wound, her fingers flashing a bright green for a moment. Not that her plant magic would do anything to help her cover up the garish wound. "It's nothing. A bee sting. One must have snuck through my window and taken a liking to my pillow last night."

Lady Barclay scowled, and Paulo had to take a bite of egg to keep from laughing.

"Where are you off to today?" Penny asked, her attention fastened on Lady Barclay's traveling gown.

"Luciana has invited me to accompany her to Claudia's this afternoon. A shipment of very fine silk should arrive from the Continent today."

Mater smiled warmly at Penny. "You're more than welcome to join us if you like."

"No," Penny answered, then hastily added, "but thank you. I have a lot of work to do today."

Lady Barclay gave her an appreciative glance.

Paulo did smile this time. "I'm sure you do, Penny." Should he warn her about what would happen in Chthonia that evening? He smirked at her inquisitive look. No. Some things were best left secret, especially where he didn't wish to meddle. Besides, he certainly didn't wish to dissuade her from her current trajectory, but the temptation to help his friend warred with the decision he'd made to stay this course.

A flash of auburn hair under moonlight flashed in his vision, followed by the twinge of a headache.

The latter course held out.

Paulo practically bounded from his horse as soon as their procession pulled up next to Eleusia's most prestigious dressmaker's shop that afternoon. His body vibrated like a struck chord on a lyre. He was in Eleusia. This was the moment that would set the course of Olympia's future.

Eleusia boasted the largest river docks in Olympia and had become a trade hub under the direction of the Barclay family. Paulo couldn't help being more than grateful for it, as it gave Delphine a port to export wool closer to the Continent, their largest consumer.

That would eventually change, but it was a problem for Peter to solve later. Paulo's cousin and heir had been put in charge of the wool empire while Paulo ran the estate and worked as Olympia's sole oracle and advisor to the Crown. A good thing too, since the man had more of a taste for the gruff work than Paulo did. Though, his son Oliver did not.

Drawing up his magic, he searched for his target. He stared at the red brick of the building in front of him. He found the string he was looking for and followed it until he came across the future of Laurel's arrival he'd seen a few weeks ago. Blinking away the vision, he looked to the sky and the shadows around him. Based on where the sun hung, he needed to get moving

Shaking himself, he spun toward the carriage. Diana had already followed him out and Mater was halfway down the steps. Paulo leapt forward and offered her his hand.

Mater gave him a small smile and stepped down. "I don't know what you're waiting around here for." She waved a gloved hand at him. "We ladies have this excursion well in hand. Off with you!"

Paulo took her hand and kissed it. "I thank the Goddess every day for you, Mater."

Diana flicked him on the forehead. "Get out of here."

"You, I do not thank the Goddess for," he said with a smirk. Diana only rolled her eyes and turned back to where Lady Barclay stepped regally out of the carriage.

With the humming in his limbs growing, he left his horse with one of the stableboys and bolted down the street toward the harbor. Paulo turned away from the dressmaker's. Eleusia's main road boasted a line of shops. When he was only two doors down from the dressmaker's, he looked up and found a flowerpot precariously perched on a windowsill. His grin widened and he bolted further down the road. He measured the shadows and carefully scanned the faces of those around him. His heart skipped at every head of dark hair he saw. Every swish of hunter-green skirts. Every flash of steel.

Until he saw her.

Paulo's lungs nearly burst as he watched her glance to either side of the road and stride across the street toward him. Golden skin glowed under the shining sun. Her dark hair was pulled back into a simple braid, but a few stray pieces framed her face. A large leather bag was slung over one shoulder, and her green dress swayed as her boots quietly crept over the cobbled street. Keen brown eyes— eyes that had distracted Paulo's thoughts more than once— scanned the faces of those she passed. Her gaze met his and he wanted to sink to his knees.

For all the times he'd seen Laurel Flumen in his visions, he could have never prepared himself for what seeing her in the present did to him.

It was like his heart had never actually beat in his chest before.

Like he'd been a hollow husk of a man until the very moment he finally laid his eyes on her. After nearly twelve years of seeing her face in his mind, of slowly losing his heart to her, she would finally be within his grasp.

Her gaze quickly moved on from his and it felt like a punch to the gut. He knew she wouldn't recognize him. Of course not. They'd never met.

But it didn't mean it was easy to endure.

She drew closer, looking up at him again. He was blatantly staring, but he couldn't help it. He couldn't stop himself from studying her lips as they tightened into a firm line, and she slowed.

Paulo had to stop himself from running to her. Instead, he turned away from her, looking up at the building next to him. When he saw her out of the corner of his eye, he stepped back, intending to knock into her.

Instead of falling into her arms, however, his heel caught on an uneven piece of cobblestone, and he fell, right onto his rear.

"Blast it." He looked up and found Laurel standing only a step away from him. "Oh, pardon me," he said, though he didn't get up.

Her brows were low as she shook her head and walked past, blatantly ignoring him. She even went so far as to give him a wide berth.

Well, the falling into her trick didn't work. Paulo didn't let her get far until he sprang to his feet, pulling a coin from his pocket. "Miss! I believe you dropped this."

Laurel looked back over her shoulder at him. "Not mine," she said quietly. Her voice was lower than he'd thought it would be on his ears. A little husky but still carrying that youthfulness that came with only being eighteen. It was better than music.

"Are you certain?" he asked. "I could have sworn I saw it drop behind you."

With a shake of her head, she continued on. *Stubborn woman.*

Paulo caught up to her. "It's my gentlemanly duty to make sure this gets back to its owner."

Laurel hoisted her bag higher on her shoulder. Paulo didn't even hear the telltale clank of steel inside. There was likely a dozen weapons in there. She looked over at him once, then back to the path in front of her. "As I said, it's not mine. Good day."

The coral-colored shop came into view and Paulo wanted to grab Laurel and throw her into his carriage— hang the consequences! Instead, he cut in front of her. "That's quite a large load you're carrying. Could I help you get to your destination?"

Laurel stopped and her brows drew together in frustration. "Listen, I don't know what kind of game you're playing, but I have places to be. So, if you'll excuse me..."

Paulo didn't move. "What makes you suspect I'm playing a game? Can't a gentleman see a lovely lady and offer his assistance without an ulterior motive?"

Both brows rose on her forehead. "You mean to tell me you didn't just try to ram into me a moment ago?"

She'd caught that, had she? Paulo pulled his lips down. "Why would I try to run into you?"

Her shoulders lifted in a shrug. "I couldn't guess. Based on your attire and the coin you drew from your pocket, you're a wealthy gentleman, so robbing me would be practically useless. As we've never met, it wasn't like you were trying to reacquaint yourself with me which leaves the only other option."

"Which is?"

"That you saw a pretty girl you were hoping to charm into your bed." She gave him another once over, obviously finding him lacking. "I'm sorry to say, however, that I'm not interested in finding out what other colors you have tucked under that hideous jacket."

By the Goddess, the gall of this woman. Paulo burst out laughing.

Laurel started, coming to a full stop, and looking at him as if he'd grown another head.

"Sorry." He pulled a handkerchief from his pocket and wiped his eyes. "That was just too good."

"Happy to have given you a good laugh, sir." The *sir* was nothing short of an insult. Someone shouted ahead of them, and Laurel swung around, hand hovering at her hip. She shook herself. "Now, I really must be off."

Paulo reached for her. "Wait—"

She grabbed his outstretched hand and pulled him off balance. He stumbled toward her, and she jammed the heel of her hand into his throat. Any air that remained in his lungs stuck in his throat and he gaped like a fish, trying to get his body to cooperate.

Laurel released her grip on him and marched away.

Paulo watched as two feet in front of her, a flowerpot smashed into the ground. Laurel looked up and frowned at the window above her head and stepped over the shattered remains.

When Paulo could finally breathe again, he laughed like a madman.

She was here.

She was in Olympia.

The game had just begun.

5
THE JOB

LAUREL'S FIRST GLIMPSE OF OLYMPIA'S CAPITAL MADE HER TOES CURL in her boots. It was like looking at a wonder of the world— the unnatural mountains surrounding the city glittering with bluish light. They had electricity on the Continent, and she'd seen a magelight once or twice, but this? There was no grasping of the amount of pure magic running through this land. It was obvious now why the Continent had never sought to take over the magic isles.

Olympia was beautiful. Gulls swept over the towering buildings. Music seemed to echo down every street. The brick-laid streets glittered like gold with the setting sun. Perhaps, Aspen would be amenable to moving their operation away from the Continent. After the rebellion took over, there would be ripe opportunity to start an assassin's guild right here. It would certainly get them far enough away from Teagan for Laurel's peace of mind.

She pulled the edge of her hood down to keep the moonlight from glaring off her mask as she ran across the street. While it wasn't necessary for scholae to wear their mask to every meeting with a client, Laurel did for a couple reasons. The first being that it was safer to conceal her identity, and the mask was recognizable enough for most clients to know who she was. The second was not many people thought sending an eighteen-year-old to do their dirty work was in good taste. It was simply easier on all accounts to wear the mask.

The directions on her map led her to a ramshackle building. The sign on the front said *Distillery* but how they were distilling anything of great quantity in the small building was a mystery. Laurel ignored the front door and made her way around the side. She found the light hanging from an iron hook and she pounded her fist against the wall beneath it. Three short knocks, followed by two long ones.

A piece of the wooden wall opened to reveal a man on the other side. The light from the hanging lantern next to her reflected on his bald head. He frowned down at her.

She drew a paper from one of the many pockets lining her jacket and handed it to him. He broke the seal and read it before stepping aside with a grunt to reveal a set of stairs leading upward. Laurel took them two at a time. A trapdoor waited at the top and it opened on oiled hinges out onto the roof.

Laurel shut the door behind her, leaving the bald doorkeeper to his post. She searched the edge of the flat-topped roof, finding the marker she'd been searching for. A small compass had been carved into the wall built to keep people from stepping off the side. If she hadn't known to look for it, she might have missed it. She looked over the edge, finding nothing. She nearly stepped away before the spot between her shoulder blades started to burn. Her tattoo.

Every assassin in Stellatus Hall had one. While the assassins didn't often face off against magic users, they came across enchanted objects regularly. When an assassin turned fifteen, they had a charm against magical influence tattooed into their skin. Laurel had hers between her shoulder blades, that patch of skin hidden most of the time. It had been crafted to burn when something was attempting to influence her mind with magic. Generally, the charm did its job in keeping the magic from working and also alerted her to the magic being used.

With a blink, she saw an outline of something hovering in the air.

Taking a breath, she swung over the side of the building. Her boots met the plank of invisible wood. The small breath she'd held slipped between her lips. Magic really did abound in the kingdom of Olympia. She steadily walked across the board, stepping into the building across from her.

They could get a magic bridge but no magic doors?

Laurel fully entered the compound. The building was much bigger on the inside than what it looked like from the outside. People bustled back and forth through the open space, racing upstairs and into doors on the second floor. Laurel stepped aside as a man swept past her, arms filled with maps.

A woman with graying hair approached her. "You're the assassin, I presume?" At Laurel's nod she said, "I'm General Nedra. Come with me."

Following behind the general, Laurel watched the operation unfold around her. Men and women stood around tables, passing papers back and forth and going over maps. Young boys scurried over the floor, delivering missives to the adults. While the room was somewhat chaotic, Laurel could see the order in it. The chain of command. She may not have particularly liked Adira, but the old spymaster certainly knew how to run an operation.

"Do you like what you see?"

Laurel returned her gaze to the general. "It's not my job to care."

General Nedra grinned.

Doors passed by on their right and General Nedra stopped at the end of the walkway. She fished a key from her pocket and opened an unmarked door. Laurel stopped in the doorway and studied the room before she entered. A desk sat to the side, a fine leather chair waiting for General Nedra while two stools squatted on the other side. Paper was pinned to the wall and stacked on the desk, but there wasn't an ambush waiting for her, so Laurel shut the door behind her.

"Please, take a seat," General Nedra said, gesturing to the stools.

Laurel opted to stand. She knew a powerplay when she saw one and this woman needed to be under no illusions that Laurel was under at The Cartographer's command. She only had allegiance to her order, to her sect as a schola. This little rebellion meant nothing to her and neither did this general.

The general pulled a thick envelope from within the confines of her desk. "The Cartographer had me collect this for you. It contains a full map of the Olympian Palace as well as the city with all rebel meetinghouses and the base. Don't lose them."

Laurel refrained from rolling her eyes. She was an assassin, not some ruddy-faced pubescent with a dull blade and a duller mind. Though, she'd seen enough of those downstairs. With the knife she had tucked in her sleeve, she opened the packet and began rifling through it.

"We've also supplied you with a false identity and references to get you into the palace."

A pristinely folded envelope with a wax seal glared up from the pile in Laurel's lap. "What's the identity?" She didn't really need to ask, since she could likely gather all that from the papers in front of her, but it was always best to hear an employer's expectations.

"A kitchen girl."

Laurel paused for a moment. A kitchen girl? Something in her chest lightened. She'd never been able to work in a kitchen before. Hundreds of recipes flashed through her mind before she stilled her thoughts. This was a job, not time to be excited about culinary experiments.

While many assassins liked the opulence of mingling with nobility, it was the unseen servants that always had the best advantage. Being in the kitchen was even better because food gave one pretty much any excuse to be anywhere. You could say there was a spill, that someone ordered a meal, or even that you forgot something in the kitchen. Laurel's skill with poisons would also come in handy. Aspen had more of an ambition for it, but it had been Laurel that taught her how to create them and how best to use them. Laurel just liked blades more. There was a semblance of honor in looking a person in the face when you killed them.

She slipped everything back into the pouch. She would sit and memorize the maps tomorrow, after she got some rest. She did her best prep work in the mornings. "When do I start at the palace?"

"You interview in ten days." General Nedra leaned back in her chair. "The palace has an advertisement going out for kitchen staff now and want to do the interviews in one go."

Laurel's brows drew together. "How many other applicants are there?"

"Six or seven. There should be a list in your packet."

Laurel rifled through the papers until she found the list of other girls applying for the job along with their places of residence. "I'll take care of it."

Laurel watched young Brooke Stephens get in line for the butcher at market, her dark-brown curls wrangled into a twist at the nape of her neck. She'd been jumping from stall to stall all morning, purchasing what looked like a small feast, likely for the large family she had at home. Brooke looked to be the oldest child, preparing to make her way into the world.

Unfortunate that she chose the wrong occupation.

Laurel got behind her in line. The woman at the front of the line was in the process of haggling the butcher down on a cut of lamb.

Brooke looked over her shoulder at Laurel, a shy smile spreading over her lips as they made eye contact.

Laurel leaned forward. "How long do you think that'll take?"

Brooke gave a small sigh. "Mrs. Naiad seems to do this every market day. We could be here a while."

Laurel feigned exasperation and pulled a small box out from the pocket of her skirt. "Much longer and these choco-lates will be a melted puddle." She opened the small box and popped one of the sugary treats in her mouth. Brooke's eyes were fastened on the other three truffles remaining.

With a smile, Laurel lifted the box. "Want to split them with me?"

Brooke gobbled down both of hers in the time Laurel ate the other. She tucked the box back into her pocket and waited. They chatted back and forth, talking about the upcoming summer solstice in a few weeks. The sweat on Brooke's upper lip was the first indicator of the poison working. Brooke made it up to the butcher for her order and left, wiping her face with the collar of her dress.

She was the first of six girls to fall ill to Laurel's poisons.

Delta and Amaya fell to rashes from a powder dusted over their hairbrushes. Marina's family all had bumps from the poison Laurel left on their doorknob, though they would clear in a few days. Avonlea got a note from the palace saying the job had already been filled. Little Coral was the last and Laurel had slipped into her house in the middle of the night with her schola mask on and spooked her parents into withdrawing her candidacy. Honestly, they were lunatics if they thought an eight-year-old should work in a palace kitchen. No child should be subject to that kind of work.

It had taken Laurel less than a day to rid herself of the competition. Now, all she had to do was get into the palace, work to establish herself as a trustworthy servant, and kill the future king of Olympia. Laying on her bed in an inn close to the palace, Laurel estimated she could be finished with the job and back to Stellatus Hall before the autumn equinox and could get her new guild set up before winter solstice.

Then, she and Aspen would finally be free.

6

THE INTERVIEW

Laurel will sit in a room across from Lady Carnation and the palace housekeeper as they listen to another girl speak. Laurel will hold the attention of the ladies well enough, but the other girl will impress them more. The girl will be offered the position as kitchen girl. Three months later, she will lose it because she is caught with the Crown Prince.

LAUREL TUCKED HER LEATHER-CORDED NECKLACE UNDER THE COLLAR of the simple dress she wore. The light-brown skirt hung to her ankles, and she draped a gray shawl over her shoulders. It was a drab outfit for certain, but it would make her invisible to most people. She tied her hair back in a simple twist at the nape of her neck and pinned back any flyaways that tried to frame her face.

Her stomach fluttered just the tiniest bit. It wasn't nerves. She hadn't been nervous about a job since she was fifteen and had to assassinate a greedy minister of trade on the Continent.

No, it couldn't be anything short of excitement.

This mission would free her and Aspen from the constraints of their order. From the people that would smile at them just as easily as they would stab them in the back or poison their supper and watch them writhe on the floor. It would give her everything she'd dreamed about since she was seven and her mother signed those cursed contracts.

She also couldn't ignore the fact that working in a real kitchen with unlimited supplies and ingredients majorly appealed to her. Her mind whirled with the recipes Father had shared with her during her childhood. Of the experiments they'd done in their kitchen at home.

Laurel turned away from the mirror and went to the bed where all her supplies were laid out. Her clothing, her mask, the garrotes, five daggers, brass knuckles, her set of throwing knives and stars, her lock picks, and her poison jacket. That was her favorite item. The black jacket looked normal from the outside, but the inside panel was lined with what looked like tea bags. Some of them were, but most of them were simply holding onto poisons. She didn't carry many that could harm her if the packets broke. Most of them were to taint food or be applied to a blade— though, there was one she carried that would be considered dangerous in any case, but that one had been secured to her jacket with specialized gold plating lining the pocket.

The Stellataen Arrow, they called it. A particular species of flower that grew in the small mountains where Stellatus Hall stood. Laurel often wondered if the order or the flower came first, but she'd yet to discover the answer. The flower itself was an ugly thing. The stem was brown and brittle looking, and the top of the plant was made up of three triangular looking bracts, all as deep blue as the night sky. It looked harmless. Unremarkable. But when one extracted the tiny white flowers within the plant, they could doom anyone to a death so long and so horrible they wished for death long before it arrived. It looked like an illness that slowly grew worse and worse, causing the body to slowly shut down in a natural yet horrific way. Untraceable, the only way one discovered it was if they looked for it in its early stages, but most people never caught it, believing they only came down with some nasty illness that would go away in a few days. But the Stellataen Arrow never missed its mark. The healthiest fae would die from the effects of it within a year, a mortal within a few weeks.

Laurel tucked the jacket along with her weapons into the bag she'd brought with her. She'd likely have to come back for it after the interview and figure out how to smuggle all of it into the palace without notice. The room had been paid for through the end of the week and the limply stuffed mattress on the bed had provided an excellent place for her to stash her weapons. She set the tripwire on the door and closed it behind her. The small knife trap she'd set would certainly run off any intruders, though it wouldn't do any serious harm. She didn't want to have to dispose of a body if she could help it.

The public room of the inn was empty, and the predawn light barely brushed the windowpanes. There was plenty of time to get to the palace before her appointment.

Without stopping in the kitchens to see about breakfast, she slipped out of the inn. There was something about seeing a city in the early morning that had always appealed to her. Night was when the seediest bits of the city came out. Daytime held the bald-faced lie of prosperity. But early morning was when the city had its true face on. The streets had yet to be cleared of the sins of the night before. The filtered light of day had yet to cast the world into life. When every creature slept, and the world was quiet. When it was no one but Laurel and the city.

She approached the palace from the south, weaving her way through the waking streets and approaching the gate. The gates opened at sunup, and her interview was at six-thirty. Even without looking at her watch, she could tell by the lightening sky that she had about half an hour before her appointment.

By the time she reached the palace, dawn had fully arrived. The sunlight splashed against the white alabaster turrets in pinks and oranges. The colors of sunsets were always more vibrant for some reason, but she could appreciate a pretty sunrise.

The palace gate was a thing of beauty though it was likely thick enough to keep the worst of a siege out should one ever attack. What looked like a tree made of thick iron twisted together over dark wood. The decoration might have even been fused to the wood rather than bolted it seemed so seamless. The entire gate opened from the middle to allow people to pass through to the palace proper and palace guards in dark-blue uniforms greeted everyone that swept through.

"State your business," a palace guard said when she approached.

She silently handed him her appointment card and continued to study the gate. All three gates were likely the same for security's sake. Even if someone burned away the wood, the iron would still pose a problem for any invaders. Was there an entrance on the cliffside? She glanced to the east, though she couldn't see the cliffs through the large houses and shops sidled up close to the palace. Those would also make siege difficult, considering an army would have to weave their way through the streets or demolish anything standing in the way.

The guard handed her card back and gestured for her to continue forward. Laurel let herself be swept away by the small line of people weaving their way through the gates. As close as she was, she trailed a hand over the thick barricade. Her assumption had been correct. The iron had been melded to the wood or vice versa. However it had been done, it was a stunning piece of craftsmanship.

She found the door to the servants' entrance on the south side of the palace. Carts sat huddled together in the cobbled courtyard as people bustled back and forth, carrying supplies. There were even several wheels of cheese that had to be carted in. Laurel's mouth watered a bit as she followed behind them and found her way to her destination.

The kitchens were a whirl of activity, yet Laurel could see the systems everyone worked under. The delivery folks brought the supplies in and left them to the servants waiting there who then scattered to put the crates and bags in their proper places. The cooks were already hard at work. The hiss of steam and the clank of pots rang throughout the large space. Counters spread across three quarters of the room along with a wide table in the middle, allowing the three people in the center of the room to hop from one dish to the next as they prepared the meal to go up to the dining room. Sprigs of herbs hung above a roaring fireplace, where a lamb turned on a spit. On another wall, a male cook pulled out a slab of *pita* and added it to a tray. The aroma of the fresh bread mingled with cinnamon and honey, reminding Laurel of her lack of breakfast that morning.

Voices came to her in bits and pieces over the cacophony, but she tucked herself to the side next to another girl to watch instead of interacting. She was early enough that she need not seek out the head cook for the interview, which she guessed was the woman with light-brown hair leaning over the center table to frown at a young man.

The man looked out of place in the hustle and bustle of the

kitchen. He wore a finely made jacket of what looked like blue velvet. While his blond hair was thin, the queue at the back of his neck was tastefully done. His shoulders were narrow, speaking to a life of little exercise, but his small paunch of a stomach spoke to his tastes for fine dining. Which was likely why he was in the kitchen, huffing and puffing about.

"If His Highness asks for that asparagus *frittata* one more time this week, I shall certainly die."

The cook swatted at him. "You most certainly will not die because I make the best frittata in the kingdom."

The man buried his face in his hands, the frilled sleeves of his shirt hanging down over his velvet jacket. "But the asparagus..."

"Not another word," she admonished. "If you want some of these flat cakes, I suggest you simply accept your fate. Prince Dion has already requested his breakfast this morning."

The man groaned and thumped his forehead on the countertop.

"Poor Galen."

Laurel looked to the girl standing next to her. She was a petite thing with hair that couldn't decide if it was brown or blond, though she had a pretty face that not even her drab dress could distract from. She couldn't be older than fifteen.

The girl's brown eyes studied the complaining man. "It must be difficult, being a taster."

Laurel turned back to the man the girl had referred to as Galen. A taster wasn't the worst thing she'd ever faced, but it would be another thing to watch out for as Laurel figured out how to assassinate the Crown Prince.

One of the other cooks shuffled toward them, her dark eyes narrowed at Laurel. "Is it just the two of you?" she asked. "You're both here to interview?"

Laurel looked down at the girl next to her. Of course there

was one more applicant for the job. If Laurel had arrived in Olympia sooner, she'd likely have done her own reconnaissance and made sure she knew everything about everyone seeking out this position. Instead, she'd trusted in Teagan's good word and the word of his little friend. She should have known better.

The girl nodded. "I haven't seen any other girls I don't recognize."

The young cook looked up at Laurel again. "Well, that'll make it easy for you, cousin."

Ah, so that was how the girl hadn't made it onto the list. She had an in with the kitchens already.

This interview just got much harder.

The head cook moved from the taster and turned in their direction.

"Ah, Deirdre," she said, looking at Laurel's competition. "I'm glad you could make it on short notice."

The young cook grabbed Deirdre's hand. "Of course she could make it. You know my family would do anything for this kitchen." Her words oozed with sweetness. This wasn't the young cook's first-time poisoning someone, she just did it with words rather than powders.

"You know I'm not the only one who gets to decide, Delilah." The head cook focused on Laurel. "And which girl are you?"

Laurel dipped into a curtsy. "Laurel, madam."

The head cook straightened her apron. "Well, since the two of you are the only ones here, we can get your interviews started." She gestured for them to follow her.

Laurel watched the back of Deirdre's head as they wove through the kitchens and into a hallway. Besides the small sconce of magelights twinkling against one wall, there wasn't much to use if she wanted to get rid of Deirdre quickly. Besides, no one would hire someone who went around bashing in the heads of fifteen-year-old girls. No, she needed to wait this out. She'd been able to rid herself of the other applicants. One more wasn't difficult.

The cook stopped at an already open door. "Just here, you two. Lady Carnation and Esther will be handling your interviews."

Laurel followed Deirdre into the room where they were met by two other women. The first Laurel recognized from the notes she'd been given for this mission. Lady Carnation of Speculo sat erect in a simple fabric chair. Half of her blond curls cascaded down the back of her pale pink dress while the other half had been pulled back from her face and pinned in complicated braids and twists. Her sharp blue eyes studied both Deirdre and Laurel as they walked in, and Laurel felt like her soul was being measured.

The other woman, Esther, sat next to Lady Carnation. Her demeanor seemed much more pleasant as she folded her hands over her simple, navy gown. She nodded to each of them and gestured to two wooden chairs positioned across from her. "Please, have a seat."

Deirdre chose the seat across from Esther and Laurel was left with the one closest to Lady Carnation, positioning herself so she could still see the door out of her peripheral. There was a small window in this room, though it wouldn't act as the best escape route if she needed one.

"Thank you for coming," Esther said. "We'd like to ask both of you a few questions together and then we will interview both of you separately."

Esther took a sheet of paper from a pile on the table next to her. She asked for both Laurel and Deirdre's recommendations as well as what their history was in the kitchen. While Laurel liked to experiment in her kitchen back home, she wasn't truly a kitchen girl, and it seemed Deirdre was—in every sense of the word. Lady Carnation nodded at everything she said and continually wrote notes as she spoke. Laurel held her own, at least she thought she did well enough, but the girl was the obvious choice if the smiles and nods were anything to go off of.

Laurel really would have to get rid of the poor girl.

It wouldn't do to simply make her sick either. She might be sick for a few days, but that didn't mean she would lose her position. Laurel wouldn't kill children or babes, but fifteen was pushing adulthood. It would be much easier to make her disappear if she didn't have to worry about her showing up again later. Or the girl could lose a limb. That would make it difficult for her to work— though it would be messier in the long run. Laurel would have to plan it carefully which would take more time than she wanted.

The door to the room opened behind Laurel.

She was on her feet in an instant.

Crown Prince Dion swaggered into the room.

The very man she'd been sent to kill right within her grasp.

Laurel nearly reached for her dagger but remembered she'd left everything but her shortest daggers back at the inn. Besides, she couldn't kill him with witnesses. She wouldn't make it out of the palace alive.

"Good morning, ladies!" he greeted, his amethyst eyes bright. A charming smile danced on his lips, but Laurel felt her own lips trying to turn down into a frown. The man exuded arrogance. She quickly searched the outline of his fine jacket and rather tight trousers. Not even a single imprint of a weapon stood out beneath, though she couldn't say the same of the guards who took their places at the door. Did the prince truly have that much confidence?

"What are you doing here, Dee?" Apparently, Lady Carnation was having none of it. Her own eyes narrowed as her betrothed approached.

Prince Dion's smile only widened. "I've received a letter from Polly." He reached into the inner lining of his jacket, making the hairs on the back of Laurel's neck rise, before withdrawing a folded piece of parchment. "He included some news for you."

"And you thought I needed this information right this second?" She gestured toward Laurel and Deirdre. "I'm right in the middle of interviews."

Prince Dion glanced at each of them, his eyes taking in both of their faces. "The note accompanying it said to get it to you immediately."

Lady Carnation frowned but took the note. Whoever this "Polly" was must have been important. The wax seal keeping the paper together snapped apart as she unfolded the missive. She quickly scanned the contents, her eyes darting up to look at Deirdre then back at the note before refolding it. "The interviews are over. Laurel will be given the position, and Deirdre will have to find employment outside the palace."

Deirdre's face fell. "Is there something I did wrong, my lady?"

Lady Carnation stood and smacked the letter into Prince Dion's chest and shoved him aside. "Not yet and you won't, should you leave the palace and find work elsewhere." She glared up at her betrothed then turned to Laurel. "You begin tomorrow at sunrise."

Laurel sat stunned as the lady stormed out the door, the prince on her heels. She heard Deirdre choke back a small sob and Esther reached out to reassure the poor girl. But Laurel couldn't look away from the now empty door.

What on Gaia's green earth just happened?

7

AN UNFORTUNATE GOODBYE

Paulo stared up at the star-speckled ceiling. Why his ancestors had chosen the constellations to decorate the underground cave, he had no idea, but it worked. The stone floor was cold beneath his spine, but he could feel the magic swell under him, as if the land itself were pushing him through time. Some of the journals and things from his predecessors spoke of the magic as if it were attached to the land. After the things he'd seen, he didn't doubt it.

The faint trickle of water to his right calmed his mind. He didn't know if the small spring was a natural occurrence or if it had been crafted by a previous MacGregor, but the splash of the small pool centered him and pulled his mind into time.

Laurel will creep through the shadows, the mask of a demon covering her face. A slip of white trails up ahead of her and disappears through a door. Laurel follows and waits at the door. After a time, she slips through a door lined with faint light. She creeps toward a settee where soft snores sound and draws her dagger...

Paulo released the magic and opened his eyes. The stars above him whirled as the headache set in. It wasn't as bad as some he'd had in the past. The further he looked into the future or the longer he gave the magic access to his thoughts, the more it hurt and the longer it would take for him to recover. Hopefully, Mater had a cup of tea waiting for him upstairs. Pushing himself up, he tried not to think about what would happen next.

He'd seen the vision of Laurel already. He knew the consequences. The thing he had to make sure changed.

"Mater, I hope you won't miss me too much while I'm gone." Paulo stuffed a lime-green waistcoat in beside one the same shade as a tangerine. His trunk was beginning to resemble a fruit salad. He grabbed his favorite dark-blue jacket and stuffed that in as well. Jenkins and Mater watched from the corner of the room, both with narrowed eyes though for different reasons.

"I'm not going to be sitting idly around while you go off to Olympia to do your duty." Mater came up beside him and laid a hand on his arm. "You've given me plenty to do, and I've never been one to dawdle."

Paulo stopped his harried packing and turned to face her. "Are you sure about this?"

Mater's brow quirked and she pulled him to the side to allow a muttering Jenkins to access his trunk. "That I need to remain to make sure our lands stay safe and to give us a fighting chance in the months to come?" She gave him that soft, motherly smile she used when she thought he was being overprotective. "Of course, my dear. Everything will be just fine here."

Paulo ran a hand through his hair, his fingers catching on

the curls Jenkins had so meticulously pomaded away from his face that morning. The muttering from his valet increased for a moment. Paulo did his best to ignore it, but a smile pushed itself onto his lips. "Just because I know everything will turn out how we planned doesn't mean I have to like it." In fact, he didn't like it at all, but he knew he couldn't change it. He couldn't stop the war that would come to his kingdom.

Mater's arms came around his waist, and he sagged into her, his chin resting atop her silvering hair. "You're all going to be just fine up there, and I'm sure there will be plenty to distract you."

Magic swirled in Paulo's head, and he saw a flash of roaring flames being smothered by shadow. "Yes, there will be plenty for me to do in the next couple weeks."

She pulled away from him. "Good. I'm sure Diana will keep you on your toes until then."

"I really wish I didn't have to take her," Paulo groaned. He needed her in Olympia with him, of that he was sure, but she could be such a... *Diana*.

"You know you would be bereft without her and call for her within a week if you didn't take her."

That was likely true. For being such an annoying little sister— even if it was only by eight minutes— Paulo couldn't really picture himself without her. She could be his greatest enemy or his best friend depending on the moment. Sometimes, both at the same time. He was glad he only had one sibling to butt heads with.

"Do you think she's already packed?" Paulo asked.

"*Do you think she's already packed?*" a voice mocked from his door. Diana slid into the doorway. Her bright hair was pulled back into her signature braid, a few wispy curls sticking out next to her ears. She had a large leather pack slung over her shoulder. "Paulo, I've been ready to leave for two hours and have just been waiting for you to get your junk in the carriage so we can go."

Paulo bristled. "I'm not taking junk."

Diana leaned against the doorframe. "Then why is Jenkins tucking a clock into your trunk?"

Paulo turned to watch Jenkins set his nightstand clock into the trunk he'd finished repacking and close the lid. Paulo whirled on Diana. "That clock doesn't click like the ones in the palace do. You know I can't sleep with the incessant clicking in my ear."

Diana rolled her eyes. "Prima donna."

"Savage barbarian," Paulo snapped back.

"Really, you two," Mater drawled as Jenkins hefted the trunk off the floor. "You act like a pair of spoiled children."

"Aren't we?" Diana asked and stepped aside to allow Jenkins through the door. "Seeing how we've never wanted for anything, and you let us do whatever we want, I would say we are spoiled, and it's definitely your fault."

Mater let out an exaggerated sigh. "The follies of young parenthood."

They followed Jenkins out into the hallway. Paulo's eyes trailed over the pattern of the burgundy wallpaper as they walked, the veins of gold making crisscrossing patterns along the wall for his eyes to trail. He always thought they looked like strings of fate, but he didn't know if it had been chosen by one of his predecessors because of that or if it was coincidence.

The family rooms weren't too far from the entrance hall and Paulo could hear the bustle of the staff as they prepared for him to leave. He wished it wasn't always such a hubbub, but he'd learned early on to just let the servants do their job. They got a bit grouchy when he didn't. The double doors leading to the entrance hall were open as they came upon it. Jenkins turned and disappeared from view. Paulo's attention was captured by the large face of a boar hanging above the front door.

"A new trophy, Diana?" he asked, frowning.

Diana set her hands on her hips. "Why yes, thank you for noticing. I bagged the beast two months ago and the taxidermist delivered the mount yesterday. When I saw it, I knew this spot would be perfect."

"Ah yes, because the last impression you want to leave our guests is that we are absolute 'boars.'" The head was somewhat grotesque, the mouth open in a squeal and its eyes wide and wild. They had several mounts decorating the halls of Iatrus Castle and he could name at least a handful that would look more prestigious above the door than a screaming boar.

Mater studied the beast. "That is a rather large trophy, my dear. It looks like it would fit marvelously in the library. You know where that blank wall is where the old painting of the wars had been?"

Paulo withheld a shiver. He'd had to have the painting put away last year. His visions had started giving him nightmares and the painting seemed to be those images brought to canvas.

"I hadn't thought about that spot," Diana said.

Mater took both Paulo and Diana's arms, tucking each of them to her side though both were taller than her by at least a full head if not a head and a half. "Don't you fret. I'll see to it while the both of you are off on this adventure."

Paulo tucked his mouth close to her ear. "You're a saint, Mater."

Mater patted his arm in silent support.

The carriage awaited them on the gravel drive outside. Paulo's stomach flipped. Their luggage had been tied to the back and the carriage for Jenkins and Diana's very patient lady's maid waited behind it. This was it.

Mater released her hold on them and swept Diana into a

hug. "Love you, dearest. Try to keep out of trouble while you're in Olympia."

Diana snorted but acquiesced. It was impossible to say no to Mater.

She wrapped Paulo in a hug next. "You too. I know this trip is important but remember to watch yourself. We all know there will be dangers lurking around every corner."

Paulo pulled back. "Are you sure you'll be all right here?" He wanted to ask her to come with them, if only to know she was close, and he could watch over her. But he knew he needed her to stay, and she did too.

Mater yanked both him and Diana into a hug. "Keep each other safe. Watch each other's backs. You two were born as a team and I expect you to come back to me whole and hale."

8

AN UNFORTUNATE
PARTNERSHIP

*The prince will meet with a young lady, their
rendezvous one of the many sitting rooms in the palace.
He will enjoy the company of this young lady, finding
companionship in her presence much as he does so
many other girls. They will make their way to one of the
sofas. Neither of them will see the masked assassin
enter the room.*

IT WOULD BE TOO SOON IF PAULO SAW THE INSIDE OF A CARRIAGE
again before next summer solstice. While it had been nearly
four months since he'd last been in Olympia, he wanted to
burn the carriage and never look inside one again.

When the footman opened the door, Paulo jumped out, not
even bothering with the steps. He breathed in a deep lungful of
fresh city air and looked up at the palace. Visions of fire and
death had plagued him for the last hour of the ride. Things
were *not* going according to plan, but he needed to figure
out why.

"How you can be eager to be back in this place, I have no idea." Diana more gracefully lighted from the carriage, though she still didn't allow the footman to help her.

"Just because you can't appreciate the luxuries of our station in life," Paulo replied, "doesn't mean I have to rough it out with you."

A group of glittering young ladies passed by, silk fans fluttering as fast as their lashes.

Diana made a small gagging sound from behind him.

He turned to her. "Will you help get our things settled? There's someone I need to see."

"Oh?" A mischievous grin stretched across her face. "You can't even wait a single minute to go harass her, can you?"

Paulo rolled his eyes. "I'm not a completely lovesick fool."

"I'll believe it when I see it."

Shaking his head, Paulo left Diana to attend to their things. He had made plans to stay for an extended period, which necessitated the large load on the back of the carriage. He was still a marquess. There were estates to run, tenants to manage, and his sheep flocks to watch over. His work never ceased, but he was grateful for the people he had around him to help.

Paulo strode through the halls, calling up his gift and searching for his quarry. His magic automatically went to the kitchens, and he found Laurel there, peeling an outrageously large pile of potatoes. He turned his attentions away from her, even if he ached not to.

The magic found Prince Dion and Lady Carnation seated in the prince's study.

Perfect.

Paulo made his way in that direction. When he arrived and saw no guards standing at the door, he waited until Prince Dion and Lady Carnation walked around the corner five minutes later.

Bowing low, he greeted them. "Good afternoon, Your Highness. My lady."

"Polly!" Prince Dion's voice echoed about the hallway. "I was just talking about you."

Paulo straightened. "I hope I haven't displeased Your Highness."

Prince Dion waved him off. "Not at all. It was merely a conversation I was having with Shaunie about what's going on down in Eleusion."

A group of courtiers came around the corner.

Lady Carnation looked over her shoulder at them, tugging Prince Dion toward the study. "Perhaps we can chat somewhere a little more private."

Paulo followed the couple into the study. He'd been in the room a few times, getting a full view of the large bookcases and merry fireplace. The walls were papered in dark blue with images of oak trees and soaring eagles painted in gold. The guards in the hallway closed the door as the prince and his betrothed took their seats behind a large desk. They really were a perfect pair, at least appearance wise. Both were the epitome of sophisticated beauty, cutting fine figures in their elaborate clothing. There would be statues made in their image. Painters from around the world would wish for the chance to paint their images on canvas.

It would happen if the next several months went exactly how Paulo wanted.

Which, at the moment, they weren't.

"Is there anything I can assist with in regard to Eleusion?" Paulo asked, taking a seat across the large desk from them. "As their closest neighbor, I feel I should help in whatever way I can."

"Do you know what's happening there?" Lady Carnation

asked. Her blue eyes met his, the steel there cutting through to his soul.

Does she have even an inkling as to what I know?

Paulo shrugged. "I know the Lord of the Underworld is there now."

Of course, Paulo had seen most of it. In fact, he had been laying down hints in the council meetings for over a year, pushing the youngest prince to eventually go to Eleusion himself. How would they get Penny to join the fight against the rebellion if he didn't train her? There were so many moving parts to the future that needed to come to pass, and Paulo had to make sure it all went smoothly.

"I knew it!" Prince Dion laughed. "I knew all your little nudges at Denny going to Eleusion weren't as innocent as you made them sound. I've been eager to know what you've seen."

Paulo crossed his foot over his knee. "He's attempting to ferret out the rebellion and discover who The Cartographer is."

Prince Dion steepled his fingers. "Do you know who it is?"

Yes. "No, though I don't doubt your brother's abilities. I saw them firsthand when we were younger." The Lord of the Underworld, only a month older than Paulo himself, had become infamous for the way he could discover information. He had been trained by one of the most nefarious spymasters in Olympia's history and had used those skills to help his brothers take the kingdom from their tyrant of a father and those that supported him. Paulo had watched many of the Tyrant King's peers face justice at the young prince's hands.

Prince Dion sighed. "Unfortunately, we haven't had much progress on that front and now we're starting to see rebel activity here in the capital. I've just called Denny back from Eleusion to help sort it out."

Paulo sat up. "You did *what?*"

"I sent him a missive just yesterday. He'll likely receive it in a few days and return home by the end of next week. Now that the rebellion in Eleusion has grown to such an extent, we will have to petition the council to rally our forces and help Duchess Dominique take back her lands."

Paulo stood and began pacing. He would need to get word to the youngest prince. The Lord of the Underworld needed to return to Barclay Manor. Needed to save Penny from the fire that would reveal things to her and put her on a path that would ultimately lead her where she needed to go.

"Was I wrong to do it?" Prince Dion asked.

Paulo stilled. "Of course not, Your Highness. I am only concerned. The murders happening within the city are most upsetting as is the knowledge of Lady Barclay's situation. It was wise of you to call back our spymaster." If only he'd waited another week. The youngest prince would have already been on his way when Prince Dion sent the missive. Paulo allowed the magic to sweep through him. He still saw the youngest Prince pull Penny from the fire. Hope wasn't lost, but he needed to make haste.

"I did have a few questions," Lady Carnation said. "Are you able to tell us about our upcoming trade deals? With Lord Hermen's people in Faerie, I'm hoping to have something in place before the end of the year, barring a complete rebellious uprising."

Paulo allowed himself to look to see if telling her would cause any hiccups in the timeline. "I don't foresee the Winter Court agreeing at the moment. There are too many decisions to be made, but I wouldn't lose hope. Devan and Angelica Elie are both talented negotiators."

Lady Carnation nodded, jotting down a few notes on a pad of paper.

"Is there anything else we should be aware of, Polly?"

Prince Dion chuckled. "While I am glad to see you in Olympia once more, I cannot help but think it a bad omen."

Paulo flashed his most charming smile, trying his best to hide the strain he felt as he returned to his seat. "There's one last thing I would discuss with you. I have seen a new arrival coming to Olympia, one I think will be able to help us."

"Color me intrigued," Prince Dion said. "When will they arrive?"

Paulo grinned. "They're already here but approaching them will take some... tact."

Prince Dion opened his mouth, but Lady Carnation cut in before he could speak. "I assume you're approaching us because you wish for us to stay out of it."

Paulo grinned. "Not to say either you or His Highness don't possess a great amount of tact, it is more that I ask for your cooperation."

"What do you need us to do?" Prince Dion asked.

Paulo clasped his hands behind his back, his fingers digging into his palms. "I simply ask that you trust me and believe that what I'm doing will work out for the best."

Lady Carnation's brows lowered. "Are you going to be causing trouble, Lord MacGregor?"

"Perhaps a bit."

Prince Dion barked a laugh. "If he's anything like his father, he'll be causing quite *a bit*."

Yes, Father had caused quite a few bits of trouble. He had been the one to nudge the princes down the path that led to the Tyrant King's downfall. Unfortunately, he hadn't lived to see it happen.

"I promise," Paulo pledged, "to make the least amount of trouble that I possibly can."

Prince Dion clapped his hands together, the sound cracking like thunder through the room. "I'll take it."

9
THE TASTER

"TONIGHT. WATCH FOR *THE SHINING RIVER*."

The words slipped by Laurel's ear as quickly as the wind. If she hadn't been slightly bumped into, she wouldn't have believed it came from a person. She didn't recognize the voice and the man was lost in the crowd before she could even get a good look at him.

But she recognized the name he'd spoken.

She should have expected this. Teagan could be patient when he needed to be, but he'd been nearly frenzied about this plan before she'd left. Of course he'd want her to be done already. Of course, he'd expect her to infiltrate the palace in a month and a half. On her own. Without another pair of eyes.

But it was for the best that she was alone.

Pushing her way through the crowd, she pulled the brim of her cap farther down her brow and tucked the stray hair sticking to her cheek up into the body of the cap with the rest of her braid. Sweat had already seeped into the lining, the summer sun beating down over the market square and adding to the tizzy. She kept her eyes on the edge of the market square.

The paper package of chalk sat awkwardly in her hands. She didn't know how much of the stuff she would need for her reconnaissance around the castle walls, but it seemed she might be back next week as well if she needed to use it to meet Teagan in two days. Climbing the cliff holding up the palace might be the quickest way down and it would be good to figure out if it was a proper escape route.

Laurel stopped at the edge of the market, taking out her small pocket watch. She had three hours until her half-day off was over. She'd been given one of those a week and everyone in the kitchens had time off on worship days— except for Galen who was still technically working as he went with Prince Dion in case of any food-related emergencies. Which would have been the perfect day for Laurel to go see Teagan since she didn't go to the temple with the rest of them. They didn't have temples on the Continent.

Why Teagan had to plan a meeting for the day prior to worship, she could only guess. Sometimes, it seemed it was the man's prerogative to make her life as miserable as he could.

Awkwardly tucking her watch back in her vest pocket with one hand, she glanced both ways, her attention falling on a woman standing across the street from her. Copper hair shone under the shining sun, contrasting with her dark green tunic. The well-made leather pants the woman wore had Laurel calculating how much money she'd brought with her. What she wouldn't give to know where to purchase them. While she didn't consider herself vain, Laurel knew good craftsmanship when she saw it. She couldn't take her eyes off the woman or her pants as both crossed the street toward her. The woman's forget-me-not blue eyes landed on Laurel before passing over her. Laurel nearly turned away, but the redhead's gaze whipped back to her, and a crooked smile spread across her face. She nudged her gentleman companion.

Laurel froze when she met the eyes of the man.

It was *him*! The odd man from Eleusia. The one who had practically accosted her on the street. She hadn't seen him in nearly five months, but she hadn't forgotten the freckles creating constellations all over his face or the brilliant red hair curling in front of his ears.

And the very direct, very smug look on his face said he hadn't forgotten her either.

Laurel told herself to look away, but her eyes betrayed her. The man drew closer, his smile widening with every step he took toward her. It would be better if she looked away. She didn't need this kind of attention. But almost against her will, one eyebrow rose on her forehead, challenging his blatant stare.

That devilish smile finally reached his eyes as he passed her. It was a smile that said he saw her, he knew her, and he wasn't going to let her scare him off. It turned Laurel's challenging eyebrow into a scowl. It wouldn't do to give the man any sense she was interested in him.

He finally let his gaze fall from her, but Laurel was left feeling like she had come out the loser.

Laurel pressed a hand to her lower back and rubbed out the ache that had settled there. The combination of bending over on a stool to peel potatoes and scaling part of the castle last night had leant to sore muscles that evening. She'd been in the palace for three months now and believed she'd sniffed out every nook and cranny there was to be found. The only room she hadn't made it into was the royal sitting room, but she already knew that was going to be a one-shot wonder. The room was practically a bunker inside the palace. Only one door led into the room and while it was usually guarded, it was also enchanted. The entire room had been carved with charms in the walls apparently.

Luckily, it seemed Prince Dion wasn't one of those paranoid types that holed up in the safe places. He traipsed through the palace daily, meeting with councilors, allowing time for public petitions, even finding a moment or two to tuck himself into a closet with a pretty skirt. That was the one thing Laurel found somewhat human about the man. In everything else, he seemed to be a paragon of leadership and princeliness, but in this, Laurel found just a man who she'd been charged to kill.

However, the cursed prince never seemed to be alone.

There was always a crowd of people wherever he went. And not just humans. Mages, fae, and water folk flocked to him at every turn. It seemed like the man was a magnet for attention and the residents of the Olympian Palace were only too happy to oblige him. It set Laurel's teeth to grinding.

The open archway leading from the staircase up into the dining room darkened and a servant stepped in, holding a tray. His eyes shone with excitement. "Excuse me, Cook, but His Highness has requested a bottle of wine along with his third plate. There's been some terrible news."

Laurel watched the man, the hairs on the back of her neck standing on end. For someone who just announced he had terrible news to share, the man looked nearly gleeful. Her eyes narrowed. While he was dressed as a servant, something felt slightly off about him. Like the uniform didn't quite fit around his shoulders.

"What's happened?" Delilah, the undercook who was now Laurel's roommate spun toward the server. "Is His Highness all right?"

The man nearly bounced. "There's been a fire! Barclay

Manor went up in flames not two nights ago and the rebellion has taken Eleusion for themselves."

Laurel's fingers tightened around her knife. Things in Eleusion were progressing quickly then. Adira had told her somewhat of the plans she was making. Eleusion was their first target, and it seemed their goals had been met there.

"Sweet Gaia! What a tragedy." Cook placed her hand on her bosom. "All that farmland, gone. And poor Lady Barclay and her daughter. They must be devastated."

The server placed the tray on the table. "Prince Dion is beside himself, which was why he requested the wine."

"I can go," Delilah offered.

"No, I'll fetch it." Cook set her spoon on a little dish to catch drips. "You get His Highness's wraps prepared, and I'll be right back with that wine."

A loud moan broke through Laurel's musings, and she withheld an eye roll.

Galen, the blasted taster with nine stomachs, dramatically spread himself over the table in the middle of the kitchen. "Why must His Highness order another plate of *souvlaki* wraps? I hate *tzatziki* sauce, and he knows it."

Cook turned back to the table. "Now Galen..."

"*Now Galen,*" the taster mocked. He closed his garnet-colored eyes— a color Laurel had thought quite strange at first — and sighed.

Cook shook her finger at him. "We've had this conversation a thousand times."

"Yes, yes. I know. Stop my whining and get the food to His Highness." Galen ran his hands down his pale face. "But he has such poor taste! Would it kill him to try some *kochlioli* and rice or even *pasta apo melani htapodiou?*"

Laurel reflexively grimaced. Snails and octopus ink sacks sounded like the last thing she would want to eat as a prince.

While she liked to experiment with food, there were some-things she wouldn't touch with a ten-foot pole— mainly anything that secreted slime in its life or had more than four appendages. And she'd been on the receiving end of Cook's art and every bite had felt like music in her mouth. There was no other way to describe it.

But Galen had the taste buds of a raccoon with a superi-ority complex.

Cook must have thought so as well. "My fare is good enough for our future king which means it's good enough for you." She nodded, as if to punctuate what she said, and swept toward the wine cellar.

Galen grumbled and dramatically smashed his face into the table.

Praise the Goddess the man's woeful life was slowly coming to a close.

Laurel set aside her potato and grabbed another, her gaze flitting to the tower of desserts on the table against the wall, closest to the door. Galen would have to take a few bites, of course, but it wouldn't matter. Laurel had made sure every dessert had been laced with blue-ringed octopus venom, one of the most common poisons used by the Aigeans. The taste of the venom was easily masked by anything with cinnamon and would take a few hours to hit those who had eaten it. The Aigean delegation would be investigated. Laurel had already planted the poison in their rooms, hidden just enough to not cause notice but found easily if someone were to go looking for it.

Delilah grinned and grabbed a clean plate. "By the Goddess, Galen, you act as if we're living in a drama."

Laurel nearly laughed. From what she had gathered in the last few months, the kitchens were nothing short of a drama-making machine. One of the butlers was blackmailing the other undercook, Dan, for ten silver pieces a month to not tell Cook about his gambling debts. The dishwashing girl was seeing one of the stableboys, one of the guards, and a gardener all without any of the other men knowing about each other.

And then there were Galen and Delilah.

Their little one-sided love story was as ridiculous as they were. How Galen would let himself be strung along after someone like Delilah, Laurel would never understand. She would pity the man if he wasn't such a lout.

Delilah finished preparing the wraps and set them on the table in front of Galen, who still had his head down on the table. She turned back to the stove and the server reached for the plate.

If Laurel hadn't been watching, she wouldn't have noticed the powder slip from his fingers and fall onto the food.

She stilled.

Great Goddess, there was another assassin out for her bounty.

By the purple tinge of the powder, it was castor bean poison. Castor bean, when ingested, was great at attacking organs. It worked better as an inhalant, but with enough powder, ingestion worked just as well. However, if it were Laurel using it, she would have mixed it with pufferfish toxin to paralyze the victim and keep them from being treated for an ingested poison.

Laurel sat back, waiting to see how this would play out. Her main objective was to remain invisible in this kitchen. She needed to act like she was there to help while also not looking too smart. She didn't need any extra attention pointed her way as it could make it difficult for her to escape after the prince's assassination. Her fingers twitched on the handle of the knife.

If someone else cashed in on her mission, she wouldn't get off this cursed island and she wouldn't get Aspen's contract.

Before she could do anything, Cook stepped back in. "Here's the wine." She set it on the table.

The assassin placed it on the tray. "I'll take this right up." He turned to walk away.

"Now wait just one second," Cook said. She pulled the tray off the assassin's shoulder and plopped it on the table. "Galen, my boy."

Galen grumbled but lifted his head and grabbed the fork on the tray.

The assassin stepped forward. "I really need to get this up there—"

Cook swatted at him. "You know very well that Galen will be the one to take it to His Highness."

Laurel watched as Galen cut into the middle of the wrap, her heart thumping in her ears. She'd watched him do it with every meal. He would find the spot in the dish with the thickest amount of food and would practically ruin the fine plating Cook had created. After he tasted it in the kitchen, he would carry the plate up to the dining hall and take another bite right before he placed it in front of Prince Dion. The guards would watch for any sign of poison and if nothing happened, he would return to the kitchen. It was a rather serious job and one that showed how loyal Galen was to his kingdom, even if he complained about everything.

Castor bean powder would take several minutes to hit Galen's lungs. It would then take hours for him to die if he ingested enough of it. However, castor bean had a very bitter aftertaste if one knew to watch out for it.

If Galen discovered the poison in the dish, she might be able to get the desserts up to the prince in the hubbub.

Galen took a bite.

The assassin took a step back.

Laurel stood.

Galen froze. In the next second, he spat out the food. "Sweet Gaia, not again!"

Oh, praise the Goddess. Laurel sagged in relief.

The assassin bolted, pushing past Cook and racing along the wall.

"Guards!" Cook hollered.

Almost on instinct, Laurel threw the paring knife in her hand. It snagged the sleeve of the assassin's ill-fitting jacket and stuck him to the wall. He jerked to a stop and had to tear his sleeve in order to get free.

But it was too late.

The guards swarmed him. They wrestled him to the ground as he screamed, "The Cartographer is coming! Be warned! We are coming!"

The man continued to scream as he was dragged away.

Laurel's heart beat like a crazed drum in her chest. It only took seconds for them to capture him. Seconds for him to get caught.

A choking gag cut through the fading hollers and Laurel turned her gaze back to Galen. The taster had gone absolutely purple in the face.

Usually, castor bean took much longer to take effect.

Cook cradled Galen's head and laid him on the floor. "It's all right, lad. It'll pass. Don't fight it." She snapped her fingers, and Delilah set to giving quiet orders around the room, and everyone returned to their stations.

Laurel's brows furrowed on her forehead. The kitchen was decidedly calm as they watched a man writhe in agony on the floor. Which should have taken his body three hours to get to, based on the bite he'd taken and the handful of minutes it had been since he'd eaten it.

Something was very wrong.

Laurel crept toward the desserts.

The growing gray pallor of his skin made the garnet color of his eyes dull.

Oh, by the blasted Goddess, the man was a cursed mage! Laurel had to keep herself from throwing her hands up. He'd likely been given the job because whatever gift he had made the poisons detectable early on.

This blasted magical kingdom!

Cook brushed Galen's thin hair to the side as he died. She didn't weep. In fact, none of the kitchen staff even looked askance at the dead body now taking up space in their kitchen. No one called for an undertaker as the man's skin turned a ghastly shade of gray. No one paused for a moment of silence. Even quiet Dan carefully took the plate of poisoned food and set to disposing of it. It seemed as if the life of the taster didn't warrant any thought at all. How many tasters had they seen fall to poisons since Prince Dion had taken down his predecessor?

A loud gasp made Laurel jump and bump into the desserts. They all fell to the ground, which solved her problem more or less.

Galen rose, spluttering and panting, his skin still the grayish pallor of death. Laurel's stomach dropped as Cook helped him get to his feet.

"By the Goddess." Galen spat out several colorful curses. "I *hate* dying!"

Laurel stuck her right hand in the chalk bag hanging from her waist as her left kept her from plummeting. The wall around the palace towered what was likely forty or fifty feet above the ground. With her right hand properly chalked, she reached up and grabbed the gap making up part of the crenellated edge. She pulled herself up, using the rubber tips of her boots to keep her grip between the mortared bricks.

The soft clip of boots sounded from her right. Laurel waited, listening. The scuff of leather on the stone brick. The clink of metal. The huff of a breath.

If she had to kill a guard, this could get complicated. She didn't need to alert anyone to a breach in the palace's security. They would start an investigation, and she didn't have time to relearn patrols or worry about extra guard rotations. It had taken her an entire month of reconnaissance to learn the patrol patterns.

Turn around. She willed the guard to go in the other direction.

The guard turned a moment later.

Laurel bolted over the walkway and slipped down the wall.

The ground on the other side of the wall lay much farther down than the castle side. Only two dozen or so feet of grassy dirt stood between her and the perilous fall to the beach below. *Great Goddess.* It was like hovering above the world and the rapid beat of her heart protested the possibility of her fall. The wind buffeted against the wall, practically plastering her to the bricks as she scaled down. How difficult would the climb down to the beach be without the manmade gaps in the brick and the consistent hand holds?

Laurel dropped the last couple of feet to the base of the wall, her heart settling as her boots sank into the wild grass beneath them. Tiptoeing to the edge of the cliff, she looked about. With the way the wall was built, there was no access to this side of the cliff from the streets of the city. This portion stuck out onto the cliff higher up than the others, creating a natural defense. Looking over the side of the cliff, Laurel's chalked hands began to sweat in earnest. The drop looked to be about a hundred feet, the cliff face worn and smooth. She followed the edge all the way around the wall and found the same on every side.

Impossible. She would be absolutely insane to climb down this way. She set her hands on her hips.

"Now what?" She fiddled with the bead on the leather band around her wrist. Teagan would likely be down on the beach within the hour. If she was quick, she could get back over the wall and go with Plan B, which was to use the guard halls within the walls themselves. She had only gotten a glimpse of those in her reconnaissance of the palace, so it would be riskier— though not as risky as climbing down this cursed cliff.

She turned away from the edge and raced toward the wall. When she reached the halfway point, the ground under her feet gave way.

It was only because of her training that she was able to dive to the side and avoid falling into the hole. She continued to scramble away as the hole widened, swallowing the grass and dirt as it grew toward the palace wall. Five, ten, fifteen feet gave way before coming to a stop.

The trickle of dirt quieted, and Laurel slowly crawled closer, staying on her stomach to distribute her weight over the ground. She slowed at the edge and peeked over the side. The moon was high enough in the sky to see what looked like a tunnel. The ground beneath sloped up toward the palace wall, as if someone had intentionally built it.

Laurel got to her feet and slowly crept toward the top of the ramp. Using the toes of her boots, she tested the stability of the dirt as she went, prodding the ground just in case. While the loose dirt moved, the foundation didn't crumble under her weight. She reached the bottom and looked up. The tunnel had a brace right next to where it had collapsed.

Reaching into one of the pouches on her belt, she withdrew a magelight and gave it a small squeeze. The things were handy, though extremely expensive on the Continent. Aspen had given one to Laurel for her birthday a year ago and she never went anywhere without it.

Magelight in hand, she made her way down the tunnel. The walls were smooth, obviously having been carved. Who had created them? Had she stumbled upon some sort of escape route from the palace?

The tunnel connected with others, going either deeper into the cliffs or toward the beach. Laurel followed the sound of wind and came to an opening in the cliff face. The beach was still too far. She retraced her steps, remembering every turn she made. Two tunnels led her to openings in the cliff that gave incredible views of the ocean below. One sent her into a large hall, the space empty and covered in dust. *What is this place?*

In what felt like hours but had likely only been thirty minutes, she followed the sound of crashing waves to an opening. Large rocks reached out of the sparkling sand below her, spaced just perfectly for her to climb down.

"Praise the Goddess." She quickly clambered down onto the sand. With her back to the water, she studied the face of the cliff. She cataloged everything for her return journey and raced for the harbor.

It likely took her another half hour before she reached the harbor. The water slapped at the wooden boards of the docks reaching out to sea, and the boats rocked with the waves like cradles. She climbed over the jetty separating the beach from where the ships bobbed in the water. A dozen trading ships sat snug next to the docks, but her eyes were only drawn to the one at the farthest corner with the red sails.

The Shining River.

Of course it was on the other side of the cursed harbor.

Laurel raced down the jetty toward where it met the harbor, stepping carefully on the large rocks and doing her best to avoid breaking her ankle. When she reached the harbor, she slowed her pace. Even this late at night, people still milled about. She set her pace to a quick clip that said she was on business but wasn't desperate. A few men whistled in her direction, but when she flashed her mask in the moonlight, they shrank back into the shadows.

A rope ladder waited for her over the edge of the ship, and she climbed aboard.

It came as no surprise to her that Teagan was already waiting for her on deck.

"Our mission timetable has moved up," he said. No hello. No asking after her health. None of those things mattered to him. He never cared about anything but the mission.

Laurel remained quiet.

"With the acquisition of the Duchy of Eleusion, plans are being set into motion that will go smoother if Prince Dion were out of the picture."

Curses. Maybe she should have simply let the prince get poisoned by her desserts and ran for the hills. It would have been riskier, but at least she would be done with this blasted assignment.

"When is the deadline?" Her mask muffled her voice slightly, but she knew Teagan could hear her over the crash of water.

"You have until the winter solstice."

10

AN UNFORTUNATE MEETING

Penny Barclay will stand across from the youngest prince at the wedding, her blue dress clashing terribly with her green eyes, but looking lovely against her bronze skin. The jewel tones always suit her. The prince across from her will not be able to keep his eyes on the officiant either, the amber flashing in Penny's direction more than twice. The portal of black will appear behind the alter. The prince will be taken. The crowd will frenzy. No one will see the dart sail through the chaos, hitting Prince Dion in the neck.

THE LYRE IN PAULO'S HANDS SOUNDED MORE FORLORN THAN HE wished it would. It had been two weeks since he saw Laurel at market. He thought the months after their interaction in Eleusia had been difficult. This was absolute torture.

He tried to pluck a different tune. A few years ago, he learned one about a woman who caught the eye of Fate and when Fate asked for her hand, she said she would only accept if she was gifted the ability to see into the future. Fate gifted her the ability, but she spurned Fate and rejected the marriage. In retaliation, Fate cursed the woman that she would see the future, but no one would believe her.

How fitting.

Paulo tossed his lyre on the table beside him and heaved himself up from his chair. "All right, I'm done waiting."

Both Diana and Donnie looked up from their projects—Diana's pile of half fletched arrows and Donnie's... Paulo squinted at the small pile of pinecones glued together with paste and decorated with what looked like a mixture of pine needles and fennel seeds.

Donnie looked up at him. "It's a bull."

Paulo tilted his head. "Are you sure it's a bull?"

"Yes, I'm certain. I saw the most beautiful specimen when I visited Lord Hermen's estate a few weeks ago and I've been trying to figure out how to capture its beauty."

"With pinecones?"

Donnie threw up his hands.

"Where are you going?" Diana asked.

Paulo straightened his jacket. "I'm going to the kitchens."

Diana scrambled to her feet. "I want to go."

Donnie followed suit. "Wait, what's in the kitchens?"

Paulo pushed Donnie back into his seat. "Nothing I am letting a rascal like you close to, of that you can be certain."

"Ah!" Donnie's eyes brightened. "It's most definitely a woman!"

Paulo rolled his eyes. "Be a good friend and stay put so I don't have to worry about extricating you from any embarrassing situations."

Donnie turned to Diana. "I want every detail down to the number of eyelashes fluttered."

"Consider it done," she said.

Paulo pulled her from the room before Donnie had the chance to change his mind. He loved the man dearly, but sometimes Paulo could strangle him. They had been friends since their years at school together, both attending the same school near the capital. Donnie had been much smaller and much fairer as a child than he was now. There were many of the other boys that called Donnie "feminine" and subjected him to ridicule in front of the rest of the school.

Paulo and his rather well-practiced fists— thanks to Diana — took care of that and they'd been best friends ever since. Donnie was a man of integrity, but he flitted about life like a hummingbird jumping from one flower to the next. Always in flight and flashing the bright colors on his wings. He made lots of tiny decisions that kept him from moving forward through life, but he moved, nonetheless. Dynamic in every sense of the word, but simple to understand. He was a man of many vices and an absolute genius when he set his mind to something, having inherited a rather large vineyard at fourteen and scaling it tenfold by the time he had turned sixteen.

They made it down the corridor before Diana spoke. "So why now?"

Paulo blew out a breath. "Because I'm tired of waiting."

"Is it right though?"

His steps slowed and he allowed the magic to take form around them. He watched several paths play out in seconds. Going to the kitchens. Running into members of nobility. Seeing Laurel's surprise. Telling her what she meant to him right from the get-go.

That particular path ended rather abruptly.

Oh, no. He definitely couldn't do that.

"We should be fine so long as no one proclaims their undying love for the other, and you don't challenge her to a duel."

"Oh, sure, because that last one is just as likely as the first, right?"

Paulo bit the inside of his cheek. There were certainly days when he wished to throw this cursed plan to the wind, take Laurel in his arms, and run for the blasted hills. It obviously couldn't happen, considering she had absolutely no idea who he was or what he knew.

But at least one of those things was about to change.

They reached the entrance to the kitchens and Paulo shoved Diana in front of him. "Go distract the cook."

Diana poked him back. "Maybe *you* should go distract the cook. No one is going to be looking at me when I'm not the one wearing a lavender jacket."

Paulo looked down at his clothing. *Blast.* He really should have worn something else.

He ran a hand through his hair. "Just go."

Diana chuckled and pushed through the entrance. "Cook! Could I have a moment of your time?"

Diana never could do anything by halves.

"Oh, Sweet Gaia!" Cook set a hand to her chest. "Lady Diana. Lord MacGregor. What can I do for you?"

"I was wondering," Diana said, leaning against the large table in the middle of the room, "about the best way to prepare quail. There seems to be a surplus in Delphine and the way you serve it puts every other quail I've ever had to shame."

Paulo stepped to the side, tucking himself against the wall. The poison taster— Paulo could never remember the mage's name— leaned away from Diana. The man's skin had a sickly gray tinge to it. Had he died recently? A young undercook came up to the table, trying to insert herself into the conversation and leaving the other undercook to watch the pots on the stove.

But where was Laurel?

He scanned the faces of those around him. He recognized several from visions he'd had of the upcoming months, but none were the face that haunted him. A tightness grew in his chest. Of all the times for him to come—

His eyes clashed with a pair of deep brown eyes peeking out between a set of shelves. Laurel stood inside the pantry, and he could just see her through the sliver of the doorway between shelves. He took a step in her direction and her eyes narrowed.

Oh, she was most definitely hiding from him.

As Diana started debating with the cooks at the table whether or not to use a brine on the quail, he crept toward the pantry. He stopped on the other side of the shelf, watching Laurel through jars of what looked like pickled fish and olives. She looked ready to bolt for the door, which he was now standing in the way of.

"Well, this is certainly a happy coincidence," Paulo said. "Here I find myself in your presence once again."

Laurel came around the shelf, a sack of aubergines in hand. "I highly doubt this is a coincidence, my lord."

Paulo remained standing in the doorway, blocking her escape. Not that she couldn't get past him if she truly wished to. "You think I planned to find the woman who throat-punched me in a town on the other side of the kingdom in the kitchen of the palace? My, that's quite a bit of work."

She stepped closer. "I don't know what you planned, Lord…"

"MacGregor, but please call me Paulo. And you are?"

"Someone who isn't going to be won over by a charming smile or a stuffy title, Lord MacGregor. Our association will not be one of friends nor any other sort of acquaintance you may wish to pursue with me."

"Oh? And why not?"

Laurel quirked a brow. "I know better." She slipped past him and returned to her work in the kitchen.

Paulo almost followed behind her, but he let her escape him. She'd set him in his place and pushing her would get him nowhere. Not yet.

Eating supper in the palace every night might drive Paulo to absolute madness. His entire body twitched as he passed by the doors leading from the palace dining room to the kitchens. He was so close to her. Only a few doors away. How he was going to survive the next several months in the palace, he didn't know.

At least for tonight, he'd endure it. There were other things he needed to worry about.

Instead of making a complete fool of himself in front of Laurel, he walked beside Diana to their table. At least her fate would keep him somewhat distracted that evening. The formal dining room in the palace was made up of several long tables, four making neat lines in the middle of the room and one at the head, perpendicular to the others. When Prince Dion and his brothers took meals with the rest of the visiting nobility, they sat there. Today, only Prince Evan took his place at the head table, the other princes taking their supper elsewhere. Prince Evan likely wouldn't have even been in this dining room if it wasn't for the Aigean delegation now mingling throughout the room.

Conversation was lively around the dining hall. Well, of course it was. Barclay Manor had burned to the ground, and the council meeting two days before had been fraught with tension. Paulo's chest tightened at the mere thought of it.

When he'd greeted Penny at the meeting, he'd nearly blurted out everything. Her shoulders had held a weight he'd never seen before, her brightness dimmed. Being in the same room as her had been difficult. Her entire world had come crashing down, just as he knew it would. He'd seen the vision of the fire over a year ago, just after Penny's debut. He didn't know how he would look her in the face when he saw her again and continue to lie, knowing she would be hurt. Knowing he could stop it if he tried.

But there was too much at stake.

Paulo pulled Diana's chair out from the table, and she sat. While she had fought him about it when they were younger, Paulo had always made sure he acted the proper gentleman toward his sister not only to show the people around them that he was honorable, but to also show everyone else that he viewed Diana as a woman of high regard. While she made choices that society didn't agree with, she was still a marquess's sister, still a daughter of noble birth. Just because she didn't strut around in crinolines and petticoats didn't mean she wasn't as glorious a woman as any other.

Diana took up her fork and stabbed a large portion of the colorful salad on her plate before stuffing it in her mouth. A piece of tomato fell from the corner of her mouth onto her black tunic.

Paulo rolled his eyes. Perhaps *glorious* wasn't quite the word to describe his sister.

The chair next to Paulo moved and Donnie gracefully fell into it. It was the only way to describe the movement as he made it look graceful but was very obviously drunk.

"Been too deep in your cups, Donnie Boy?" Paulo whispered.

Donnie chuckled. "Couldn't be helped. The drinks came

with two beautiful ladies, and I was held hostage until I paid my ransom."

"I'm sure it was a hefty sum."

Donnie sighed. "Such is the price of being this astonishingly good looking."

Paulo picked up his fork and moved the food around on his plate. "What plans do you have for this evening?"

"Like you don't already know." Donnie grinned at him.

Paulo didn't rightly know. Donnie's line of fate was somewhat... fuzzy. Like a piece of yarn, it had tiny strands that would pop up all down the line and twist around so many other strings it was hard to keep track of.

They continued through the courses that slid onto the table in front of them. How many of the dishes had Laurel helped prepare? He could picture her standing over a cutting board, her nimble fingers chopping vegetables at an astounding rate. The thoughts were a sweet torture.

Paulo took only a few bites of each dish, his stomach tight. Talk of the fire and rebels still ricocheted around the room. Speculation abounded. What would happen to the crops? Where would the rebels go next? What were the princes going to do? Was this revenge for the Tyrant King's death?

When dessert finally came around, Paulo couldn't even pick up his fork, though the orange cake was likely delicious. Diana traded her empty plate for his not thirty seconds after the servants had put it in front of him.

Once the dishes were finally cleared, Paulo stood. "Come on, you two. I say we mingle a bit."

Diana groaned but Donnie jumped to his feet, a bit wobbly. Paulo led them toward the doors, though they didn't leave the dining room. Paulo had no intention of leaving until he did what he'd come to do. He spotted a head of dark-brown hair in the crowd gathered there.

"Adam!" he called over the hubbub.

Adam Cyrus turned from the selkies he was talking to, and a smile spread over his face. "Good evening, my lords. My lady." He took Diana's hand and bowed over it.

Diana drew it back and wiped it on her pant leg as if he had kissed it.

If Adam noticed, he didn't say anything. "It's been too long since I've seen any of you."

Paulo slapped him on the shoulder. "I was thinking just that thing."

As ambassador in the Aigean Isles, Adam was often gone from court. With new trade agreements being made between the two lands and the tedious court systems in the isles, Adam had his hands full trying to bridge the cultural divides. It likely also didn't help that the man was labeled excessively handsome by most of society and often swarmed by the young ladies of the court.

Adam gestured to the men next to him. "Allow me to make some introductions. Lord MacGregor, Lady MacGregor, Lord Abrams, allow me to introduce Kai Delcharco and Caspian Delrio, both illustrious members of the Aigean Trident."

Paulo did his best not to show any kind of recognition on his face. Sometimes that was the hardest thing about his gift, not giving away that he knew who people were before they'd ever been introduced. Especially people he knew impacted much in the future. As leaders in the Trident— the elite fighting force from the Isles of Aigean— these selkies had a major role to play.

The Isles had signed the accords created nearly five years ago by Prince Dion and the Council. Olympia, Faerie, and the Isles had become allies after years of turmoil between the three kingdoms. And now, all the work Prince Dion had put into creating harmony between them would shatter.

Paulo held out a hand. "Pleasure, sirs."

The tallest of the water folk, Caspian, clasped his hand. "Likewise."

The urge to smack the selkie surged in Paulo's mind, but he dropped his hand instead and tried to keep the pleasant expression on his face. He needed to remain unsuspicious.

Adam smiled and Paulo didn't laugh when one of the ladies near them fanned herself. All right, he may have chuckled a little. Adam either didn't notice or deigned to ignore it. "Lord MacGregor is the Marquess of Delphine, the lands just east of the Black River from Eleusion."

Paulo nodded, though he wanted to grimace. He knew the Aigeans weren't all they appeared to be. In fact, The Cartographer had a fairly good relationship with the water folk based on what he'd seen. One the rebellion would rely on in the coming months. How much did Adam know of their discussions with the rebellion? Was he suspicious as to why such a large delegation had come with him to Olympia this time?

"Ah." Caspian adjusted the dark seal pelt around his waist and clasped his hands behind his back. "It seems Eleusion is all anyone is talking about this evening. Do you know the Barclays well, then?"

Paulo matched the selkie's stance. "We're very good friends of the Barclays and mourn with them at this time. It's an absolute tragedy what has happened to their lands, but if anyone is strong enough to overcome such adversity, it's Lady Barclay and Lady Penny."

"You can say that again," Diana agreed. "If anyone can send the rebels packing, it'll be those two."

Caspian smirked. "You sound so sure, my lady."

"I am sure," she said, leaving no room for argument in her tone. Paulo could only say so much though. He'd seen a few of the possible futures when it came to Lady Barclay and Penny.

Those women were a force to be reckoned with, but he only knew what the Goddess showed him.

Adam's expression turned grave. "It's quite alarming. I was there with Prince Dion when the youngest prince arrived with the news. I've never seen the spymaster get so worked up over something, and I've been around him for a good portion of my life."

Yes, Paulo could imagine the youngest prince was overwrought. A flash of the prince standing in a group of trees outside Barclay House in the predawn light took form in his mind. The image didn't completely take over his senses, but overlaid what was actually going on around him. He could still laugh at the joke Donnie made while watching the youngest prince cast himself in shadow when one of the curtains of the windows shifted at the house. The vision faded and a small twinge took root behind Paulo's eyes. The headache wouldn't last long, praise the Goddess.

"Will you be staying in the capital for a while?" Adam asked. "It would be good to get to spend more time together."

"We have no plans to leave anytime soon," Paulo said. He didn't turn to look at the door leading to the kitchens. "I have some business here that will take up quite a bit of time."

"Nothing too serious, I hope."

Diana snorted. "He's only in a bit of trouble, I can assure you."

Donnie straightened. "What kind of trouble are you in? You haven't told me anything about this."

Paulo glared at Diana but shrugged. "I'm here to hopefully stop trouble, not fall into it."

"I see," Adam said. He turned to the selkies. "Lord MacGregor is Olympia's oracle."

Kai, the other selkie, turned back to Paulo with wide eyes. "You can see into the future?"

Paulo straightened the lapels of his green dinner jacket. "But of course. I was the one who foretold the metaphorical death of the bustle in women's fashion."

"Praise the Goddess," Diana muttered. She never cared for women's fashion, but some things she thought were absolutely ridiculous— the bustle being one of them.

Caspian's brows lowered. "You can see everything?"

"Sweet Gaia, no!" Paulo gave his most charming laugh. He needed to turn this conversation, catch these fish in his trap. "That would be miserable. Imagine having to watch your sister every time she used the little girls'—"

Diana shoved him. "Paulo."

"What? I was going to say little girls' target growing up." Paulo tried not to look at the selkies. *Bait.* "What did you think I was going to say?"

She rolled her eyes.

"Target?" Caspian asked.

Hook.

"Yes." Paulo groaned. "It was bad enough having to watch her practice with her bow in real time. Can you imagine having to watch every single moment she shot at a target for the rest of her life? I would have been driven to an early grave with boredom."

Caspian looked at Diana with renewed interest. "You shoot, my lady?"

Paulo kept himself from smirking. *Catch.*

Donnie slung an arm over Diana's shoulders. "Our Diana is a remarkable markswoman, if you'll forgive my pun."

"Yes, I shoot." Diana shrugged Donnie's arm off with a glare. "I also stab, maim, and dismember."

Donnie laughed like she said the funniest thing in the world. By the Goddess, it was probably wise to get him out of the feasting hall before he did something stupid.

"Perhaps we can face off with one another sometime," Caspian said, a wicked gleam in his eye.

Diana gave him a very unamused once over. "You're not the first male to come looking for an easy ego boost only to be sorely disappointed. I can assure you, a match against me will result in one of two ways."

"Which are?"

Diana sighed. "You crying to your mother over being soundly beaten by a girl or your nose bloodied by my fist because you couldn't take your loss like a good boy."

Caspian's grin widened. "I guess we will just have to see, won't we?"

Diana shrugged. "I guess so."

Fate pushed itself into Paulo's mind once more. An arrow pulled back to the corner of Diana's mouth. Caspian's swagger. Laurel's brown eyes flashing with delight.

Everything was going according to plan.

"A duel to the death then?" Donnie cackled.

"How about a friendly wager?" Adam offered.

Diana grinned. "You're on." Paulo's fists clenched behind his back. He might have achieved what he'd come to do that evening, but that didn't mean he liked it.

He searched the line of Diana's fate.

Diana, kneeling on the rubble-strewn ground with blood on her hands as she roars up at the smoke-colored sky.

No, he didn't like it one bit.

11

THE FIRST

Laurel will creep through the shadows, the silver mask covering her face. A slip of white trails up ahead of her and disappears through a door. Laurel follows and waits at the door for several minutes. After a time, she slips through a door with faint light lining its edges. Laurel strides with silent steps toward the settee, draws her dagger, and stabs down. Her knife meets its mark and Prince Dion doesn't even stir.

LAUREL CROUCHED AT THE END OF THE HALL, KEEPING HER BACK pressed to the wall and sliding her cheek around the corner so she could see down the perpendicular corridor without being spotted.

Delilah, Laurel's *charming* roommate, carried a tea tray beside Galen, who held a platter of sweet meats. The prince had ordered a late night snack fit for an army and Delilah had had no choice but to assist Galen in delivering it to the prince.

Or rather, she begged until Cook acquiesced.

And instead of heading to bed like the rest of the kitchen, Laurel had slipped into her gear and trailed behind them. She needed to figure out a way to get to the prince.

Delilah admired herself in a mirror she passed, flicking her hair over her shoulder and biting color into her lips.

Galen watched Delilah with growing concern.

The guards at the end of the hall opened the door for the pair, casting light into the hallway and giving Laurel a good glimpse into the royal sitting room. By the Goddess, she was so close. She regretted not being the one to beg Cook to let her take the tray, though it wouldn't have mattered since Delilah had looked like she was ready to go to blows over it with the other kitchen girl that offered.

Delilah took the lead and swept into the room, Galen following quickly behind. The guards shut the door behind them, submerging the corridor in darkness once again.

Laurel waited.

But Galen came out alone, his head hung low as the guards clicked the door shut behind him.

A smile stretched across Laurel's face as she quietly crept back to her rooms. Her roommate had just made a rather fatal mistake.

"Laurel, get that filling set. We don't have time to waste."

Laurel whipped the whisk in her hand faster. She'd been promoted from potato peeler to whisk whipper that morning. If she was an actual kitchen girl, she'd have been thrilled. As an assassin, she was not. While the position gave her more access to the food, cursed Galen made any plans to poison the prince void. It drove her a bit mad.

But she'd be done soon anyway.

Laurel stepped closer to where Delilah was standing at the stove stirring a pot of milk, lemon, and vanilla for the *bougatsa* they were making for dessert that evening.

"You got in quite late last night," Laurel whispered.

Delilah's eyes darted around, and she pulled Laurel's arm to bring her closer. "Hush! Cook doesn't need to know how late I was." A small stain of pink spread over her cheeks.

Laurel feigned confusion, slowing her whisk. "But why would it matter when she was the one who had you deliver the food?"

Delilah bit into her bottom lip. "Because he asked me to stay."

Laurel didn't even have to guess who "he" was. She tried to show surprise. "He did? What did you do?"

The blush on her face turned beet red. "Swear you won't say anything?"

"Of course. Who would I tell? Galen?" Not that she wanted to go anywhere near him. Since the incident with the poison two weeks ago, she'd done her best to avoid his attention. Having a taster in the kitchen was an obstacle for any assassin set on poisoning a prince. One that was a mage with the power to come back from the dead was more than an obstacle.

"Sweet Gaia, do *not* tell Galen. He wouldn't understand."

"I won't. I swear."

Delilah looked about, checking for extra eyes or ears. "Prince Dion said he wants to see me again."

Laurel tried to gasp appropriately while keeping it quiet enough to not draw attention. "When?"

"I'm to meet him tomorrow night."

Which meant Laurel could finally make her move.

"Laurel! Delilah!" Cook's voice boomed over the kitchen. "Quit your chit-chatting and get those desserts done!"

They both nodded, and Laurel took a step away, returning to her bowl.

She had to keep the grin from spreading over her face. It would be simple to kill the prince and lay the blame at the young undercook's feet. Laurel wasn't against making the entire thing look like a death of passion followed swiftly by the girl's own demise. Laurel would then return to the kitchens for a month, maybe two, then disappear. Most assassins didn't linger, but Laurel was smarter than most. No one suspected a killer who stayed around after.

The custard— egg yolk, sugar, vanilla bean, flour, and milk — in the bowl finally mixed together with the stiff egg whites and Laurel grabbed the pans with the crust of layered *phyllo*. She poured the mixture into each pan and set the bowl into the pile of dishes for the dishwasher. She left the pans and went to the cold room to grab another brick of butter. It was still unbelievable that there was an entire room enchanted just to keep food cold. Hadn't the engineers of the palace thought about a dry larder?

When she found the butter, she returned to the kitchen to find they had a guest.

Lady Diana stood at the table next to Galen, who was obviously trying to create as much space between them as possible.

Cook turned around and nearly leaped to attention. "What can I do for you, Lady Diana?"

Lady Diana smiled, leaning one hip against the table, making Galen nearly fall out of his chair. "My brother was wondering if we could borrow a few extra glasses this evening. It seems our small gathering in one of the parlors has grown quicker than we thought."

Laurel did her best to ignore the odd flip in her gut. Lord MacGregor was an absolute menace. The man obviously had no boundaries and seemed to delight in causing others as much grief as possible. Like sending his sister to disrupt the kitchen for glasses.

Cook scrubbed her hands on her apron. "And he sent you down here with such a request instead of calling for one of the maids?"

Lady Diana shrugged. "I didn't want to sit around and listen to a bunch of men preening about their paltry hunting escapades and figured I could at least smuggle a biscuit or two into my pocket if I came myself."

"I suppose I do have a few biscuits you can take with you." She looked about. "Laurel, fetch that tin—"

"I can do it, Cook!" Delilah set to grabbing a small tin only a few inches from Laurel's head and gathered a few different desserts from the small cache left over from tea Lady Carnation had cancelled earlier in the day. Laurel kept her face empty of expression as Delilah continued to send Diana charming smiles. "What exactly are the gentlemen gathering for?"

Lady Diana frowned. "I don't care about what a bunch of pea-brained, silky-palmed gentlemen are doing."

Delilah ducked her head. Apparently, her brand of charm only extended to the men. A smile threatened to break Laurel's blank mask. When Delilah returned with the tin, Cook wrapped it all in a bit of cloth and passed it to Lady Diana along with the glasses she'd requested.

"You are a saint among women, Cook." Lady Diana blew her a kiss.

Cook chuckled and waved her off.

Lady Diana headed in the direction of the door, but before she left, she turned around.

And winked right at Laurel.

Laurel laid in her bed, keeping the rise and fall of her shoulders even as the hours ticked away. She counted out every second, taking inhales for four then exhales for seven. She didn't stir. Didn't even twitch as she waited for Delilah to make her move. They were nearing two in the morning, the kitchen staff having made their way to their beds ages ago. The palace operated at all hours, guards making rotations and advisors working late into the night to prepare for the slew of meetings scheduled the next day.

Yet, Delilah stayed in her bed, her breaths hitching at every sound.

Laurel waited.

This was the part of the job she was good at. She could stay in one position for hours, allowing her joints to lock and her muscles to seize. Laying in a bed necessitated the opposite, forcing her to relax her body but keep her mind alert. The math of counting her breaths then converting it to time helped, but the pillow under her cheek did not.

When Laurel was moments away from just letting herself go to sleep, the bed next to her squeaked.

About cursed time.

Laurel watched Delilah creep from their room, a bright shawl wrapped around her shoulders. She was the epitome of a fair maiden making her way through the halls of a darkened castle to meet a paramour.

And Laurel was the harbinger of death following right at her heels.

She threw off her covers and pulled her nightdress up and over her head, revealing her gear beneath. She grabbed the mask from under her pillow and crept to the door. Delilah's steps padded toward the kitchen.

Laurel snapped her mask into place and slipped out the door.

Delilah crept ahead of her, not even stopping to look if anyone was about. When they reached the main staircase, Delilah ducked back around a corner like a skittish mouse. Laurel stopped several feet away, ducking low so Delilah wouldn't look back and see her. A set of guards passed, not noticing the trembling undercook tucked in a doorway. Praise the Goddess. Laurel waited for Delilah to move forward, but she took a step back instead.

Keep going! Laurel kept herself from screaming the words but prayed Delilah heard them anyways. If the girl got skittish now, Laurel would have to replan. This was going to be such an easy job if Delilah continued forward.

The undercook took another step away from the corner, her head shaking. Laurel silently cursed. Of all the times for the girl to allow good sense to steer her!

Voices echoed from the hall behind them.

Laurel crouched down as Delilah swung around. The air in Laurel's lungs froze. If she got trapped between Delilah and any guards, there would be trouble.

But Delilah must not have seen her because she dashed forward.

Laurel grinned and followed right behind her.

The voices faded as Laurel trailed Delilah through the servants' passageways until they entered into the more elegant hallways of the palace. They were in the guest wing with its high ceilings and illustrious artwork. Delilah tiptoed past several doors before stopping at one lined with light. A sitting room. Laurel had seen it on one of the maps she had tucked away. Delilah lifted her hand to knock but thought better of it and simply pushed through the door, softly closing it behind her.

Laurel glided forward, pressing her ear next to the crack between the door and its frame.

The sound of hushed voices— a man and woman— slipped through the door. Laurel listened as the voices quieted and movement in the room slowed. She heard the thud of someone falling into a chair. A man's warm chuckle. A sigh. Then...

Laurel pulled her ear away from the door. The amount of lip-smacking happening was nearly nauseating. She cringed. It sounded... messy, for lack of a better term. The wet noises continued, only broken up by soft moans.

Perhaps killing both Prince Dion and Delilah would put the both of them out of whatever misery this was. By the Goddess, how Prince Dion had retained the reputation as the best lover in all of Olympia, Laurel had no idea. She'd seen her fair share of sensual trysts in her time as an assassin, and this had to be one of the most embarrassing ones she'd ever had to listen to.

When the noise died down, she nudged the door open slightly. If she had to kill them both, she wouldn't regret it as much as she thought she would. Not after listening to whatever *that* was for nearly a quarter of an hour.

She slipped into the room.

A magelight sat on one of the tables, the soft glow casting shadows around the room. There were no windows in this room, only a sleeping magelight chandelier hanging from the ceiling. There was another door, but it was shut and locked based on the twist of the key sitting beneath the doorknob. Could the evening get any simpler? Laurel quietly slipped her longest dagger from the sheath against her thigh. It made no sound as it rubbed against the tight leather holding it in place. Soft snores sounded from the settee set in the middle of the room. Laurel saw Delilah's shawl draped over the back of it. A pair of booted feet perched on the arm of the settee.

Laurel stayed low as she made it to the settee, creeping to the side where Prince Dion's head would be.

She checked her surroundings once.

Twice.

Dagger in hand, she stood.

A small tin with a large swan on the front came flying from the dark confines of the settee at her head.

Laurel ducked before it could hit her, and the tin hit the floor with a clang. She scrambled to the back of the settee and popped up, her dagger swinging down.

A man's gloved hand shot up and wrapped around her wrist.

Strong arms pulled her down over the back of the settee and onto a very warm, very awake body.

"A dagger is absolutely no way to say hello," a voice rumbled against her back. He twisted her wrist until the dagger dropped from her fingers.

Laurel shoved her weight into the back of the settee, sending it toppling. The man's grip on her wrist loosened as they fell, and she rolled away from him. She sprang up next to a chair, putting it between her and the man.

The man was on his feet, her dagger in his hand. "While I don't mind a bit of ferocity when meeting a woman in a darkened room in the middle of the night, I don't think daggers play part in any of my fantasies."

He stood with his back to the magelight, but Laurel could see he was hooded, wearing very similar apparel to her own, but it obviously wasn't Stellataen made. And he obviously wasn't the prince. A black mask covered the top half of his face, but she could see the outrageous smirk stretch across his mouth. Was he another assassin? An elite guard to the Crown Prince? Where had Prince Dion gone?

Laurel drew one of the small blades at her wrist and flung it at him. While Aspen might have been the expert markswoman with throwing knives, Laurel could use them in a pinch.

The man moved as if he could see the blade coming before they even left her fingers.

He stepped to the right and angled his head just slightly. The knife passed through the air by his face, right where his left eye had been a moment ago.

The dagger now stuck out of the wood paneling behind him. His gloved fingers plucked it from the wall. "Another gift? You really shouldn't have."

Who is this man?

Laurel vaulted over a low table and ran for the door. This man wasn't her mark, and she wouldn't be caught dead in here when he called for help. Sprinting for the door, she felt more than saw the knife fly by her face. She caught it right before it could hit the wooden door and spun to throw it back.

The man was already on top of her, his hands wrapped around each of her wrists as he pushed her up against the door.

"I need you to listen carefully, Laurel."

She froze. He knew her name. By the Goddess, how did he know who she was? She brought her knee up toward his groin, but he only twisted so he could pin her to the door with his hip.

He chuckled, his face coming within an inch of her ear. "I'm going to take a step back. When I do, don't try to stab me and leave. You need to walk straight out the door then take a sharp left. You'll find a small breakfast room with a small door leading to the servant's stairwell. Take that back to the kitchens and tuck yourself back into your little bed before your roommate returns. If you don't, you will be found out."

Her skin burned at every point of contact their bodies made, and her mind caught up with her body. How had this evening gone so wrong? Where was the prince? Delilah?

Who on Gaia's green earth was this man?

"Do you understand, Laurel?"

How did he know her? She gritted her teeth and gave a small nod.

"Excellent." He took a step back.

Laurel pounced, knife in hand, and sent him sprawling. They knocked into one of the short tables, but instead of landing in a heap, the man had been ready. He wrapped his arms around her then rolled to the ground, landing on top of her. Her head smacked into the hard floor.

The man drew in a hiss through his teeth. "Sorry. I did try to talk you out of it."

She tried to headbutt him.

He shifted his head, so she missed. It was like he'd trained with her for ages. Could see every one of her moves. Cold sweat broke out along her back. She'd never fought someone like this before.

He laughed, bringing his head up to look at her. His eyes— his very colorful and magical eyes— met hers.

A mage. She knew enough about them to know each one had a tell. Some physical manifestation of magic. No one's eyes naturally swirled a million colors at once.

Panic swept through her like a bucket of freezing water. She flipped the knife in her hand and attempted to bring it up between them. Without hesitation, he rolled off her, springing to his feet.

She mirrored him.

The man gestured toward the door. "After you, my lady assassin."

She hadn't taken the invitation the first time, but she did now.

It took seconds for her to be through the door and only minutes to get back to the servants' quarters, the sound of his laugh seeming to chase her through the halls.

She crept back into her room, cursing Teagan, Adira Durant, and the blasted geas they'd put on her. Coming to Olympia had been a mistake. She unclipped her mask and threw it down on the bed. Fighting ruthless warlords was one thing, but mages that could fight like that? This had to be why Teagan had offered such a payment. He planned for her to fail and be trapped on this cursed isle. To keep her from Aspen. From their future.

Soft footfalls echoed from the other side of her door. Quickly, she pulled her nightdress on and dove under her covers, tucking her mask out of sight.

The door opened slightly, and Delilah slipped into the room. Her eyes met Laurel's.

"Delilah?" Laurel asked, feigning grogginess.

"Oh, Laurel," Delilah sighed like a lovesick debutante. "I've just had the most exciting night of my life. I have never felt so alive."

Laurel almost winced at the irony. "Where were you?" They obviously hadn't been in the room Laurel watched Delilah go into.

Delilah giggled. "Prince Dion showed me one of the best stained-glass windows in the palace. The way the moon shone through the colored glass made the room look like I was walking into a rainbow. It was magical."

Laurel's training kept her from snorting, but it was dark enough to allow her to cringe. She knew the window. She'd heard of at least three other girls he'd taken into that room in the almost five months she'd been in the palace. The man was an absolute rake.

Delilah continued to blissfully sigh across the room.

Had the prince planned to leave the sitting room the entire time? How had the masked man known she would come that night?

This mission would kill her before the cursed geas ever got a chance.

Withholding a groan, Laurel rubbed the bump on the back of her head and stared up at the ceiling. The events of the evening played in her mind over and over, but one stood out above all the others.

The pearlescent whirl of the man's eyes.

12

AN UNFORTUNATE PAIR

EVERY PARTICLE OF PAULO'S BODY TINGLED AS HE TRIED TO SET THE room back to rights, picking up toppled furniture and tucking very sharp knives into the inner pockets of his jacket. While he'd talked to Laurel in the kitchens only two weeks before, it hadn't been anything like this. He hadn't smelled the small trace of wisteria in her hair. Hadn't felt the press of her body against his. By the Goddess, he wouldn't be able to think about anything else for days. His thoughts rarely strayed from her for long, but now? Now that she was here, and he could touch her? Talk with her? Feel her breaths against his cheek? It was enough to send a man to his knees.

He spotted the tin he'd thrown at Laurel's head earlier. The same one Diana had brought back from the kitchens. A flash of Diana's angry face when she would discover the cookies missing from her hiding spot in her room had him grinning. Paulo picked it up as the door to the sitting room opened once more. Prince Dion prowled in, his eyes gleaming.

Paulo held back a sigh. "I trust your evening went off without a hitch?"

Prince Dion fell into the settee Laurel had toppled less than an hour ago and grabbed the undercook's shawl. She'd left it on the ground and Paulo had used it to his advantage. The prince folded it and set it on his lap.

"I've just come back to thank you, Polly. I appreciate your warning about my brother's late-night walk this evening. He's been extra broody since Barclay Manor's fire— even for him. Evan and I think he simply needs a girl to distract him, but he's such a baby about it."

Paulo bit the inside of his cheek. Lying to his prince went against everything he'd been taught as a boy. He sighed. "I'm sure a girl will distract him soon enough."

Prince Dion spun around in the settee to look at him. "What do you know?"

Curses, he'd almost let too much slip. He took off his gloves. "I'm only saying he's a man and there's bound to be a girl eventually."

The prince pointed a very threatening finger at him. "If you ever see any kind of vision about Denny's love life— no, *either* of my brothers— I want to know about it."

Paulo bobbed his head. "Of course, Your Highness."

Prince Dion spun back around with a laugh. "With ammunition like that, I might finally be able to get the upper hand on Denny. He's ruined a good number of my romantic moments. It would be nice to return the favor one day."

A flash of a room covered in paintings came into focus, a head of dark hair closing in on a girl with emerald eyes.

Paulo blinked the vision away. "The Royal Gallery seems to be a place your youngest brother might take a girl, Your Highness."

Prince Dion scoffed. "Denny *would*."

Paulo did his best to ignore the swirling in his gut as he stood on the front step of Barclay House. Now that it had been a month since the fire that took Barclay Manor and the Barclays were receiving calls, he didn't think it fair of him to avoid his friend any longer. Not after the pain she'd had to endure.

"Are you going to knock or keep staring at the door like it killed your favorite puppy?" Diana asked from behind him.

Paulo took a deep breath and rapped his knuckles on the wooden door. The same sound beat against his skull. Using his gifts to defend against Laurel's attacks last night had left him with an agonizing headache. The door opened a moment later, Barclay House's short butler standing sentinel in the doorway. Paulo could never remember his name, since he didn't often call at Barclay House. Barclay Manor's butler was Rogers— or at least it had been. Where was Rogers now? "Good morning, my lord." He stepped back and gestured for them to enter the house.

Paulo removed his hat as he stepped inside. "Is Lady Penny taking callers this morning?"

The butler took Paulo's hat, then reached for his coat. "Both Lady Penny and Lady Barclay are in the green parlor."

Paulo refrained from asking if there was any other colored parlor. While always tasteful, The Barclays had a penchant for green he would never fully appreciate. Beige and gold were the only accents, and honestly, it wasn't much.

Diana followed the butler ahead of Paulo, her boots silent on the stairs as they were led to where the Barclay women waited for them. His hands started to sweat. That was fine, so long as nothing else gave him away.

The liar.

The betrayer.

He took a fortifying breath. The night before had set him on a course that he needed to see through. He couldn't be sorry about that. Not even a little. The fire wouldn't be the last tragedy any of them faced, but it would get Paulo what he wanted. He would stop Laurel from killing Prince Dion and he would get closer to her in the process.

The butler announced them at the door to the sitting room and Paulo allowed Diana to proceed him. He pasted his most charming smile on his face and followed on her heels.

Lady Barclay sat at a writing desk, a small stack of correspondence at her elbow. The older woman lounged in the small chair as if it were a towering throne and she the reigning monarch. She was a striking woman, her auburn hair and bronze skin in contrast to her bright green eyes, but the elegance was sharp.

The younger copy of the duchess sat in a window seat, a book in hand. Penny Barclay looked every bit like her mother except her elegance was soft and brimming with liveliness and curiosity. However, both were slightly dimmed. Paulo could see the scars of the fire in her countenance. The shadows that night had left behind. He swallowed back a lump in his throat.

Both women stood and Penny crossed the room to them. "If it isn't my two favorite twins."

Diana wrapped her in a hug. "I've been worried sick about you."

Penny returned the embrace, her eyes closing in what looked like pain. "I'm all right."

She pulled away and turned to Paulo. If he could, he would wrap her in a hug, but he knew better. Lady Barclay would have his head on a pike before he could utter a single word.

Penny knew it too, so she saved them both from a miserable fate and simply curtsied. "It's good to see you, Paulo."

He pushed that smile onto his face with everything he had. "And you, Penny. Once we heard you were finally taking visits, Diana and I raced over."

Penny frowned. "You know neither of you would have been turned away if you'd come to see us."

"We know." Diana clasped Lady Barclay's hands in her own, not quite at the same level of familiarity with the duchess as she was with Penny. "But we also knew you both needed time to gather yourselves, and we didn't wish to be underfoot."

Lady Barclay patted Diana's hand. "You wouldn't have been. In all honesty, it likely would have been good for Penny to have some friends to talk to after... well, everything."

Penny's frown only deepened as she looked at her mother. Paulo could feel the tension there, see the glint of anger in Penny's eyes. She suspected Lady Barclay had something to do with the rebellion. Paulo had seen it. He wouldn't contradict her suspicions. Not now.

Conversation continued, bouncing from one inane topic to the next. The weather. The fashion trends. The horrible traffic on the west side of town due to some construction. All depthless topics. Paulo kept up with the conversation, but he tried to distract himself from the pain he saw in Penny's eyes. He tried to think of anything else. The surprise in Laurel's eyes when he caught the knife. How nicely she had fit into his arms when they'd toppled to the floor. Her angry breathing as he'd pressed her up against the door last night...

Sweet Gaia, he sounded like a lunatic.

What woman would ever fall for a man who obsessed over her when she had done nothing but try to kill him? It was the epitome of madness, but none of what he felt for Laurel had ever come by sane means.

"I only pray the council can band together in order to eradicate the people trying to harm our kingdom," Lady Barclay announced. "Olympia is destined to fall should this conflict continue."

Penny's face didn't betray her feelings on Lady Barclay's words, but the clenched fists in her lap did. "I wholeheartedly agree. The rebels need to be stopped."

Paulo sipped at the chamomile tea in his hand. The pounding headache subsided slightly. Perhaps he could bother Barclay House's cook for a bowl of mixed nuts. Something in nuts always helped get rid of the headaches faster, especially almonds or cashews. He'd likely need to sleep a bit of it off before supper as well if he didn't want to be dealing with it the next day.

"What do your visions say, Lord MacGregor?" Lady Barclay asked. "Have you discovered a straight path through this little conflict we find ourselves in?"

"I would hardly call this a 'little conflict,' Mother," Penny muttered.

Lady Barclay turned sharply toward Penny, but Paulo cut in before they could start snapping at one another.

"There seems to be too many moving pieces at present. I haven't seen anything concrete yet."

The pounding in his head beat out a rhythm.

Lie.

Lie.

Lie.

"That's a shame," Lady Barclay said. And that was all she said. She didn't cast blame at Paulo for not knowing. She didn't berate him for not trying harder. She only stated her opinion on the matter then moved on. It was one of the things Paulo liked most about the older woman. She understood why he hid what he knew and because she understood, she allowed

Paulo to simply be instead of pushing her own agendas on him.

"How long are the both of you staying at the palace?" Penny asked.

Diana sighed. "At least until this whole rebel mess gets figured out or the council doesn't need Paulo for his rainbow-string magic."

Paulo sent his sister a scowl. "Why do you always have to make it sound weird?"

Diana grinned mischievously. "Because it is weird. Listening to you talk about all your magic strings makes it sound like you're a member of some kind of supernatural knitting club."

"I ought to take offense to that."

"Oh, don't get your knitting needles in a knot."

Leaning back in his chair, he feigned an overly grumpy attitude while the three women chuckled. He couldn't actually be angry. Their little tiff had lightened the tension in the room considerably, as it always did. It was their twin superpower— diffusing tense situations by being utterly ridiculous and distracting everyone from their own problems.

"You ought to come up to the palace more, Penny," Diana said. "It would be nice not to be the only woman there with an actual brain in her head."

Lady Barclay hummed her agreement but shook her head. "Penny's still healing."

Penny herself rolled her eyes. "Even the worst of my burns have completely healed."

The look Lady Barclay gave Penny told her that wasn't all she was talking about. Penny met her mother's expression with an equally stubborn one. However, Paulo could still see the pain there. Lady Barclay likely could too.

The tea in Paulo's gut sloshed uncomfortably. He'd seen

the vision of the fire. Of the evidence she found in Lady Barclay's study. Of the prince revealing himself to save her. What else had the fire subjected her to?

While the headaches were a rather painful price to pay for the visions the Goddess gave him, the pain of watching those he cared about hurt and not be able to do anything about it might have been worse.

Penny set her teacup on the small table at their feet. "I've been thinking about taking walks around the palace gardens. I haven't ever really been able to experience all of them and would like to see how the palace staff manage such large and enchanted grounds. I might be able to gain some perspective on how to best help our lands, as we'll have much to do once the rebels are stopped."

Lady Barclay studied Penny for a moment. "Yes, perhaps it would be good for you to go."

Penny startled. "Really?"

Lady Barclay nodded. "So long as you take Philo with you and you stay away from those womanizing princes, I think it should be fine."

"Mother, really—"

"Splendid!" Paulo said. "You'll have to let us know when you're about. We can keep an eye out for womanizing princes together." He gave her a wink. There was at least one prince she would be wanting to keep an eye out for, of that Paulo was certain.

The line between Penny's eyebrows deepened but she said nothing. She'd always been a smart girl. She'd get it figured out.

Though that didn't ease the tightness in Paulo's chest.

13
AN UNFORTUNATE RENDEZVOUS

AFTER SPENDING THE AFTERNOON WITH PENNY AND LADY BARCLAY, Paulo could feel the previous night's escapades really start to weigh on him. The pounding in his head had eased with the tea, but the glaring sunlight outside felt like a needle was sewing the back of his eye to his head.

"Do you want me to call a carriage?" Diana asked.

Paulo shook his head but stopped when the jarring motion sent pain shooting through his skull. "We aren't far from the palace. I'll be fine until we get there."

"Will you have enough time to recover before tonight?"

"As I said, I'll be fine."

Diana harrumphed. "You can't pretend with me. I have twin sense you know."

"Is that twin sense telling you that your questions are unwanted?"

"Yes, but just because I'm bothering you doesn't mean I'm not right."

Paulo gritted his teeth. She was right and he knew she had good grounds for it. The headaches were terrible, but there wasn't anything anyone could do about them. Both Diana and Mater had been there through some of his worst, when the visions had played out in front of him so vividly, so clearly, and for hours. That had only happened twice. Once, before the Tyrant King was deposed. The second, almost two years ago. He'd been in his bedroom for a week after each of them, curtains drawn in absolute darkness. The smaller, involuntary visions happened more frequently and left him with much easier prices. However, when he pushed himself like he did last night, the headaches were worse. The dizziness and nausea would start up if he wasn't careful. It was just part of his life. He couldn't let time slip past him. There was so much to do and allowing something as small as a headache to deter him wouldn't help anyone.

They reached the palace before suppertime, though that wasn't any great achievement. Supper in the palace happened well after the sun went down. Mater had always made sure supper was served before the clock struck eight at Iatrus Castle. The MacGregor's had always been early risers, though Paulo seemed to not carry that particular family trait. While Diana would wake before the sun, Paulo decided the world didn't exist until after nine o'clock. It also didn't help that his visions regularly came to him at night.

"Lady Diana! Lord MacGregor!"

Diana turned and Paulo's hand twitched to reach out to her. He knew having Caspian burrow his way into Diana's stone heart was important, but sometimes he didn't want to do the important thing. He wanted to throw Diana over his shoulder and roar at Caspian to stay away from his twin.

But he didn't.

Instead, he straightened and pulled on his most lordly smile. "Ah, Mr. Delrio! What a pleasant surprise."

Diana didn't smile, but her head tilted in curiosity.

The selkie reached them, a broad grin stretched across his cheeks. "I have been meaning to speak with you before I leave."

"Where are you headed?" Paulo asked.

"The delegation is to return home for a few weeks and report on what is going on with our allies. Our queen is very interested about this rebellion and what Prince Dion and the council are doing about it."

Paulo pinched the bridge of his nose. Of course Queen Bestia would be. By the Goddess, she was working against them.

"I had wondered," Caspian continued, "if you would humor me, Lady Diana with that friendly competition we talked about. I have heard nothing but marvelous things about your skill with a bow and am most eager to see it for myself. Would you be amenable to facing me when I return?"

Diana smirked. "Ready to get that selkie pelt beat?"

Caspian chuckled. "We shall see."

By the Goddess, the pounding in Paulo's head was beating an excruciating rhythm, fogging his thoughts. "Sorry to cut this little chat short," he said, "but Diana and I were just headed in."

Caspian gave a short bow. "Of course. I will let you go."

Paulo gave a small wave in conjunction with Diana's farewell and trudged his way back to their rooms. By the time he had shucked his boots and untied his cravat, his head had gone from the beat of a drum to the thunder of a gong. He even waved Jenkins off from helping him out of his jacket and simply slumped onto his bed with the orders to wake him for supper in a couple hours.

The night would have enough excitement waiting for him.

Diana folded her arms over her chest. "Are you sure I can't go?"

Paulo quickly tied off the mask pressed against his face and straightened in the mirror. The head piece covered most of his hair, the faintest wisps peeking out the back which would be covered by the hood on his jacket. There was nothing he could do about his abundance of freckles, but he wouldn't be meeting with Laurel in the light of day, so he could maintain some anonymity. He twisted back and forth in the mirror. The entire ensemble made him feel like a rogue living in the woods or perhaps a pirate. Mater had the jacket and pants crafted for him, and he thought the whole thing rather dashing. Perhaps someday, Laurel would too.

"Stop preening, Paulo, and answer me."

Paulo grabbed a few of the peppermint leaves out of the bowl on the table next to him and stuffed them in his cheek. The herb would fight off the bit of headache still lingering after his nap. And his breath would smell amazing.

Diana had thrown herself over the coverlet of his bed. He frowned when he noticed the flakes of mud stuck to the bottoms of her boots. If she got dirt on his bed, he'd throw something at her.

"No," he said, "you really can't come. Laurel only thinks there's one of us to worry about in the palace. If she sees two, she's going to get spooked."

"I don't see why it's fair for you to be the one to get to sneak around fighting assassins at night."

Paulo checked his clock by the bed. Blast, he'd slept too long and was going to be late. He grabbed the hooded jacket off the bed. "I really shouldn't have to defend my decision to you."

Both of them knew why. Laurel might be someone Paulo cared about— all right, that may be a very moderate term for how he felt— but she was still a *trained assassin*. One who didn't have any connection to him or anyone else in this kingdom. She didn't care if she stabbed Paulo or Diana in the back and left them to die.

At least, not yet.

"Besides," Paulo continued, "it's not like you haven't gone sniffing around her." He tossed the cookie tin he'd taken on the bed next to her.

She snatched it up. "I knew you stole it!" The lid quickly popped open, and she growled. "And you ate them all?"

Paulo shrugged, though he felt the smug grin trying to break out across his lips. "I had to do something while I waited for her." He pretended to eat one, smacking his lips ridiculously like he had when Laurel had been standing at the door.

Diana's outrage turned into disgust. "I sincerely hope you didn't make those noises in front of Laurel. That's just plain embarrassing."

Paulo laughed and pulled the hood up over his head. "I guess I'll just have to add lip-smacking to my long list of obnoxious traits."

"Don't worry, I've already slotted it between 'sneezes like a troll' and 'wetted the bed until he was eight.'"

"Hey! You can't hold the bed-wetting against me!" Paulo folded his arms over his chest. "Not when you still slept with Fuzzy until you were fourteen."

Diana rolled her eyes. "A stuffed bear is not the same and you know it."

Paulo grabbed the gloves off the edge of his vanity table. "We'll have to finish this conversation later."

"Fine, but I expect to hear every detail when you get back."

Paulo couldn't help shaking his head as he slipped out

into the hall. For all the things Diana didn't do like normal girls, her nosey nature could rival even Lady Clarice's, the daughter of Lord Discordia and the kingdom's resident gossip hound.

Paulo slipped through the palace hallways. His nap earlier in the evening had banished the headache, but he knew he'd have another by the end of the night. He kept his magic open as he surveyed watch rotations through the palace and kept the timeline open for Laurel. He saw a vision of her in her costume, creeping after one of the kitchen girls. The same one that had met with Prince Dion last night.

The prince really had no shame.

The vision faded and he leaned against a wall to wait, keeping himself out of the moonlight peeking through the window across the hall. This particular part of the palace was home to a plethora of the guest chambers, many of which were empty at the moment. Everyone was holding off their arrivals to the capital until the winter solstice celebrations at the end of the year. Not that it would stay that way. If Paulo calculated his visions correctly, the full council would be called back to the capital in eight weeks or so. A good month before the solstice celebrations. Though many of the nobility had their own residences in the city— like the Barclay's— there were several that still resided in the palace— like Paulo. Having a bit of royal blood in his family line didn't hurt when it came to asking for favors, and the royal family had always kept a suite of rooms available for the MacGregors to stay in the palace whenever they wished.

It certainly made it easy to get to know the palace well enough to sneak around.

The scuff of a slipper against the carpeted hallway sounded just around the corner. Paulo pulled himself farther into the shadows where he stood. A woman in a white nightgown swept past the moonlit window, the shawl she'd worn the night before likely still in Prince Dion's possession.

A shadow followed, ducking underneath the window.

Paulo grinned and chased after them.

He watched Laurel, both in the present and future. It was a hard skill to master, as he had to consciously keep his reactions up with what was happening while also planning what to do next. Like reading the notes of a musical piece ahead so one could look up to see what the conductor wanted them to do. While the instrumentalist knew the song, they had to follow the direction of the maestro right that moment.

The undercook turned down a hallway and Laurel followed her. Paulo slowed at the turn, pushing his gift to watch where Laurel went next. She stopped at the door, this time only waiting to confirm Prince Dion was in there before rushing in.

But Paulo had other plans for that evening.

He turned down the hallway, seeing the faintest glimmer of Laurel's mask by the reflection from the light coming through the small crack under the door. She drew a long dagger from her left thigh, the sheath on her right thigh still empty. That knife was tucked away in Paulo's room.

Paulo used the plush carpet under his boots to mask his steps. Diana had helped him pick out his boots and had taught him how to walk on silent feet. It took a lot more effort than one might think, but he knew he needed every tool in his arsenal if he wanted to stand a chance against Laurel.

As he got closer, he saw her tuck the knife up against her arm. She was nearly ready to pounce.

He snuck up behind her and carefully snatched the knife from her hand. "You know, we really ought to stop meeting like th—"

Laurel spun and threw a punch at his throat.

He saw it, of course, and dodged out of the way.

Without another thought, he tucked his new toy into his jacket and raced back the way he had come.

He cast his vision out a little further into the future, making sure she would follow behind him.

She did.

And it was a lot sooner than he anticipated.

She grappled him to the ground at the end of the hallway.

He fell and twisted, getting a grip on her before he landed on the ground. If he hadn't, she would have stabbed him with a little knife in the back of the neck.

Instead, he caught her hands and used his hips to send her flying over his head, still holding onto her hands. She landed on her back instead of wrenching her shoulders out of place.

He released his hold and rolled to his feet. She was already there, knife in hand.

He watched her as the future scrolled through his vision.

She kicked out, reaching again for a knife.

He dodged it and swept toward her.

There was a knife at his throat.

He deflected the knife and brought her arm up over his head, slamming her forearm on his shoulder and plucking the knife from her hand. Knife number thre. He was really starting a collection now.

Another knife, this one aimed at his kidney.

He twisted to the side, letting go of her right hand to grab her left. He pulled her past him as if in an intricate dance only the two of them knew how to perform.

Her knife slashed toward the arm that held her.

Sweet Gaia, how many blasted knives does she have?

He let go, allowing the momentum to pull her away from him.

She recovered and drew another knife.

She stopped.

"Who are you?" she asked.

Paulo's lips split into a wide grin, and he almost wanted to laugh at the absurdity of it all. "Me? I'm a friend."

He heard the tiny scoff, but he was already moving, stepping close. He had no weapons in his hands. He leaned in so his mouth paused only an inch from her ear.

"I know you don't believe me, but one day you'll understand. One day, you'll realize that I'm one of the only people in this entire world you can actually trust."

Laurel shoved him away. "Then take off your mask."

Paulo chuckled. "I think this mystery is one you need to solve on your own, love." It wouldn't do for her to know yet. Not when they'd just begun.

Laurel took a step toward him, but he was already moving. He counted down the seconds as she chased him through the palace.

Good.

He raced past the guest chambers and into the servants' halls. She knew her way around the palace already, which made it difficult to lose her, but he knew where all the guards would be. Only six or so feet ahead of her, he pulled himself into a closet as guards swept into the hall. He heard her curse from behind the door and run back the way she'd come. Paulo waited until the guards were past the door to sneak away, leaving Laurel to wonder which way he'd gone.

A grin stayed on his face the whole way back to his rooms.

14
THE MATCH

Laurel will stand at the edge of the crowd, unable to see a thing over the heads of so many. Her eyes will alight on one of the many guard towers in the practice yard. Not waiting for anyone's permission, she will make her way there. The room will be full, but she will quickly work her way through. Shouts will go up when she arrives at the window, missing what would have been a fantastic sight.

LAUREL SWALLOWED BACK HER ANNOYANCE AS SHE WATCHED DELILAH twirl around the kitchen. The girl thought herself in love, though she teased the rest of the girls in the kitchen with who she was seeing. Like it was really a mystery. Like none of the women in that room suspected she'd gone off to meet with the Crown Prince every few days. Laurel shook her head and turned back to the vegetables she was chopping. The knife in her hands moved in a blur, cutting through the flesh of the carrot with practiced ease.

Chop. Chop. Chop.
Scrape.
Chop. Chop. Chop.
Scrape.

Though the motion would soothe her any other day, today it only fed the fire that had been growing in her belly over the last couple of weeks. The man had thwarted her again and again. Every time she got close to Prince Dion, the masked man would pop out of thin air like he knew she was coming. Had Prince Dion told this man to watch out for intruders on his nightly escapades? Where were his guards? Why hadn't they started looking for her yet?

"Sweet Gaia, Laurel," Cook said from beside her. "You'll lose a finger moving at that pace. We aren't in a rush, dear."

Laurel slowed her chopping, but her mind still whirled. This new opponent was making her job difficult. Was it all a trap? Had Teagan actually set her up from the very beginning? *Of course he did.* It was Teagan. But she knew him. While he was conniving, he couldn't have accomplished something of this magnitude without her knowing it was him. This felt greater than either of them. It felt like something else was going on and she didn't appreciate being a pawn in anyone's game.

One day, you'll realize that I'm one of the only people in this entire world you can actually trust.

Laurel beheaded another carrot top. *As if!* She knew who she could trust. Aspen and herself. That was it. It was them against the world, and no one else mattered. Laurel would get this job done, and she would get off this cursed isle to claim her prize. She just needed to outsmart the masked man trying to play hero.

The sound of running footsteps and excited chatter grew from the door leading to the grand dining hall. Galen burst into the room, face bright and chest heaving. "There's to be a competition!"

Cook wiped her hands on her apron. "What's this?"

The servers behind him pushed forward. "Mr. Delrio is back and challenged Lady Diana to a competition. They're to meet out at the archery ranges in less than a quarter hour and Prince Dion said everyone in the palace was invited to attend."

Laurel's hands stilled over her pile of carrots. The excitement practically vibrated in the room, whispers ricocheting off the stone walls and the server's toes bouncing with anticipation A competition was exactly what she needed to get rid of this awful fire in her stomach.

"Well!" Cook placed a hand to her chest. "I suppose, if His Highness has invited everyone..."

Delilah harrumphed. "Is that even proper? A woman being challenged to a duel and paraded about for entertainment?"

"It's not a duel," Galen scoffed. "It's a friendly competition and will be loads of fun— something you could certainly use more of."

Delilah pouted even more, and Laurel had to keep herself from snickering as she stepped toward the door. Galen had grown a bit snippy at Delilah recently. If it was because Delilah was being extra annoying or Galen was feeling spurned, Laurel couldn't say. She followed the crowd out of the kitchen, Cook's orders to be back in time to finish preparing supper fading as they stepped out into the open air. The maids tittered as they all scurried toward the archery range.

It had been set up in one of the gardens near the guard barracks. They were quite close to the servant quarters but had their own entrance on the north side of the building. Laurel let herself be swept by the tide of people, soaking in the competitiveness brewing within their group. Stellatus Hall had seen its fair share of friendly and sometimes unfriendly competitions.

Assassins were naturally blood thirsty— it came with the job — but there was nothing like watching two skilled opponents go against one another. There was a deadly beauty in it. Hopefully, Olympian nobility had at least half of the rivalrous spirit Stellatus Hall did.

The crowd entered the shooting range near the palace wall. The distance from the palace to the wall had to be around two hundred yards and half of it was teeming with people. It seemed they'd summoned every warm body in the palace— and perhaps even those from the dungeon— to watch the spectacle. Someone had had the foresight to block off the shooting area, giving the competitors plenty of space while also guarding against an international incident should one of the arrows go astray.

A cheer went up as a man with a black pelt wrapped around his waist emerged from the palace. A selkie, then. Laurel watched him as he swaggered toward the shooting line. There was a lot to be discovered in the way one faced a challenge, even when they faked confidence. His white teeth flashed as he passed by his admirers, the puff of his chest proud. Oh yes, this was a man used to winning. Lady Diana would certainly have her work cut out for her if the selkie's bravado matched his skill, which based on the calculating tilt of his head and the sure measure of his gait, it did.

One of the footmen ushered everyone to the south side of the range and out of the way of the nobility and higher-class attendees.

Biting her lower lip, she glanced around the crowd. The royals were seated just behind the archers, three heads of golden hair glittering in the sunlight. Only the youngest prince seemed to be missing. Prince Dion and Prince Evan sat next to one another, their smiles wide as Mr. Delrio took his place.

Lady Carnation sat on her betrothed's other side, her expression pinched.

Did the woman ever smile?

Another cheer went up as Lady Diana strode from the depths of the palace. Her gait did not carry the sashay of her opponent but the straightforward trod of a woman who meant business. There was no falter, no hesitation. She marched through the crowd with unbridled fervor that made Laurel grin.

When Lady Diana made it to the line, the crowd around them surged forward, doing their best to get a good look at the opponents. The sound hushed as someone began calling out the rules of the competition, stating the bout was to be only three shots and listing the rules of the game.

"This view is awful," Galen grumbled.

Delilah stretched up on her tiptoes. "I can't see a thing." While Laurel was a bit taller than the undercook, she could still only see the top of Lady Diana's fiery red hair.

Laurel turned away from the competitors and glanced about. Her gaze caught on a flash of orange through the crowd, and she saw none other than Lord MacGregor weave his way through the audience toward one of the small towers standing near the wall. After their short interaction in the pantry, Laurel had looked into Lord Paulo MacGregor of Delphine. A marquess. A mage. One with the ability to see into the future and the high enough standing to do something about it.

Could he be the masked man?

Laurel took a step in the direction he'd gone, but Delilah grabbed her arm.

"Where are you going?" she hissed.

"Come on," Laurel whispered. "We can probably see better from that tower over there." And it would give her a moment to watch Lord MacGregor. It was too much that she'd met him on her first day in Olympia and nearly halfway across the kingdom before arriving at the palace. Coincidences were rare in her line of work and even rarer when the man in question could see into the future.

"What are you two up to?" Galen asked, following behind them.

Laurel shook her head, but Delilah answered him. "We're going to the tower to get a better view."

"Is that allowed?" he asked.

Laurel ignored them and pushed through the crowd quicker. If it wasn't allowed, then they would hurry back, but in Laurel's opinion, it was better to ask for forgiveness later. They reached the bottom of the tower as the guard at the firing line called for the competitors to ready themselves.

"Hurry!" Delilah hissed. "They're going to start any moment."

Laurel charged up the steps. Wooden stairs wrapped around the stilted legs of the tower and up to the top where a small enclosure stood over the area. Laurel reached the opening and found a group of men standing at the window on the far side.

Galen bumped into her. "Guess we weren't the only ones with the idea."

Laurel took a step back, but Lord MacGregor suddenly appeared in front of her, pushing past the guards and grabbing her hand. Laurel nearly broke his wrist before stopping herself and grabbing Delilah's hand as the man pulled her forward, the guards shuffling out of the way.

When they reached the window, Laurel yanked her hand away from Lord MacGregor's and attempted to rub away the weird tingle that had taken root in her fingers. "Pardon me, my lord, but I don't think our short acquaintance merits you touching me."

"My apologies." He grinned at her. "It's just the view from the door isn't nearly this good."

Of course, he was right. Laurel could see the entire field from their vantage point. Lady Diana's hair blazed gloriously in the autumn afternoon, matching the reddening oak leaves on the trees next to the palace. She stood proud, the quiver at her back fletched in brilliant colors, two bows in her hand. Based on the sizes, one was for her and the other for Mr. Delrio.

"Oh dear," Lord MacGregor said, looking away from her.

Laurel looked up at him then back to the line where Mr. Delrio took his place. "What?"

The nobleman shook his head. "She's really not going to like this."

"Who?"

The answer came a moment later. Mr. Delrio didn't take the bow Lady Diana offered. Instead, someone tossing him a spear. Mr. Delrio caught the weapon in the air, using his momentum to then send the spear hurtling toward the target.

The red-painted rings exploded in a cloud of straw.

The selkie twisted again, catching another spear. Then another. The last two targets followed in the same fashion as the first. Straw rained down over the ground, the spears stuck into the stone wall behind the targets.

"Things are about to get violent." Lord MacGregor turned and headed for the door.

"Wait!" Laurel couldn't let him leave. She needed to question him.

Delilah and Galen called after her, but she lost them in the herd of people around them. Cheers were still going up from Mr. Delrio's decided victory and bets being paid out. Laurel followed the man through the crowd, keeping pace as he cleared the crowd ahead of her. She nearly ran right into his back as he halted at the partition.

"Let me through," he ordered the guard standing on the other side.

The guard moved without question and Lord MacGregor nimbly vaulted over the thick wooden fence. Laurel didn't wait for the guard to tell her she couldn't and followed right after him. It might have been a tad presumptuous, but her curiosity was getting the better of her.

Lord MacGregor approached where Lady Diana was standing toe-to-toe with the selkie. The lady wasn't short by any means, but she barely met the man's chest as she bared her teeth up at him.

"You are a cursed *cheat*, and you know it!"

Mr. Delrio only frowned. "There were no rules pertaining to what weapon I used."

If Lady Diana's finger could wound, it would have with how she stabbed the selkie's chest. "But blowing up targets completely destroys the bullseye, ruining any chance of checking for precision. Even if I was to shoot now, no one would be able to tell whether or not I even hit the marks."

A smirk grew on Mr. Delrio's face as he gestured to the decimated targets. "I think my victory was pretty precise, don't you?"

Lady Diana snarled and lunged forward, but Lord MacGregor caught her by the waist and dragged her back a step.

"Bad Diana!" he admonished. "No biting the selkie brute!"

Laurel blinked. Had he really just said that? To Lady Diana no less? Her steps slowed and she looked about, waiting for anyone to come to Lord MacGregor's aid. Everyone watched with wide eyes, several looking curiously at her,

Curse it all! She shouldn't be anywhere near this spectacle.

Lady Diana growled. "Let me go, Paulo, so I can rip that smug smile off his stupid face!"

15
AN UNFORTUNATE QUARREL

PAULO NEARLY LET DIANA ATTACK CASPIAN JUST SO LAUREL WOULDN'T have the chance to escape. She'd finally engaged with him— well, properly this time— and the world was slowly being set to rights. Of course, his cursed sister had to go and ruin it.

"He's a blasted cheat, Paulo! Can't even be decent enough to make it an even match and instead had to make a fool of both of us in order to keep his big head inflated."

Caspian's *big head* reared back. "Excuse me?"

"You heard me!" She reached for his throat, but Paulo yanked her back once again. Though, if she'd really wanted to gouge the selkie's eyes out, she wouldn't have let Paulo stop her. They both knew she could break his hold for long enough to at least land a hit to Mr. Delrio's very prominent nose.

And Paulo wanted to let her.

The selkie really was a cheat. And a liar. He would cause so much heartache; Paulo would love nothing more than to let Diana at least get this little bit of justice for it.

But that wasn't part of the plan.

Paulo sighed. "Perhaps we can all take a little breather and talk about it tomorrow." He turned to Laurel, who had taken a few steps back. "Will you grab Lady Diana's bow and help me escort her to our suite?"

Laurel froze, her gaze bouncing about. Likely looking for a means of escape. She must not have found one because she met his eyes and did her best to portray her frustration. Her brown eyes shot sparks at him even as she walked over to grab Diana's things. Usually, Diana would be spitting mad that someone was touching her precious bow, but it was Laurel. She was an exception to quite a few rules.

Caspian made a hasty retreat, diving headfirst into the crowd of well-wishers still standing at the edges of the field. *Coward.* The man couldn't even face the consequences of his choices, but he would eventually. Of that, Paulo was sure.

The selkie was fully submerged when Paulo let go of Diana. She didn't even stumble as she swung around, seething. "You should have let me at least break his nose."

"But you might have gotten blood on my new waistcoat." He tugged at the fine blue cotton fabric he'd just purchased the week before. "The red would have clashed horribly."

Diana barked a humorless laugh. "Has no one ever told you what a condescending egomaniac you are?"

"Usually, such epithets are reserved for Thursdays or when I attend the theater in my bright salmon suit jacket."

A small snort came from where Laurel stood holding Diana's bow and quiver.

"Oh, Laurel." Diana sent Paulo a look that said *You really need to hurry along your whole wooing thing so we can all not feel the complete awkwardness of this situation.* Or at least, that was the gist he got. Twin sense and all that.

Laurel gave a small curtsy. "My lady." She held up the bow with the ease of someone who had held one many times before.

Diana took the weapons from her. "What did you think?"

Laurel blinked. "I'm sorry?"

Diana flapped her hand at the crumbled targets. "About what Caspian did. Do you think it should count as a victory?"

Laurel's very soft-looking lips pulled down in a frown as she looked at the targets. "I don't know..." Her dark brows pulled down as she thought.

By the Goddess, she was lovely.

"Don't try to play off your intelligence, Laurel. I just want your honest opinion."

Paulo's heart jolted and he refrained from shooting a glare in Diana's direction. He could have strangled his twin. Her surly attitude was going to expose them.

Shock widened Laurel's eyes, and she looked back and forth between both Diana and Paulo before looking at the targets. Her eyes, the color of the dark stones under water, narrowed. "From the way I was raised, yes. But for me? It would depend on how well he actually shot."

"The judges all agreed they were perfect marks," Diana said.

Laurel turned and took a step closer, angling her head as she studied where the spears still hung in the wall, forgotten in Caspian's new victory. "Well, if my memory is as good as I think it is, the second and third spears would have been a few inches off the center marks."

"I knew it!" Diana crowed.

Paulo studied Laurel. "How do you know?"

Laurel shrugged. "I have a very good memory. I recall that the center of the middle bullseye sat below that chipped brick just there." She pointed at a brick in the palace wall, and sure enough, one of them sported a rather large chip in the white stone.

Paulo studied her. "I'll have to take your word for it." By the

Goddess, he was going to have to up his game. If she had that good of a memory, he would need to figure out how to better keep her from discovering his identity.

Laurel's chin lifted slightly. "You don't believe me?"

"It's not that. My memory just isn't nearly so precise." In fact, his visions took up a good portion of that memory and details were often lost in all the hubbub inside his head. Not to mention how many versions of a future he saw. By the Goddess, sometimes things really did get muddled in his brain.

However, he could easily recite every word to the bawdy song he'd heard pouring out of a tavern when he was ten and recall every detail he learned from his tutor of King Jovan III, who had been the third king after the end of the Faerie Wars and had ruled over a poverty-stricken kingdom and had married the first mage in the royal line to help end the mage hunts after the war. He'd also lost his leg in a horseback riding accident. Him and his wife had five daughters and one son— who had not had any mage gifts and inherited the throne at the age of fourteen because his father had died in a hunting accident...

All important things, of course.

"Paulo, how are we going to get revenge?" Diana paced the grass like a caged lioness in the circus. "He has to pay."

Laurel took a step away, and Paulo sidled up next to her, blocking her path. "Since you seem to be the paragon of wisdom at the moment, what would you do if you were in my sister's position?"

Laurel stilled. "To enact revenge on someone who just humiliated me in front of at least two hundred people?"

Paulo smiled. "Yes."

She nibbled at her bottom lip, and Paulo couldn't take his eyes from the spot. By the Goddess, it was the sweetest torture, the most bitter delight. Did she have any idea how lovely she was? How intriguing? He'd known years ago that there wasn't a single woman that would capture him as fully as she would, but having it happen in the present might be too much for him to fully handle.

Diana kicked his boot.

He shook himself. He wouldn't gain her trust if he stared at her like a maniac.

She nodded. "Probably stick some kind of poison ivy in the toes of his boots."

The tension in Diana's shoulders had eased a fraction. "Oh, that's brilliant. He'd never figure out why he kept itching and he'd be absolutely miserable for ages, or at least until someone figured it out. You're a genius, Laurel."

Laurel gave a little bow and turned to Paulo. "What about you?"

"Easy," Paulo said. "I'd rip his seams."

"Yes!" Diana cheered, then paused. "Wait, what does that do?"

Paulo smirked. "I'd figure out when he wouldn't be anywhere near his wardrobe, sneak in, and tear out a few of the seams in his clothing. He would put his clothes on, none the wiser, but they would slowly fall apart during the day."

Diana laughed, but Laurel looked at him curiously. "No murder? No maiming? No venomous snakes in his bed or hiring thugs to beat him to a bloody pulp?"

Paulo shook his head. "I'm a firm believer that a punishment ought to fit a crime. He humiliated her. He needs to be humiliated. Can you imagine him running through the palace, his clothes slowly falling to pieces as he ran past every courtier in the corridors?"

Diana rubbed her hands together gleefully. "All right, how are we going to go about it. Do we do one? Both?"

Paulo chuckled. "Diana, you can't enact a revenge plot against a visiting dignitary."

She stopped maniacally rubbing her hands and folded her arms over her chest. "Why not?"

"Because Prince Dion explicitly told us not to start an international incident while we're still trying to figure out what to do about this rebellion." Paulo grabbed Laurel's hand and tucked it into his elbow. "Let's go inside and we can have Donnie paint the selkie's likeness on a target board for you to shoot at."

Laurel slipped her hand from his arm, and he had to refrain from snatching it back up. He did allow himself a small sigh. He'd seen that it wouldn't work, but he couldn't help himself.

She gave a quick curtsy. "I'll leave you both to your revenge plans."

"Nonsense," Paulo said. "We'll walk you back."

"I wouldn't expect you to—"

"Just give it up, Laurel," Diana cut in, walking in the direction of the palace. "When Paulo wants something, he usually gets it."

Laurel gave him a look that clearly stated how unimpressed she was with that particular statement.

He grinned and fell into step with her. "Of course I do. I'm a marquess. It's a requirement of my station to get everything that I want."

"I believe that's just called being spoiled," Diana snapped back.

"I think I prefer the phrase 'entitled' more." He looked to Laurel. "Gives it a certain air, don't you think?"

She shrugged. "If you're into appearing like a pompous upstart, sure."

Paulo clutched his neatly tied neckcloth in feigned distress. "That is the second time you've both insulted my good name. I shall have to write to Mater about this immediately and bemoan the obvious lack of good taste in the women of my company."

"Apologies, my lord," Laurel said, but her lips said she was anything but sorry. "I simply hoped my teasing would lighten Lady Diana's mood."

"Well, I cannot fault you for that then." Paulo let one finger touch the back of her hand in what would seem an innocent brush of their skin as they walked, though it was anything but innocent. It was difficult to not pull her into his arms and kiss her silly, especially when she was teasing him. He was a man just begging for torture.

She stepped further away. "Thank you, my lord."

Diana groaned. "Donnie's going to be insufferable once he hears."

Paulo held back a snicker. *Yes, Donnie will be.*

The three of them walked back toward the south side of the palace. The doors to the kitchen came too soon and Paulo felt himself dragging his feet even as Laurel maintained her quick pace.

Diana swung an arm over Laurel's shoulders, slowing her for one more moment. "You know, Laurel, we should hang out more."

Laurel visibly stiffened. "I don't know if that would be wise, my lady. Besides, I have a lot of work to do—"

"Bah! They've got plenty of people crammed in that kitchen. I'm sure Cook could spare you every once in a while."

Laurel looked up at Diana. "Begging your pardon, but even if Cook could spare me, I don't see why you would desire my company."

Diana threw her hand toward the palace. "You think there's someone in that peacock parade that would interest someone like me? Not a cursed chance."

Laurel shook her head, sliding out from under Diana's arm. "I'm sorry, but I really don't see how any of that would work out." She spun to glance at both of them. "I appreciate you walking me back, but we really should part ways here. Good afternoon."

She turned and scurried away as fast as her feet could carry her.

Paulo reached Diana's side and shook his head. "She's a tough egg to crack."

Diana bumped him with her elbow. "Yes, but it's going to be worth it. It has to be."

16
THE COLLISION

Laurel will be in the kitchens when Diana returns the cookie tin she'd borrowed. She will spend an entire week asking questions about the MacGregor family. She will set a trap for Paulo, and he will be caught by the guards in order to save her from her own foolishness. When he removes his mask to identify himself, she will know for certain. With an oracle on the loose, she will run to the ship with red sails witting in Olympia's harbor and reveal what has been happening to a man with dead eyes.

"Oh, Lady Diana! Lord MacGregor!" Delilah gasped. "You've come again."

Laurel looked up from the chicken she was tearing apart and dipped into a curtsy. Kitchen girls didn't ignore the presence of nobility even if they were planning to metaphorically raze the entire palace to the ground. From what she'd seen of the woman, Laurel had quickly deduced Lady Diana didn't follow the fashions of the other young ladies in Olympia. She wore tunics and trousers more fitted to the gentlemen Laurel had seen, though the attire wasn't in any way scandalous. At least, not to Laurel. She almost missed getting to wear trousers on the regular, though she always wore some under her skirts just in case. But Lady Diana walked about freely in men's attire, ready to jump into action without skirts hampering her. In fact, Lady Diana looked like she was always ready for a hunt, her blue eyes flicking over every nook and cranny of a place.

But the man next to her, while similar to Lord MacGregor, wasn't him. He glanced around the kitchen, making eye contact with Laurel before quickly looking away. Where Lord MacGregor was a whirlwind of color and chaos, this man was a tempered version— even his hair a darker shade, almost brown, instead of bright red. He still carried that vibrancy she'd come to recognize from the MacGregor family, but he wore it with simplicity rather than the extravagance the brother-sister-duo did.

Lady Diana stuck a thumb in his direction. "This is Lord Oliver MacGregor, the son of Lord Peter MacGregor. He might look similar to my brother, but I can assure you, they're nothing alike."

Lord Oliver frowned. "I don't know whether to be delighted or offended."

"The former, obviously." Lady Diana turned back to Delilah. "Where's Cook?"

"Apologies, my lady, but Cook is meeting with Esther this morning." Delilah wiped her hands on her apron next to Laurel. "Is there anything I can do for you?"

Lady Diana held out a metal tin. "I simply wished to return her tin and apologize that I haven't returned it sooner. It did come in quite handy."

Delilah took it. She turned, and with no one else close

enough to foist it off on, passed it to Laurel. "Will you set this for Jeannie to wash?"

Laurel stared. A large swan was engraved on the lid of the tin. The same one she'd dodged the first time she'd gone up against the masked man a few weeks ago. Her attention swiveled back to Lady Diana who gave her a daring smile, though if she was being friendly or she knew something, Laurel couldn't tell.

Delilah gave Laurel look that said she was running out of patience. Laurel plucked the tin from her hand. It really was the same one. How did Lady Diana get it back?

Delilah then returned to their guests. "Is there anything else we can do for you?"

Lord Oliver piped up. "I did hope there was some leftover baklava from last night. No one makes it like Cook does."

Delilah puffed up her chest. "Actually, I made last night's baklava. I'm glad to know it was enjoyed. I'll fetch you some straight away." She bobbed a curtsy and hustled to the pantry. Dan, the other undercook, frowned after her from his place at the stove.

The girl was bold, Laurel would give her that. If anyone in Stellatus Hall tried to take credit from their master, word would get around and there would be consequences for such impudence.

Lady Diana leaned against the table and met Laurel's stare once more. "Is there something you want to ask me?"

So, she did know something. Laurel's heart went from a trot to a gallop as she glanced between the lord and lady. There absolutely was something going on with this family and Lady Diana was involved. Was Lord Oliver as well? Could he be the masked man? Their statures were similar.

But their eyes had been so different. Lord Oliver's were hazel, unlike his twin cousins' forget-me-not blue. The masked man had eyes of pearl or opal, a thousand colors swirling in their depths.

Laurel shook her head taking a step toward where Jeannie's pile awaited her after she returned from her half day. She would have to investigate the possibility.

"You could you know," Lady Diana said.

Laurel turned back around. "Could what?"

"Ask me." Lady Diana spread her arms wide. "I'm a completely open book."

"Why would I need to ask you anything?"

Lady Diana shrugged. "You just have the look of someone who has too many questions and not enough answers. Figured I could help with that."

Laurel studied her for a few seconds until Delilah returned with a small plate of baklava and her best smile. "Here you are, my lord. Let me know if there's anything else you need."

Lord Oliver raised the plate as if offering a toast. "This will be lovely, thank you." He turned to leave, Lady Diana stepping behind him.

"Lady Diana?" Laurel blurted.

Delilah gave a sharp inhale, but Lady Diana turned with an eager smile on her face. "Yes?"

Laurel nodded at her leather trousers. "Would you tell me where you bought those? I'd love to get myself a pair."

Delilah scowled beside Laurel, but Lady Diana laughed and gave Laurel directions to what she proclaimed to be the best shop in Olympia.

It was two weeks— and several firm talking-tos from Delilah the Hypocrite about not trying to befriend people above their station— later that Laurel took her half-day to go pick up her new pants. She'd ordered three pair for herself and three for Aspen. She couldn't help herself after she'd visited the shop and seen them on the racks of the clothier shop. The supplest leather she'd ever touched. The clothier had a good relationship with the seamstresses that created the clothing— though, Laurel didn't know if they were magically influenced or not— and could alter them as needed. The longer Laurel spent in Olympia, the more she understood why Teagan would agree to Adira Durant's schemes. He would be a rich man if he could figure out how to export this culture.

Laurel raced through the market square, excited to try on her new wares at the shop. She would have to ship them back to Stellatus Hall when she could figure out how without anyone tracing it back to her. If she couldn't, she would have to take them home after she finished the job.

A tightness took root in her stomach. She would finish this job. She would figure out who the masked man was, assassinate Prince Dion before solstice, and get home to Aspen before Teagan did anything maniacal.

Laurel shook herself as she passed a man peddling copper pots. Who the masked man was didn't matter. What did matter was that she only had two months left of a job that should have taken her half the time she'd been there. First, the mage taster. Then, the prince who couldn't seem to be alone for longer than half a second. And now, this cursed masked vigilante! It was like someone was attempting to play a cruel prank on her and would come jumping out from around a corner screaming "Surprise!"

However, she was notorious for ruining surprises. She wouldn't be caught off-guard by this job, and whoever was trying to meddle in her affairs would rue the day they crossed her.

But first, she wanted to try on her new pants.

The oak trees lining the streets had turned red and gold, their acorns crunching under her boots. She'd seen the gardeners in the palace harvest the acorns and store them in large barrels, saving some for planting. Cook had even set to leaching vats of them to use for flour and roasted several pounds of them. Laurel had snuck a handful from one of the pans. They'd been sweeter than she thought they would.

The biting air of the autumn morning had slowly thawed into a crisp afternoon only warm enough for a sweater. Tantalizing aromas of cooked squash and warm spices drifted through the air. Fall had always been her favorite season. The colors of the changing leaves, the crisp air, the shortening days. While the air grew colder, the spirit of the season grew warmer. She'd never really been able to explain it. Aspen thought it morbid of her, stating that everything just smelled of death, but Laurel couldn't help but see it all as a preparation for something grand. A death of one life to make way for the beginning of a new one.

Her hand strayed to the lead weight hanging around her neck. Father had loved the season too.

Laurel arrived at the clothier's shop and held the door for a trio of young ladies and their chatty mothers. Once inside, she headed straight for the man behind the counter. He was at that middle-aged stage where you couldn't really figure out how old he was based solely on his looks. His hair still retained a good portion of its dark curls and was only striped through with silver. The wrinkles framing his eyes and mouth hinted at years of laughter.

"Ah, Miss Naiad," the shop owner greeted. "You've come just in time. I just finished wrapping your parcels."

Laurel pulled her pleasant smile out of her arsenal. Expressions were weapons as well. Aspen had always been quite proficient in wielding a simpering smile or a teary eye. Laurel's best weapon was her ability not to show anything on her face, but she could emote when needed— as she did now to put the man at ease.

"Good afternoon. I couldn't wait to try on my new wares." She bounced on the tips of her toes. "I do hope the new alterations weren't a problem."

The man waved her off. "Not at all. The seamstress claimed it was a pleasant challenge." He leaned down behind the counter and retrieved two packages, handing the one on top to Laurel and directing her to the dressing room behind the counter.

Laurel pulled the curtain closed and set to shedding her dress. She'd decided if she was going to order specially tailored clothing, she'd best do it as a woman so it wouldn't be suspicious of her to try them on. She pulled the first from the package, a pair of dark brown trousers that felt like something she would sleep in. She set to fastening the brass buttons on the front. Those could be easily replaced with specialized buttons that had needles or poison, but she enjoyed the contrast of the bright buttons on the dark leather.

She stopped and listened to the clothier on the other side of the curtain, making certain the man was nowhere near for what she was about to do. When Laurel pinpointed his location near the front of the shop, she grabbed her petticoat. The entire underskirt was weighed down with weapons stuffed into pockets and sewn into the lining. Laurel took the garrote line she had and slid it into the small space between the seams on the pant legs. The fall front on the trousers was double padded and the inner layer had six small slits for blow darts. It would need a little tinkering since she wouldn't want to risk getting stabbed by the darts, but that wouldn't be difficult to do on her own. The pockets were also double-lined, and she asked the seamstress to sew a rather generous hem on each pant leg so she could slip envelopes of poison into them. She would have to limit them to ingestible poisons, but that wouldn't be too much of a trial.

Finished, she twisted and looked at herself in the mirror set against the dressing room wall. It really was too bad the trousers were somewhat scandalous in Olympia. She would wear them everywhere if she could.

With a grin she didn't have to fake, she tried on the other two. A black pair and a lighter brown pair. Both received their own garrote wires in the small seams. She would put her nightshade powders in the black pair and her mountain laurel in the dark brown. Which poison she would put in the tan pair was a toss-up between the almond paste and water hemlock.

She threw her dress back on over the dark brown trousers, not yet ready to part with them. After rewrapping the other two in their package, she stepped out of the dressing room. A pair of women walked in right after Laurel stopped at the counter and paid. They eyed the dove-gray dress hanging in the window as she passed them.

Packages in hand, she meandered back to the palace. She still had a few hours before she had to return to the kitchens, but she found herself walking in that direction anyway. How had she come to this? All her reconnaissance had been completed. She'd seen nearly every inch of the palace. Knew the guard rotations. Had a good relationship with her pseudo-employer.

Yet the cursed prince still lived.

Laurel turned from the direction of the kitchens and walked toward one of the many gardens. After Lady Diana had come with the tin, Laurel had investigated the possibility of the family's involvement. As Laurel was sure she would recognize Lady Diana in men's clothing, the male members of her family seemed the best fit at the moment.

Firstly, Lord Paulo MacGregor. The man was certainly a conundrum.

Known as one of the wealthiest men in the kingdom, he still oversaw his family's wool company even after having many other businessmen offer lofty sums to take it off his hands. He was seen carousing with gentlemen like Lord Donaldson Abrams, who was known for being one of the most salacious men in the kingdom, yet Lord MacGregor— while not a virtuous man when it came to wooing young ladies based on the rumors Laurel had collected— stayed far from any scandalous activities himself. And while he was the only oracular mage in the kingdom, the only things he seemed to foretell were the fashions of next year and if they would have good crop that fall.

Based on the information she'd gathered, it made no logical sense that he was the masked man.

But Lord Oliver MacGregor? Possibly.

There wasn't much spoken about the other lord. Not like his cousins. Even though he was two years the twins' senior, he played the role of Lord MacGregor's spare heir, falling in line after his father as first cousin once removed. He was involved in the wool business with his father— Lord MacGregor's first cousin and heir apparent— who seemed to be in charge of managing much of the business beside Lord MacGregor. Lord Oliver wasn't married. Had no rumors circling any of the rumor mills.

Unlike his family's line of succession, he was, in essence, a simple man.

Which were always the ones to watch for.

Could Lord Oliver be the one who donned the mask? Was the entire family in on it? Was that why Lord MacGregor and

Lady Diana had such an interest in her? Because of their cousin?

The questions tumbled over one another like the surf she could hear on the other side of the palace wall. She followed the wall as much as she could, staying far from the nobility strolling through the gardens. It seemed to be a popular activity for the members of high society. Didn't any of them have anything better to do than wander around waiting for the next spectacle? The next scandal?

Laurel found a secluded path into the rose garden on the eastern side of the palace. The bushes had long lost their spring splendor, now resembling clawed fingers reaching for the warmth of the sun. The leaves had been swept away and the paths cleared until spring came. But with the lack of color came a distinct lack of people. Laurel made her way to what looked like a small gazebo situated in the middle of the bushes. Perhaps she could take the moment of quiet to figure out what she was going to do about the prince.

She wove through the bushes and stepped up into the gazebo. When she reached the top of the steps, she found a very dainty boot sticking out from the pillar beside the stairs. She froze, but the damage was done.

A head of golden curls darted out from behind the pillar. Lady Carnation's lips turned down into a frown.

Laurel took a step back, but the red around the lady's eyes stopped her in her tracks. "Do you need help, my lady?"

Lady Carnation gave a beleaguered sigh. "Do you have a remedy for stupidity?"

A small laugh bubbled up in Laurel's chest. "Do you think I'd be working in a kitchen if I did?"

"Fair enough."

For reasons she couldn't even begin to comprehend, Laurel

sat on the top step so she could be on the lady's level. "Are you hurt?"

Lady Carnation shook her head. "Just my pride and foolish heart."

"Grievous injuries, those." Laurel set the packages on the step below her and settled her forearms over her knees. "They take the longest to heal if you ask me."

Lady Carnation smoothed out the crumpled handkerchief in her lap. "I believe we often think they scar thicker than they do. We allow ourselves to be hurt in the same way over and over again, believing we're stronger because we overcame it the first time, but instead we keep reopening the wound and making it deeper."

"That's very true." The words were profound, and Laurel found herself prodding deeper. "And it's often the people plagued with stupidity that continue to pick at the wound."

"Why on Gaia's green earth are they the ones immune to the heartache?" Lady Carnation gave a very unladylike growl. "Shouldn't stupidity cause them to fall on their own swords?"

Laurel laughed. "One would think, but life never has been fair."

"We can certainly agree on that score." Lady Carnation dragged her fingers down her face. "All right. I should probably stop whining and get back to firing."

Laurel's stomach dropped. "*Firing*, my lady?"

"Yes. One of the scullery maids was seen with Prince Dion a few nights ago. I'll have to have her removed from the palace immediately."

A knot formed in Laurel's gut. Is that what happened to the young ladies Prince Dion fraternized with? Had anyone seen Delilah? Seen Laurel? Her stomach continued to tighten, but she wouldn't allow herself to spiral.

Lady Carnation stood and looked down at her. "You work in the kitchens, correct?"

"Yes, my lady."

"Then I certainly couldn't ask you if you knew about it." Lady Carnation clenched her hands in her skirts. "I hate that this is how it has to be."

Laurel studied the woman before her. It truly must have been so difficult to be the betrothed of a man like Prince Dion and have to do everything in her power to keep scandal out of her future marriage. Who could such a woman trust?

"I'm sorry I can't be of more help, my lady. Though, I could have Cook make up one of the recipes Galen has been dying to try. That might put His Highness in his place."

A laugh burst out of Lady Carnation. It was a laugh of someone who didn't use those muscles very often. Rough and out of shape, but beautiful in its rawness.

The lady wiped her eyes. "No, I suspect we would all regret that by the end. I can't tell you how many times Galen has come to me with wild recipes for the weekly menu. For a man who hates dying, he takes some rather interesting risks when it comes to cuisine."

"I suppose we all have our vices." And that was the problem, wasn't it? Prince Dion's lust made him untrustworthy. Lady Carnation's pride kept her from leaving a man she couldn't count on. Laurel's arrogance had her believing she could get around this masked bandit. That she was better than him. But she wasn't. He would beat her every time.

Lady Carnation sighed and got to her feet. "If only some of us were strong enough to simply leave our vices behind and try something else." Laurel watched as the lady slowly walked back to the palace.

She was right. There had to be something else.

Laurel simply needed to switch tactics.

17
AN UNFORTUNATE TRAP

SOMETHING WAS DECIDEDLY OFF. PAULO COULDN'T QUITE concentrate on the papers in front of him. It wasn't so much a knowing as it was a feeling. It settled in his gut, neither beneficial nor malevolent. He knew better than to ignore those feelings, but at this point there wasn't much he could do. His visions had been muddled all day and it was making his eye twitch.

Though, perhaps the twitching was in response to his cousin.

Well, his cousin's son.

Peter had insisted Paulo start working with Oliver in the particulars of the business. As Peter was growing older, he thought it best to get his heir involved in the running of the estates— especially if nature took its course and he died before either of them.

Paulo prayed daily that that particular day would be a long time coming. Peter was a fine heir, if a bit of a troublemaker. He had married into the Hermen family, his wife claiming Lord Stone Hermen as an eldest brother, and it seemed they were a bad influence on him. Paulo had been the victim of several pranks by both Peter and Lord Hermen over the years, but taking Oliver under his wing might have been the worst prank either of them had ever pulled.

Though, at this point, he was pranking himself. He needed Oliver, but it wasn't because the man could help him with the sheep.

Oliver leaned across the desk, the light in his hazel eyes making Paulo's stomach churn. It was always a stressful day when Oliver got that spark. He'd been bouncing in his chair since Paulo had begun the quarterly reports.

They'd done well that year.

Wool had always been a MacGregor business. While many of the nobility didn't run businesses, the MacGregors had. With their abilities to see into the future, they could make rather sound investments and start lucrative businesses. Textiles was one of the steadiest. Everyone needed fabric and wool had withstood the tests of time. Generations of MacGregors had raised sheep, providing the greatest supply of wool in the kingdom and filling MacGregor coffers for hundreds of years. Paulo was only the most recent lord to take advantage of his forefathers' gifts.

Oliver shut the ledger in his lap. "I think we should expand."

And there it was.

Biting back a sigh, Paulo closed his own ledger. "Why would we do that?"

"Have you ever heard of alpacas?"

Paulo nearly threw his ledger at Oliver's head. "Yes, I've heard of alpacas, you dolt. We have a small herd at the menagerie at Iatrus Castle." All Diana's fault, of course. She couldn't seem to keep her collection to dead creatures and had a plethora of live ones as well. If hunting was her life work, the menagerie was her hobby. Mater even helped her run it, and many of the nobility would take tours of it during the summer months. It was quite lucrative.

Oliver ignored Paulo's insult. "I believe we could expand MacGregor Wool by including alpaca wool to our exports."

"Oliver, the fibers cannot be woven into a yarn." At least, not yet. There was a young manufacturer on the Continent that would have it figured out in three years. "Besides, maintaining an alpaca herd in Olympia is next to impossible. The creatures are temperamental and do not fare well in our climates without extreme care." He'd had to pay a fortune to equip the enchanted enclosure for the twelve alpacas they had. Paulo would not invest in alpaca wool trade if his life depended on it. Not after he'd been spit on so many times. *Nasty creatures.*

Oliver sagged back in his chair. "I suppose it was a long shot. I simply thought we could do something else besides sheep for once."

For a man whose estate made a lot of money from the little beasts, Oliver never did like them. Though, that might be because he'd awoken one morning to a sheep chewing on his hair after Diana had smuggled half a dozen of them into his bedroom when they were children. That could cause a bit of trauma.

Paulo looked at his pocket watch. "Is there anything else?"

"I suppose not." He slapped the ledger on his knee. "Father and I will make sure to have the men start moving the herds toward the castle for the winter. Now that we expanded the west pasture, we should be able to get the Wolf Flock closer to the castle."

Paulo dug through the papers on the temporary desk he had set up in the palace. He didn't often take business meetings at the palace, preferring to meet at the warehouse they

had just south of the city, but Oliver claimed familial privi-
leges, as he and his father were also staying at the palace until
Prince Dion decided they could all go home and, therefore,
could pester Paulo at their leisure.

Paulo pulled out the sheet listing the flock rotations for last
quarter. There were three flocks, ranging from two hundred to
seven hundred sheep. Paulo's grandfather had allowed Diana
to rename the flocks after a disease nearly wiped out half the
flocks and he'd had to rearrange the sheep. She'd named them
after her three favorite animals at the time— wolf, raven, and
dolphin. The names were absolutely ridiculous, but Diana
would murder Paulo if he ever changed them.

"Excellent. I have a meeting scheduled with Cypress
Company at the end of the week to negotiate another
contract." Cypress Company was one of the largest buyers of
MacGregor wool and Paulo knew they would be taking some
heavy hits in the coming months. Paulo wanted to renego-
tiate their contract to protect both his business as well as
help them as much as he could. He'd met with them the
previous week and it seemed as if they would have it settled
quickly.

That stirring in his gut heightened.

Oliver straightened. "Oh? Do you think they would be
interested in alpacas?"

Paulo rolled his eyes and stood, showing Oliver to the door.
He had quite a few things to do before he met with Diana and
Donnie that evening— but it seemed his mind had other ideas.
It wandered constantly as he worked and the churn in his gut
grew.

The feeling followed Paulo through supper and far into the
evening, the heaviness moving from his gut up to his chest.
The fine line between excitement and anxiety was still foggy.

"...and Paulo likes to dress up like a woman and enter

beauty pageants in the winter. The higher necklines of those gowns hides his lack of—"

"What?" Paulo cut in. "I do not dress like a woman!"

Diana gave him a questioning look. "Finally caught that, did you?"

Donnie laughed. "Paulo, she said at least half a dozen more ridiculous things before you heard her."

Sweet Gaia, what else had she said? Paulo blinked. "My apologies. I didn't realize we were playing the 'ridiculous things' game."

"Not to worry," Diana sang. "Donnie and I can certainly continue playing if you want to keep having a moment with the wallpaper over there." Paulo followed her gaze and squinted at the powder blue walls of the parlor. It was a fairly elegant paper, if not a bit plain. He understood the choice. The room would look positively gaudy if there was a pattern beneath all the finery decorating the room.

"What plans do you have this evening?" Donnie asked. "I received a few bottles of my newest wine this morning and was looking for someone to test them out with me."

A vision slammed into Paulo, and he sucked in a breath. Donnie curled on the ground in another auspicious parlor, his fingers clawing at his hair as a scream tore from his throat.

Paulo shook himself from the vision. He'd seen several variations of it recently, but this one held a little more substance. It was approaching and it seemed there was nothing Paulo could do about it. Or perhaps there wasn't anything he *would* do about it.

"Do you think they'll keep until tomorrow night?" Being with his friend could prove critical in the next several weeks, but there were many moving pieces on the board. "I already have plans this evening."

"The wine might keep, but I don't know if I will!" Donnie

groaned. "It's fine. I'm sure there's one or two people in this place that wouldn't mind spending time with me and some good wine."

Diana snorted. "If there are, you're certainly the man to find them."

"Thank you, Diana Doll."

"I wouldn't take it as a compliment, Donnie Dearest." Her eyes gleamed with promised pain if he didn't quit teasing her. The long hunting knife in her hand shone with the same promise.

Paulo stood. "I should probably leave you." It would be good to get a little rest before that evening. He'd seen the vision of Laurel's next attempt that morning and while he couldn't wait to see her again, he still couldn't shake off whatever this feeling was.

"Fine," Donnie acquiesced. "I suppose I'll start my hunt then."

Diana scowled. "Please don't call it hunting."

"What? You think seducing isn't difficult?" A grin stretched across his face. "Well, the best seducing can be quite rigorous."

"Ew!" Diana's face wrinkled in disgust. "By the Goddess, why do you have to say things like that?"

Donnie stood, laughing. "I live to get people riled up. Get their blood pumping. Passion can ignite from the smallest spark."

Diana set to fake gagging as Donnie sauntered toward the door. Paulo only shook his head. Both of them were ridiculous sometimes. But if he was being honest with himself, so was he.

Prince Dion left the confines of his study late that evening. Paulo watched from the shadows of the corridor as the prince stretched and swung an arm over his youngest brother. Paulo expected the infamous spymaster to shrug him off, but he didn't. They simply kept walking, their low voices growing fainter as they left the study behind.

Paulo let his head fall back against the wall, settling in for a long evening. Laurel would arrive in this corridor within the hour. How she knew where the prince was, he didn't rightly know. He guessed it was the undercook Prince Dion had been meeting with, but he couldn't be completely sure.

It was forty-five minutes after watching the princes disappear that he felt it.

The air around him changed.

The feeling that had taken root in his chest twisted. He watched the shadows, waiting to glimpse the small shine of her mask or hear the small brush of her hands against the wall. His magic started swirling and his vision doubled.

Something slammed into him before the visions could settle.

He twisted on instinct, lifting his hips to dislodge his attacker. Her mask glittered above him as she locked her ankles together and pulled him with her. They rolled over the marble floor. When they came to a stop, Laurel landed on top with Paulo beneath her. One of his hands rested at her hip and the other held her wrist where she poised a blade at his throat.

His visions finally caught up and he was able to see things a few seconds into the future.

But nothing happened.

They simply sat in that position, his hands on her and that knife at his throat.

"We really need to stop meeting like this," he finally said.

"If you let go of me," she answered, "perhaps we can have a civilized conversation."

Paulo grinned and he tightened his hold on her waist. "I can't say I'm feeling very civilized at the moment."

He could barely make out her eyes widening before she scrambled to her feet. He remained on the floor as she tucked the dagger back into its spot on her thigh. With a sigh she offered her hand. When he hesitated, she wiggled her fingers.

"Come now. I promise I won't bite."

A pity. Paulo grabbed her hand and let her pull him up. Once he stood on two feet, she yanked her hand away as if he had burned her. He flexed his own fingers, feeling a little burned himself. He crossed his arms over his chest to try to dispel the feeling, but it didn't help one bit.

"So," he said, "if you aren't going to bite me, is there something I can do for you?"

She mimicked his stance. "I'm here to counter your employer's offer."

"What?"

"You heard me. I want to buy you out. How much would it cost me?"

Paulo laughed, taking a step toward her. "What's your offer?"

She matched his step. "I can get you four thousand gold pieces in two weeks if you will leave me alone in a room with Prince Dion for five minutes."

Four thousand gold pieces? Paulo let out a low whistle. "That's quite the ransom."

"I know what this is worth," she said.

He tapped his fingers on his chin, as if considering. "But what happens if I don't want money?"

"Position? I have connections."

Another laugh bubbled up, but he kept it down. "Are you so sure I don't?"

Laurel shrugged. "I don't know anything about you, so I can only guess."

Paulo took another step toward her, bringing them within only one step of each other. "And what if I asked you to take that shiny mask off as payment?"

"I would counter and say you'd have to do the same."

"I didn't realize this was a 'I'll show you mine when you show me yours' negotiation." The desire to close the distance between them grew, but he kept his feet firmly planted. "Glad to know I'm not the only one tossing and turning at night."

She didn't roll her eyes, but he felt as if she wanted to. "Please. I have more important things to do than wonder about what you've got hiding under there."

"And here I thought we were having a bonding moment."

"If you wanted a bonding moment, you should have let me stab you earlier."

"Ah yes, the bonds between a murderess and her very dashing victim. Nothing like connecting over an untimely death."

She took the last step toward him, standing only a hairsbreadth away. "If you don't like my suggestions, perhaps you should find someone else to thwart."

Paulo dipped his chin so he could look her straight in the eye. "Perhaps I like thwarting you. Have you thought of that?"

Her eyes narrowed as she studied him. He saw it happen twice in quick succession and he couldn't tell if the sensation was so visceral because he got it twofold or if it was simply that she was really looking at him.

Finally, her fingers came up and brushed against his jaw. "You have so many freckles."

He almost chuckled. He'd made Jenkins paint a few more

on his face. Laurel didn't need to memorize the layout of his freckles.

The skin under her fingers scorched and he had to keep himself from closing his eyes to relish in it. Her finger moved from his jaw over to his chin and up to his nose.

He saw her slip those fingers under his mask.

His hand snapped up and stopped her before her fingertips finished their travel up his cheek.

"Now, now. That really isn't fair."

She ripped her hand from his. "What did you think I was doing?"

"You've already burrowed your way into my heart, you maddening woman. At least give me the decency of revealing myself to you when I'm sure you can handle it."

Laurel scoffed. "Have some hideous scarring, do you?"

"I simply don't think you can handle the magnitude of my glorious face. Safest to keep the mask on so you don't allow your overwhelming desires to cloud your judgement."

"Or send me screaming in the other direction, hm?"

Paulo sighed and grabbed her hand. "Ah, Laurel, how you flatter me." He kissed the tips of her fingers. "However, our time this evening is about to be cut short."

Laurel yanked her hand away again.

Light blossomed down the hall.

Paulo took a step back.

"Wait!" Laurel grabbed his arm. "What would it cost me to get you to stop thwarting me?"

Paulo smirked and drank her in. By the Goddess, this woman was glorious.

"Now, what's the fun in telling you? When you offer me the right price, you'll know."

18

THE SPARE

LAUREL THREW THE MASK ON DELILAH'S EMPTY BED WITH A SNARL.

What on Gaia's green earth was she going to do with this ridiculous masked man?

The more she looked at him that evening, the more she believed he was Lord Oliver. They were so similar, even the freckles on his face attested to his possible involvement.

But that also meant it could be Lord MacGregor.

"Who the blasted curses is it?" she hissed into the darkness.

Laurel began shedding her gear, trying to be quick, as she knew Delilah wouldn't be gone much longer. One would think a girl would wish to be around her paramour for longer than two hours, but Laurel was sure the prince had other... *appointments* that night.

With her gear tucked into the hole she'd carved into her mattress and her sheets and nightgown in place, Laurel slipped into her blankets. The small room held a semblance of peace when Delilah wasn't there, snoring like a pack of wild pigs. The stone walls kept the room dark, and it would have been cold if it wasn't so close to the kitchens. It was small, only big enough for two beds with enough space to walk between them. Their trunks sat at the ends of their bedframes. The walls to either side also held long shelves for them to place things on. Laurel hadn't added much besides a few hairpins, but Delilah's boasted dozens of tiny trinkets. A small box. A collection of seashells. A fabric doll.

Laurel flipped over onto her side, looking away from Delilah's busy half of the room. It distracted her from the matter at hand.

How would she convince Lord Oliver to give up this charade?

Or Lord MacGregor.

Whoever it blasted was.

Laurel's body had nearly settled when the door opened. Delilah snuck in and frowned down at her.

"Do you wait up for me or something?"

"No. You're loud."

"If I was loud, I would've been caught by now." She closed the door and flipped her hair back over her shoulder. "You're just jealous."

A laugh almost broke from Laurel's chest. Delilah really was a piece of work. The girl couldn't even see the lies she was telling herself. How could she believe that a prince, one who had been betrothed to the same woman for years and was set to inherit a throne, would fall for someone like her? Yes, there were foolish people out there, but from what Laurel had gathered about Prince Dion, he wasn't one of them. He may have let his desire for a light skirt go to his head, but he knew what he was about the rest of the time.

Not to mention that Lady Carnation seemed to be on his side. *That woman would make for quite a queen if she ever makes it to the alter.* Too bad her betrothed wouldn't. Laurel would make sure of that.

Laurel turned her back to Delilah. "You're going to get caught."

Delilah grabbed her shoulder. Laurel turned with the pull but kept her hand at her thigh where one of her small daggers was sheathed.

"You better not go tattling to anyone about this," she sneered. "I'll have you kicked out of the palace if you dare try anything."

"I'm not going to tell anyone." At least, not yet. Delilah was Laurel's sure path to the prince. It would be remiss of her to take her out of the picture unless completely necessary. Laurel jerked her shoulder away. "All I'm saying is that what you're doing is foolish."

"It's not me who's the fool. You are. You sit there and judge me for finding love against societies expectations while you scrape and beg at the MacGregors for every bit of attention they'll give you. Not that they're even worthy of proper society's regard. While Lord MacGregor barely seems to fit into his station, his family certainly doesn't."

By the Goddess, this woman. Laurel tried to keep the annoyance out of her voice. "I can see how that comment would apply to Lady Diana, but what about Lord Oliver?"

Delilah snorted. "Not much to say about him. It doesn't help that the rather outrageous members of his family take up the gossip. Though, from the little gossip I've heard, the man could be a simpleton or a genius."

Another conundrum then? Perhaps he wasn't so unlike his cousins. It seemed the MacGregors had a knack for snubbing societal expectations while also keeping within the bounds of propriety.

Great Goddess, Laurel's head hurt. "So, which is it?

Delilah gave a long-suffering sigh. "The gossip is divided. See, the women think him charming if somewhat naive, while the gentlemen can't tell if he takes after his father or his cousin."

"That's ridiculous."

Delilah propped herself up on her elbow. "No, it's politics. These people are all playing a game, shifting pieces around to get what they want and leaving the rest of us to pick up the scraps. But I know how the game is played. That's why, some-day, I'll be the wife of a gentleman and you'll still be slaving away doing everyone else's dirty work."

Laurel let the conversation die off. Delilah was right, to an extent. If Laurel didn't figure out the game, she really was going to be trapped in a life where everyone else made deci-sions for her. Where Teagan could continue to sink his claws into Aspen. Where he could send Laurel across the world just to assassinate someone he found inconvenient. Delilah was playing a game, but Laurel was on an entirely different board — the one crafted with shadowed corners and bloodied floors. But Laurel would prevail. She'd been playing this game for eleven years.

And she never lost.

It was the next day that she saw it. The silver flag flicking in the wind atop the largest mast on *The Shining River.*

Teagan had summoned her.

It wasn't difficult to lace Delilah's cup of tea with a bit of laudanum after supper. Prince Dion didn't like to meet every night, so the undercook wouldn't be missed anyway. However, she would wake up in a mood, but such was the price of Laurel getting out of their room without being seen.

The wind whistled through the tunnels of the cliffs, filling the dark path with a haunting sound. After her first night in the maze of tunnels. Laurel could easily recall how to get down to the beach. She found the opening and climbed down the set of rocks below the mouth of the cave. Her boots sank into the rocky sand at the bottom as the low tide crashed over the beach several yards away. The wind whipped off the ocean in freezing gusts, bringing in a sea fog. She couldn't even see the palace on the cliffs above her. It made perfect sense that the weather would mirror the cold taking root in her limbs. She kicked at a small stone in her path, watching it crash with a spray of sand ahead of her. The silent harbor came into view through the thin fog, the docks like long-legged monsters trying desperately to return to the sea. They were trapped to this place, reaching for things completely out of reach.

Just like she was.

She found her way down the docks, watching the small silver flag whip in the wind. Once again, a ladder hung over the side of the ship. She climbed to the top, but Teagan wasn't waiting for her there.

Instead, it was Adira Durant.

Praise the Goddess Laurel hadn't left her mask back at the palace.

Adira leaned against the mast of the ship, her eyebrows raised. "I wasn't sure you'd show up. Considering how long this job has taken, I figured you'd be dead, and we've been wasting weeks waiting around to hear about the assassin found in the palace."

Laurel ignored her and walked toward Teagan's quarters. She'd had her fill of self-serving humans for one night. By the Goddess, she'd hit her quota for a lifetime, and she still had to go home until she could get Aspen out of Stellatus Hall. The thought spurred her toward his door. She would see what he needed and get back to work before anyone else could ruin her plans.

The fog moved out of the corner of her eye.

She caught the wrist holding a dagger that would have sunk into her arm. Not a killing blow, but one to cause pain.

Adira smiled up at her. "At least I didn't hire a complete idiot for this job."

"You didn't hire me." Laurel shoved her away. She didn't take her eyes off the rebel leader as she took the steps up to the captain's quarters.

The woman's green eyes flashed with violence as she turned and climbed down the ladder Laurel had just used. If Adira was willing to try to intimidate her, things between her and Teagan must have been tense.

Laurel made her way to Teagan's door. While *The Shining River*'s sails were somewhat eccentric, the rest of the ship was rather modest. Only a few curves decorated the railing and the iron knocker on the door formed only a ring. A pair of brutes framed the door. Teagan wouldn't have been permitted to bring any scholae. Not while she was here. Laurel tapped the knocker on the wood.

"Come."

Laurel swept into the cabin. Like his office at home, Teagan's decorative tendencies leaned heavily on books. There were several maps on the table in the center of the room and a candle-laden chandelier hung from the low ceiling. Teagan sat at the end of the long table, his fingers joined over his mouth.

"Why isn't he dead, Laurel?"

Her spine stiffened. "I haven't been able to reach the prince."

He stood abruptly. "One of the youngest and brightest

assassins to come out of Stellatus Hall can't take down one measly prince?"

Laurel didn't allow herself to even twitch. "There have been unforeseen circumstances, but I'm taking care of it."

Teagan stepped so close his nose nearly brushed hers. "You do realize if you don't get this job done, there won't be anywhere for you to go, right? You'll be stuck on this Goddess-forsaken island for the rest of your miserable existence, and I'll find someone else to do the job."

"Yes." Not that he would be saddened by that in the least.

He tapped the part of her mask that covered her forehead. "Aspen will still have to fulfill her contract. You won't ever be able to access that nice little vault with that fortune you've been squirrelling away. There won't be anywhere I can't find you."

Laurel's teeth creaked with how tight she was clenching them. "Yes."

He stepped away. "Whatever it takes, Laurel. Slaughter every nobleman, poison every milkmaid or stableboy or doddering old dowager, I don't care."

Laurel kept her posture straight even as every word landed a blow. It wasn't often that Teagan got this involved in a mission, but when he did, no one was safe. Laurel had seen him stab a man through the heart, then slaughter his entire family simply because he'd been asked to. No questions. No remorse. Every person was a number to him and if the numbers weren't falling into line, he got rid of them.

He had climbed to the top of Stellatus Hall on a mountain of dead bodies. Laurel was under no illusions that he wouldn't add her to the pile if she got in his way.

His gray eyes cut into her. "Kill the prince, Laurel, and kill him before he has the chance to take the throne."

19

AN UNFORTUNATE MAZE

Paulo checked his watch for the third time in the last five minutes. His quarry should arrive right—

A small yip punctured the silence of the hall.

Paulo stepped out from around the corner, swinging his watch around on its chain as if he were simply taking a stroll through the palace halls. He smiled as the Lord of the Underworld, his very brainy dog, and Lady Delmar stepped into view.

The youngest prince had a scowl on his face, obviously brooding about whatever he and Lady Delmar were discussing. Paulo had three guesses as to what he was scowling about.

Penny.

Penny.

And Penny.

Truly, a man like him only brooded so hard about one thing and it was always of the female persuasion.

Paulo prayed he hadn't become that broody himself.

With a small skip in his step, he approached them and gave a flourished bow when they finally met his gaze. "Good afternoon, Your Highness." He gave another bow. "Lady Delmar."

"Hello, my lord." Lady Delmar answered with a curtsy.

The prince took a step forward, ready to pass by with as little interaction as he could manage. It wasn't a snub, but simply a man looking to be on his way.

Paulo flashed a smile at Lady Delmar. "My lady, I hope I don't sound impertinent, but I recently heard of your connection with a good friend of mine. Mr. Adam Cyrus?"

The prince stiffened and Lady Delmar smirked. "Why, yes. I consider him a great friend."

"I am happy to hear so." He took a step toward her as if to impart a secret with her. "I consider him to be a very likeable gentleman. He is graced with an ability to make friends wherever he goes."

Lady Delmar's expression softened. "I agree."

The prince mumbled something under his breath that Paulo couldn't make out, but by the way it hissed between his teeth, it likely wasn't something complimentary.

Lady Delmar smacked him lightly on the arm.

Paulo ignored it and continued. "It's been so wonderful to have him here for so long and be able to introduce him to one of my dearest friends." Great Goddess, things were about to get very tense. "Have you had the privilege to meet Lady Penny Barclay?"

His Highness whipped back around and came within a handspan of Paulo. "*You* introduced them?"

Lady Delmar cautiously touched Paulo's arm and drew him back a step. "Yes, we recently heard they'd made one another's acquaintance." She widened her eyes at the prince in a way that suggested he find his calm before she turned back to Paulo with a grin. "Though I haven't heard much else except they were regarded as a darling couple at the recent garden party."

Paulo held his shoulders relaxed instead of ducking his ears into them. There was something quite unsettling about being glared at by a prince who could kill him quicker than Paulo could counteract it.

"Yes, well I recently heard they would be taking a walk about the palace gardens this afternoon. I know Lady Penny has had designs on finding the center of the hedge maze, though I don't know if Mr. Cyrus has been shown the path to the secret garden."

"Oh really?" Lady Delmar gave the prince a knowing look.

The prince spun on his heel and marched off without another word, his dog following behind him.

Lady Delmar turned her bright smile back on him. "Thank you for your candor, my lord. This information is most help—"

"Rissa!" the prince barked from the end of the hallway.

Lady Delmar curtsied and glided toward the prince. "You can't challenge anyone to a duel, Aiden!" she called to him.

Paulo waited until they were well on their way before he turned and raced in the other direction. He allowed his gift to surface, sifting through the strands to find the emerald one he recognized. If nothing changed, Penny was due to arrive at the palace with Adam in three minutes and would enter the formal gardens in five more.

Paulo's shoes slipped over the polished marble of the west wing as he tried to stop at the gilded double doors of the library. He pushed one open with a little too much force and it nearly whacked one of the librarians passing by.

The head librarian's gaze snapped in his direction, her dark eyes narrowed over her thin spectacles and her painted lips pursed in disapproval.

Paulo gave her a little wave and tiptoed through the bookcases. The library in the palace was a marvel. It was so big it had its own collection of staff that tended to it. There were books as well as glass cases showcasing pieces of history. While Paulo's gifts didn't allow him to view the past, it was almost like he could feel it when he looked at the old relics.

He found Diana near the corner window, her nose pressed to the glass.

"Are they there yet?" Paulo asked, pressing his own nose against the windowpane.

Diana pointed at a spot to the west. "They just entered the spring garden."

Paulo stood on his toes to see over Diana's head and spotted Penny's familiar hair and Adam's hat. He stepped back and raced along the wall, nearly running headfirst into one of the library's handful of patrons. He stopped at the window near the main desk and knelt on the seat there. He had to really push himself against the glass to see the prince standing near the oak tree below him.

He raced back to Diana. "He's in position."

Diana huffed. "Adam is certainly taking his sweet time. Hopefully His Highness doesn't get bored standing there."

Paulo smiled. He wouldn't. Everything was going exactly according to plan.

"What do you think they're saying?" Diana asked.

Paulo watched as Adam pointed out a spot on the palace turret above them. He cleared his throat. "Oh, Lady Penny," he said in a false bravado, "do you see that chip in the bricks there? Why I learned that exact chip was the cause for the Battle of Sea Turtles, where everyone threw live turtles at one another."

Diana snickered but stopped when Penny turned to answer Adam. "My lord, that's absolutely ridiculous. How could it be turtles when the indentation is obviously from the shell of a tortoise?"

Both of them snickered now.

"What are you two giggling about?"

Paulo whirled from the window and found Laurel standing there, holding a small stack of books in her hands. He'd known she would be there, yet his heart still leapt at the sight of her.

Her brown eyes locked onto his and she quirked an eyebrow as if to say *Thought you got the best of me, did you?* She stepped forward and glanced out the window.

"Who are they?"

Paulo nearly sagged against the wall at the feel of her so close to him, but he locked his knees in place.

"The girl is Lady Penny Barclay," Diana answered, "and her companion is Mr. Adam Cyrus."

"And why are two people walking about a garden cause for such laughter?"

For a number of reasons, but Paulo wasn't about to lay out every detail of Adam's sad courtship of Penny for all to see. Instead, he poked Diana. "Oh, she's talking."

Diana took up the role quickly. "Why, Mr. Cyrus, I didn't realize there were so many people we had to talk to before we could do something stimulating."

Adam nodded and started talking, prompting Paulo. "Well, since I'm a stuffy ambassador for a kingdom that can't seem to get the stick out from out of their—"

"Watch it, Lord MacGregor," another voice joined in.

Now all three heads turned to find Caspian leaning against a bookcase.

"Finally brave enough to show your face?" Diana snipped.

Caspian rolled his eyes and joined them at the window. "It is not I who should be unwilling to face the public. I won after all."

Diana bristled, but Paulo ignored them and grabbed Laurel's sleeve. "They're on the move." He pulled her toward the next window, and she followed behind, though she did yank her sleeve out from his grip.

They stopped and watched the couple's progress, all four of them squished against one another.

"Oh, look!" Diana said as Penny pointed toward a set of bushes. "Do you think this bush was here when the Faerie Wars happened? Perhaps it was home to pixies or even a brownie."

"What a silly idea," Paulo retorted in his best Adam voice. "Of course, this bush wasn't here when the fae still were. It's much too small."

They followed them from window to window, the fake conversation carrying them until they reached the window where the prince waited. Both Diana and Paulo went quiet.

Caspian stretched to see over Diana's head. "What is it?"

"Shh!" Paulo hissed. He watched Penny pass by the maze. He saw the exact moment she noticed the prince. Her entire countenance shifted from "pleasant Penny" to "real Penny."

"Who's that?" Laurel asked, pointing to the left.

"That," Caspian sighed, "is Amarissa Delmar, one of the most beautiful women of the sea and one of the worst souls to ever cross."

Laurel shifted further forward. "Why is that?"

Diana chuckled. "She's a siren and acts as a member of Lady Carnation's ladies-in-waiting. She's also married to one of the most fearsome knights in the kingdom. You cross her and she can sing you off a cliff while her husband cuts you from throat to navel."

"Be quiet!" Paulo hissed. "She's going in for the distraction." Even as Penny turned to see Lady Delmar approach, anyone could obviously see she was tuned in to the prince. Paulo leaned forward and pointed at the prince as his shadows wrapped around him and formed a glamour that cloaked him and the pup in invisibility.

Caspian pushed forward. "Where did they go?"

"He glamoured them," Laurel answered. Her eyes flicked in Diana's direction likely hoping her slip-up went unnoticed. A normal kitchen girl wouldn't have known the youngest prince had glamoured them away.

Paulo smirked but took pity on her and redirected the conversation. "He can't get into the maze without Penny knowing. He obviously wants to draw her out."

Laurel squinted toward the opening to the maze. "So, why are we watching this random melodrama?"

Paulo scoffed. "What you are seeing before you are the beginning acts of a great romance. Well, at least the beginnings of a second chance."

"What?" Caspian asked, obviously not following.

Diana elbowed him. "Broody prince is in secret love with beautiful heiress but messed it all up by lying to her. She, however, is absolutely brilliant and he realized he can't live without her, so he's here to convince her to give him a second chance."

"Ah," Laurel said. "Yes, that seems to be a regular occurrence with young love."

Diana snorted. "I don't get what's so difficult about telling people how you feel about them from the get-go. It's ridiculous. Why can't we all just say what we feel?"

"There's no excitement in that!" Paulo protested. "There are so many little things when it comes to romance and it's easy to be nervous. You know? All the butterflies in the stomach?"

Diana scoffed. "Digest them."

Laurel tapped the glass. "There she goes."

They all turned to watch Penny follow the dog, who had regained his visibility, into the maze. Paulo leaned closer to Laurel, pretending like he was trying to get a better view but really using it as an excuse to lean into her. From the way the window was situated, they couldn't see the center of the maze, but it didn't matter.

Paulo had seen all he needed to.

Diana spun, hands on her hips. "If you think it's such a problem, you should just tell her."

Paulo gently plucked at the strings of his lyre as he laid out on his bed fully dressed. Tonight, Laurel would be staying in the kitchens as Cook had kept Delilah up to help with Prince Dion's late supper with the Barclay's. Laurel stayed in her rooms, sharpening blades and mixing poisons. So, Paulo watched.

It seemed it was all he was good for at the moment.

"She's not going to poison Oliver."

Diana snatched the lyre out of his hands. "Then why is it a problem?"

"Because if she discovers it's not Oliver, she'll realize it's me. If she learns it's me too quickly, she'll run."

"Because of your gift."

"Yes." Because of his cursed gift. Everyone always talked about how great it must be to see the future, to know what comes next. How great it was that he could stop great calamity, to see happiness before it comes, or to even know what needed to change to create the best outcome. It was one of the reasons he wore his foppish façade. It wouldn't do for people to come to him for everything. For them to realize that under the guise of tomfoolery, he was wiser than they could ever believe. That, like they believed his ancestors to be, he was a god among men, gifted with the greatest magic the Goddess had put on Her planet.

He wasn't. It wasn't.

Knowing the future, truly understanding what things had to happen in order for other things to come to pass, then having the option to tweak things to get what he wanted was a power no man should ever have. Yes, Paulo was able to accomplish great things, things that saved people, but at what cost? If he walked down the street and saw a man being attacked by another man, he shouldn't be able to know the man having his teeth knocked out of his mouth would go home and beat his wife. That the man raining blows was the wife's younger brother. That if Paulo stopped the brother from killing the husband, it would allow the husband to go back to mistreating his wife. He should be able to decide based on his own judgments of right and wrong, not on what the Goddess showed him. While he was glad he could help people, there were so many factors that he should have no part in. He wasn't the judge, jury, or executioner. He was a man who had been cursed to see every mistake he would ever make and still have to make them so others could succeed.

It was exhausting.

And telling Laurel before it was right would cause her to run.

He needed more time.

He needed to convince her to trust him.

"If she figures it out now," he said, "she'll run back to her boss and the assassins will sweep through the palace before the solstice. If that happens, Penny doesn't leave for Faerie the day after and all the plans I've made for the past several years will be for naught." He wouldn't even tell her what happened to everyone else.

"So, what are you going to do?"

"It's not so much a 'you' but more of a 'we.'" He sat up and swung his legs over the side of the bed. "Come on. We need to talk Prince Dion into reconfiguring the guard rotation, get Donnie six bottles of wine, and steal Oliver's favorite pocket watch."

Diana grinned. "Finally."

20
THE MISDIRECT

Sir Heff's smithy will be sweltering. Sweat will pool on Laurel's soft upper lip. They will talk about all sorts of different weapons, the two of them finding a kindred soul in the other. Lady Delmar will tease them and return up the stairs to the house above. The door to the smithy will burst open. Fire will rain down at the table where Laurel is standing. She will be engulfed in flames.

LAUREL STRODE DOWN THE HALLWAY, HER STEPS SILENT ON THE PLUSH carpet. The MacGregor's rooms were positioned in the middle of the residential wing of the palace. Nobles still tittered through a couple of doors, but the magelights hanging from their sconces along the walls were asleep.

There were three weeks until winter solstice. She needed to know who the masked man was, and she needed to know now.

Light waved at her from under the door she sought, and she could hear the strain of voices from within.

"Paulo!" Lady Diana snapped. "You know better than to let Donnie talk you into one of his afternoon drinking games. The last time this happened, Mater had to order you into an ice bath."

A groan punctuated the air.

Laurel pressed her ear closer to the door. Lord MacGregor must be decidedly hungover to sound so miserable. Odd. He hadn't struck Laurel as the drunkard type.

Lady Diana scoffed. "Honestly, Paulo, you're the biggest baby Olympia has ever seen. I pity whichever woman finds herself eventually trapped into being your wife."

"Please, Diana," Lord MacGregor's voice slurred, making it unrecognizable. "You're talking too loud."

"AM I?" she yelled.

He moaned his obvious displeasure.

Laurel took a step back and bumped into someone.

"What are you doing?"

She spun around, facing her masked man. "Snooping."

Those pearlescent eyes narrowed. "I thought you were a murderess, not a nosy busybody."

Laurel shrugged. "A girl needs her hobbies."

The masked man leaned forward. "And yours is listening to sisters berate their brothers for their vices?" He tutted his disappointment.

Laurel shoved him.

He fell back a step. "Ow!"

She reached to shove him again, but he caught her hands.

"What was that for?"

"Trying to ruin my life." She ripped her hands away from him. "Listen, I don't understand what kind of perverse pleasure you get out of this, but it needs to come to an end."

He spread his arms wide. "Take your shot then."

Laurel drew her blade but stopped. This was what he

wanted. He wanted to fight with her. To distract her from her job, from doing what she'd been meant to do this whole time.

She turned and ran down the hall.

If she could stay ahead of him, she could find the prince. She could stop playing this ridiculous game.

Running in a circuitous route, she made her way up the residential wing and toward the royal suites. The halls were strangely empty for that late in the evening. She stopped at a corner, waiting for the sound of the guards that were supposed to be on patrol in this hall right then.

Nothing.

She peeked around the corner. Where were they?

Prowling down the corridor, she found the hallway to Prince Dion's study empty.

Something wasn't right.

The click of boots sounded from behind her.

She spun, finding two guards walking down the hall in her direction.

Curses!

Their swords remained in their sheaths, so they hadn't caught sight of her yet. She slipped around the corner, finding the first small door and tucking herself into it. It looked like a clerk's room, a small desk tucked as far back as it could be in the room to allow for a set of chairs and a small table. The guards' boots echoed on the hardwood floor on the other side of the door. She faced the door once more.

A hand came up over her mouth and another encircled her waist.

Her elbow drove back, digging into the abdomen of her attacker.

"Ow, Laurel!" he hissed. "Quiet, or they'll hear us."

Laurel froze. How? How had he gotten in here before her? Where had he even been hiding?

She did the only thing she could think of.

She bit him.

"Curses!" he hissed as he let her go.

Laurel reached for the door. Guards or not, she needed to get away from him.

His arm wrapped around her waist, and he lifted her off the ground.

She reached for her knife.

Which was missing.

"Honestly," he whispered, "I'm shocked you think I haven't learned anything in the last two months."

That was the fifth knife he'd taken from her!

She twisted, using the momentum to put him off balance and shove him backward. He fell, though he kept his arms around her as he did. They tumbled into one of the chairs in a heap.

A flash of silver slipped out of his pocket and thumped to the ground. Her knife.

Laurel threw her elbow back, which he dodged.

But it didn't matter.

She rolled off the chair, grabbing at the knife he'd dropped.

Her fingers met chain.

"Why do you continue to fight me, woman?" He pushed himself out of the chair. "Haven't I proven enough already that it's futile?"

"I have no choice," she said, slipping whatever she'd found into the pocket near her knee. Whatever he'd dropped, she would look at it later.

"Don't you? You can simply stop. Change professions. Switch loyalties. You could do a million other things than try to kill Prince Dion."

How dare he? He didn't know what she'd sacrificed to be here. What she was sacrificing by being in this room with him.

This was for Aspen, for someone she had given everything to. Something a stuck-up noble with family coffers as big as his overinflated ego would never understand.

She gritted her teeth and pounced.

He dodged her attack once more, using the chair as a shield against her.

"You can't win, Laurel."

"Not with you in the way." She slid a small throwing knife from her wrist and drew her hand back.

He ducked, almost like he knew which direction her knife would go.

At the last second, she changed the trajectory, aiming for the sleeve of his jacket.

The knife pinned him to the chair.

"*Blast*," he hissed.

She raced out of the room.

By the Goddess, she was tired of running in circles, trying to stay one step ahead of the cursed man. Tired of the threats looming over her. Tired of fighting for something that felt so far from reach.

The worst part? The masked man was absolutely right.

She could change her life. She could let go of the obligations of her past. Switch sides. Join Prince Dion and fight against everything she'd grown up hating. They might even win. She could tell them all about Adira and it would be over.

Except she would be abandoning Aspen. The reason she did everything.

Laurel stopped at her door. The small weight in her pocket drew her attention and she drew out whatever the masked man had dropped. It was a pocket watch. She turned it over and found an engraving on the back.

For Oliver.

She pulled off her mask and wiped the sweat from her brow. She knew it was him!

She tucked her mask into the folds of her jacket and stepped into her room.

Delilah sat up in her bed. "Where on Gaia's green earth have you been? And what are you wearing?"

Laurel stilled. By the Goddess, Delilah had been gone not long before Laurel had left. She shut the door behind her.

"I thought you went to meet Prince Dion."

"I did and he could only see me for a little while. I got back here not ten minutes ago to find you gone." Her eyes fastened on Laurel's hand. "What is that?"

Laurel walked forward and tucked it under her pillow. "If you don't want me poking into your business, don't stick your nose into mine."

Laurel watched Delilah out of the corner of her eye. The girl watched her just as much.

Delilah grinned. "You look exhausted. I'm glad you have your half day to catch up on some rest. One would think you didn't get any sleep last night."

Laurel turned back to the pistachios she was cutting up.

It had been like this all morning.

Delilah continued to pick at her. Kept a steady stream of words that would sound innocent to anyone else, but both of them knew better. The comments continued to grow bolder as Laurel kept ignoring her. When Delilah would let the boot drop, Laurel didn't know. What she did know was that now she had two obstacles to get through if she wanted to have a chance at taking out the prince.

"What are you going on about now, Delilah?" Cook asked. "Laurel's getting her work done just fine, unlike you, who keeps pestering the poor girl."

"Sorry, Cook," Delilah murmured and went back to prepping the dough for the rolls they would need at suppertime.

A few minutes passed and Cook started humming a tune.

"Galen," Delilah chirped, "have you seen Lord Oliver MacGregor this morning?"

Laurel's chopping slowed.

Galen sighed. "No. He doesn't usually eat with His Highness."

"Oh, well I found this."

She drew out the very pocket watch Laurel had tucked under her pillow the night before.

Cook held out a hand and Delilah dropped it into her palm. "Where did you find it?"

Delilah met Laurel's eye. "It was right here in the kitchens. I hope it hasn't been here for long. Do you think he's missing it?"

Laurel's grip on the knife tightened.

"We'll have to return it at once," Cook said. "Where did you say you found it?"

Delilah's grin turned sharp as she leaned against the counter. "Well, actually Laurel—"

Laurel moved without really thinking it through. The knife flew from her fingers. Laurel stared as it buried itself in Delilah's shirt sleeve, pinning her to the table.

Delilah screamed.

Galen started yelling.

The other kitchen servants turned to stare.

Cook rushed over to them.

Laurel jumped back, lies flicking through her brain. "Where did it go?"

Cook stopped. "What on Gaia's green earth, Laurel?"

"A mouse!" She pointed to Delilah's sleeve. "There was a mouse right there. I was sure it was going to bite Delilah. Who knows what kind of nasty diseases it carried?"

Galen's hollers stopped, but Delilah continued screaming, face white with terror.

"She's lying! She tried to kill me!"

Cook yanked the knife out of the counter. "Don't make trolls out of brownies, girl." She set the knife on the counter. "Laurel, I think it'd be best if you took your half day early."

No. She couldn't let Delilah even whisper in Cook's ear.

"But—"

Cook held up a hand. "No arguments. Galen will take Delilah to the infirmary to make sure there wasn't any injury—mouse bite or otherwise. I'll take the watch to Lord Oliver myself and we can all put this little incident behind us."

Delilah met Laurel's eye, her face white with fear.

Laurel toyed with the lead weight hanging from her wrist. "As you say, Cook. I would hate to disappoint you or lose this position because of a silly misunderstanding. I'm glad Delilah wasn't harmed. Who knows what could have happened? That little mouse could have killed her if it wanted to."

Delilah's face went white as the flour coating her hands. "You know, I don't think anything is wrong with me. Laurel must have scared the mouse off. Thank you, Laurel. I'm glad to have your trust."

At least Laurel's message had been received.

She left the kitchen, only stopping by her room to grab the things hidden in her mattress. They weren't safe there if Delilah decided to do a little snooping. It didn't look like the girl had touched the leather sleeve she kept her gear in, the knot still tied how she'd left it that morning. Tucking it under her arm, she grabbed her cloak. She'd have to figure out a new place to hide her things later, but she wouldn't let Delilah go digging into her things any more than she already had.

Laurel found herself walking down the market street once again, her coins weighing heavy in her pocket. With all her amenities paid for by her position and nowhere for her paychecks to go, she'd actually saved up quite a bit of coin. Enough for a day of good food and perhaps a few new toys. That should cheer her up and at least give her a moment's joy before she returned to the guards waiting to throw her in the dungeon. With a small, paper bag of *loukoumades* keeping her hands warm, she found a stall selling an assortment of blades. There was a rather nice-looking filet knife. She brushed the cinnamon from her fingertips and picked it off the stand. The blade was incredibly balanced, even for a filet knife. The steel had a swirling design, something she'd learned had to do with the mixing of metal alloys when forging. It was a difficult process, as the temperature of the metal had to be quite high. Only a few of the assassins at Stellatus Hall had such blades. Laurel was in possession of two— a short dagger Aspen had given her for her birthday and a short sword she'd had made when she had joined the scholae. She twisted the blade and found the maker's stamp near the hilt. A pair of membraned wings.

She turned to the merchant. "Excuse me, but could you tell me who this stamp belongs to?"

The merchant grinned, his yellowed teeth bright under his thick black mustache. "That'll be Sir Heff's work. Best blades in the kingdom, if you ask anyone that knows anything about a blade."

"Oh? Does he have a shop here in the city?"

"Of course. Sits right outside the palace." He chuckled. "Has to if he's to keep an eye on that wife of his." He told her what building to look for.

Laurel left him with a word of thanks and headed back toward the palace. Her fingers twitched as she thought about what she could order from the smith. Another sword? A set of throwing knives for Aspen? Perhaps a small hand scythe. With the talent the man seemed to have, he could likely do a number of things.

A shadow passed by over her and she looked up to see a large bird swoop down near one of the buildings ahead of her. The shield and sword sign hung above the door. She grinned as she skipped to the front step and knocked on the door. Laurel heard an odd squawk from within. A moment later, the door burst open, and Laurel nearly jolted.

A woman stood on the doorstep, her long red hair falling in waves down to her waist. Her sea-green eyes flashed with vivacity as she met Laurel's gaze.

"L-Lady Delmar?" Laurel asked. "I thought this was a blacksmith's."

Lady Delmar tilted her head to the side, her smile sparkling. "It is. Can I help you?"

"Uh..." Laurel's brain couldn't catch up with her and something between her shoulders burned fiercely. She'd seen her fair share of beautiful people, but something about Lady Delmar seemed to muddle her thoughts. "I don't think so?"

"Oh, wind and waves! Hold on." Lady Delmar dug into the small pocket of her skirt. A shell hung from a string and Lady Delmar slipped it around her neck. When the shell settled beneath her clavicle, Laurel felt her mind sharpen once again and the burning between her shoulders cooled.

By the Goddess, it had been her tattoo.

Sweet Gaia, Lady Delmar's magic must have been something else if it still affected Laurel even with the charm.

Lady Delmar smiled once again, but the beauty of it before was muted. "Sorry about that. Heff is down in the forge, and I can usually relax without causing him any grief."

Laurel studied the lady a little closer. "Your husband is the blacksmith?" No wonder the merchant had made that comment about Sir Heff's wife. Anyone with a wife as gorgeous as Lady Delmar must be fighting off less honorable people left and right.

"Yes. I can take you down to him." Lady Delmar locked the door behind her and tucked the key into her bodice. "He's with another customer, but I'm sure they'll be wrapping up soon."

Laurel followed her around the house and toward a set of thick cellar doors on the side. Laurel looked about. What blacksmith had an underground forge? Laurel picked up the hem of her skirt and descended. The air grew warmer as they got further down. The sound of male voices became distinguishable as they reached the bottom of the steps.

"A harpy? Isn't that some sort of bird woman?"

Laurel took a deep breath. *Is he going to be showing up everywhere now?* She crossed the threshold to find Lord MacGregor standing across a table from a hulking man. Laurel had seen her fair share of men from all walks of life, but this particular man likely hit close to seven or eight feet in height without the additional inches his wild hair gave him.

"Yes," the man said, his voice rumbling in the stones under Laurel's boots. "But 'harpe' with an 'e' is a sword."

"Ah, so we are talking about a sickle sword."

"A harpe."

Lady Delmar leaned in toward Laurel. "No one appreciates the classification of swords like they used to, much to Heff's frustration."

Truer words had never been spoken. Laurel took a step forward and cleared her throat. "A harpe is a sword with a straight, single-edged blade that ends with a curved tip, not to be confused with a khopesh which is shaped more like a sickle but where a sickle is sharpened on the inside of the curve, a khopesh would be sharpened on the outside."

The giant's gaze fastened on her, interest sparking in his dark eyes. "Yes."

"Laurel!" Lord MacGregor greeted. "What brings you to see Sir Heff this fine morning?"

She stopped at the table and looked down at the sketch of a harpe sword. Whoever had drawn it had done a fine job, even going so far as to add the shine it would have if held under sunlight. It was a beautiful blade.

"Laurel, is it?" Lady Delmar asked, coming to Laurel's side.

"That's me," Laurel answered.

"You know, just a few weeks ago, Lady Carnation was talking about a new kitchen girl that was the first servant in years that seemed to have a head on her shoulders."

Laurel swallowed. "It is very flattering to know Lady Carnation has taken notice of me."

Lord MacGregor gave a noncommittal hum next to her.

"Hopefully, you can stay in her good graces." Lady Delmar wound a hand around Sir Heff's elbow. "I only know a select few who have ever been able to accomplish such a feat."

Sir Heff nodded. A man of few words it seemed. Laurel would keep that in mind.

"So, what do you think about this sword, Laurel?" Lord MacGregor asked.

She sighed and looked over the drawing again. "It's a classic harpe. Am I supposed to notice something in particular?"

Lord MacGregor shook his head and passed the picture to Sir Heff. "When could you have one for me?"

Sir Heff scratched at his bearded jaw. "Six weeks."

Laurel's jaw nearly dropped. Six weeks for a blade? The blacksmith at Stellatus Hall would take that long for a simple sleeve of throwing knives.

"Excellent," Lord MacGregor chirped. He dug into the pocket of his outrageously lime-green jacket and pulled out a pocketbook. "How much for the deposit?"

"Three hundred," Lady Delmar supplied. Sir Heff gave her a frown as Lord MacGregor counted out the banknotes, but she squeezed his elbow and gave a subtle shake of her head. When she saw Laurel watching, she winked.

With the transaction finalized, Lord MacGregor turned back to Laurel. "Come, Laurel. We have much to do." He grabbed the edge of her cloak.

She pulled back, but he had a firm grip on the thick fabric. "Wait, I haven't been able to discuss an order with Sir Heff."

"Well, now you know it's a six-week wait until he can even start on another project. Best to come back later." He led her to the bottom of the steps when a crash sounded behind them.

Laurel whirled as a blur of gold zipped across the room, followed closely by blue.

"Halt!" Sir Heff boomed. The table where he and Lady Delmar had been standing was lit up with orange flames.

The colors stopped in midair, and Laurel gasped.

Two miniature dragons hovered above the flaming table, where a purple dragon was beating back the flames with its tail. Their size could be comparable to a medium-sized dog. If a medium-sized dog had a tail as long as its body and was covered in shining scales. The purple dragon on the table was a bit larger, but not by much. She hopped down once the flames were put out. The blue dragon turned Laurel's way, little wisps of smoke trailing from its nostrils.

Lady Delmar set her hands on her hips. "What on Gaia's green earth do you think the two of you are doing? We have customers!" She gestured toward Laurel and Lord MacGregor.

The two dragons chirped, but before they could finish, a black shadow whipped into the room, knocking them both to the ground. A new dragon stood on top of them, growling.

Laurel couldn't take her eyes off them.

The black dragon growled once more, then stepped to the side. The blue and gold stood and skittered back toward the door at the back of the forge. The black one puffed out a cloud of smoke and turned back to Sir Heff. He gave a few sharp chirps.

"How many?" Sir Heff asked. The dragon responded as if they were having a conversation. Sir Heff glared at the door the two dragons had escaped through.

Wait, were they actually having a conversation?

"What happened?" Lady Delmar asked.

Sir Heff sighed. "The new gems."

"Ah," Lady Delmar said, as if that explanation made absolute sense. As if her husband talking to dragons was simply a normal happenstance.

Laurel nearly tripped on the stairs as Lord MacGregor led her out of the forge. "I really did want to talk to Sir Heff about something."

Lord MacGregor didn't slow. "What does a kitchen girl need with a blacksmith?"

She huffed. "I have a life outside of that kitchen, you know."

A bark of a laugh burst from him. "I'm sure you do."

21

AN UNFORTUNATE REALITY

Paulo set the letter down on the desk and opened his drawer for a fresh sheet of parchment and his pen. He dropped the pen back into the drawer, hitting his extra inkwell and nearly knocking it over. Mater's latest letter had set his hands to shaking.

The rebels were moving.

He'd seen this coming. Seen their camp move through his lands months ago. Seen what path they would take next. He had more time, but it didn't feel that way.

Picking her letter back up, he read over it again.

...remains of a dozen sheep just north of the western pasture. It looks like the thieves only took the mutton... Peter has set a double watch around the sheep for the next two months as you've asked... don't know where the Coronas or the O'Malleys have disappeared to...

Paulo dug the heels of his hands into his eyes, trying to rub the words away. Everything was starting. All the seeds he'd planted were beginning to root. All his work was coming to fruition. He should have been happy about it. He'd made it all happen, yet the tightness in his chest and the lump in the back of his throat told him differently.

The vision hit him with a viciousness he hadn't felt in months.

Penny, laying on rough cobblestones, an arrow protruding from her leg.

The youngest prince, running through the streets, shadows bleeding from him.

A young man, another arrow, but this one in his neck.

Adira Durant barking orders.

He stood from the desk and went to the door. He needed out of that room. Needed to breathe and remember why he was doing it all in the first place. Which was how he found himself at the door to the kitchens, watching Laurel hover over a small pot on the stove.

The day had somehow turned to night, as all the other kitchen workers were gone. He crept forward, tucking himself against the wall. Magic swept over the room, his visions overlaying. His newer boots would squeak on a wet part of the floor a few steps away and Laurel would spin toward him. Or he passed over that and moved through the room. She would reach for the small plate on the counter. The sound of whatever was in there falling into the small pot would cover his steps and he could get within a few feet of her before she felt him there and spun, the spoon in her hand about to smack him.

He chose the first option.

At the squeak of his boot, she spun.

"What are you doing here?"

Paulo shrugged and took a seat at the large table in the middle of the kitchen. "Where are all the other kitchen workers?"

Laurel turned back to the stove, grabbing the plate and pouring the little nuggets into whatever was boiling in the pot. "Most of them have gone to bed. Cook is meeting with Esther and Dan in the offices. I'm hoping they'll be busy long enough for me to finish this."

Paulo strained to see into the pot but couldn't from where he sat. "What is it?"

"Candied chestnuts. It's Cook's birthday tomorrow and I was hoping to have a few to give her."

By the Goddess, this woman. Did she not see how amazing she was? "So, you decided to pilfer from the palace pantry to give her a birthday treat?"

She shrugged. "Figured I could be put in the dungeon for worse crimes. Best to take the chance now." With a slotted spoon, she fished out the small lumps and placed them on a parchment-lined tray laid out on the counter next to her. The little nuggets of sugar glistened in the magelight Laurel had hanging above her. The kitchen had been updated with the lights long before Paulo had ever walked the halls of the palace. At least, he couldn't remember a time when there hadn't been magelights there.

"That didn't take long," Paulo said.

Laurel snorted. "What you just witnessed was the last of four days of work, and now these little beauties get to sit on a top shelf of the pantry until tomorrow to set."

Paulo straightened. "You mean, we won't even get to taste them tonight?"

Laurel chuckled. "Sometimes, your *marquessness* really shows."

"What is that supposed to mean?"

"You know, how you march into a room and demand to be handed sweets and fawned over."

Paulo smirked. "Well? I'm waiting for my sweets and fawning."

A laugh followed Laurel into the pantry, where Paulo heard her shuffle about.

"Curses," she hissed.

Paulo was on his feet a moment later. He stopped at the door to the pantry, finding her standing there with the tray hovering in one hand as she tried to push a large platter to the side. He took a step to help her, but she placed the tray on top of her head and balanced it there while she slid the platter aside and moved several bowls to other shelves, never once jostling the tray on top of her head.

"Anything I can do to help?" Paulo offered, though somewhat belatedly.

"Absolutely," Laurel chirped. "You can stand right there and stay out of my way." She finished clearing a space and placed the tray of sweets on the shelf.

Paulo gave a light applause as she turned to him. When she frowned, he said, "I had to offer some form of support. That was exceedingly well done."

Laurel rolled her eyes. "What? No 'you should have let me use my manly arms to help' from you?"

"You think I have manly arms?" He flexed his right bicep and waggled his eyebrows. It wasn't like he didn't know he had good arms. As the oldest sibling to a crazy-strong woman, he had to make sure Diana couldn't ever beat him to a pulp like she could all the other men of their acquaintance. He'd also been the only one around for her to spar with. It hadn't helped that Diana had been taller than him until he was fifteen.

Though, when his gift had come in when he was eight, it had certainly leveled the playing field.

Laurel walked past him out of the pantry, patting said *manly arm.* "At least they're enough to fill out that ridiculous jacket. Honestly, how you find someone to make you these costumes is beyond me."

Trailing behind her, Paulo said, "I'll have you know, my wardrobe is said to be the talk of Olympian high society."

"Perhaps, but I'd wager the talk is nothing good." Her eyes trailed over him. "Who wears a floral waistcoat with a striped jacket?"

Paulo folded his arms over said waistcoat. "Are you claiming to be a fashion expert?"

"No, simply claiming to have a working pair of eyes." She stopped at the stove and retrieved the pot of glaze she'd been using. "The fact that one is green and the other purple doesn't help either."

Paulo followed her to the sink on the other side of the room. "What colors would you suggest then?"

"Blue," she said automatically, grabbing a brush to scrub out the thick syrup from the bottom of the copper pot.

Paulo leaned against the edge of the sink next to her. He found himself fascinated by the beauty mark on her jaw. She had a small scar on her neck and another near her ear. Would he ever have the chance to get to know every one of those marks? To truly get to know her?

"And why blue?" he asked.

She sighed. "It compliments you. It brings out the gold in your hair and the blue in your eyes. And, considering how often you use it, I'd also wager it's your favorite color."

How this woman could see straight through him, he would never know. She'd only known him for a few months really and yet, even with the years he's gotten to know her, she always had the upper hand on him.

He tapped his finger to his chin and feigned a very ponderous expression. "Perhaps I'll order a pair of blue boots next time I see my cobbler."

Laurel set the pan on the drying rack with a clang. "Of all the ridiculous..." She shook her head. "You know what? Never mind. That makes perfect sense."

"I am a marquess you know." He grabbed the lapels of his jacket and struck a pose. "Of course I would have a long ancestry of good sense."

She laughed, wiping her hands on a towel. "Yes, which is why you would order blue boots."

That laugh slithered into the broken pieces of his chest and sewed something crucial in there back together. He closed his eyes at the sound. Sweet Gaia, it had to be his favorite sound.

"Laurel! What are you doing?"

Paulo's eyes flew open. That was most certainly his least favorite sound.

The undercook stood in the middle of the kitchen, arms folded over her chest and a furious expression twisting her otherwise pretty face. What was having a rakish prince good for if he couldn't even keep the girls away for long enough for Paulo to enjoy one conversation with the girl he wanted to make laugh?

Laurel grabbed a jar off the shelf and stopped in front of him, dropping into a curtsy. "Pardon me, my lord, but I should get to my rooms." She handed him the jar. "Here's that jar of pickled octopus you asked for."

She swept past him and the undercook, who gave her a vicious glare as she walked by.

Paulo lifted the jar in toast and left the undercook to her glaring.

He'd gotten what he'd come for. Laurel had laughed, and it had reminded him what all of this was for. She was the balm to his broken soul, the woman who would save him from becoming the man he feared he would. He knew it.

He'd known it when he first saw her face when he was eight years old.

22

THE MARQUESS

Laurel will leave the confines of her tiny room in the servants' quarters. She will meander the halls of the palace in her nightdress with a white shawl draped around her shoulders. The moonlight catches on the bright fabric through one of the windows, casting its glow around her. She haunts the halls until shadows skitter over the floor and a voice calls after her. She ducks down a hallway and finds Prince Dion and the undercook there. The undercook starts screeching about her being a thief. Laurel draws a throwing knife and sends it spinning toward the prince. Prince Dion zaps it from the air, sending it right back in Laurel's direction. She dodges the blade, but the distraction has given the guards enough time to arrive. They surround her.

DELILAH STRAIGHTENED THE FRONT OF HER NIGHTDRESS AND TURNED to Laurel. "You're such a little hypocrite, Laurel. First Lord

Oliver and now Lord MacGregor? And then you turn around and judge me for taking one man for myself?" She shook her dark hair from its braid.

Laurel had to consciously loosen her jaw. She'd been listening to Delilah talk to her about the MacGregor cousins for nearly three days straight. The only time she wasn't speaking was when she was sleeping or running around with Prince Dion— though she hadn't had a rendezvous with him since Lord MacGregor had visited the kitchens. Perhaps Laurel could slip her more of the laudanum somehow. Or strangle her.

"Don't even get me started on the clothes you wore to meet Lord Oliver. The family really must have some kind of barbaric tendency if they like all their women to walk around in trousers. It's scandalous! What kind of woman are you? If you threaten Cook's work, I'll have no choice but to report you."

And that was the reason Laurel wouldn't be looking for the prince that evening.

She could take the slander. Sweet Gaia, she'd been dealing with that her entire life. It didn't matter. She knew how to bite her tongue and simply let it slide off her back.

It was the threat to her mission that Laurel couldn't abide. If Delilah realized what Laurel was, there was no way the girl wouldn't go straight to the prince and Laurel would find herself rotting in a dungeon.

So, Prince Dion's imminent demise would be put on hold for the evening.

Delilah was the mark.

"Now listen," Delilah said, laying both of her shawls out on her bed. One was a stainless white while the other was a light lavender. "We can't both be out at night at the same time anymore. You'll just have to settle for the nights when I'm here. We can both cover for one another that way. Work as a team."

Laurel nearly rolled her eyes. Even if she didn't drug

Delilah anytime she needed to go out, the girl wouldn't help Laurel if she wouldn't gain anything from it.

"All right, I'm off." She wrapped the lavender shawl around her shoulders. "Don't wait up!"

Laurel watched her slip out the door without a word.

One.

Two.

Three...

Her count reached three hundred before she threw back her blankets and walked over to Delilah's bed. She snatched the shawl from the bed and wrapped it around her own shoulders. Honestly, it was like the girl was begging Laurel to get her caught that night.

The door opened on silent hinges, and she slipped from the room. There was no way to tell where Delilah had gone, but it didn't really matter. Laurel just had to make sure to find her on her way back from seeing Prince Dion.

Though, she wouldn't begrudge a run-in with the prince if it came to that.

There was one week left until solstice. The ticking clock in the back of her mind grew louder with each minute. One week for her to assassinate the prince and set Aspen free. One week to fulfill this ridiculous geas. To finally find her own way in the world.

The halls in the palace were quiet again that evening. A hush had come over the palace throughout the last few days, like even the turrets at the top were holding their breath. She'd seen a contingent of guards leave a few days before, but for what, she didn't know. Even Galen had commented on the solemness of Prince Dion's supper party that evening.

But everything was drowned out by the hours ticking away to solstice.

Laurel crept past the open door leading to the grand ballroom. The smell of fresh polish and the chill from open windows attested to the preparations being made for the Solstice Ball. The room would likely be greatly changed in a couple of days, but for now, it stood empty. There was something to be said about a sparkling ballroom. The glittering lights, the glamorous dresses, the intimate dancing. The feel of the music under slippers and the brush of a man's hand against the small of one's back. The smell of delectable food and thousands of fresh flowers.

Being an assassin hadn't leant to Laurel getting to attend many balls, but there had been a few over the years and none of them simply for pleasure. Sometimes, the masters took the older trainees to a ball to help them with their sleight of hand, seeing how many drinks they could spike or how many necklaces they could snatch. It was chaotic and somewhat nerve-racking.

Laurel stepped into the open doorway of the ballroom but didn't cross the threshold. While there was beauty in the tumult of a ball, the empty ballroom was something else. While the moon didn't shine through the tall window taking up the back wall, there was certainly enough light to see by. Three chandeliers hung near the floor, chains stretching up toward a painted ceiling. Angels looked down on the dance floor, standing vigil over the silent room. Marble pillars held up a second story balcony, which likely led to a number of card rooms and parlors for attendees to take a break from the crush that likely took over the ballroom at every event. Tables were pushed against the walls, all covered with white cloths to prevent dust until they could be filled with towers of Cook's finest treats. The poor woman had already started cooking for the event and likely wouldn't stop until the morning after.

The cold breeze coming from the open doors leading to the gardens outside fluttered the tablecloths.

Laurel let the breeze push her from the room. There was no sense in allowing the quiet of the palace to wrap her up and keep her from her quarry. If she had her way, the quiet wouldn't last much longer.

A shadow skittered across the hall.

Laurel stopped, her blood running cold. While she didn't know much about fae magic, she knew to watch out for oddities in light and shadow. Another shadow shot past her, brushing over her slippered foot. She jumped back at the contact. It almost stung. That one was followed by another. By the Goddess, what was happening? There was a fae somewhere and they were using magic in a palace full of royals and nobility.

Guards would start swarming any moment.

She jogged down the hallway, keeping her steps quiet as she tried to figure out where Delilah had met with the prince. They seemed to stay in the residential wing of the palace, though the rooms changed more times than not.

The sound of men's muffled voices echoed from behind her.

Blast. She needed to find Delilah. The guards wouldn't have cared about a girl wandering the halls so much on any other night, but the shadows told Laurel they wouldn't be as forgiving this evening.

Her jog turned into a sprint. She stopped at intersections and listened for the telltale clip of boots or the clink of chainmail. Noise seemed to shuffle about her, not close enough to catch her but close enough to make the hairs on the back of her neck stand on end. The shadows only grew in intensity as well.

She made it almost all the way to the royal wing before a hand shot out of an alcove and pulled her into it. Her hand automatically came up.

"Don't hit me," a voice hissed.

She looked up, expecting to see the pearlescent gaze of Lord Oliver in his mask, but stilled when she met a pair of tourmaline eyes.

"Lord MacGregor?" she whispered.

He pulled her farther into the alcove, the large decorative urn making it difficult to move about. He expertly pressed her toward the back and blocked her in, making escape next to impossible.

She pressed a hand to his chest, trying to keep distance between them even if they were pressed against one another. "What are you doing?"

"I could ask you the same thing," he whispered back. "I saw the shadows and came to investigate, but then I spotted you."

"And hiding us in this tiny space occurred to you because?"

"Because anyone caught in these halls will look quite suspect. Especially tonight." Lord MacGregor readjusted his footing, but it put little space between them. She hadn't realized how large the man was until he was pressed against her. He might not have been as broad as Luc was, but she could feel the muscles coiled under the dark jacket he wore— likely in some ridiculous color she couldn't see in this lighting. For a man used to convenience, he had the familiar body of a fighter.

Perhaps Delilah was right. The MacGregors were an odd lot.

Laurel's pulse took up residence in her throat. "What's happened?"

Lord MacGregor shook his head. "Nothing good."

"That's hardly an answer." Laurel poked him in the ribs. If he was going to trap her in an alcove for the rest of the night, she would prove the worst sort of companion. She obviously couldn't tell him off and be on her way. Who knew what he would do if she provoked him? He could be petulant enough to tell the guards she was sneaking about.

He hissed. "Don't do that."

"What? Poke you?" He provoked the most outrageous feelings in her. She wanted to poke him simply because he riled her. It made her feel ridiculous. *He* made her feel ridiculous. The only other person that could drive her as mad was Aspen.

She could blame the close quarters or the twisting shadows, but whatever it was that drove her to it, she went to poke him again.

He stepped back. "Don't—"

The decorative urn crashed to the ground behind them.

Laurel froze as Lord MacGregor cursed.

A shout went up at the end of the hall.

Laurel didn't think. Didn't even really consider it as she dropped Delilah's shawl at her feet and grabbed the lapels of Lord MacGregor's jacket. Next thing she knew, her hand wrapped around his neck, and she pulled his mouth down to hers.

By the Goddess, this could backfire so badly.

He was a marquess. If he didn't want to be kissed, he could tell the guards she attacked him. Cry off and leave her for the guards to rip apart. She knew plenty of other men who would, simply to get out of a smack on the hand.

But Lord MacGregor didn't.

While she may have initiated the kiss, he took it over.

He groaned like a starved man and pushed her up against the wall. Every inch of his strong body pressed into hers. One hand splayed over her waist, her hip, somehow gentle yet demanding as he pulled her even closer to him. The other hand came up to cup her cheek.

Her hand on his neck moved to the soft curls at the nape of

his neck. How could a man have such soft hair? She lifted her chin the slightest bit, deepening the kiss.

He met her stroke for stroke.

The hand at her cheek moved to her hair, tugging it back to give him better access to her lips.

A small noise came out of the back of her throat.

His mouth moved from her lips to the skin under her jaw, leaving a trail of heat as his stubble scratched the sensitive skin of her throat.

She gasped.

His lips captured the sound.

Her hand returned to the front of his jacket, pulling him closer to her.

His heart beat thunderously under her hand.

Hers beat at the same rapid pace.

"Lord MacGregor?"

The voice was a cold bucket of water over Laurel's head. Her eyes flew open, and she broke away from the kiss, though she couldn't move far, pressed against the wall as she was.

Lord MacGregor's entire body stiffened, but he didn't move much. Instead, he kept his nose only a hairsbreadth from hers, his eyes closed. She couldn't see anything else but him.

"Yes?" Lord MacGregor asked, the sound of his voice rough. It vibrated down her spine and she couldn't help studying his lips as he said it. Those lips that had just been pressed against hers.

"Sorry to interrupt you, but we've been commanded to ensure all the hallways are clear.

Lord MacGregor's brows furrowed, but he didn't open his eyes. Instead, he pressed his forehead to Laurel's. She couldn't decide if she liked the feel of him so close to her or wanted to rush from the small alcove like it was on fire. The heat in her cheeks definitely made the place feel sweltering.

"All right. We'll leave. Please, continue your patrols."

Lord MacGregor's word must have held some clout, because the guards didn't wait to escort them. The sound of their steps faded as they strode down the hall and around the corner.

Laurel waited until she was sure they were gone, then removed her fingers from Lord MacGregor's hair and pushed him back a step.

"Thank you for playing along with my little ruse, my lord." Did her voice sound as breathless to him as it did to her? She patted him on the chest, straightening his lapels, and swept her hair back from her face before she let herself speak again. "I don't know what Cook would have thought if she'd known I was wandering the halls. I appreciate your discretion and for not revealing me to the guards."

Lord MacGregor finally opened his eyes, blinking a few times as he fully took a step back. "Yes, of course. We wouldn't want anyone thinking you were up to anything nefarious, would we?"

Laurel's stomach knotted. "No, of course not."

Lord MacGregor reached down and picked Delilah's shawl off the floor. His arms came around Laurel once more, though this time he only wrapped her in the shawl. When he finally stepped out of the alcove, he offered her his hand. The hand that had been pressed to her waist.

By the Goddess, had she ever been kissed by a man like that? Yes, she'd kissed and been kissed— more than she would probably like to say. Sometimes, seduction was part of the job. There were places a woman could get to for a mission that men couldn't, and a bed was certainly one of them. Sure, there were male assassins that used their wiles on marks as needed, but it just didn't happen as often. Laurel's skills weren't as suited for seduction. There were other assassins in the Order more versed in such things.

Laurel took a deep breath and placed her hand in his.

He didn't pull her back in for another kiss. He simply drew her from their hideout, then set to returning the urn back to its place.

"Oh dear," he said, looking at a large chip in the likely priceless piece. He twisted it so the chip was at the back and wouldn't be seen by anyone passing by.

Laurel chuckled. "At least that was the only damage done."

"For now." He turned away but not before Laurel saw his smirk. That look promised something she wasn't quite sure if she liked or not.

She cleared her throat. "Well, I suppose it's time for me to return to the kitchens." She swept past him.

His fingers caught on the edge of the shawl. "You'll want to take the main staircase from the residential wing."

Turning, she looked up at him. His face was turned away from her, his light lashes catching the light from the window behind her.

"All right." She tugged the shawl from his grasp. "Again. Thank you."

His eyes shot to her face, the blue dark and heavy as he looked at her.

"Don't thank me yet."

With those cryptic words, he spun and swept down the hallway away from her. He turned the corner, not even looking in her direction.

"All right," she whispered to herself. *What an odd man.*

She shook herself. If the guards were sweeping through the palace, then Delilah was likely already on her way back to their room.

Laurel took off back the way she'd come.

When she came to the place where the servants' staircase led out of the residential wing, she swept past it, remembering that Lord MacGregor had told her to until she was halfway down the stairs. She stopped. Was she really listening to something he'd said?

By then, the guard had spotted her.

"You there! What are you doing out and about?"

Laurel turned the other way and ran back to the servants' staircase.

Why had she listened to that idiot? Of course she should have taken the servants' stairs. The guards were likely swarming the entire palace. Did he want her to get caught?

Footsteps pounded behind her as she flew down the steps. Thankfully, the light here was much darker than it was out in the open paths of the palace.

She turned a corner and saw a flash of white on the stairs ahead of her.

Delilah.

Perhaps the Goddess really did care about her children.

Laurel slowed her pace, following quietly after the undercook down the stairs. Delilah reached the bottom and kept moving toward the kitchens, but Laurel took the first door she found, sequestering herself in one of the many broom closets situated along the servant hallways.

At least three pairs of boots thundered down the stairs.

Laurel peeked out of the door as they passed. She could just see the other end of the hall through the crack.

"Halt!" she heard one of them call.

But they weren't shouting at her.

Delilah paused at the end of the hallway as the guards descended on her.

Laurel smiled. There was more than one way to assassinate someone, and sometimes the murder of their reputation was better than sliding a knife between their ribs.

23
THE COUNTDOWN

DELILAH SNIFFED AGAIN AS SHE STUFFED HER FAVORITE APRON INTO her trunk.

Laurel scooted her own trunk back into place. The last three days had come with a storm of people and emotions.

Laurel picked up the small wooden box that sat on the shelf above Delilah's bed. One of the hinges was still broken after it had been tossed on the floor a few days ago. An investigation had taken place, as that same evening there had been an attack in the city. The guards had come in when while the captain of the guard had been interrogating Delilah after they caught her. They'd ripped apart the room, looking for any proof of ill intent.

Thankfully, Laurel had moved her gear. After Delilah started getting into Laurel's things, she'd moved her belongings out of their room. While she kept quite a few weapons on her person, most of her gear was now generously spread throughout the kitchen. If anyone found them, they'd think it odd, but not so suspicious as a cache of weapons hidden in a mattress.

She would have had to move it before she got Delilah caught anyway. It only made sense for the guards to search their rooms after they'd discovered Delilah so close to the prince.

Laurel carefully picked up the broken shards of the seashell that had also had a home on Delilah's shelf and put them in the box. Cook had ordered Laurel to help Delilah clean up their room and pack, saying it best to get her out of the palace as quickly as they could to avoid any more of Lady Carnation's very pointed ire.

Lady Carnation had learned of Delilah's late-night traipse through the halls. The lady had materialized in the kitchens with a retinue of guards to question Delilah in Esther's office that morning, only three days after Delilah had been caught. They'd come back into the kitchens, Delilah sobbing as Lady Carnation announced her immediate removal from the palace and the stripping of her position. It had been absolutely humiliating for Delilah.

Laurel carefully set the box next to the pile Delilah worked on.

Before she could step away, Delilah grabbed her arm in a vice. Red rimmed eyes met Laurel's with a fury she could only blink at.

"You know," Delilah whispered, "when Lady Carnation screamed at me like the jealous harpy she is, she mentioned how the guards had discovered me. It was so odd. She said the guards had to chase me through the halls. Said I ran from them. I told her I didn't. That when they discovered me in the servant's passage, I stopped. One of the guards practically scoffed in my face, saying he'd been the one to trail me from the main staircase, but I never took the main passages in the palace. They called me a liar, saying they recognized me because of my shawl. I was so confused. That is, until I remembered."

She drew out the folded shawl from the pocket of her skirt. "I found it the morning after, when you had already gone to the kitchens, though it had somehow been tucked into the very corner of my bedframe. How it got there, I have no idea since I distinctly remember laying it out on my bed when I went to see Prince Dion. However, when I went to hang it up, I was shocked to find this."

At the edge of one corner, the fabric had become discolored. Half a boot print.

Laurel held her expression still.

Delilah barked a laugh. "I haven't worn this shawl since I washed it last week. How did this happen?"

Laurel shook her head. "I don't—"

The vice Delilah had around her hand tightened. "Don't even try to deny it, you little witch. I don't know how you escaped, but you were the one running from the guards. You were the one they should have caught."

Laurel ripped her hand from Delilah's grip. "You're crazy."

"I'm right and I know it. You're up to something, and I'm going to prove it. When Lady Carnation asked if I knew anyone else sneaking about the palace, I told them about you. I tried to tell the guards you had been snooping around too, that you had weird stuff in your mattress. I looked like a complete fool when they found nothing. Lady Carnation called me a liar and told me about how she knew you. How I couldn't fool her because she trusted you."

Her voice rose. "How you've weaseled your way into everyone's heads, I don't know, but I'm going to expose you. If I have to lose my position, you should too."

Laurel shook her head and turned away. The gall of this girl. Praise the Goddess she would be gone.

A hand grabbed Laurel's braid. "Don't turn away from me, you little—"

In the blink of an eye, Laurel's fingers jabbed the girl in the throat.

Delilah's screeching voice cut off and her hands came to her neck. She wheezed as she tried to get air back into her lungs.

Laurel didn't give her the chance to catch her breath. The fire in her chest turned to steel as it ran through her veins. She dug her fingers into Delilah's jaw with one hand and forced her to meet her gaze.

Delilah's face had gone from purple to white. Laurel knew why. Knew what she looked like. Her congenial mask had finally slipped. Aspen had told her about it over the years. There was a look Laurel got. She'd seen it once after she'd found an older assassin had cornered a younger one in an empty training room when she was fifteen. There had been a mirror and she'd seen the look as she slit the throat of the older assassin.

Luc called it her "Killer Face."

Aspen called it her "Reaper Mask."

"Listen to me, you little wretch," Laurel whispered. "You have no proof of anything, and even if you did, you wouldn't ever have the chance to expose me. Do you know why?"

She brought the girl's face closer until their noses nearly touched. "Because you would be dead before you so much as gagged on that sad, weak lump of flesh you call a heart that I will have ripped from your chest and stuffed down your tiny throat. Do you understand?"

Delilah sucked in a breath. "Yes," she practically wheezed.

"Good." Laurel dropped her hand. "I don't want us to go away from this without being on the same page."

Delilah's face was pale as she finished packing and left a half an hour later.

Laurel returned to work in the quiet kitchen. Cook stood at the stove, her mouth turned down in a frown. Dan, the other undercook stepped about on tipped toes. Even Galen was despondent, sitting at the table and staring at the door Delilah had walked out of.

Laurel marched across the dock; her ears tucked into the collar of her jacket. Winter would make her official debut in three days, but it felt as if she had slipped into the sky pretending to be autumn and making fools out of the world.

Great, now I'm acting maudlin. She shook her head. The hours following Delilah's removal from the palace had been fraught with tension. With the ball only four days away, Cook had escalated from a tizzy to a full-on cyclone.

And now, she found herself summoned to *The Shining River.*

This time, she kept a dagger within easy reach. No need to let Adira get the upper hand on her. Not when her time was almost up.

She scaled the side of the ship smoothly and quietly crept across the deck of the ship. Large shipping boxes now took up most of the extra space. Were they going somewhere? The light under Teagan's door greeted her instead of the brutes that normally did. She guessed they weren't far away, though, if their master was inside.

Laurel slipped into the room and found Teagan once again seated at his desk, this time a with a pair of spectacles on the bridge of his nose and a pen in hand. She closed the door behind her but remained standing near the threshold. He hadn't invited her to sit, and she could feel the very thin ice stretching from where she stood and where he sat.

The pen scratched for several minutes, Teagan not looking up once. He was definitely upset if he was wasting both their time. Laurel didn't allow herself to even breath louder than she had to.

It was ten minutes before he spoke.

"I can't decide if you have been bought out by the Olympians or if you've somehow fooled me all these years into believing you're more competent than your peers." He looked up at her. "Take off your mask."

Laurel unclipped her schola mask from her hood and held it at her side.

"Do you think I was a fool to give you this assignment?"

Laurel gave a small shake of her head, keeping her expression placid.

"Are you betraying me?"

Laurel shook her head again, meeting his eye.

He sighed. "No, of course not. I still have Aspen. You won't do anything that would put her in jeopardy."

It wasn't a question, so Laurel didn't need to answer. He knew her. He knew what made her tick. He was the master of the clock in her head, after all. He wound the mechanism with his very hands.

And she was failing him.

They both knew it.

He stood, going to the bed in the cabin and picking up a box as long as Laurel's arm. "You've somehow been unmatched for years and this mission has truly made me wonder if Adira Durant has fooled me into a war she won't win. That her own ambition has clouded my judgement. When you last met me here, I was upset, but after the last few weeks,

I realize I've put you in a difficult position. I should have strived to show you what you mean to our Order instead of making you feel like you had to leave. You're considered one of the greatest assassins on the Continent. If not even you could do this job, no one could. It's the impossible quest. The greatest achievement of our order."

Laurel watched him, keeping her expression smooth. The compliments again. He was trying a new tactic. Trying to make her feel like something greater than she was. She'd seen it used on younger assassins, used to make them feel like they could take on the world.

It always brought their deaths.

She stayed quiet. Anything she said would either motivate him to keep complimenting her or would send him into a rage.

Box in hand, he walked over to her. "Imagine being the one to take down the mage prince. The one to bring glory to our Order. To free your sister from the life you despise so much."

He handed her the box.

She took it.

"I'll be leaving. Adira Durant is set to take down the Mist between here and Faerie." He went on to explain what the next few weeks would entail.

Their plan was actually simple in essence. Laurel would assassinate Prince Dion. As the princes scrambled to get the council in order, the youngest prince would be summoned to Faerie. Somehow, he was the heir to the Faerie throne, though Laurel still couldn't quite grasp all of that. It would leave Prince Evan behind, who would go to his people for help.

That was where the true deception would pay off.

Adira Durant had gotten the Aigeans on her side.

From how Teagan explained it, the kingdom across the sea was looking for more land. Their population was expanding and the islands that made up a good portion of the hospitable land beginning to sink into the water, the coasts eroding and falling into the sea. Apparently, islands could be pulled under the water over long periods of time. While merfolk couldn't leave the water, selkies, sirens, sea hags, and others had to have some land to dwell on or they would fall prey to the predators of the oceans or even drown.

They needed more land.

And they'd set their sights on Faerie.

After all, why not? They'd supposedly been citizens of Faerie hundreds of years ago. It was the home of their ancestors. They simply wished to return to the lands of their fore-fathers.

The fae, though, they had to go.

So, Adira struck her bargain. She would give them Faerie if they helped her take Olympia and subjugate the fae.

"The war will truly begin once we have Olympia," Teagan said. "If the job hasn't been completed in time, there will be serious repercussions. I've been very patient. Don't disappoint me."

He walked back to his desk and returned to his work.

"You have four days, Laurel."

She ran from the ship as fast as she could.

It wasn't until she returned to her rooms that she opened the box.

A gown of dark blue silk winked out from between the folds of white tissue paper.

24

AN UNFORTUNATE INJURY

PAULO LOOKED BETWEEN THE TWO VASES OF FLOWERS. ONE VASE held a beautiful collection of sunflowers and roses that looked like a sunset while the other highlighted an assortment of lilies and mums in golden hues. He chuckled and grabbed the latter.

"That's a lovely arrangement, my lord," said the florist. "I'm sorry for your loss."

A smile nearly crept over his face, but he pulled his brows together and turned down his lips to cover it up. "My loss? Why should I celebrate loss when I'm about to give these to a lovely lady who will undoubtedly fall head over heels in love with me the moment I arrive with them in hand?"

The florist's mouth opened and closed like a fish gasping for breath. Paulo didn't even allow the woman a word as he dropped a couple of coins on the counter and sauntered away from the flower cart.

Another flash of lightning ripped across the sky. The crack of thunder followed shortly after. Prince Dion had been in a foul mood since the council meeting the day before, and the sky wasn't the only sign of his frustration. He'd nearly gone to blows with some of the council members over discussions about the wedding in five days and his imminent coronation.

Things were starting to fall into place. Things Paulo could have prevented.

But the simple remembrance of Laurel's lips on his was enough to make him question every bit of his sanity. By the Goddess, he'd thought he'd been dreaming. He hadn't foreseen the kiss, likely due to the improvised nature of it. If he had, he might have done things differently, but now that it had happened, he didn't regret anything. Every vision he'd had of the two of them together paled in comparison to experiencing it. His blood still burned every time he thought about her waist under his fingers. The way her body fit so perfectly against his. His magic had gone completely out of control, flashing across his mind's eye faster than he could take it in. He hadn't even been able to look at her for fear she would see the pearlescent sheen of his tell and it would ruin everything. It had taken a monstrous amount of effort not to meet her gaze, to see if she had been as affected by the kiss as he was.

Another peal of thunder sounded above him. Rain would strike within the hour. He would have to hurry. His walk turned into a jog as he reached the palace gate. Green clouds circled the topmost spires of the palace, likely the result of Prince Dion's growing agitation and the weather mages attempt to mitigate the damage of such a storm. If the crab-apple-sized hail hit the palace, it would do little more than shatter windows, but if it made it into the city, it had the potential to harm the citizens.

The first drops of rain hit the palace steps as he swept through the door, flowers in perfect order. He looked over them again. One of the stems had bent in his hurry. Curses.

He swept up the stairs leading to the guest chambers. He passed one, two, three doors before he stopped and knocked on the fourth one. The sound of giggling slipped through the seam between the door and the jam. Paulo rolled his eyes and knocked again.

A moment later, Donnie opened the door enough for his head to slip through and little else. "Paulo! I've been looking everywhere for you."

A smear of lipstick stuck out from under the man's undone collar. He gave his friend a pointed look. "Clearly."

Donnie frowned. "Who are the flowers for?"

A small titter echoed from the other side of the door.

"I'll certainly tell you once we get there. You have two minutes to get properly dressed and sneak your guest out before I come back here."

"Two minutes isn't nearly enough time!"

Paulo turned, pulling out his pocket watch. "One. Two."

The door shut behind him.

Donnie joined him down the hall one minute and fifty-five seconds later. "How did I do?"

"Five seconds to spare. I knew you could do it." Paulo started down the hall, passing by the scenic paintings of waves crashing onto a beach of white sand and mountains guarding the sun as it made its decent below the horizon. This part of the palace was full of artwork and every bit of the finery the members of nobility expected.

Sometimes, Paulo missed Iatrus Castle's eclectic collection of mounts and old furniture.

"Are you going to tell me who the flowers are for?" Donnie asked.

"Are you going to tell me which lady you had in your room?"

Donnie's grin widened. "Wouldn't you like to know?"

Paulo grinned back. "If you can keep up, then you'll find out the answer to my mystery for free." They turned a corner and found a set of double doors at the end of the hallway. Paulo stopped and knocked. Movement on the other side of the door proceeded the arrival of Lady Delmar.

Donnie nearly turned to a puddle as he dipped into a low bow. "My lady," he demurred. "It is a great honor to see you this morning."

Lady Delmar smirked and turned to Paulo. "I hope those flowers aren't for me."

Paulo met her smirk with one of his own. "If I told you they were?"

She gave a playful glare. "Then I'd have to tell Lady Penny she kept awful company and insist she kick you out on your rears." She pushed the door wider and stepped aside.

Paulo dragged a very boneless Donnie through the doorway. Honestly, it was like the man had never seen a woman before. Once they were in the sitting room, Lady Delmar led them through the suite to an open door. She knocked on the wall and announced both Paulo and Donnie.

"The most honorably ridiculous Lord MacGregor and his overly excited friend, Lord Abrams."

A laugh sounded from within the room and something in Paulo's chest eased a fraction. It would be all right.

He stepped over the threshold and found Penny sitting up in bed, a deck of Cruin cards shuffling between her fingers. Light bruises under her eyes and a small speck of shadow in her green gaze were the only signs of the pains she'd suffered only a few days ago.

But her smile did a very good job hiding it all.

"I hope both of you brought your coin purses," she teased, waving the deck in the air at them. "I'm on a winning streak and Rissa's poor purse won't last much longer."

Lady Delmar folded her arms but stayed by the door. "Much longer? My coin purse was empty three rounds ago."

Penny chuckled and began dealing out the cards on the coverlet in front of her. "Come now, you two. Come keep a poor, injured girl company for a little while."

Donnie took a step forward. "You're injured?"

A flush stole over Penny's lightly freckled cheeks. "I got into a fight with a rake and found myself on the losing side."

"How did that happen?"

Penny looked down at the coverlet in front of her. "It's rather embarrassing actually. I slipped and fell on a rake one of the gardeners had left out in the garden."

Donnie turned to Paulo. "And you didn't see it in time to warn her?"

Paulo ignored him and held up his bouquet. "I brought you some flowers."

"I noticed. You can put them there if you like." She pointed to a small sitting table next to the door. "An interesting choice, picking flowers more suited for a funeral than a get well. Are you trying to tell me something, Paulo?"

Donnie's head whipped in his direction, but Paulo shook his head. "I only thought they would be well received. I particularly liked the almost amber color of the mums as well as the message of life and death the lilies give. I feel like they remind me of someone, but I just can't put my finger on it." He set the vase down on the table and met her very wide green eyes.

Oh yes, he absolutely knew about what she'd been getting up to with the prince and now she knew that he knew.

Donnie looked between the two of them then shrugged. "Well, are we going to play or not?"

Lady Delmar took another step toward the door. "I'll just be out here, Penny. I've got some letters to write. Hopefully, I can scrounge up enough coin to pay for the postage."

Laughing, Penny held up her cards and pointed to the chair

closest to her bed. "Paulo, you take that chair while Donnie runs to grab another from the sitting room."

Paulo sat and Donnie raced out of the room after Lady Delmar.

Penny waited to speak until he'd made it through the doorway. "How much do you know?"

Paulo picked up his own hand of cards and begun shuffling them around. "Enough to know that your prince sent out an army's worth of glamours three nights ago and your injury isn't from some rake."

Penny's eyes darted to the door then back to him. "Will you tell my mother?"

He reached for her hand and squeezed her fingers. "Penny, you can trust me. I have no intentions of telling Her Grace anything."

She blew out a breath, but their conversation was cut short as Donnie returned with a chair which he placed on the other side of the bed. He rubbed his hands together playfully. "Now all we need is a bottle of wine and this will be a real party."

Penny laughed and tapped his cards. "We'll see how long it takes for me to win all your coin before I let you anywhere near any wine."

The game started and Paulo couldn't help watching his friend as she played. In four days, she would be gone, off to face great peril. He should warn her. Should tell her of the things she would face. Of the dangers waiting for her.

But Laurel's face flashed into his mind, and he kept his thoughts to himself.

Though, he may have let Penny win a game or two.

The following day passed in a blur of one meeting after another. With the announcement of Prince Dion and Lady Carnation's impending nuptials, the palace was in a bit of a tizzy. Paulo hadn't even been able to stop in at the kitchens to see Laurel. Every time he tried to go down there, someone would stop him with some trivial matter or snippet of gossip. It was as if the Goddess didn't want him anywhere near her, and he really couldn't figure out why.

So, he kept Penny company. He took Diana with him and the three of them played too many games of Cruin and listened as Diana read one of the novels Penny had sitting on her bedside table. The gruff manner Diana used to portray the dastardly pirates in the story left both Paulo and Penny in stitches.

As they chatted about the festivities around the city—mainly what Diana had seen as she'd been running around and Penny or Paulo asking about it since neither of them had stepped foot out of the palace walls— a knock came to the door. Paulo's vision flashed of him opening the door to the cursed Adam Cyrus.

He truly loved the man, but in this one instance, he was an absolute nuisance.

Penny turned to look at the door and Paulo grabbed her arm, shaking his head. "It's Adam," he whispered.

"And I shouldn't speak with him?" she whispered back.

"Not unless you are willing to accept an invitation to the solstice ball from him."

They waited a few moments before Diana nodded that he was gone. Her observation skills, while somewhat frightening, were often a boon.

Penny's face fell. "I truly feel terrible about what's happened with him. I feel as if I owe him an apology for leading him on, but I don't know how to break off things without Mother growing suspicious."

Diana snorted. "You say, 'Mother, I don't want to marry the puffed-up ambassador, and you should be happy about that because you're the one who's pounded good sense into my brain.'"

"I don't think that would go over as well this time." Penny looked back at the door, a real look of pity on her face. She really was too good for this world, and Adam Cyrus would only keep her from reaching her fullest potential. At least, that was what Paulo kept telling himself as he sat there and acted as if nothing would ever change.

Diana dragged Paulo from the room so she would have time to make it down to the city for the parade that evening. They passed Lady Delmar with baskets of flowers as they made their way down the hall.

When they turned the corner, Diana stopped him. "What really happened to Penny?"

"What do you mean?"

She smacked his arm. "You know exactly what I mean. I don't believe for one second she fell on a rake. I've known her since we were all young enough to hide from our nursemaid whenever she came to Iatrus Castle. She's lying and I want to know what happened."

Paulo sighed. "She faced off against The Cartographer and came away injured."

Diana shoved him this time. "And you knew and didn't warn her?"

Paulo laid his head back against the wall. "If I told her, other things wouldn't be able to come to pass. There's too much at stake."

"Fine, but you also ignored Adam when he came to the door. Is that part of all this too? Don't think I didn't notice that you set him and Penny up and then basically flipped around and began discouraging it. I feel like there's a lot going on that you're not telling anyone, and I'm starting to worry."

"I've got it under control." He straightened and took another step down the hall. "Now, don't you have a parade to go to?"

While she didn't bring it up again, he could still feel Diana's judgement long after she left for the parade. The feeling followed him into supper as well, but when he looked into the plate of carefully arranged pastries, he couldn't find it in himself to be sorry.

25
THE SOLSTICE

Laurel's face will turn sallow quickly. Her gaze will go hazy, and she will blink the dizziness from her eyes. Sweat will drip from her temples. Cook will look at her with concern, placing the back of her hand on her forehead. Laurel will try to brush her off, but Cook will guide her toward the hall leading to the servants' quarters. Laurel will be sick on the floor of the hall.

THE DAY OF THE WINTER SOLSTICE CAME QUICKER THAN A PUNCH TO the gut and Laurel was seeing stars.

She'd never experienced anything like this. Having a deadline had always been motivating to her. It gave her something to beat. She relished being able to report a job done weeks or even months in advance. She'd been invited to join the scholae at sixteen because of it.

If she'd had more time to think about her mission, she might have been able to come up with something. She might have merely razed the palace to the ground— curse the consequences— but Cook flapped about the kitchen, blades and towels swinging. She hadn't nicked anyone, but it seemed only a matter of time.

Laurel still tried.

For the last three nights, she'd raced out of her room and searched the palace every minute she could.

The Crown Prince had vanished.

At least, it seemed like he had. She searched high and low for him every night, but it was like searching for a phantom. Not even Lord Oliver and his mask showed up, much to Laurel's frustration. She was working hard to take out the prince and the nosy lord hadn't even the decency to show up to at least pretend to try to stop her.

Then there was the youngest prince.

Laurel had only crossed his path once while she was helping prepare a breakfast buffet in the royal dining room. The hairs on the back of her neck had stood on end at just the sight of him.

He prowled through the palace like a big cat Laurel had seen in a traveling circus once. A lot of people talked about the majesty of lions. Their strut, their roar, the way they led their prides of lionesses. They were considered the greatest of all vicious felines.

While Prince Dion might have been a lion, his youngest brother was a tiger.

Tigers were more solitary creatures. They didn't use the masses to take down prey. No, they hunted, stalked, and struck when their prey least expected it. And while lions roared loud and ferocious, when tigers roared, you knew your life was most certainly about to end.

Yes, the youngest prince was most certainly a tiger, and he would go right for her neck if he figured out who she was.

She avoided him completely after that one interaction, but that made crossing paths with Prince Dion nearly impossible.

So, she sprinkled a cinnamon-sugar mix over the pan of hot *loukoumades* as sweat began to pool at her clavicle. She shivered and looked at her pocket watch. The solstice ball was set to take place in just under three hours. Cakes had been frosted. Hors d'oeuvres plated. Ice carved. Punch mixed and cooled.

The ball came like a silent killer, slowly tightening the noose around Laurel's neck.

Or perhaps all these symptoms she was experiencing were linked to the khat poison running through her veins.

She'd go with that.

She checked her watch again. Once it had hit the quarter hour, she pulled a small vial from her pocket. Without looking to see if anyone was watching, she drank it quickly, nearly gagging on the thick liquid. She tucked the vial back in her pocket and breathed through her nose.

Just a bit longer.

"Curses!" Cook hissed. She slammed her spoon down on the counter.

Dan stepped to her side. "What can I do?"

"Lady Carnation requested an Aigean delicacy, but I can't get the texture right."

Laurel looked over at the bowl, blinking away at the fog trying to take over her brain. Thin red soup sloshed about. From what Cook had put in there earlier, she would guess it was *gazpacho*, a soup of finely pureed vegetables. Laurel peeked in closer and took in a lungful of the cold puree. Garlic, vinegar, and cumin all tickled her nose, but yes, the consistency was off.

"Did you add the bread?" Laurel asked, her words slightly breathy.

Cook turned. "I have it cut up on the plate over there."

Laurel followed Cook's gaze to the platter of perfectly laid out bread sitting on a tray. She shook her head, though it made her vision swim. "No, you put it in the soup." She walked over and grabbed two large handfuls of the bread, avoiding the pieces with crust. She came to the pot and dumped them in.

Dan took a step toward her, but Cook stopped him. "Laurel, are you feeling all right?"

Laurel wiped her brow with her apron. Her body had gotten hot quickly, and her stomach cramped. "The texture is off because the bread acts as a thickener."

"The recipe called for bread, but I didn't know you were supposed to put the bread *in* the soup."

Laurel took Cook's spoon from the counter and pushed the bread down. "Let it sit in there for about ten minutes, then it should dissolve enough to mix in properly. I might have accidentally gotten a little bit of crust in there, but it should still thicken up the soup without leaving chunks. Then it will be ready for the cold room." She checked her watch again. It had been less than five minutes since she'd drank the vial.

She stepped back to her last tray of *loukoumades*, but Cook grabbed her elbow.

"Laurel, my dear, you're slick with sweat and your eyes... Perhaps you ought to go lie down for a bit."

Laurel squinted at her, trying to hide her blown out pupils just a bit. "Are you sure?"

"Absolutely. You look like you're about to lose your lunch."

And Laurel did, thirty seconds after Cook said so.

At least the antidote was working how it should.

The antidote she'd drank in the kitchen took all of forty-five minutes to start working. Praise the Goddess she'd built up such a resistance to khat over the years and could avoid the worst of the mania that came with it. Laurel would have two hours to get ready. While she wouldn't be in peak condition, she would get better as the night went on. She wiped the sweat from her skin with a soapy rag. Hopefully, her quick spot wash would rid her of any stink.

After another thirty minutes, she pulled on a light layer of gear. She'd need a selection of poisons as well as a handful of blades. She dearly missed her matching set of daggers. *Cursed Lord Oliver.* She still slid a few in the sheathes attached to her legs and even tucked a pair of decorative ones into her hair.

She grabbed the box with the dress and quietly snuck from her room. If she'd put it on and run into one of the other servants, her object in poisoning herself would be discovered. A servant walking about with a box was much more believable.

She swept through the servant's quarters and up the stairs to the guest chambers. Most of the guests would already be down at the ball, eager to soak up the magic Olympia's royal family had to offer.

After passing the first few, she stopped at a nondescript door and knocked, a ready lie about a delivery for a made-up Lady Thessalia on her tongue.

But no one came to the door.

Laurel slipped inside.

A man's room greeted her, the strong scents of amber and cedar practically burning away the hairs in her nostrils. How she hadn't been able to smell it through the door, she had no idea. The man had to bathe in the scent.

She quickly ducked into a corner of the room, keeping an eye on the door and shedding her outer layer of clothing along with the leather strap she had wrapped around her wrist, which she moved to her ankle. She would tuck her clothes somewhere in the servant's staircase on her way to the ballroom. Thankfully, she had stopped sweating, though the antidote made her mouth awfully dry. She pulled the dress out of the box.

A note slipped to the floor.

She placed the gown back in the box and picked up the scrap of white paper.

> *If whoever you're meant to kill isn't dead yet, they will be when they see you in this.*
> *—A*

Aspen.

Tears gathered at the corners of Laurel's eyes, and she had to blink them away. How had Aspen snuck this into the box? How had she even known the dress was for her?

Laurel tucked the paper into a pocket on her trousers and returned to the dress. She held it up, noticing a few wrinkles from how it was folded. It looked easy enough to put on herself. The full skirt spread to the floor, the blue nearly black in the faint light of the room. There was a small line of buttons along the back, but nothing Laurel couldn't handle. The three-quarter length sleeves would make it easy to tuck a dagger near her elbow and the embellishments around the neck and cuffs were elegant but not so gawdy to draw too many eyes. She quickly threw on the also blue petticoat and pulled the gown over her head.

When she noticed where the neckline reached, she realized why Aspen thought the dress deadly.

Laurel couldn't help but grin when she imagined the look

on Lord Oliver's face when he saw her in it. His snarky comments would fall quite flat, she was sure.

With the buttons in place, she pulled out a pair of slippers and a matching masquerade mask that would only cover the skin around her eyes. By the Goddess, Teagan had thought of everything. She tucked the box under the bed. Whoever eventually cleaned the room would hopefully think it the gentleman's that resided in here. Laurel could burn the dress later.

Next, she set herself to fixing her hair. She thanked Father for her straight locks. It was easy to pull from its braid and settle around her shoulders. Aspen often complained about the odd waves in her hair and how she could never get it to sit right. Laurel's wouldn't hold shape for longer than a few hours, but that was all she needed. She pulled back the front, leaving a few tendrils to frame her face, and used sharpened hair picks to hold it all in place.

She checked over her appearance in the vanity mirror. While it wasn't anything to fuss over, she looked presentable enough not to stick out like a sore thumb in a ballroom full of Olympia's elite.

Though, the plunging neckline would definitely draw eyes.

She checked over the placement of her weapons. She still wore her pants under the long skirts, which held a garrote wire and her thigh sheaths each held a dagger. There were pockets on either side of her skirt, where she tucked a couple of paper tubes, each filled with one poison or another. The Stellataen Arrow still sat in the lined pocket of her jacket. She couldn't risk carrying that around and it wouldn't kill the prince fast enough. She needed something that would end him before morning broke. Each of the papers were ingestible poisons, so her options of administering it to the prince were very limited.

But she would do it. She would kill the prince.

Then she would go back to Stellatus Hall, pack up her things, and get Aspen out of there.

Slipping from the room, a small bundle of clothes under her arm, was as easy as slipping into it. She prayed the rest of the evening would be just as uneventful.

26

AN UNFORTUNATE DANCE

Paulo shook his head. "I can't, Penny. I can't tell you."

The dancers around them glided toward the edges of the dance floor, the last strains of the quadrille fading and the cacophony of the crowd taking their place.

He'd already said too much. He'd revealed his hand. She knew that he saw things about her future. Things she needed to do. His façade wouldn't last much longer if she kept pressing him. Not even the glittering mask on his face would be able to hide it.

Tonight was a night of revealed secrets, and it made his hands sweat.

His gaze flicked over the crowded ballroom. Everything about this ball made him sweat.

The youngest prince, glamoured to conceal his identity, took a step toward him.

"Tell her what?" the prince growled. Yes, that was the best way to describe it. Violence radiated from him.

Paulo's magic rushed through him, casting another layer over the ballroom. The glittering gowns around him sparkled even brighter with the magic, like a thousand constellations swirling around the room. He'd get a headache just trying to watch where he was going. He stepped away from Penny and the prince as they turned to one another. By the Goddess, the two of them would have been adorable if Paulo didn't feel like he was about to go into cardiac arrest. Best to leave them to the rest of their very promising evening.

They had a reservation with fate that evening that Paulo would do everything in his power to ensure would happen.

Even stopping a gorgeous assassin from killing the prince she'd been sent to kill.

By the Goddess, he wished he could just let her. If it was any other prince with any other future, he would. If it secured her future, if it saved her from her fate, he would let her. He'd let people die for the betterment of others before. Such was the natural order of things. But in this, he couldn't relent. He couldn't simply let the chips fall where they may.

Because if he didn't stop her, she would most definitely kill Prince Dion. Sweet Gaia, she could have done it ten times over if Paulo hadn't had his gift. She was smart, she was resourceful, and she was cursed good at her job.

Which was why tonight would be difficult.

Paulo swept through the crowd, doing his best to conceal himself from Penny and the Lord of the Underworld, which could prove to be difficult considering the man had the eyes of a blasted eagle. Honestly, the Goddess probably got a laugh out of watching him escape dismemberment from the people She continued to foist on him. He switched out his mask, changing from the glittering half mask that only concealed the skin around his eyes to the hooded mask he'd worn on the nights he'd gone to thwart Laurel.

The swish of a dark blue skirt caught his eye.

He followed it straight to the dessert table.

He watched in real time as Laurel poured a glass of the punch and took a sip.

Then, the magic showed her walking in the direction of Prince Dion and bumping into him, bringing their glasses together and allowing a bit of hers to splash into his. She was such a good poisoner it would have been impossible to catch if he'd not been watching for it and if his magic hadn't shown the Crown Prince taking a sip and falling to the ground not five minutes later, foam gathering at his mouth.

Paulo spun away from Laurel as she glided past the buffet. He shoved through a group of giggling debutants and knocked shoulders against one or two gentlemen. He lurched in Prince Dion's direction.

And ran straight into her.

The poisoned drink splashed all over the front of his dark blue waist coat and black jacket.

Laurel's brown eyes widened as she looked up at him in shock. Then they narrowed into dangerous slits.

He grinned. "Hello, Laurel. Have you missed me? I've certainly missed you."

She gritted her teeth and spun away from him.

He snatched her wrist, plucking the glass from her hand. "I don't think you'll be needing that where we're going."

Laurel tried to yank her hand away without causing a scene, but Paulo could read the obvious distress on her face. "Where are we going?"

He waved down one of the servers and put the glass on his empty tray. "Please have this glass disposed of. There's a crack in it that leaked all over my favorite waistcoat."

The server nodded and swept away, hopefully in the direction of a trash receptacle. Or a fire.

Laurel twisted her wrist, effectively breaking his hold on

her without anyone's notice. He bit back a curse. She swept through a pair of ladies.

Paulo followed right after her.

She darted through the crowd. Sweeping past giggling ladies and grinning gentlemen.

Paulo let his magic carry him forward and guide his path to her.

They collided at the edge of the dance floor just as the first strings of the waltz struck.

He swept her onto the floor.

"Let go of me."

"No."

He pulled her into the whirl of dancers as the music increased in tempo.

It was then he realized his mistake.

This wasn't a waltz.

"What are you doing?" Laurel hissed.

He pulled her closer, watching a handful of Aigeans and other aristocrats dance to the fast-paced music, their partners held closer than they would be in a waltz.

A small chuckled drew Paulo's eyes to Laurel. She quirked a brow at him. "Never seen an *Aigean Val* before?"

The name sounded familiar, but he couldn't say he kept up with all the dances brought to court. Donnie did a much better job of that, obvious as he glided over the floor with a young lady in his arms. Paulo's magic swept over the dancers, watching the way they twirled and how they swung their partners away from them before bringing them closely. He saw the way their feet moved, quick with the tempo of the music.

Laurel's spine straightened under his hand. "Maybe there is something I'm finally better at than you."

He met her eye. "Oh, I don't know about that."

Her mouth parted as he drew her close, their hearts pressed close to one another.

His magic melded with his body, fixing his mistakes before he made them. Dancing and fighting weren't so different, especially with the way Laurel moved.

She danced as beautifully as she fought.

Her hips swayed in time with the music, her skirts brushing over his boots as he led her over the marble dance floor. Her feet were quick, demanding as much of him as the music.

That was when she struck first.

She used her fingers to crush one of the pressure points in his hand.

He gasped and did his best not to draw attention to them. Instead, he used the heel of his boot to crush her toe.

She barely stumbled, but she did let go of the insanely painful grip she'd had on his hand. "That *hurt*, Lord Oliver."

Paulo pushed her away, grabbing one of the pins from her hair as he did. He tucked it in his pocket as he brought her back to him.

"I tried to tell you before. I think you have the wrong man."

She gritted her teeth and jabbed him in the neck with the hand that was laying on his shoulder. "Don't try to deny it now. I had all the proof I needed when I found your watch."

It took a few moments to regain his voice, which he used to spin her and pluck the other pin from her hair and reunite it with its partner in his pocket. When she came back and tried to reach inside his jacket, he dipped her back. Not his brightest idea. The daring neckline of her dress only grew more eye-catching. He swallowed and met her eyes. She practically dared him to look. He grinned mischievously and pulled her back up. She easily kept up with him as he swayed, their feet moving quickly under them.

Paulo tried to remember what she'd been saying. He'd stepped on her toe. His blasted cousin's name.

Oh, right. The pocket watch.

"Who says I didn't simply steal the watch?"

"Did you happen to steal the man's face as well? You look just like him."

Paulo cringed. "Oh dear. He's got an ugly mug if I've ever seen one."

Laurel frowned. "I don't think him ugly."

"So, you think I'm handsome? We're making excellent progress."

Her mouth opened with a retort, but he pushed her back, sliding a knife from her sleeve to distract her. By the Goddess, the woman could arm an entire company of palace guards with the steel she had smuggled into this ball. Paulo would have to have a word with Prince Dion after all this was over.

She grabbed his elbow and pressed her thumb into it. The pain had him hissing and he repositioned again, so she had to spin under that arm, letting go of the pressure point. He would be battered and bruised by the end of this cursed dance.

The song reached its climax, each instrument in the orchestra straining with the speed at which the musicians played.

She spun again and again under his arm, her feet constantly moving under her skirts as she matched the intensity of the song.

Paulo brought Laurel so close his cheek was pressed against hers. "Would it be presumptuous of me to say I think you might be the most beautiful woman in this room? That I would do anything to keep dancing with you?"

Laurel pushed him away that time, pulling him back violently enough to wrench the elbow she'd already likely bruised. The song took on its last strains.

"You can't distract me. I know who you are, and I'm more than prepared to take on a march's spare heir as long as I get what I want."

The final notes of the song played out and Paulo's feet moved in time with hers until the very last note, which he used to dip her back once more.

However, he made sure her gaze followed his.

"Then who's standing next to Diana and his recently acquired fiancé, Miss Aria?"

He knew Laurel found Oliver when she stiffened in his arms.

Paulo had asked Oliver to attend the ball with his fiancé. He'd also asked him to wear the same mask he did now, saying it would be great fun to confuse everyone.

However, anyone that looked at them side by side could see the obvious differences. Oliver's shoulders were broader, built from the hard work he'd done with the sheep. He stood a bit shorter than Paulo, too, not that anyone noticed until he stood next to Diana, who ended up being taller than him by at least half an inch. Paulo had two more inches on her, praise the Goddess. Oliver also had hazel eyes and slightly darker hair from his mother's side, though both boasted just as many freckles.

In a dark room and with a little bit of cosmetics, anyone would confuse the two of them.

Which had been Paulo's intent all along.

The song ended and the crowd around them clapped.

Paulo slowly drew Laurel up. The moment stretched out between them, his magic finally settling as it snapped into the present and faded into a dull ache behind his eyes.

Laurel finally straightened from the dip, her brown eyes meeting his. And it was with certainty that she finally spoke.

"Lord MacGregor."

27
THE MASK

Laurel had seen it. She wasn't a complete idiot. She had been on his trail. Had been moments away from discovering him.

But he'd known. He'd known she would figure it out and so he threw her a red herring.

And she'd been fool enough to chase after it.

The clapping around them slowed, the dancers shuffling off as the musicians started the next set.

"It's been you all along. You've known who I was from the very beginning— from the moment I stepped foot into Eleusia seven months ago. *You knew.*"

Lord MacGregor didn't move. He only held her gaze, finally ceasing his denials. Why would he try to distract her now? He wanted her to know who he was, now that he'd finally brought ruin to her. Now that he'd destroyed every chance she had of freeing Aspen.

The Master of Ceremonies called over the crowd, summoning the attendees to the center of the ballroom for Prince Dion to make a special announcement.

Laurel tried to break from Lord MacGregor's hold, but he

held firm. His eyes flicked about, and he shook his head the slightest bit.

"Not here."

Without another word, he pulled her through the crush.

She let him.

Why not? It wasn't like she had a chance of escaping him. She'd never had a chance. He had been hundreds of steps ahead of her the entire time.

He pulled her into one of the private sitting rooms. There wasn't a soul in the room, and he quickly locked the door behind him.

She ripped the mask from her face. "Why?"

Lord MacGregor followed suit, removing the mask from his head and setting his wild red curls free. "Why what?"

She threw the mask at his face, which he dodged. The glimmer in his eyes made her want to throw something else. "Why the ruse? Why all the secrets and everything? Why make me think it was your cousin?"

"You would have left."

Laurel threw her hands in the air. "Well, all your hard work was for nothing." Her tongue froze in her mouth, the geas enacting its magic to keep her from spilling its secrets.

Lord MacGregor took a step toward her. "You would have left, Laurel. You would have gone back to your master and everything I've been trying to accomplish would have been wasted."

"Well, sorry to say that's now going to happen. I'll be telling my Order everything, and all your scheming will still get your little prince killed in his sleep, only this time he will be most certainly joined by his wife and every other member of his family."

Lord MacGregor shook his head. "It's too late, Laurel. Your

master is already beyond the Mist, and I can assure you, he's not coming back any time in the near future."

Laurel clenched her skirt in her fingers. Her heart skipped. "What is that supposed to mean?"

Lord MacGregor took another step toward her. "It means that I got what I was after. Now, you really can't leave, and you and I can accomplish what we need to together."

She scoffed. "You are a lunatic! How can you think for one moment that I will want anything to do with you after this?" She strode for the door. "In fact, if I ever see you or that stupid mask ever again, I'll kill you."

Before she could open the door, he spun her around.

"I've seen your future, Laurel. Yours was the first I ever saw."

His lips captured hers.

But she only allowed him to cage her for one beat of her heart.

She shoved him away. "Don't ever try to kiss me again."

And she left.

Laurel stared at the dress laying on the empty bed across from her along with all the supplies she'd had scattered about the kitchens. Months' worth of work, relegated to a small pile of items on Delilah's stripped bed with nothing to show for it.

By the Goddess, she really had been such a fool.

And now, she was an even greater one.

There was nowhere for her to go.

She couldn't stay in the palace. Lord MacGregor knew about her, knew everything she would ever do. She had no chance to kill the prince even if she had a lifetime to do it. He'd been blasted waiting for her, and for what? To convince her to switch sides? To fulfill some sick fantasy of his that his magic made him think could be real?

And she'd kissed him.

Cursed blasted idiot!

She flipped over on her bed to stare at the ceiling.

Why was she the one who had to go on this mission? Why couldn't everyone just leave her and Aspen alone for once? She wiped frustrated tears from her eyes. She needed to come up with a plan. If she was ever to get word to Aspen, she needed to wait for Teagan to come back from taking down the Mist. She could explain what happened. He could remove the geas. She would go back to scrimping and saving for a few more years until she could buy the contracts.

Her thoughts stilled. No, he wouldn't let her out of this

This was exactly what he wanted. This was why he'd put the geas on her in the first place. If she couldn't do her job, he got to trap her. He would wait until she was desperate, then he would come to her with a deal. And it wouldn't be easy. After she disappointed him, it wouldn't be enough for her to simply come back. She would have to sign away the rest of her life. There would be no picking through jobs and appeasing her honor. She would be his puppet and there would be nothing she could say no to.

So that left two other routes.

She could stay here in Olympia, find a job in some remote corner of the kingdom where no one would ever find her, and live a life of solitude until she died of old age and regret.

Or she could kill the prince who was about to become king.

She sat up slowly in her bed.

That also meant she would have to kill the oracle that could stop her.

Sliding out of her blankets, she gathered up the few

weapons she had left. Cursed man hadn't given her back her blades. She had three throwing knives, a pair of brass knuckles, and her poison jacket. Not to mention the handy garotte wire in her trousers. By the Goddess, they really were such a great investment.

She ran her fingers over the pocket with the Stellataen Arrow. If she gave it to the prince, would it count as her killing him? Would the geas release her from its binding? She recalled the exact words from the geas.

Laurel Flumen will remain within the bounds of Olympia's borders until she assassinates Dion of Olympian royal blood, and if she leaves, will forfeit her life and die the moment she crosses the border.

No, he had to be dead.

She looked over the other poisons. She truly didn't wish to kill any innocents, and Adira had clearly stated Laurel wasn't to kill the other princes, so using a breathable poison wasn't an option, considering they were all in the same place at any given moment. Why did the princes have to be such supportive brothers? She shook her head. There was no reason to blame people for their good choices. If anyone understood the bond between siblings, Laurel did.

The wedding was supposed to take place at the temple that morning. She put the jacket on and buttoned it to her chin. If she was able to get into the temple, she might be able to poison something. The altar. The king's crown. Something.

The sky outside the room's only window lightened the smallest bit as she picked up the dress and started to fold it up. She had time. The coronation hadn't started yet. She had until then to kill Prince Dion. She just needed to be quick about it.

The snick of the doorhandle cut through the silence of her room.

Her gaze whipped to the door as a shadow slipped in.

The dress in her hands didn't hit the floor before she was on her assailant.

He smashed against the wall with an audible *oof*.

"By the Goddess, I didn't expect you to be this pleased to see me."

Laurel's entire body both flared with heat and trickled with cold.

"I am going to kill you," she said between her teeth.

Lord MacGregor yawned. "I can't tell you how many times I've been on the receiving end of that threat."

She pulled a knife from her waist.

"Oh yay! Hopefully I can add this one to my collection as well."

She stabbed at his neck.

He dodged it of course, grabbing her and spinning her around so her back was pressed to the wall. "Really, Laurel. I thought we've been through this already."

She dropped, using her body weight to slip from his grasp. She took a stab at his knee, but he jumped back.

"I really only want to talk."

Laurel flipped the blade in her hand. "And I really only want you to stop blasted talking."

Her blade flew in his direction. He leapt to the side, landing on Delilah's bed, and the blade ricocheted harmlessly off the stone wall behind him.

"I know you're mad."

Laurel barked a laugh. "You're right. I'm absolutely furious. How dare you come in here and act like we're old bosom pals. How dare you show up again when I'm at my lowest point. How dare you show up to stop me from doing the one thing that will save my family. *How. Dare. You.*"

"Laurel—"

"No, *my lord*." She threw a punch. He diverted it and sent it into the headboard. She didn't even hiss at the pain. "You think that you know me because of some crazy visions you've had in the past, but you don't."

He used his boots to shove her back. The backs of her legs hit the bed, and she fell onto her blankets. He leaped across the small space between them and pinned her to the mattress.

A knock sounded on the door.

Both Laurel and Lord MacGregor stilled. By the Goddess, was the door even locked? Could whoever it was simply walk in? What would they see?

"Laurel?" Cook's voice was muffled through the door. "Are you all right in there, dear?"

Laurel didn't take her eyes off Lord MacGregor. He watched her, though the pearlescent sheen had faded.

He also didn't let her go.

"I'm fine, Cook," Laurel called back. "Just dropped a pin on the side of my bed."

Other voices joined Cook in the hall. "Well, I'm glad to hear you're feeling better. We're headed up to the temple. Do you want us to wait for you?"

Ah, yes. The wedding. The coronation. Laurel's imminent loss of freedom.

"I seem to be in a bit of a bind." She gritted her teeth as the corner of Lord MacGregor's mouth turned up in a smirk. "No need to wait for me. I'll find you down there."

The voices grew louder. "If you're sure..."

"Absolutely," Laurel said in her cheeriest voice.

They didn't move as the voices faded away. Laurel studied Lord MacGregor as they waited. He still wore his punch-stained waistcoat. His red hair curled boyishly at his ears, but the eyes he studied her with were anything but boyish. They seemed to hold lifetimes in their depths.

What horrors had he seen? What joys? Why didn't he use

his gifts to take over the kingdom? Was it simply that he wanted to be a good man? Then why wouldn't he tell the princes about Adira Durant. If he knew about Laurel and why she was in Olympia, then he had to know about Adira's plans.

"I can practically see the gears in your head spinning," Lord MacGregor said.

She narrowed her eyes at him. "Aren't you supposed to be at a wedding? Aren't there lordly things to do and allegiances to swear and all that?"

"I can assure you, everything is going exactly according to plan down at the temple. Besides, I would think stopping the woman who was intending to murder the groom is all the help they need."

Laurel sighed and closed her eyes. "Why haven't you turned me in?"

Lord MacGregor took a moment, his brows drawing down, before he rolled to the side and sat next to her on the bed. "If I told you, you wouldn't believe me."

Laurel wiped a hand down her face. "After having seen your magic at work, I think I would believe anything you say."

Lord MacGregor gave a humorless laugh. "Then perhaps you would run for the hills instead. It is a bit of madness on my part, and I don't think our relationship has developed to the point where I feel the need to reveal all the skeletons in my closet just yet."

"I'm a skeleton now, am I?"

Lord MacGregor's expression turned solemn. "No and it's my fervent prayer you never will be."

Laurel shook her head. "I really don't understand you."

"Sometimes, I hardly understand myself."

Maybe he really was a lunatic.

"So, what are we going to do now, my lord? You won't

allow me to fulfill my mission, and I can't simply give up. What are the two of us to do?"

"Do you truly want to know what I think we should do?"

"No. I just asked to fill the silence."

Lord MacGregor heaved a dramatic sigh and went to stand. "Well then, I suppose I'll just be going…"

Laurel sat up. "Sit back down." She grabbed the sleeve of his jacket. "What are you trying to accomplish here?"

"Honestly?"

"Obviously."

A sad smile tugged at the edge of his lips. "I'm trying to gain your trust."

He certainly had a funny way of showing it. "Why? What does my trust matter to you?"

The light from the window highlighted the deep planes of his face. His chin, his cheekbones, his brow. She watched his expression flick from emotion to emotion. Heartache, fear, frustration, determination. Her heart sat in her throat. What had he seen?

"All I can say, Laurel, is that your future is yours to seize, yours to take from those who have kept it from you for so long, and I want to be there when you finally steal it back from them."

His words held her mind captive. She couldn't speak, her tongue cemented to the roof of her mouth. Even if she could speak, what would she say to that?

So, she stayed silent, staring out the small window of her room, waiting for the bells of the city to ring in their new king.

Lord MacGregor left once the sun was fully in the sky.

The first chorus of bells sounded just after he closed the door.

28

THE PROMOTION

Queen Carnation, Cook, and the palace housekeeper will be gathered around a table, their brows drawn together as they speak. Laurel's name will be on their lips. The queen will set her cup down and politely command Cook to fetch Laurel as quickly as possible before the day truly starts.

THE WEEK FOLLOWING THE WEDDING PASSED BY IN A BLUR.

The youngest prince had been taken, just as Teagan had said he would be. An entire contingent of guards had gone to the border. Speculation about what the King and Prince Evan would do to fetch their younger brother bounced around the palace.

That was it then. She'd officially missed the deadline. Soon enough, the Mist would be gone from the border and Teagan would arrive back to get the job done. While the thought of Teagan's incoming punishment made her stomach twist uncomfortably, the only regret she felt was for Aspen. If only Laurel could have freed her.

And while she could have given Aspen the money to buy off her own contract, now Laurel couldn't even do that. She should have simply done it the moment she could instead of being greedy and trying to make sure both of them got out. That they could be together.

Laurel needed to figure out what she was going to do next. Where in Olympia she could even go now.

But word had come back from the border three days later.

The Mist still stood.

And it was locked. One couldn't even cross into the magic fog.

Laurel watched for *The Shining River* to return to the harbor for three more days. It never came.

Teagan was as trapped as she was.

Somehow, Laurel knew this was simply a hiccup. The Mist was likely to fall any day now. It meant she still had time to figure out what her next steps would be. She couldn't kill the prince outright, but maybe she could still come up with something. Still figure out how to fulfill the terms of the geas. To get back to Aspen.

One week after King Dion's coronation, Laurel woke to a knock on her door.

"Laurel, dear? You awake in there?"

Laurel withheld a groan and went to the door. Cook stood in the hallway, a clean apron tied around her waist and her light-brown curls still tucked into their pins. This polished look of hers only ever lasted until she got to the kitchens.

"Is something the matter?" Cook didn't often come to the doors in the morning, usually relying on the threat of unemployment to get the rest of the staff out of bed in time to prepare breakfast for the palace.

"Nothing's the matter, but I'd like to have a word in Esther's office this morning."

Laurel's stomach sank. "Of course. Let me just throw on my frock."

Cook nodded and Laurel closed the door. By the Goddess, what now? Would she finally lose this job too? Had Lord MacGregor turned her in? She nearly tore her dress as she shoved her arm into the sleeve. The man left her with too many questions for her liking. She should have tried harder to kill him.

With her attire more appropriate for a meeting with the housekeeper— *palacekeeper?*— Laurel joined Cook in the hallway.

"Is there anything I should be worried about?" Not that she wasn't worried already. "I hope this isn't about what happened with Delilah."

It had been almost two blissful weeks since the ex-under-cook left the palace, and Laurel hadn't heard one peep about where she'd gone or what happened to her. There was no doubt that Delilah could have found someone to take her in. She was determined and ambitious, though she went about using those particular skills in a very selfish way. The girl's threats from the last time Laurel had seen her popped up in her mind.

I'm going to expose you. If I have to lose my position, you should too.

Cook pursed her lips, her distress about Delilah's termina-tion evident. "I suppose it's in relation to her situation."

Oh, dear.

Laurel followed Cook through the servants' quarters and into the small set of offices used by the housekeeper, the seneschal, and other higher-ranking servants. The corridor wasn't ostentatious like the rest of the palace, but it wasn't in any sort of disrepair. The dark wood gleamed with fresh polish and a wide vase of purple asters set on a table.

Cook knocked on a door before pushing it open. Light bloomed out into the hallway and Cook gestured for Laurel to proceed her. Never a good idea to go into a room first, but Cook didn't look to be hiding one of her wicked cleavers under her skirts.

Laurel stepped through the doorway. Esther as well as Queen Carnation were seated around a small table, similar to how they'd been during her interview. This time, however, Queen Carnation greeted her with a small smile. Laurel returned the expression with a deep curtsy.

"Good morning, Laurel," Esther greeted her. "I'm sorry for the early wake up, but I hope you're feeling rested."

Laurel bobbed her head, remaining near the door. Any traces of exhaustion she might have felt fled at the heart racing she experienced in front of these women. Women who held her future in their hands. They could ruin any chances she had of deciding what she was going to do about her situation and figure out how to get to Aspen.

Cook took one of the empty seats and took up one of the cups on the table in front of them. The queen reached forward and poured Cook a cup of tea as if the servant was a great lady deserving of such regard.

"Sit Laurel," Cook said, nodding at the seat between her and Queen Carnation.

Laurel slowly stepped toward the chair. It would be more difficult for her to run if she had to leap out of a chair.

One of Queen Carnation's golden eyebrows curled up. "You look as if you're walking to the gallows."

"Until I'm sure of why the three women who could hand me a letter of termination without blinking an eye have invited me to sit down with them before the workday has even started, I think I'll remain a tad wary."

Cook snorted. "Please. If we wanted to be rid of you, we would've come when you least expected it."

Esther chuckled. "The first time Shaunie here attempted to schedule a firing, the server ransacked the kitchens and stole a dozen bottles of wine before the guards caught him."

Queen Carnation— or Shaunie as Esther referred to her— shook her head ruefully. "And I never did it again. Instead, I slap them with a termination letter as soon as the ink dries and have a guard escort them out with their belongings."

Laurel's shoulders relaxed, but only slightly. "So, may I ask what's caused you to invite me to..." She looked down at the table set with cups and little pieces of toast with cheese and jam. "Tea?"

"Actually, most of this is coffee." Cook plated one of the small pieces of toast, spreading a liberal amount of butter over it. "Tea is for those who have time to sleep in the middle of the day. Coffee is for the warriors."

Both Esther and the queen hummed their agreements and reached for their half-empty cups.

Laurel withheld a grimace and opted for the peppermint tea rather than drink the bitter concoctions in the other pots. She'd never really liked coffee. It was one of those flavors she could always taste no matter what she paired it with. Bananas, the few times she could get her hands on them, were the same.

"Now, to business," Esther said. She placed her cup down and picked up a small ledger. "As all of you know, we had to let go of Miss Delilah Westley and Cook is in need of a replacement."

All eyes turned to Laurel.

"Me?" She gaped. "You can't be serious."

"At least she's humble," Her Majesty quipped.

Cook patted Laurel's knee. "Of course we're serious. I need help and you're the best girl for the job. I've seen the way you move about the kitchen. You have recipes perfected after one glance at the cards and can wield a knife better than anyone else. Not to mention how you saved the *gazpacho* the other day. You've got a knack for cooking and it's about time we put it to use."

"I can assure you," Laurel said, "there are other girls more qualified than me and with much more experience." Not to mention more loyal.

The queen set her cup back on the table. "Yes, but how many of them will try to find their way to my husband's bed by the end of the year?"

At that, Laurel did grimace. "Who says I won't?"

Cook swatted at her, but the queen laughed, the sound still rough from disuse. It made Laurel want to help her laugh just so it could stretch its legs more. "I think that very question is an answer in itself. What woman with designs on my husband would ask that? Besides, after our conversation in the gardens a few weeks ago, I think you'll be the perfect fit."

Of course, that encounter had come to bite Laurel. She stared at the still steaming cup in her hands. "Am I allowed to refuse the position?"

Cook frowned. "Yes, but I'll do my best to convince you to reconsider. Your responsibilities will grow, but there are perks. The position comes with a raise and more time off. You'll have pick of your roommates. You'll have say in the menu. It will also reflect nicely on a letter of recommendation should you need to go find employment elsewhere for some reason."

Esther smiled. "Though, we hope to keep you for as long as we can."

Laurel closed her eyes. She didn't need a new position. Everything they offered her would tempt even the best of kitchen girls, but she wasn't one. Her small bit of anonymity would become null with such a position. She wouldn't be able to sneak out as much without eyes on her. She couldn't just be another face in a sea of servants. Too many people would know her.

If she took it, the chances of her figuring out a way to get back to Aspen would become that much harder.

She opened her mouth, a denial on her tongue, when Lord MacGregor's words from the night before popped into her mind.

Your future is yours to seize, yours to take from those who have held it back from you for so long, and I want to be there when you finally steal it back from them.

Curse it all! Did the man have to understand her so well? Couldn't she do anything in this kingdom without him popping up? She wanted to say no to the offer. To say she was leaving right then and there and race to her room to pack her things. All of it was enough to drive her to madness.

She sighed and opened her eyes. The trio of women looked at her with a mix of curiosity, acceptance, and anxiety.

"When would you need to know by?" she asked.

The queen pursed her lips. "We were hoping you would simply say 'yes' now and we could be done with it."

Cook patted Laurel's knee. "We aren't so understaffed it'll hurt anything for you to think on it. How about three days?"

She nodded. "I can have an answer for you by then."

Traversing the tunnels to the beach was easier than sneaking out through one of the gates, especially with the palace security on edge after the young prince's abduction. The lights from the palace sparkled even from the beach below the cliffs.

Laurel's boots left deep prints behind her. Olympia had received its first real snow for the season right before solstice—which apparently could stretch out into late spring according to Cook. While it had mostly melted in the city, it still stuck to the sand close to the cliffs. Stellatus Hall would get a bit of snow once or twice, but it stayed in the mountains for the most part and never made it to the coast. Snow on the beach was a peculiarity Laurel hadn't decided whether or not she liked.

The wind grabbed at her hood and blew it back onto her shoulders. She probably should have put on her mask, but she didn't feel like she deserved it at the moment. She wasn't worthy of such recognition.

By the Goddess, she really had been such a fool.

And now, she was an even greater one.

There was nowhere for her to go.

The offer of undercook would have thrilled anyone else in her position, but it only caused her a stab of pain. Being on a job for so long let assassins form bonds with the people around them. No one was immune to the desire to be well liked. Not even the smart assassins. Attachments made one weak. They led to mistakes.

Laurel didn't make mistakes. Not since she was a child.

The small lead weight hung heavy on her wrist. *Take care of Aspen*. It was the last thing Father had asked her to do.

She wanted to get back to her sister. The one attachment in this world she did have.

Two shapes appeared out of the fog, a couple bundled in a blanket on the beach. How they thought tonight was appropriate weather for such things, she could only guess. Perhaps Olympians were more insane than she even realized.

"Laurel?"

She stopped cold and turned back toward the bundles.

"It is you!"

A shape leapt out of the mist and practically tackled Laurel to the ground.

Laurel wobbled but kept her footing. *"Aspen?"* she whispered.

"Of course!" she exclaimed, pulling away. "Who else would it be?"

"How?" Laurel pulled away, looking her over. "You should be in Stellatus Hall. What are you doing here?"

The second bundle took shape through the fog. Luc took his place at Aspen's side. "We've been freezing our butts off for two days waiting for you to show your face here."

Laurel grabbed her sister's arm. "Why on Gaia's green earth didn't you reach out the moment you arrived?"

"You know we couldn't. Teagan has been very hush-hush about what you've been up to and doesn't want to risk anything. He said you hadn't reached out either, which either meant you were nearly finished with your assignment, or something went very wrong— which we all know it had to be the former since you've never had an assignment go wrong."

Laurel didn't quite have the heart to let her down at the moment, so she ignored the last bit. "But why are you here?"

Luc wrapped his arms tighter around himself. "He had to go to Faerie with the rebels, which you probably know already. He said he would be back after solstice, but he wanted us to start laying plans before he gets back."

Laurel's head swiveled between the two of them. "Plans? What plans?"

Aspen beamed as she bounced on her toes. "We're going to take over the palace!"

29
AN UNFORTUNATE SIBLING

Laurel will meet Aspen at the inn. Aspen will argue with her, saying Laurel should be able to get the job done and berating her for being selfish. Laurel will tell her about the king and what happened with the previous undercook. That same undercook will burst through the door and tell Laurel she's going to tell the king. Aspen will put a knife in the girl's throat.

SHADOWS SWIRLED ON THE PAGE UNDER PAULO'S PENCIL. THEY writhed in a circle, casting the entire page into darkness. Paulo could barely see the forms in the middle, the youngest prince holding Penny to his chest as his magic swirled around them.

His own chest ached. He'd seen too many reflections of this very moment in the string of his future, though his ending was not quite the same as the young prince's.

"How do you think Penny is doing?"

Paulo added a lighter stroke of color along the edges, the

gray of mist rather than the black of shadow. "She hasn't even reached Faerie yet."

"Really? What has she been doing this entire time?"

"From what I've seen, she's still in the Mist, though it will feel like only moments to her when she gets out." Time in the Mist was interesting that way. It was one of the few places in the world that followed its own rules. Paulo would know. Penny would arrive in Faerie in a little over a month. The Goddess needed to accomplish a few things before She could set Penny on that kingdom, it seemed. There were quite a few things that needed to happen in Olympia as well.

He turned back to his drawing. By the Goddess, his friend truly would be fighting for her life for the next several months. Hopefully, the youngest prince— well, now he would be High King— would come to his senses sooner rather than later and let Penny help him accomplish what they needed to together.

Not that they wouldn't. There were some things that were more certain than others. After the solstice ball, things had been set in motion that couldn't be undone unless someone knew to keep it from happening.

Which Paulo did and he wouldn't.

However, sometimes there were those that tried to fight Fate and ended up causing themselves much more turmoil than they had ever probably wanted.

Which Paulo was and he would.

The closest of the city's clocktowers chimed the noon hour. The small square where they sat circled a large fountain, one of the waterways for the citizens to access clean water for their businesses or homes. The cold weather from the past several days had left the top layer of water frozen, icicles dripping down from the tiered bowls where water usually poured out of to splash into the larger basin.

Several young ladies burst from alleyway next to an inn, *The Breezy Lady*.

"Which one is Aspen?" Diana asked.

A girl with ashy-blond hair skipped across the street, headed for the fountain in the center of the square ahead of them. Several girls stood along the edge, each collecting water to take home for the day. Paulo flipped a few pages back in his sketchbook and found the exact moment she touched a finger to the half-frozen water sketched onto the page.

"That one there." She really didn't look much like Laurel. There were similarities in the shape of their faces, but besides that and their dark brown eyes, there was little that revealed the two women as siblings.

Diana cracked each side of her neck. "Are you sure? I didn't think she'd be so tall."

Paulo snapped the sketchbook closed. "You can tell it's Aspen because of the way she is."

Diana looked over at him. "What does that even mean?"

He nudged his chin in the girl's direction. They both watched as she plucked an icicle from the edge of the fountain, twirling it in her hand, before throwing it at the wooden sign hanging above the door of the local newspaper. It stuck out right of the middle of the O in *Olympian Tribune*. With a satisfied nod, she filled the bucket she'd been carrying and headed to the inn where she'd taken temporary employment.

"Have you told Laurel?"

Paulo shook his head and tugged his wool cap down over his ears. He didn't need to. She already knew. He stood from the crate he'd been using as a chair and dusted off his pants. They weren't part of his regularly flamboyant attire, but this outfit would help him blend in. The scarf covering the bottom half of his face and the dirt he'd scrubbed over his freckles would hopefully keep Aspen from recognizing him in the future. Diana handed him a bucket of paste and the small stack of flyers he'd had printed the day before. He stepped onto the street and walked in the direction of the inn.

Voices hushed as the bell above him rang and he strode toward the back counter where a young man stood, wiping out glasses and nodding at customers. Aspen had stopped next to him and was shooting him a pretty smile reserved for those who held a girl's special attention.

The man looked up as Paulo approached. "Good morning," he said. "How can we help you?"

"Got an advertisement to put up in your window." Paulo pulled the stack of flyers out from under his arm. "The palace is looking for another kitchen girl."

Aspen visibly perked up. "Oh, really?" She came around the counter and took one of the flyers. Her eyes lit and she looked back to the man behind the counter.

"Mind if I stick one in the window there?"

The man shook his head. "Sorry, but I don't think the owner wants anything in the windows. Blocks the view of the street for customers."

Paulo nearly rolled his eyes. "Are you certain? It would really help me out."

Aspen held up the flyer still in her hand. "Perhaps I can keep this one and give it to the owner?"

Paulo bobbed his head. "I suppose that could work." He tucked the flyers back under his arm. "Good day, then!" He didn't allow himself to glance back at the couple as he swept out the door.

When he'd made it halfway down the street, Diana joined him. Paulo scanned the street and saw the group of young boys tucked near the outer wall of a chimney. They huddled close to the bricks, their eyes flicking warily over each passerby.

Paulo pointed toward them. "There's our little messengers."

Diana took the rest of the flyers and walked over to the group. Paulo would have taken them himself, but Diana's presence was much less abrasive. For all the times she wished she didn't have to be relegated to the societal standards of womanhood, there were benefits to being a member of the fairer sex that Paulo could not acquire. He smiled as she gave the boys orders then handed each of them a small bag of dried fruit and nuts. The treat would be sweet without upsetting their hungry stomachs. Coins would only get them attacked by bigger thugs on the street. The boys snatched up the flyers and the paste and raced down the street like a herd of wild geese.

Diana returned to his side, a grin on her face.

"Hopefully, they can get a few of the flyers up before they toss them into the street." Paulo watched a few of the papers fall from the stack and land in the middle of the road.

They turned away from the square.

Diana straightened the collar of her long coat. "So, what's next?"

Paulo sighed. "Once Aspen gets into the palace, there will be things that need to get setup. We need to sit down with Lady Delmar. There are several things she will need to be aware of in the next few months and as she will become the new Lord of the Underworld, it's best we meet with her sooner rather than later."

"I can ask Caspian about becoming friends with her. He seems to know quite a bit about her."

Paulo bit his tongue. It seemed Diana had finally forgiven the selkie for humiliating her at their match. Not that Paulo was surprised in the least. Even if he hadn't had visions of the future, he couldn't count the number of times Caspian had popped up to talk to his sister recently. The two of them had certainly gotten closer over the last several weeks. Not that he was worried about romantic attachments. Diana wasn't looking to woo anyone, least of all a selkie with a competitive streak. No, the two of them were simply becoming fast friends and there was nothing Paulo could do about it.

Not now.

"I'm sure a simple invitation to tea will do the trick," Paulo suggested instead. "We could even see if Adam can come." Penny's disappearance would leave a mark on the man. Paulo knew it was all for the greater good, but he also knew Penny was one of the best women in the kingdom. He was sure the blow to Adam's pride would have him questioning his own worth for a while. Which, unfortunately for him, would help things move along in the next few months.

If only Paulo could save everyone and make everything better just with the snap of his fingers.

"Fine, you can invite Adam, but I can't do tea until tomorrow. I'm going spear fishing this afternoon."

Paulo smiled, but he felt how flat it was. "And leave me all by my lonesome up at the palace? Who knows what kind of trouble I could get into?"

Diana punched him on the shoulder. "You get up to plenty of trouble with or without me being in the palace. Besides, we both know you can't avoid talking to her for forever. The more I leave you alone, the faster you'll realize you just need to have a real conversation with her."

Paulo groaned. "She tried to stab me, Diana."

"So? I try to stab you all the time and you don't whine about it nearly this much."

"Maybe I'm tired of getting stabbed at."

"Maybe you need to get stabbed at more."

She would suggest that.

But perhaps there was a little wisdom in what she was

trying to say. He couldn't gain Laurel's trust if he waited for her to come to him. Just because they no longer had their nightly run-ins when she was trying to kill King Dion didn't mean that he couldn't find other ways to see her, to let her get to know him. While she may not have accepted the position as under-cook quite yet, that didn't mean she wouldn't. He'd worked too hard to let her go now. If letting her take a few more stabs at him kept her close, he would risk it.

"Your silence is very telling you know," Diana said. "You're deciding how to tell me that I'm right and you will be returning to wooing our Laurel with the stabbing."

Paulo rolled his eyes. "Heathen."

"Pompous crybaby."

30
THE INN

THE FOLLOWING DAYS WERE FULL OF LAUREL MEMORIZING RECIPES and new techniques. Being an undercook came with many more lessons than being a kitchen girl had. There were protocols to be followed, more recipes to memorize, and meals to plan. Laurel fell into the rhythm of it, rising early and falling into her bed late. She barely remembered to take her full-day off and when it came, she realized she didn't know what to do with herself. She'd eventually decided to track down where Aspen was staying and started a line of communication between the two of them. Laurel had been away too long.

She stretched her arms over her head as she walked over to the table and helped Cook layer flour over the entire tabletop. However, it put her close to Galen who glared at her. His garnet eyes held a promise in them that Laurel didn't wish to look too deep into. She grabbed one of the aprons hanging on the wall and threw the loop over her head.

"Oh, I forgot to get the *hummus* going." Cook wiped her hands on her apron. "You get these *pitas* flattened, and I'll be back to help get them in the oven."

Cook scurried into the pantry and Laurel grabbed her rolling pin.

The screech of stool legs on the floor had her turning back to where Galen had been sitting. He strode toward her, that promise still swirling in his eyes.

He stopped only a step away from her and folded his arms over his chest. "I don't know what your game is, but I know you're the one who got Delilah fired."

Laurel set a hand to her chest. Her training set in. "I didn't get Delilah fired."

There were a million ways to lie, and most people chose the wrong ones. Many tried to distract from a conversation. Many spoke in circles or even went on the defensive from the get-go. Laurel had learned to read those little tells, watch how people recounted stories or what their bodies did differently. She'd trained herself to ignore all those tendencies, to believe what she was saying and say only the lies in truth's form.

Besides, Delilah got herself fired by fraternizing with the Crown Prince turned king. Laurel just expedited it.

Galen's jaw tightened. "We know it was you. I didn't even know that Delilah and the king..." He shook his head. "I didn't know why she would get fired and she said you were the only one who did."

Laurel kept eye contact with him. "She did tell me, and I helped her. I didn't want her to get fired." And that was true. She didn't want to ruin Delilah's life, but that didn't mean she wouldn't do things she didn't like to accomplish her goals.

"It was you," Galen swore. He stuck a finger in her face. "And I'm going to expose you and get Delilah her job back."

Laurel blew out a breath. *Time to press some buttons.* "Galen, I'm truly sorry for what happened to Delilah. I don't know how it all went down, but I don't think Queen Carnation would give her the job back. Not after what she was doing. She won't be allowed back into the palace."

"Delilah belongs here!" he snapped. "You are the one who needs to go!"

"Galen!" Cook barked. She dropped the bowl of chickpeas and bottle of olive oil on the table. "You've no right to talk to Laurel that way. You can't blame the girl for taking Delilah's position when I practically begged her to."

Galen shoved a finger in Laurel's face, and it took everything she had not to break it. "She's a liar and I know it was her that got Delilah fired."

Cook grabbed his arm and pulled him to the side. "She did no such thing. In fact, it was one of the guards who caught Delilah coming back to her rooms. He reported the incident to Esther who had to report it to Lady Carnation. It all came out after that."

"I know it was her." Galen's chest rose and fell in quick breaths. "Delilah knows it was her."

Cook set her fists on her hips. "Delilah made her own choices and got caught. You can't blame someone else for the misbehaviors of another. We all have to face our mistakes, whether in this life or the next. Delilah made a poor choice and now she has to deal with the consequences."

With a final glare at Laurel, Galen stomped from the room.

Laurel bit the inside of her cheek. It was too bad she couldn't simply poison him and blame it on pretend assassins. Getting him fired would be next to impossible as well. Laurel would have to lie low for a little bit to avoid giving his suspicions any credence.

Cook patted her shoulder. "Don't put too much stock in his words, dear. He's hurt and simply trying to come to terms with it."

"Do you think he could get me fired?" She pushed a bit of worry into her voice. "He has the king's ear."

Cook waved her off. "Nonsense. Even if he could get His Majesty to try something, the queen has full power when it comes to the staff. She was the one who suggested you for the position in the first place, and she will fight to defend her choices, whether her husband approves or not. Usually, he acquiesces to her in the end, so I would praise the Goddess you have such a champion on your side."

Laurel nodded and gave Cook a small smile. "I really do hope Delilah is able to get back on her feet and Galen can find peace with what has happened."

"As do I, my dear."

Laurel continually checked over her shoulder as she walked down the street. Aspen had asked to meet that night, but Galen's threats whispered from the shadows.

Of course, Delilah would still be causing grief. It wasn't like the girl could quietly fade into nonexistence and never bother Laurel again. No, she had to keep her threats fresh in Laurel's mind and make her second guess herself at every turn. Even now, when she was supposed to be helping Aspen, she had to worry about Delilah or Galen sniffing about.

Lying low, indeed. Honestly, she should have stayed in the palace that night, but she couldn't say no to Aspen.

The capital had returned to its normal pace after the events surrounding solstice. The garlands of evergreens and holly had been taken down from the magelight posts. The smell of cinnamon and cardamom still hung in the air but was subdued by the stench of smoke from the houses and factories returned to normal. Even the snow looked dirtier than it had that week, though snowflakes were already building up to hide away the muck of the past.

While Laurel had used the tunnels to get out of the palace, she hadn't gone to the docks. Luc had apparently found employment with an inn that also acted as a rebel front in the city. While Laurel couldn't involve Adira's people in her mission, she understood Luc's predicament. And while Aspen would meet Laurel wherever, it had been clear for years she didn't want to leave Luc out of anything if she didn't have to.

Laurel nodded as she passed by a pair of watchmen. It felt as if their presence in the city had grown as well. Like everyone could feel the coming conflict, and while their words reflected ease and safety, their actions did not.

The Breezy Lady came into view. A crowd of men stood on the front stoop, their voices low as they smoked their pipes. How many of them were rebels, Laurel couldn't rightly tell, but more than a few of them had blades hidden on their persons.

She ducked around one of the other buildings on the small square, taking a more discrete route toward the back of the inn. When the building came back into view, she found Luc and Aspen huddled together, their faces not far from each other.

Laurel rolled her eyes. "Don't the two of you have enough time to flirt when I'm not here?"

Aspen turned to her, a grin on her face. "One of these days you're going to find a man who looks at you like you hold the very future in your hands and then you'll have to eat your words."

Why the image of Lord MacGregor popped into Laurel's head, she couldn't say. She plucked it out and sent it far, far into the recesses of her mind where she would hopefully never think of it again.

"Not likely," she said. "Now, I'm assuming you didn't ask

me to come simply to talk about our romantic lives or the lack thereof."

Luc smirked, settling an arm over Aspen's shoulders. "If it wasn't so blasted cold and I didn't only have five minutes for a quick break, we would."

With a groan, Aspen stuffed her hands farther into her long jacket. "Let's make this quick then. I think I figured out how to get into the palace and start our siege."

"What did you find?"

Aspen withdrew a piece of paper from her pocket and unfolded it. An advertisement for a new kitchen girl at the palace.

Aspen grinned. "How would you feel about working with your little sister?"

"Are you sure you don't want to look for a scullery maid position first?" Laurel made a face. "The last time I tried to let you cook, you put the sweet pudding in the *tzatziki* sauce instead of the yogurt."

"That was one time!" Aspen gave her a little shove. "And I distinctly remember you nearly burning down the Hall's kitchen cooking *kleftiko*."

Laurel laughed. "I had hoped I got the oven low enough to cook the lamb since I couldn't do it the way Father had in the pit behind our house."

Father had left the entire lamb they'd gotten for summer solstice in the ground on a bed of coals for hours. Laurel remembered her six-year-old stomach nearly bursting. They'd laughed and sang, four-year-old Aspen's braids swinging as she danced to Father's deep baritone. Then, Birdie, their mother, came home and put an end to their frivolity. As she always had.

Laurel rubbed the small lead weight she'd wrapped around

her wrist that morning. "When are you supposed to hear about an interview?"

"Who says I haven't already?" Aspen grinned. "They said they wanted to see me in two weeks. Apparently, I was their first applicant."

"Of course you were." She'd always been able to do anything she set her mind to with ease. It was a magic all her own.

The back door to the inn opened. "Luc! Your break is supposed to be over."

Laurel's entire body stiffened. She would recognize that voice anywhere.

Delilah.

"Sheesh, I'm coming." Luc slid his arm from Aspen's shoulders and turned, exposing the back door.

And Delilah's seething eyes.

Luc gave her an odd look as he passed but shrugged and swept into the inn.

Delilah followed after him, but Laurel wouldn't forget the way Delilah's eyes had gleamed when she'd noticed her there.

"Poor Luc. He's been dealing with that little witch since she started here a week ago." Aspen shook her head and turned back to Laurel. "You've already been through the interview process at the palace. Any tips for me?"

Laurel kept her eyes on the back door. "Yes. Don't make cow eyes at the king."

31
AN UNFORTUNATE VISION

Sometimes, Paulo wished he had magic like other mages.

Most mages had full control over their gifts. King Dion could control his lightning and storms at a whim, using as little or as much as he wanted at any given time, so long as he was prepared for the consequences. Penny could fill a room with ferns if she got anxious enough, but even still she could control herself and her magic. Even the youngest prince— oh sweet Gaia it was going to be difficult for Paulo to remember the man was now High King of Faerie instead of simply Olympia's spymaster after telling himself not to for months— had control over both his mage and fae gifts. Though, Paulo couldn't imagine how he did it. Every mage or fae or water folk in the world seemed to be able to pick and choose when their magic was used.

Not Paulo.

No, he was at the Goddess's whims, and it didn't matter where he was or what he was doing, visions could take over his mind at any time. While he could use his magic to a certain extent, he never knew when the Goddess would play with his head.

Paulo was sitting in the middle of a council meeting, staring at Lady Barclay's empty chair, when the visions hit him.

The palace overrun by men and women with compasses sewn onto their sleeves.

Aspen stealing a small box from a safe behind a map.

Blood spattered on the walls of the entrance hall.

The king, his expression broken and eyes haunted.

A silver mask next to a bottle of dark blue poison.

The queen, staring lifelessly at the ceiling above her bed.

Laurel's angry face, staring back at him behind bars.

He shoved away from the table, knocking his chair to the floor.

Every head turned in his direction. A servant scurried forward to right his chair, but he didn't sit back down. What had he just seen?

"Lord MacGregor?"

Paulo looked up to the head of the table.

The king's brow furrowed. "Is something the matter?"

Paulo blinked. Something was most certainly the matter, but he didn't know how or what or why yet. He straightened his jacket and finally retook his seat. "No, Your Majesty. Apologies for my disturbance."

King Dion frowned but turned back to Lord Hermen. "So, there has been no contact with your people in Faerie since solstice?"

"No, Your Majesty," Lord Hermen replied. "My daughter wrote just before the Mist locked, saying they were expecting to be in Winter for some time. The Court there had certain rules they had to follow, considering the lack of a ruler there, but Angelica was hopeful they would figure out a way to broker some sort of agreement."

Paulo dug the heel of his palm into his chest. Angelica Elie — formerly Angelica Hermen before she had been married— had gone to Faerie almost a year ago to establish trade between Olympia and the various Faerie Courts. While she and her husband had been successful with Spring, Summer, and even some places in Autumn, getting the Winter Court to sign anything would be worse than pulling out goblin teeth.

Which Paulo had known when he'd first put it into the council's mind to start negotiations there.

Which was why he had rallied the vote in favor of sending them right after they'd been married. Perhaps it hadn't been the most romantic idea for a honeymoon, but Paulo had been able to convince even her father to send them, and the rest of the council had voted in favor of it.

And praise the Goddess they had.

Penny was going to need her third best friend since her two best friends— Paulo then Diana, respectively— had to stay in Olympia while she raced around Faerie looking for the prince — The High King. *High King.*

"I'm most concerned about not being able to reach my brother," the king said.

"Do you wish to attack, sire?" asked General Draco. His eyes gleamed with the thought of violence

The king sighed. "No. We don't even know if an offensive strategy is possible with the Mist closed as it is. Besides, it isn't wise to go in, swords flailing, if we don't know what's going on there. The fae can't lie, so what they said when they took him had to be true. If he is to be their king, then they won't harm him. It's only the unknown I worry over. If this rebellion is not squashed, we may need to call for aid, and I don't wish for communication between our allies to be cut off when we need it most."

Lady Alvis cleared her throat. "We don't only rely on Faerie for their alliance with us, Your Majesty."

Paulo looked down the table to where Adam sat. "Yes, sire. The Aigeans have been valiant supporters of your reign. I would be remiss not to remind you that they aren't blocked off as the fae are."

King Dion waved a hand. "Yes, and I won't forget. There are simply too many variables, and it seems we are walking straight into the dark without any hope of illumination."

A piece of a vision skittered past Paulo's view just before the doors to the council chambers burst open.

Lady Barclay stormed in. "Where is *my daughter*?"

The guards at the door stepped toward her, but the king waved them off. "What do you mean, Your Grace?"

Lady Barclay approached the end of the table and stopped, hands on her hips. "What I mean is that my daughter has not been seen by anyone since your cursed coronation and I would like to know why."

Murmurs started up around the table.

Paulo did his best to look confused, though he met Lady Alvis's eyes across from him. She knew as well as he did where Penny went. He'd recruited her to help him after all. She had taken Penny to the portal that would get her through the Mist before the High Council of Faerie was able to lock the border down.

He gave the advisor a subtle shake of his head. Lady Barclay couldn't know yet. It would cause too many problems. There were things that needed to happen that a hunt for Penny would distract from.

King Dion stood. "I was under the impression she had returned back to Barclay House after my brother was taken."

Lady Barclay scoffed. "What would the prince's disappearance have to do with it?"

The king and queen met each other's eye but said nothing. They both knew what had been going on between Penny and the king's younger brother. Especially after her injury only days before the solstice. They also suspected Lady Barclay of being in league with the rebellion, which Paulo would happily let them believe for a bit longer.

Queen Carnation stood. "We haven't seen Lady Penny since the wedding."

Lord Hermen also stood. "I saw her, Your Grace. She took my horse outside the temple."

"Where did she go after that?" Lady Barclay demanded.

Paulo held his breath. Lord Hermen knew more about Penny and the prince than anyone at this table, including the king and queen. He could likely deduce exactly where Penny had gone, and Paulo couldn't let the man know how much he knew. That would play a hand he wasn't ready to give the Minister of Trade— especially with his propensity for mischief. Paulo had to keep as many secrets as he could with that man.

Lord Hermen looked about the table as if at a loss. "That I can't say, Your Grace. I assumed she would have returned here."

Paulo let out the breath. Good. The man could be wise when the moment warranted it. He wouldn't reveal anything. Lady Delmar likely would have had his head if he had. Penny's involvement in the Underworld had been a closely guarded secret. *Praise the Goddess for that.*

"So not a single one of you has seen my daughter in the month since the coronation? I knew this council could be stupid, but I didn't know the lot of you were blind."

"Enough!" King Dion barked. "I understand your distress, Your Grace, but you are not to speak so to anyone in this room." He stood. "This council is adjourned for the day. Lady Barclay, please meet myself and Her Majesty in my study."

The king took his wife's hand in his elbow and strode toward a side door while the rest of the council slowly got to their feet, speculation about Penny bouncing around.

Paulo darted for the door, but before he could make it out of the room, Adam cut him off.

"Did you know Lady Penny was missing?"

Paulo shook his head. "No, I didn't know." Because she wasn't missing. He knew exactly where she was.

Adam ran a hand through his dark hair. "What are we to do?"

"What can we do?" Paulo shrugged. "She could be anywhere."

"I did not know you to be a man of such inaction," Adam huffed. "We ought to search for her. Someone must have seen her." He twisted his fingers together with anxiety.

Paulo nearly burst out laughing. He'd never seen the man so ruffled over something. "I'm sure she'll be found eventually."

"*Eventually?*" Adam stormed up to Paulo, dark brows low. "What if she's injured? What if the rebellion found her? She could be trapped somewhere with no one to help her. By the Goddess, there's a rebellion running amok! She could have been taken. She could be dead!"

Paulo grabbed Adam by the shoulders. "Calm yourself! Penny Barclay is smarter than the rabble making up the rebellion. I'm sure she's fine and all will be well soon enough. The best thing we can do is take care of our kingdom and do our blasted jobs until she's found, all right?"

Adam's chest heaved with whatever frenzy of emotion was boiling within him, but he closed his eyes, took a deep breath, and nodded. "You're right. There's no reason to let fear rule our heads. Lady Penny is wise. I'm sure she's well."

Paulo slapped him on the arm. "That's a good man. Now, get all those papers ready to send to Queen Bestia to ask for their aid against the rebellion for when King Dion needs them."

Adam blew out a breath. "I'll go, but I'll be praying for Lady Penny the entire time. I sincerely hope this is all just a huge misunderstanding."

Paulo agreed and pushed the man toward the door. He would be praying for Penny, but first, there was another precocious woman with whom he needed to have a very extensive talking to.

Instead of heading toward his rooms like the rest of the council did, Paulo marched toward the kitchens. The vision of Laurel's silver mask next to the bottle of poison stabbed at not only his head but his heart.

When he burst into the kitchen, he was surprised to find everyone in a state of mild panic. Cook sat on the ground, holding a foaming-mouthed Galen as the man writhed in the throes of death. One of the dishwashers was crying into the shoulder of the other undercook and another girl looked like she was going to lose her lunch. Each person in the kitchen was in some state of shock.

All except Laurel, who stood by the stove stirring whatever was in a pan with a spoon as if a man slowly suffocating to death was a normal occurrence.

Actually, to her, it probably was.

Paulo shook his head and slowly crept toward her. While watching a man die would turn away even the most stalwart souls, Paulo had seen enough death in his life that he was probably more desensitized than Laurel was.

Was that a good thing or a bad thing?

He came up next to her. "A word, Laurel?"

She looked up at him, not at all surprised to find him there. She'd probably known the moment he walked into the kitchen, though she had seemed not to be paying attention.

"Excuse me, my lord, but we are in a bit of a crisis at the moment. Perhaps another time."

Paulo plucked the spoon from her hand and moved the pan away from the fire. "Pardon my intrusion, Cook, but I must speak to Miss Laurel right this moment." He grabbed Laurel's arm and pulled her toward the door leading out to the kitchen garden, not even hearing if Cook gave her agreement before ushering Laurel out of the room.

Once they were through the doors, Laurel twisted herself out of Paulo's grip and took several steps away. "What on Gaia's green earth are you thinking? I can't have some random lord show up and drag me out of the kitchen whenever he likes."

"What happened to Galen?" Paulo asked.

"I'm not the only one trying to kill the king."

Paulo closed the distance between them, coming so close he could shake her, but he didn't touch her. "Are you planning on poisoning the queen?"

She looked startled. "Why would I need to poison her?"

Paulo's chest tightened. "I don't know, but I saw your mask next to a bottle that looked like poison."

Her eyes narrowed. "Not every nefarious looking bottle is poison, my lord. It could have been anything."

"What normal looking liquid is the dark blue color of midnight?"

Laurel's shoulders sagged. "You saw Stellataen Arrow."

"Is it poison?" Paulo asked.

Laurel nodded. "One of the deadliest. But I don't have a bottle of it, and it's only made in one place. There are several members of my order with a silver mask and access to that poison. It could have been anyone. Anywhere."

Paulo grabbed her by the shoulders. "Listen to me, Laurel. You can't poison the queen."

She shook him off. "I have no plans to. My mission isn't to get rid of her, and I don't enjoy taking the lives of innocent people even when my job requires it. I'm not just going to randomly start poisoning the queen for no reason."

"Don't poison the queen for *any* reason, all right?"

She stared at him. "What did you see?"

Paulo swallowed. "Too much. There's so many variables, and they could all go awry. Anything could happen and there's nothing I can do to stop it." He grabbed at his hair. Penny could die. The queen could die. Iatrus Castle could go up in flames. There were so many futures, so many possibilities. How could he make sure the right ones happened?

Instead of offering him a comforting touch like any other sane person, Laurel slapped him. "Stop spiraling."

Paulo lifted a hand to his face. "*Ow.*"

"Are you done now?" she demanded.

He rubbed his cheek. "I suppose."

"Great." She stepped around him. "Now, I'll get back to work *not* poisoning any queens and you can go back to thwarting my attempts to get off this cursed island."

He grabbed her arm without thinking about it. "Laurel."

She looked down at his hand and then up at him.

He let go. "I don't want it to be like this between us."

She gave a long sigh. "Someday, you're going to realize that you can't get everything you want."

32
THE LIAR

LAUREL SCOOPED OUT THE MIX OF BEEF, ONION, AND BARLEY FOR THE *yourvarlakia* soup Cook had on the menu for that evening. As interviews had taken place for the kitchen girl that would replace her, Cook had put her and Dan in charge of preparing everything for dinner. It had been a true test of her cooking abilities as she continued to stare at the door, waiting to see if Aspen got the job or not.

Galen's death glare at the back of her neck didn't help either.

Had Delilah told him about seeing her in the city meeting with Aspen and Luc? Would they figure out what she was?

She set the meatballs on a tray for Dan to cook and moved onto making the egg and lemon broth to go on top of the meatballs. There was a chicken roasting on the spit that would be served in a similar soup, though for the staff. Beef was expensive and usually saved for the upper class, though Laurel had had her fair share of it while working in the palace. Apparently, the ranches in Olympia were some of the best, though Laurel wouldn't know enough about the beef industry to form any sort of opinion. All she did know was that Cook worked magic with the meats she cooked.

Dan set to browning the meatballs and Galen gave a cough behind her. She ignored it until Dan turned next to her and gave a short bow. "My lady. Sir."

Laurel turned then and found Lady Diana and Mr. Delrio standing in the doorway. She gave a slight curtsy. Dan looked to her, face pale, as if he expected her to do something.

She sighed. Delilah had certainly been the one to throw herself at the feet of every aristocrat that walked through the door. Laurel was not Delilah.

But Lady Diana wasn't any other aristocrat either.

"Hello there, Laurel." She took a seat on one side of Galen while Mr. Delrio took the other.

Did Lord MacGregor know that his sister was fraternizing with a potential traitor to Olympia? She nearly snorted. Of course he did. It was all probably part of some master plan to get close to the Aigeans and help something in the future. Lord MacGregor had his fingers in every proverbial pie on the table.

Laurel set a pleasant smile on her lips. "Good evening, my lady. How can we serve you?"

Lady Diana's eyes gleamed. "Mr. Delrio and I were discussing the merits of using a full meat cleaver verses a cimeter for butchering meat. Neither of us can come to an agreement, so I thought who better to settle the matter than our illustrious undercook?"

Laurel slowly walked to the sink and washed the grease from rolling the meatballs from her hands. She used the small pump to bring the water in from outside. How the water got there in the first place, she could only contribute to Olympia's magic touch.

She grabbed a towel to dry her fingers. "I don't know that I'm the best person to answer such a question. Perhaps Dan—"

The undercook shook his head vehemently.

All right. Dan was not to be relied upon.

"Come now, Laurel. Would a cleaver or a cimeter be better used for butchering?"

Laurel sighed "It depends on what you would be butchering."

"A cow," Lady Diana said.

"A shark," Mr. Delrio offered at the same time.

"Well, there you go." Laurel set the towel back on its ring. "A cleaver is better suited for the thick meats and tendons of a cow while a cimeter would be better suited to a shark since the flesh is softer with nothing to really cut through but the meat."

Lady Diana smirked at Mr. Delrio. "I told you she would know."

The selkie gave Laurel a once over. "Are you sure you're a kitchen girl?"

She could guess what he saw. Fighters recognized one another, if only on a subconscious level. There was little Laurel could do to hide the scars on her knuckles or always mask the way she moved. There was also natural biology to consider. Even the most clueless prey could feel when a predator swept into a room.

Galen's eyes flicked over to Mr. Delrio.

Laurel pushed every ounce of demureness onto her face that she possessed. "I would think my proper knowledge of how to butcher meat would recommend me for such a job, don't you?"

Diana chuckled. "Of course. Laurel is quite suited to being an undercook."

Galen's garnet eyes promised pain.

"Was there anything else I could help you with?" Laurel asked, coming around the table to usher them out by whatever force necessary.

Lady Diana allowed her to help her from her seat. "Have you seen Lord MacGregor recently?"

"He came two days ago, but that's the last time I saw him."

Lady Diana grumbled under her breath, but Laurel only heard the words "thickheaded idiot" and nothing more. Not that she wanted to hear anything else about Lord MacGregor. Their conversation had not left her mind.

She really wanted to know what he knew about her and why he was so set on her staying in Olympia.

"Thank you for humoring us, Miss Laurel," Mr. Delrio said. "With only a sniff of whatever it is you all are cooking, I am looking forward to suppertime."

"I'll pass your compliments along to Cook." She nearly shoved them through the door in the most appropriate way for a servant to push two members of high society out of a room.

"See you around, Laurel!" Lady Diana said in farewell, dragging Mr. Delrio by the arm and out of sight.

"Was that Lady Diana?"

Laurel whirled around to see Cook standing at the other door, a beaming Aspen at her side.

"Yes, Cook." Laurel shook herself. "And Mr. Delrio. They had a question."

Galen crossed his arms over his chest. "Yes, they asked about butchering meat. Horrible questions."

Cook gave Galen a frown but turned her attention back to Laurel. "I hope you were able to give them a satisfactory answer."

"I believe I did." She pushed a smile onto her face. "Have you found us a new kitchen girl?"

Cook set a hand on Aspen's shoulder. "Everyone, this is Aspen, the newest addition to our kitchen."

Laurel held out her hand. "Welcome to the kitchen, Aspen."

Aspen took it. "I'm happy to be here."

It wasn't until the entire kitchen had been scrubbed top to bottom that Laurel and Aspen were able to retire to their room.

A happy circumstance.

With Delilah's bed free, it had been obvious that Aspen would take it, and Laurel couldn't be happier with the arrangement.

Aspen crossed her legs under one another. "You got me a present?"

Laurel dug down to the bottom of her trunk. "I've been holding onto these for two months with no idea how to get them to you." She found the parcels and shut the trunk.

"What are they?" Aspen asked.

"Just open them."

Aspen tore into the paper and gasped. "How is it that you've held onto these for months? You should have sent them right away."

Laurel laughed. "I wasn't going to risk my cover just to send you a couple pairs of pants."

"The fact that they've been sitting in the bottom of that trunk is a *travesty*."

"Well, you got them much sooner than I thought you would."

The mood in the room soured. Aspen set the pants aside.

"What are we going to do, Laurel?"

Laurel sat on the edge of her bed, hands hanging between her legs. "I really don't know. I can't beat someone who can see into the future. Not on my own. I've tried everything I can think of to get this job done, and I've failed every time."

She couldn't have been more grateful that Aspen knew

about the geas. However she found out— Teagan probably figured out a way to tell her— now Laurel had someone she could confide in. The weight felt a little lighter.

Aspen mirrored her pose. While she might have been barely seventeen, her face held the gravitas of someone far older. "We're going to get it figured out. Luc and I have already been making plans to take out the king when we take the palace. We've got tons of planning left and Luc has some ideas to help escalate things for the rebellion beforehand. We'll just make sure you're there to help us when it gets to that point. We can both accomplish our goals and return to Stellatus Hall as heroes."

"And is that what you want?" Laurel asked. "To return to the Hall?"

Aspen tilted her head. "Where else would we go?"

Laurel slipped her feet out of her shoes. "If you could go anywhere in the world, where would it be?"

Aspen's expression turned contemplative. "I know it's going to sound ironic, but I've always wanted to see Faerie."

Laurel chuffed a laugh. "You're kidding."

"I'm not!" Aspen giggled. "Just think about it. The magic, the Seasons, all of it! I bet it's one adventure after the next."

"Until the fae decide to enchant you into thinking you're some kind of cat and you forget your name for several decades."

"Such a killjoy." Aspen tugged at a loose string in her blanket. "If Faerie is off the table, where would you want to go?"

Laurel looked out the window. "Somewhere far from magic and mayhem." Away from cursed geases and oracular mages that made her second guess every aspect of her life every time he spoke.

Aspen rolled her eyes. "*Boring* you mean."

"We would make it far less boring than it had any potential

to be." She turned back to Aspen. "We can cook all the food we want, buy clothes we'll never wear, and sit on a beach somewhere without caring if the sun will bake our skin off our bones."

Aspen flopped back onto her pillow. "That does sound like paradise. Luc would love it. We could travel around for a bit before going home."

"And where would you like home to be?"

Aspen settled her hands behind her head. "Stellatus Hall, of course. That's where we belong. You, me, and Luc. All together."

"You wouldn't want to live anywhere else? Maybe find a seaside cottage or a small hamlet in a different territory?"

Aspen frowned. "Why would I want any of that? Besides, Luc would never give up his post. He's too honorable for that. It wouldn't be a perfect fantasy without him."

Laurel turned to look up at the ceiling, staying silent. Luc didn't have any place in her fantasy. In fact, he didn't have a place in either of their futures. She didn't have anything against Luc except the fact that he would never leave Stellatus Hall. His loyalty to the Order bordered on overzealous.

Aspen would understand once everything was said and done. They would get off this island, go back to the Continent and claim their future.

Together.

33
AN UNFORTUNATE REVELATION

Penny will sit in that blasted camp for weeks, the hollows of her cheekbones growing with the shadows in her eyes. Adira Durant will laugh, goading her to speak and exchange verbal blows. When Penny goes back to the prisoner tent, Teagan will come into the tent, bringing word from a few of the assassins he'd brought with him. No one is able to find a way through the Mist.

"Paulo, you need to get out of this room."

Diana's face came into view overhead, blocking a perfectly good view of the blue ceiling above him.

Paulo tried to shoo her away. "Don't mess with my process, Diana. I'm trying to see what's going to happen."

For days, he'd been trying to get all the pieces of the next several weeks lined up, watching every possibility play out over and over again until he felt his brain would explode. He had to know what happened. Had to know how to save Laurel.

How to stop Queen Carnation from dying. How to keep every-thing balanced so he could save those he loved, and Olympia's future didn't crumble into a million pieces. So he didn't crumble along with it.

Diana walked away and Paulo tried to regain his focus.

Until she yanked the curtains open, and sunlight hit him square in the face.

He sat up from his spot on the floor. "Curses, woman! Are you trying to fry my eyeballs out of their sockets?"

Diana moved to the next window. "If that's what it takes for you to get out of this room and take a proper bath, then yes. Jenkins has been muttering nonstop for a week."

"Jenkins always mutters," he mumbled.

But Diana heard him anyway. "You know very well Jenkins is more than justified in his mutterings recently."

Jenkins could be such a worry wart. The man needed a hobby. Maybe a cat or something. Paulo ran a hand through his already very mussed and greasy hair. "It doesn't matter what Jenkins thinks if the entire palace goes up in flames and all of Olympia falls under the tyrannical rule of an anti-magical radicalist."

"Is that even a real word?"

Paulo threw his hands in the air and nearly smacked himself with the baggy sleeve of his robe. "Does it matter whether or not it's a real word if we're all going to be dead in a few weeks?"

"Now you're just being dramatic."

Paulo got to his feet. "What do you want? You can't have come in here just to interrupt what could have been a very important vision." Diana generally left him alone when he was on one of his vision binges as he left her alone when she went on her hunting sprees. Each of them had their passions and were more than willing not to get in the other's way unless it didn't suit them.

Diana opened the door, letting in a very twitchy looking Jenkins. The man had to put his hands up next to his eyes to give himself blinders so he could walk through the room without getting distracted by the mess.

Paulo looked about at the piles of dishes from meal trays he'd had ordered when he remembered to eat and the random articles of clothing strewn about. He also couldn't identify where the strange odor tickling his nose came from either.

Water splashed in the washroom attached to the bedroom.

"You're right," Diana said, walking to his wardrobe. "I didn't just come in here to irritate you, though it brought me no small amount of pleasure to do so."

He threw off his robe and added it to one of the piles of clothing around his room. "The suspense is killing me."

Diana rolled her eyes and set his emerald-green suit on a hook. "The king has summoned you."

Paulo froze. "Curses." Of course, the king had summoned him. There was much to prepare for. So much to wait for.

Jenkins popped his head out of the washroom, a hand over his eyes. "The shower is ready, my lord."

Paulo pulled his shirt over his head and threw it at Diana, the stench of three days with no change of clothing practically wafting off the fabric.

She gave an outraged screech, and he darted into the washroom before she could retaliate.

Paulo approached the king's study not ten minutes later, polished to a near blinding shine. He'd left an increasingly frantic Jenkins to see to his room. The poor man would likely have an ulcer by the end of their sojourn in the capital.

The guards at the door knocked gently and the door opened, allowing him entrance. Paulo flashed both the pair of guards on the outside of the study and the ones on the inside his most charming smile. He didn't know what the princes could have called him for, but none of the guards openly glared at him, so that had to be a good sign.

The king, queen, and Prince Evan all sat around the desk, looking up at Paulo's approach.

He dipped into a low bow. "Your Majesties. Your Highness."

King Dion gestured to the empty seat beside Prince Evan. "Thank you for joining us, Polly. We hope it wasn't too much of an imposition to call on you."

"I am but your humble servant." Paulo theatrically plopped himself into the chair.

The king leaned over the desk. "There are things I wish to discuss in this room that can't leave it. Is that going to be a problem for you, Polly?"

Paulo mimed locking his lips. "Not for me, Your Majesty. I am an impenetrable safe."

He leaned back. "As I thought. I just wanted to make sure all of us were on the same page."

Queen Carnation cleared her throat. "We first want to ask if you've had any news of Prince Aiden. It's been over six weeks since his abduction and we wish to know if he's been harmed in any way."

Paulo straightened in his chair. "I can't promise that the futures I've seen have come to pass. I don't see which path the subjects of my visions choose, only the repercussions of them."

Is he alive? Prince Evan signed with his hands.

Luckily, Paulo had learned to read his signed language early on in his childhood. As the half-mer prince had never been able to speak in his partial human form, Father had ensured Paulo's fluency of the language.

"As far as I can see, yes." Paulo crossed a boot over his knee and leaned back in the chair. "I haven't seen much, but I haven't seen his death."

Another lie. He had seen the High King's death. He'd seen what would happen should Adira Durant win this war.

"So, we are just to sit on our haunches while he deals with this situation on his own?" The king folded his arms over his chest. "I don't like that one bit."

"The only assurance I can give is that the Goddess does have a plan."

The queen pursed her lips. "And what of Lady Penny?"

Paulo held very still so he wouldn't flinch. "Your Majesty?"

"Have you seen Lady Penny in any of your visions?" Her blue eyes narrowed. "Lady Barclay has been insistent something nefarious has befallen her."

Paulo licked his lips. "Does that 'don't speak of anything we say outside this room' apply to what I say as well?"

"Yes," King Dion said.

Paulo sighed. They would find out eventually. "She has gone to Faerie after the prince."

All three of them straightened.

"What?" the queen snapped.

How did she get through the Mist? the prince signed.

"When did she leave?" King Dion asked.

"She left the moment the portal shut in the temple. If you would like witnesses, both my sister and Lady Alvis attended to her. I can assure you, she made it through." At least, she would. If Paulo's calculations were correct, she would arrive there in two weeks. *Cursed Mist magic.*

The king's brows lowered dangerously. "What else have you been keeping from us, cousin?"

Paulo kept a pleasant smile on his face even as his insides squirmed. "I couldn't let you know about Lady Penny as there was nothing anyone could do about it and trying to reach her would be a distraction from the things going on here. There will be more trials in the near future, though I can't say when or what will happen exactly. There are too many variables yet to fall into place."

The queen's face was as serious as her husbands. "You will tell us the moment you know anything else, Lord MacGregor. It's not your call whether or not we can handle certain information."

It was not a request.

Yet, Paulo could not agree. He knew exactly what would happen if he told visions at the wrong time. If he didn't follow his path with exactness.

Paulo nodded. "Of course, Your Majesty."

"I have one last question for you." The king pulled out a sheet of paper. "Do you know where Adira Durant is located?"

"No, sire, I can't say that I do."

A lie. Again. If the king knew she was trapped in Faerie, he wouldn't be on his guard, which he very much needed to be. Especially as both Flumen sisters now lived under his roof.

The king deflated. "Can you tell us anything about her operation?"

Paulo shook his head. "I'm sorry, but I don't know anything. My gifts are somewhat limited when it comes to people I don't know."

Lie. Lie. Lie.

The queen scooted forward in her chair. "And what about children, Lord MacGregor?"

The king whipped in her direction. "Shaunie."

She smacked him on the arm. "I'm more than obligated to ask."

A tremor started up in Paulo's hands. "Children, Your Majesty?"

"Yes." She set a hand to her stomach. "Have you seen anything about children coming into the royal family soon?"

The king sent an unhappy glare at his wife, but he still turned to Paulo. His amethyst eyes spoke of a hope there. Of a secret that Paulo should have foreseen.

For a moment, all he saw was the queen staring up at her ceiling.

He hadn't thought about all the blood.

"I can't say I've seen anything of report, Your Majesty, but I imagine it is early yet."

She blew out a breath, her lively eyes lining with tears. "I suppose you're right."

King Dion glared. "That information is definitely not to leave this room, is that clear, Polly?"

"Of course, Your Majesty. Your secret is safe with me."

They talked for a few more minutes after that, but the ache in Paulo's chest didn't abate.

Not only was the queen's life in danger.

But the life of her child as well.

34
THE DRUNKARD

HAVING ASPEN WORK IN A KITCHEN WASN'T NEARLY AS DISASTROUS AS Laurel had thought it would be. Aspen couldn't tell the difference between flour and confectioners' sugar, but she could peel a cucumber faster than Laurel could. The entire kitchen knew. There had been a competition between a few members of the staff the first week she'd been there.

Over the course of two weeks, they fell into a rhythm. They would wake in the morning, cook for the day, then head to bed, plans rolling around in their heads and jokes on their tongues. Laurel hadn't been on many missions with Aspen, her being younger and Laurel not wishing to involve her in some of the unsavory things she'd had to do. But their undercover work in the kitchens held a semblance of what their future free of the Order would look like.

It felt like paradise.

Aspen came back from her half-day, her cheeks pink and eyes shining with excitement. The weather mages' report claimed the winter weather would last for several more weeks, but that wouldn't stop Aspen from enjoying herself. Laurel hadn't wanted to ask Cook to let them have the same day off. They were already so close, she didn't want anyone getting suspicious about their history. According to the rest of the kitchen, they'd only met for the first time when Aspen started working with them.

Laurel pulled the large dish of *youvetsi* from the oven. The tomato sauce had fully saturated the orzo, and the small hint of cinnamon mixed with the beef. Her mouth watered.

Aspen came over and took a large whiff. "That smells divine."

Laurel set the dish on the counter. "How was your half-day?"

Those brown eyes brightened. "Fantastic. I made lots of progress on my little project."

Laurel tilted her head. "Is this a different project than the one you were working on before?"

Aspen tapped the edge of Laurel's nose. "You'll just have to wait and see."

Laurel shook her head as Aspen bounced over to where her apron hung on the wall.

"Laurel!" she heard called. "Where have you been?"

And, as if Laurel's perfect paradise needed a good shaking, Lord MacGregor arrived.

She spun toward him, dipping into a curtsy at the last moment. "My lord?"

He plopped himself in Galen's chair. The taster had taken a tea tray up to His Majesty.

"Why is it that I haven't seen you in weeks?"

Laurel's gaze flicked over to Aspen, who gave her a wide-eyed *what on Gaia's green earth?*

Cook bustled forward. "It's always a joy to have you in our kitchen, my lord. Laurel has been busy at work, making our kitchen proud."

Laurel frowned at Cook, who returned the expression with a mischievous one of her own. Meddlesome woman.

"Is there something you needed from me, my lord?" Why was he acting insane? Well, more insane than normal. She hadn't seen him in a few weeks, but there was no reason for the two of them to interact, not if she wasn't making jabs at King Dion.

Lord MacGregor sighed dramatically. "I need you to trust me with that little heart of yours, Laurel."

Laurel blinked, taking him in. His skin had a slightly flushed look, and his eyes were glassy. "My lord, are you *drunk?*"

"Laurel!" Cook admonished.

But Lord MacGregor cackled. "Oh Laurel, you're so perceptive. So wise. So pretty."

She strode toward him. "Please stop talking." By the Goddess, what would he say in such a state? He could expose her right there and then.

He pulled out a lyre from out of nowhere and started plucking at the strings.

"Laurel, with eyes like chocolate
With lips sweet and delicate..."

She grabbed him from under his armpits. "Come now, you."

He got to his feet, though he kept singing.

"Would you give me your trust?
Even if our future's a bust?"

"Sweet Gaia," Laurel heard Aspen whisper behind her.

Laurel got him to the door. "For the love of Gaia, could you *please* stop singing?"

"Only once you tell me you'll marry me."

"Sure, you and I can run away together in a minute." She swung one of his arms over her shoulders. By the Goddess, the man weighed a ton. "First, let's find your sister and get you out of public."

He blew out a noisy breath with his lips. "She'll come down the stairs in threeeeee, twoooooo..."

Lady Diana appeared at the top of the stairs. "Oh good. You found him."

Laurel gaped and Lord MacGregor took the opportunity to nuzzle his stubbled cheek against hers. "You mean he's been missing? What's wrong with him?"

Lady Diana came down the stairs and took his other arm. "Donnie caught him at a bad time."

The image of Lord Abrams popped into Laurel's mind. "What does that even mean?"

Lady Diana sighed. "It's happened before. Paulo will see something, and Donnie has a propensity for sniffing people out when they're at the worst, offering a quick fix to their woes."

"An entire barrel of ale?"

Diana chuffed. "Try bottles of his most potent wine."

Lord MacGregor laughed and nearly took all three of them to the ground.

Laurel readjusted her hold on him. "How are we going to get him to his rooms?" The residential wing was all the way across the palace and the MacGregor's were staying on the top floor.

Lady Diana grimaced. "We're not. We'll have to find somewhere to hide him until the worst of it passes."

That was the moment he started crying.

Lady Diana growled, pulling his head up so she could look into his eyes. Laurel had never seen his irises do what they did then, the pearlescent color practically swirled.

"He's about to go into full stasis mode."

Laurel's chest tightened. "What does that mean?"

"When he lets his gift take this kind of control, he becomes unresponsive. He must have been suppressing it the last few days, so now it's coming back with a vengeance."

"Does this happen often?"

Lady Diana shook her head. "No, but it happens. We need to hurry." She started to turn down another corridor.

"Wait, there's a small music room for the servants this way." Laurel pulled them in the other direction. "There's some old sofas, but it should be private enough."

Lady Diana nodded and followed Laurel's lead.

Lord MacGregor's crying had slowed, but he'd started to mumble.

She started to listen when he said her name.

"Laurel. Don't trust him.

"Laurel. The box is in the safe behind the map.

"Laurel. The watchtower has a man behind the door.

"Laurel. They'll come after the grinning taster.

"Laurel. She's been poisoned.

"Laurel. Choose the knife.

"Laurel. Come with me.

"Laurel. Laurel. Laurel Laurel Laurel Laurel Laurel Laurel..."

All his body weight sagged into them, and his spinning eyes rolled back into his head.

"Curses!" Lady Diana hissed. Her knees buckled, but she kept him aloft. "Why do you have to weigh as much as a blasted ox?"

Laurel gritted her teeth and helped drag him the last few steps toward the music room. She had to use her elbow to open the door while also keeping hold of the unconscious lord.

They burst into the darkened room. This particular room only had one small window which had been covered by a heavy curtain. Carefully, Laurel led Diana to one of the sofas and they dropped Lord MacGregor onto the cushions.

"Should we send for a physician?" Laurel asked.

Lady Diana plopped onto the floor next to Lord MacGregor's head. "No. There's nothing they can do. Father and Mater tried for years to get him help, but it seems this is simply one of those things the Goddess has decided needs to happen for no logical reason other than Paulo is probably supposed to learn something from it."

"That's a very positive outlook on such a difficult situation."

Lady Diana shrugged. "There's no point in dwelling on the sad bits. Sometimes, the only way to make something better is to have a better attitude about it."

Laurel walked over to the window and moved the curtain aside to let in the late afternoon light. Well-worn instruments stood about the room. A small pianoforte took up one corner and there was a table with several flutes and even a set of bagpipes. Laurel had heard the piano played every once in a while, and Dan could fiddle like nothing she'd ever seen, but that was the extent of it in the servants' quarters. There wasn't much time for hobbies when one worked in a palace.

Lady Diana got to her feet. "Well, I ought to track down Donnie and give him a proper dressing down. Might even bloody his nose a bit. The man really should know better by now than to let Paulo get this bad."

"You think he'll be fine by himself?"

"Great Goddess, no! That's why you're going to stay here and I'm going to smack Donnie upside the head. I'll send Jenkins when I track him down. He can help get Paulo back to his room when he wakes up."

Laurel was already shaking her head. "Excuse me, my lady, but I can't stay here with him."

But Lady Diana was already headed toward the door. "You'll be fine, Laurel. Just make sure he doesn't choke on his own vomit."

She disappeared out the door.

Laurel raced after her, but by the time she made it into the hallway, Lady Diana had already disappeared. What was it with MacGregors? With a deep sigh, she propped the door open and turned back to the lord draped over the sofa.

In the light of day, she could see every individual freckle on his face. His neckcloth was completely askew, his hair tousled over his brow. He looked younger there. When he was awake, there was this heaviness, this tension he carried with him. It was in the lines between his brows and the sardonic curve of his lips. In sleep, he had none of that. His dark freckles covered his face. Was his entire body covered in the little spots? He had them on his hands too, all the way up his fingers. He looked almost boyish, though his breaths were slightly quick, and his eyes flicked behind his eyelids. She'd never seen eyelashes the color his were, almost golden. Aspen, with her blond hair, had nearly invisible lashes, but Lord MacGregor's were a gold that looked like he'd caught sunlight in them.

His lips moved the smallest bit, likely in reaction to whatever he was seeing.

She'd kissed those lips.

Why that particular thought had struck, Laurel couldn't say, but it needed to be squashed immediately. She'd kissed plenty of other lips. There was no need for her stomach to do a little flip at the memory of his kisses. Or the way he'd trailed them down her neck. The feel of his hands at her waist. He made her feel so small...

"Stop it," she muttered. By the Goddess, she was ogling a very drunk, very unconscious man.

He was completely asleep.

And Laurel was alone with him.

Her spine stiffened.

The oracle was completely indisposed.

Lady Diana wouldn't be back for at least half an hour, if not more.

Laurel could easily sneak back into the kitchens, grab her poisons, sneak something between his lips to leave him incapacitated for days. He wouldn't be able to interfere with her assassinating the king. She could complete her mission right there.

She took a step back in the direction of the door. Yes. It would be so simple. This was the moment she'd been waiting for.

Her heart galloped and she finally turned away from him.

Right as he decided to start retching.

"Sweet Gaia, you have got to be kidding me." She really ought to let him asphyxiate. It would solve a number of problems for her.

She went to his side and kept him from falling off the sofa. He'd had enough wherewithal to at least lose his lunch onto the floor. She pulled him back up to the couch when he stopped, and she set to untying his neck cloth. He groaned and tried to swat her hands away, but she brushed his fingers aside.

"Really, my lord. You are being most unhelpful. Here I was, about to take back my future like you told me to, then you had to go and make a mess."

His body seemed to relax at her voice. He stopped fighting her and she was able to get the fabric away from his neck and undo the first few buttons of his shirt.

Brushing the hair from his eyes, she sighed. "I really don't know what I'm going to do with you, Paulo MacGregor."

35
AN UNFORTUNATE CONSEQUENCE

Laurel will die. Over and over again, she will die.

PAULO'S HEAD WAS SWIMMING. NOT JUST A CUTE LITTLE PUPPY PADDLE about a pond, but a raging whirlpool in the middle of an ocean. He hadn't even opened his eyes and he could imagine the kaleidoscope of colors waiting for him on the other side of his eyelids.

By the Goddess, he hadn't felt this poorly since the last time Donnie had talked him into going on one of his signature drinking sprees.

Oh.

That's exactly what had happened.

Again.

Paulo groaned and turned onto his side. His pillow felt scratchy against his cheek. The stubble along his jaw caught on the threads, and he shifted to try to escape the wretched sensation.

"Are you finally awake?"

Paulo squinted out of one eye and found Diana propped up

on the pillow next to him, a book in her hand. Thankfully, she sat between him and the glaring light coming from the mage-light on his nightstand.

He closed his eyes again, the headache behind his eyes pounding fiercely. "What are you doing in here?"

"Making sure you don't do anything stupid. Like die or run back to Laurel in the kitchens and expose her to everyone."

He opened both of his eyes and stared up at her. "What happened?"

Diana shrugged and flipped her page. How she read and held a conversation with him he would never be able to understand. "From the little that Laurel shared, you walked into the kitchen and started saying the strangest things. She realized you were drunk when you started professing your love in front of the entire kitchen staff. Then she said you started singing." She pointed to the end of the bed where he found his lyre.

He groaned and smashed his face into his pillow. Faint recollections of Laurel telling him to be quiet and dragging him out of the kitchen mingled with random flashes of time. "What happened after that?"

"She hauled you out of the kitchens and then your visions took over. Oh, then you nearly vomited on her."

Sweet Gaia.

"Is she going to be all right? I didn't ruin anything did I?"

"Give the girl some credit. I arrived back after fetching Jenkins and she had already cleaned up the mess. She even fetched your lyre from the kitchen and brought it up here after."

"Was she terribly angry with me?"

"I can tell you that *I* was terribly angry with you." Diana turned another page. "Letting Donnie get you so drunk your magic took over? Again? I thought we'd gotten past this. Mater would be in here with Father's best belt if she knew."

Paulo flipped onto his back and pinched at the bridge of his nose. "You won't tell her?"

"So long as you don't do anything like that again. It's scary, Paulo."

He blew out a breath. "I'm sorry."

She gently closed the book and set it to the side. "What made you lose control like that?"

The image of the queen's body flashed through his mind once more. The wine had only purged it from his thoughts for a minute. He knew better. He knew his magic wasn't something he could simply drink away, but the moments of relief were as tantalizing as the visions themselves. A conundrum, to be sure, but that seemed to be his modus operandi.

"It doesn't matter. I'm hoping I can change it."

That didn't satisfy Diana in the least. "Has it anything to do with Laurel?"

Paulo shook his head, though he understood her line of reasoning. The last time Donnie had helped him deal with a difficult vision it had been when he'd seen Laurel's future. It was the first time he'd ever seen her die. He'd been seventeen.

With a sigh, he took Diana's hand. He pushed the vision of the queen's vacant eyes into her mind, praying she might be able to tell him something, anything that might help. He'd shown her some of his worst visions. She had more of a stomach for them than Mater did.

Diana sucked in a breath when the magic released her. "Are you going to be able to stop it from happening?"

The backs of Paulo's eyes prickled, and he tried to blink away the oncoming tears. There were some things he couldn't stop from happening. He'd learned that lesson as a child, when Father had suddenly collapsed, his heart failing and the Goddess taking him from the world before Paulo could even realize what was happening. There were some things he couldn't stop.

He pressed the heels of his hands into his eyes. "I don't know."

Paulo sat down at his desk the next morning, staring down at the reorganized piles of correspondence waiting for him. Jenkins must have come in while Paulo had been in his drunken stupor. He hadn't left this room tidy when he'd gone to find Donnie the day before.

He drank a large gulp of the glass of water in his hand. He'd already drank what had to be a gallon of tea to try to suppress the headache still pounding against his skull, but he knew drinking as much liquid as he could possibly stomach would help flush everything from his system.

The letter sitting at the top of the pile was from Mater. The postmark told him it would have come yesterday, so at least he wasn't too behind on replying to her. He set his glass down and broke the seal. Her looping handwriting covered the page.

> Paulo,
> I don't like the idea of not coming to the capital to celebrate you and Diana turning twenty this next week, but I understand the situation is delicate, and I will adhere to your wishes. I do hope my package arrives in time for both of you, though I imagine this letter will proceed it by a day or two.
> As for the bailiff reports you asked for, they

discovered a small group within Delphine proper, though we don't know if they were the same men who took the sheep weeks ago. The rebels were put under arrest, but somehow escaped the bailiff cells a couple days later. We haven't found where they ran off to, but the local magistrate has been made aware of the situation and we're working together to make plans for any future outbreaks.

By the Goddess, it sounds like some kind of plague, but I can't come up with any better description.

I've sent Diana a separate letter but would appreciate it if you would pass along my love to her as well. I know she doesn't always get to correspondence in a timely manner. I'm eager to have the two of you home soon so I can properly smother you. I hope you both have a wonderful birthday.

Stay safe.

Love,

Mater

Paulo set the letter down and took another long drink of water. The news about the growing rebel presence was worrisome but not surprising. Even if Paulo hadn't seen the potential moves the rebels would make in Delphine, they were Eleusion's closest neighbor and had plenty of business along the Black River. It was only logical they would strike there sooner rather than later. Paulo just prayed the measures he'd taken to prepare the march would be enough.

A knock sounded at the door and Oliver stuck his head in. "Busy, cousin?"

Paulo shook his head. "Come in."

Oliver stepped through the door and closed it behind him. "I just wanted to let you know that Miss Aria and I have set a date for the wedding. I figured it best to let you know in person."

Paulo waved toward the chair. "You were able to procure a special license then?"

Oliver froze halfway into the chair. "No, we decided to go the old fashion route. Have the appropriate engagement period."

"Didn't I tell you to get a special license and do your best to marry the girl next week?"

"There's no way I was going to convince her parents to sign off on that." He sat. "Miss Aria is a respectable young lady. What would it look like if we rushed into things?"

Paulo's chest grew tight. "It means that you actually care about the girl and want to marry her. It shows that, as I am the highest-ranking member of our family, you care about what I tell you to do in such matters."

"And I took it under advisement."

"It was not *advice*, Oliver. It was an order."

Oliver frowned. "My marriage is not something you can order, Paulo. I get that you're used to playing puppet master for the rest of the kingdom and think you can order everyone about as much as you want, but there are some things you don't get to meddle in."

So, this was the thing the man would have a spine about? Sweet Gaia, his family was going mad. "Oh really? You think I can't meddle in your marriage?"

"You can't meddle in love. You can't make people fall in or out of love no matter what you fabricate. No matter what you do, you can't come between it."

Paulo stood, what little patience he had snapping into tiny

bits in his lungs, making it hard for him to breathe. "If you want to have any chance of making that girl your wife, you'd best listen. Go to the king, today, and get that cursed license so you can marry the girl tomorrow. If you want, I'll even pay for all the flowers in the palace hothouse just as long as you get it done."

All color fled from Oliver's face. "What have you seen? Is Aria all right? Are her parents going to reconsider?"

"By the Goddess, no! Just stop being such a blasted moron and do what I say!"

Oliver matched his stance. "How am I supposed to know what to do if you won't tell anyone?"

"You shouldn't need to know. You should just believe I have your best interest at heart and take my words at face value."

Oliver scoffed. "My best interests? When have those ever been a priority for you?"

The words doused the fire burning in Paulo's chest. "What? Of course they've been a priority. I've only ever done anything to help our family."

"Oh? Like when? Do you think you're helping when you're drinking yourself into a stupor and chasing after kitchen girls? Or when you're playing the rakish marquess in the capital while your own mother runs your household? *Your* home? Or when you pretend to be an idiotic fop in front of the entire kingdom, so you aren't inconvenienced by anyone while you play your little games?"

Paulo opened his mouth, but Oliver held up a hand. "I may be a simple man, Paulo, but I'm not a fool. I've known you since we were babes. I've never been bitter that you were the heir to the march or that you inherited the family's powers, but I am bitter that you would sit there and say that you've only ever had our family's best interests at heart when I've seen you throw our good name into the mud. I've been cleaning up your messes for years, and right when I'm about to take something for myself, you seek to stick your fingers into that too."

Without even waiting for Paulo's response, he whirled toward the door. "I'll be procuring the license because I do trust you know things and that if I don't, I'll regret it, but I expect you to show up to the wedding in your best and leave behind the stupid fop."

He strode out of the room, leaving Paulo standing at his desk with a heavy heart and a twisting stomach.

36
THE PLAN

"Laurel."

Laurel flipped over in her bed, seeing Aspen standing at the foot of it. Wise girl. Laurel had a dagger in her hand under her sheet.

"What is it?"

"I'm supposed to be meeting with Luc tonight and something's come up. Can you meet up with him?"

Laurel tucked the knife into the small sheath at her thigh. "What's come up?"

Aspen pulled her cloak tighter around her shoulders. "I have another meeting I can't reschedule. I swear I would go see Luc, but this is important to the mission too."

Laurel threw her blankets off her legs and put her stockinged feet on the cold floor of their room. "Fine. What time do I need to be there?"

"In an hour."

At least Aspen had given her plenty of time to get ready and go. "Are you even allowed to say where you're going?"

Aspen pursed her lips. "I worry if I tell you, your little oracle will know."

"He's definitely not *my* oracle." Laurel stood and went to her trunk. She really should have taken advantage of his inebriated state. She could have walked out of that room and killed the king. Finished her mission. Why hadn't she? Why hadn't she just left him there in that room?

"You don't need to get defensive. He definitely looked like your oracle when he was professing his undying love to you through song."

"Lord MacGregor is a silly man who doesn't know how to hold his drink." By the Goddess, she still couldn't believe he'd done that. It was a good thing he hadn't come back down to the kitchens in the week following the incident. She probably would have stabbed him. Which he likely saw, so he avoided coming.

Aspen giggled. "He's a silly man with the shoulders of a swordsman and the face of an angel. I can easily see how he and the king could be related."

Laurel pulled her tunic over her head. "When have you seen the king?"

"We live in his palace, remember?" Aspen rolled her eyes. "It's not like I can walk around without getting a glimpse of him."

True enough. Though, Laurel still had trouble tracking him down. It seemed he was locked up with the queen in their rooms more recently. Hopefully, the man had let go of his more promiscuous habits now that he was married. Laurel pulled the band of leather off her neck and tied it around her ankle before slipping into her boots.

"Where am I supposed to meet with Luc?"

"Just at the inn. He told me he's got some big plans set for the next couple of weeks. We're so close to being done."

The undercurrent of excitement in Aspen's voice was infectious. Laurel felt the spring in her step as they walked toward the door. "I'm so ready for this job to be over."

Laurel tucked her mask into the inner pocket of her jacket. While it was smart to wear out in the city, Luc didn't know she was a schola and it was best to keep it that way. Schola didn't generally know one another personally, only by their masks. They could also identify one another by the hand signals.

I am watchful.

I am focused.

I am silent.

She hadn't been any of those things for months.

If she could solely blame it on Lord MacGregor, she would. But it was her fault too. She had multiple chances to thwart the marquess, but she hadn't.

Why hadn't she?

She stepped through the back door of the inn, expecting to find the place empty, but was surprised to see several people gathered around a table, the windows around the inn covered in dark cloth to give the illusion all was quiet in the public room.

"Ah, Laurel," Luc greeted. He looked over her shoulder. "Where's Aspen?"

"She had something come up, though she told me to tell you you're a big, tough guy and can go without seeing her for a bit longer."

Aspen hadn't said that, but both Luc and Aspen knew better than to send love notes through her.

Luc grinned, likely guessing at Laurel's lie. "No worries.

You can relay anything we need to her later." He straightened and introduced everyone at the table. There were two men and two women, each one of them different from the next. The first man had broad shoulders and stood a whole head shorter than Laurel. The woman next to him had her brown hair pulled back into a braid that hung at her waist and a jaded look in her eye. The woman next to her had eyes dark as coal and a thick scar around her neck. The last man had gray hair and seemed the least conspicuous of the company with a pair of spectacles perched on his nose and a fatherly air about him. Laurel hadn't met any of them before, but her mission hadn't necessitated any interaction with the rebellion. Not that they would have given her a job like that.

That was Luc's specialty.

While Stellatus Hall trained assassins, they also trained provocationists. Luc had been involved in several regime takeovers over the last few years, helping clients take down warlords and toppling government structures from the inside out. He specialized in warfare rather than poisoning like Aspen and Laurel did. Which was likely why Adira Durant had come to Stellatus Hall for help with her rebellion.

"We've come up with a plan to start a series of riots that will happen over the next couple weeks." He pointed down at a map, lines and schedules colored to coordinate with certain days. "There will be three. We have plans to strike the city's council hall first. That will happen in six days."

Laurel looked over the plan. A small force would attack the city council building one night, lighting the grounds on fire while attempting to maintain the building's integrity. It would certainly send a message, though Laurel wasn't sure how they could promise not to harm the building.

Luc continued, "Nine days after that, we will launch our second."

This one consisted of attacking several noble estates within the city, making a stand against the aristocracy. It was a bold move as many of them had magic of their own. The fatherly looking man passed Luc a sheet of paper listing which houses were magically protected.

"The third, and last, will take place another nine days after the second."

They would attack the watchmen towers around the city.

"And what are you hoping to accomplish here?" she asked.

"It should accomplish two things. The first, provoking the monarchy to attempt to seize control over the citizens, which will, in turn, anger those that may be on the fence about joining our side. The second will be introducing ourselves as a true threat to the monarchy and finally express how severe this rebellion is. The Crown has done a good job covering up the few incidents The Cartographer instigated before she left, but this will be a show of power that the king and his council won't be able to sweep under the rug."

Laurel could see how that might work, but there were quite a few things this kind of show could threaten. "How does this help prepare us to take the palace?"

"People often think it best to stage an attack when no one is expecting it. Since the rebellion took Eleusion, we've lost that element of surprise. Now, we must draw out their fear. We must be brutal and frightening, taking the boogeymen from under their beds and showing them the demons come to take their kingdom. If you can't catch someone by surprise, you terrify them into making mistakes. And there will be plenty of mistakes to exploit once this is over."

They talked about the logistics of each day assigning groups within the city to different places. While the rebellion felt somewhat disorganized, their plans were not. Laurel watched Luc work his own kind of magic over the plans, and they all ironed out wrinkles as they went.

When they got to the third riot, Laurel pointed at the map. "Those are a lot of towers for the amount of firepower you're wanting to use. How are you expecting to get so many explosives around the city?"

One of the men waved her off. "We've got the fae for that."

Apparently, their collection of fae slaves from the Day Court far exceeded those from the Night Court, which meant they had unlimited access to light and fire. Laurel couldn't help being slightly impressed. It seemed their plans were well thought out, if a little barbaric.

But she was an assassin for a reason.

The rebels talked for a total of three hours before they finished their plans and left to spread the word. The logistics of it all had Laurel's head spinning, but she could see the wisdom in every step they took. They had contingency plans for each piece and weighed every risk carefully. It all looked like a successful coup.

Luc sagged back into the chair next to her after the last woman left. "I appreciate you coming, Laurel. While Aspen is wicked smart, she doesn't think as logistically as you do."

Laurel shrugged. "You seemed to have it all in order. I really don't know why you asked Aspen to come in the first place."

"I'm hoping the two of you will accompany my team in taking out the western watchtower." He leaned forward and slid the map from the table. "It's the largest one in the city, and I'd appreciate having people I trust to watch my back. I didn't want to say anything in front of the others, but I don't like the idea of running around with a group I don't know very well."

Laurel pressed a hand to her heart. "You flatter me."

Luc caught her obvious sarcasm. "I'm serious. You and

your sister are like family to me. I'd do anything for either of you."

"Like take down a monarchy?"

He grinned. "Precisely."

Laurel laughed. "And I should believe you don't need me for anything else except helping take down a guard tower, which you could do one handed?"

"Like I said. One big happy family." He sighed. "All right, perhaps I had another motive."

"As I thought," Laurel said, suppressing a smile.

He looked about and pulled a slip of paper from his vest. "I've been thinking about what we'll need to take the palace, and I discovered something."

On the paper someone had drawn a somewhat detailed sketch of a box. The sketch wasn't nearly as well done as the one Lord MacGregor had done for the harpe he'd drawn in Sir Heff's smithy—

Focus, Laurel.

"What is it?" she asked.

"Teagan said it's a magical nullifier. It's a device enchanted to basically suppress fae or mage gifts in a particular area."

She took the paper. "Like a charm?"

"Yes, but where a charm has to be created wherever you are, this doesn't. All you have to do is open the box and all magic within a hundred-foot radius ceases to work."

"Who has it?"

Luc scratched at his jaw. "That's the thing. The last anyone heard, it was sold to Lord Discordia nearly five years ago. It disappeared from his house around his daughter's birthday that year, but no one has seen it since. We did find out that Sir Heff and his wife, Lady Delmar, visited Discordia Park around that time."

"You think one of them has it?"

Luc smirked. "You haven't heard? Lady Delmar just became the new Lord of the Underworld. She's been part of the youngest prince's team since the beginning."

"You think it's somewhere in the palace."

"It has to be."

Laurel studied the drawing for a few more seconds then handed it back. She wouldn't need it in order to find the box. What she would need was a miracle. She'd been able to find the Underworld headquarters within the palace, though it had only been after she discovered the entrance to one of the tunnels in the kitchen almost two months ago. Adira hadn't listed those in her extensive maps, likely thinking Laurel would need to avoid the youngest prince more than use them. Not that it mattered now.

A creak sounded behind them.

Laurel twirled, her fingers reaching for a blade, but Luc grabbed her arm.

"Don't. It's just Delilah."

Laurel narrowed her eyes as Delilah peeked up again over the top of the back counter. "Is she part of the rebellion?" she whispered. Had Laurel just blown her cover in the palace? Would Delilah use this against her?

"Praise the Goddess, no," Luc hissed back. "What do you want, Delilah?"

She stood all the way up. "I want to know why the kitchen's golden girl and you are sitting in a dark public room."

Laurel narrowed her eyes but didn't say anything. She didn't have to give the girl any explanations. Praise the Goddess it seemed like she hadn't heard anything about the rebel's plans before she arrived in the room. If she had, she likely would have already started throwing accusations around.

Luc rolled his eyes. "Go back to bed before Mr. Rivers catches you down here."

Delilah narrowed her eyes and swept out of the room.

"That girl drives me crazy," Luc said under his breath.

Laurel continued to stare at the door the old undercook disappeared through. "You and me both."

37
AN UNFORTUNATE COUNCIL

Fire will bathe the streets of Olympia in orange.
Men and women sporting compasses on their clothing
will break into houses, pulling out the tenants within
and smashing in the windows. A sparkling dome will
cover the palace. On the rooftops, a woman with a
silver mask watches on.

THE KING CALLED A COUNCIL THE DAY AFTER THE FIRST RIOT.

Paulo sat beside his cousin Peter as they accepted a report from Lady Delmar, who had taken the up role as Lord of the Underworld, much to the surprise of several council members. The seat next to him was empty. Usually, Lady Barclay sat near him at the table, her patience for a number of the council members limited. Paulo counted himself lucky to be considered tolerable by the fierce duchess.

"If our intelligence is correct, which I have no doubt it is," Lady Delmar said, "the fire on the city council lands was created by Day Court magic. How many were brought in to start the fire, we cannot tell."

Paulo had seen the young fae woman, bound in chains. They'd suppressed her magic for so long it had nearly consumed her when they released her from the charmed shackles. Paulo had been taught about judging others— friends, organizations, rulers— by the fruits of their actions. It was the one way he was able to say without a doubt that he was fighting on the right side of the war. He'd also been taught that there were no winners in a war. It was a bloody business, fought because someone believed they had a right, an entitlement, to something they didn't. The Cartographer believed everyone should have magic, that those with magic were to be used to better the lives of those who didn't possess it. But if that were the case, the Goddess would have given everyone the magic the fae had.

She hadn't.

It wasn't part of Her plan.

But no one understood that.

And that was part of the plan too.

Peter stirred in his chair beside Paulo, bringing the world around them back into focus. Lady Delmar still stood by the maps that had been pinned to the council room wall. She explained that the fire had originated on the west side of the city council building and had spread due to the dry shrubbery around the building as well as the rebels who had used flammable fluids to create paths for the flames to follow.

It had been masterfully organized. Only the west side of the council building had been charred and none of the buildings around it had caught fire. The smoke had sent people scurrying from the area, but there had been no reported injuries. Not that that would continue. This was a warning, a tease and everyone at the table knew it.

"And this attack was spearheaded by the rebellion?" Duke Speculo asked.

"Yes, Your Grace. There were several witness accounts of people with compasses sewn onto their clothing or on armbands who were spreading the fire themselves."

They are getting bolder, Prince Evan signed.

The king's amethyst eyes flashed with his suppressed magic. "Have we been able to infiltrate their organization?"

Lady Delmar nodded. "It has taken us several months, but we've made headway. For the safety of our operatives, that is all I'll say for now."

The king nodded.

Paulo picked at the edge of the table where it looked like someone had damaged the wood with a chair or something. Those operatives would be useful in the coming months, but by the time they were able to infiltrate the higher positions in the rebellion, it would be too late for the palace.

"So how are we to punish them?" General Draco asked. "We cannot allow something like this without striking back. I suggest a curfew and a few public floggings in the streets."

Lady Alvis looked over the top of her spectacles at him. "While I agree that there needs to be precautions made for future riots, I don't see the wisdom in punishing the entire city for an attack made by a minority. You may anger the rest of the citizenry into rebellion with such action."

"How do we know they are in minority?" Lord Discordia asked. "We haven't been able to even get a proper accounting of how many rebels we're dealing with. It could be a hundred or a thousand."

The king's advisor leaned back in her chair. "If they weren't a minority, do you think the lot of us would still have chairs at this table?"

Murmurs trickled around the room.

The king grabbed one of the papers in front of him. "How many rebels were the watchmen able to apprehend during the attack?"

"Five, Your Majesty," Lady Delmar answered. "All of them have been placed in the dungeon, and their interrogations are still ongoing."

"Do you know if we caught the orchestrator of the attacks?"

Lady Delmar admitted they hadn't as a vision of Aspen's beau flashed through Paulo's mind. Luc, if he recalled correctly. The man stood around a table, maps scattered in front of him. Paulo had seen similar images of the man over the last few weeks. While he would readily offer the assassin up to Lady Delmar, he kept the information to himself.

The council went back and forth about what to do in retaliation of the attack on the city council building, but in the end, the king made the decision to allow Lady Delmar to continue her interrogations of the rebels and would call for the city watchmen to double patrols around the city. They would show concern, but not force, as Lady Alvis had suggested. It was a wise course and would make the job harder for the rebellion.

How long that would last, only the Goddess and Paulo knew.

After two more hours of strategizing for another riot and coming up with a plan to help restore the city council building, Paulo stood with the rest of the council when the king called the meeting adjourned, but he turned back to the table when someone caught his sleeve.

Prince Evan stood at his side.

A word, Paulo? The prince made the sign of Paulo's name, the sign for the letter P pressed to the corner of the prince's eye, a reference to the way Paulo's eyes changed when his magic was in use.

"Of course, Your Highness."

Paulo followed Prince Evan out of the council room and into the hall. The other members of the council watched them as they passed. Paulo pasted a congenial smile that he prayed didn't look slightly demented onto his face. He dropped the expression when they turned down another corridor, likely headed for the king's study.

How is Mater?

Not even the royal family was immune to Mater's charms. Paulo's smile was genuine that time. "From the sound of her letters, she's well, but you know Mater. She'll face down a troll head on and say she was taking a jaunt. She expressed her wish to visit the palace this summer, though I worry about her traveling alone with this rebellion running about."

I would worry too. She is safer in Delphine.

"I agree." Though for how long that would be true could be debated. Paulo didn't know exactly when the rebellion would strike his march, but he knew the castle wouldn't make it through this war unscathed.

They reached the door to the king's study and Prince Evan pushed into the room without knocking. King Dion seemed to be waiting for them anyhow.

Queen Carnation's seat behind the desk was empty this time. She hadn't been at the council meeting either. Paulo's gut twisted.

"I hope Her Majesty is well?" he asked.

King Dion nodded. "She's been feeling under the weather, but the midwife said that happens sometimes."

Doesn't make it any easier, the prince signed.

Had she been poisoned? Was the future he saw speeding toward them like a charging bull? He hadn't seen the vision again, but there were too many pieces. Too many fractures in Fate's timelines.

The king grunted his agreement. "But my wife's health isn't the main reason we invited you in."

Paulo's gut twisted further. "Oh?"

The prince tapped the table to get Paulo's attention. *We have decided that I need to go to the Isles of Aigean. After this latest attack, it is time to begin treating with what allies we can reach.*

Of course, the king would wish to start gathering his allies. It only made sense. That didn't mean that Paulo was happy about it. Not when those allies where simply waiting to throw a spear at his king's back and burn Olympia to the ground for no apparent reason. They probably believed they had a reason, but the fact they were reneging on their part of the accords they had signed only five years ago rankled him.

That was probably Paulo's biggest issue with it. It had been the blink of an eye— especially for an Aigean— and they were already going back on their word.

"Are you both in agreement?" Paulo asked.

The king nodded. "It seems to be the best course of action. We've had the Aigean delegation here to begin communications. It only seems natural to further those talks as the situation with the rebels continues to escalate."

Paulo smoothed out the creases in his trousers. "When are you planning to set out for the Isles, Your Highness?"

I was thinking one week. I don't want things to be able to escalate too far before I can get the help we need.

Paulo blew out a breath. "I think you are wise, my prince. What can I do to help?"

"We wish to know," said the king, "if there is anything you can tell us about the future of the next few weeks."

Nausea stirred in Paulo's gut. There were a hundred things he could tell them. Sweet Gaia, there were thousands. They passed over his tongue one by one. He could tell the prince about the Aigean's plans with the rebellion. Tell the prince about what the Trident was actually doing in Olympia. He could expose Caspian Delrio and his comrades. He could tell the king about what was going to happen to his wife. His child. His home.

Paulo closed his eyes, though if it was to act like he was looking into the future or if he was trying not to let their hopeful expressions loosen his tongue he couldn't say.

What would Father have done if he had been put in a situation like this?

He would tell the truth. He would tell the royal family what they could expect because they were men to be trusted with that future, to move forward with wisdom and bravery. The brothers were the greatest rulers Olympia had had in generations. They could handle the broken future Paulo saw, that needed to come to pass.

He opened his eyes.

"I'm sorry, but I don't see anything else."

38
THE HEIST

Laurel moved around Aspen, who stood at a cutting board chopping tomatoes and cucumbers for luncheon that day. Neither of them spoke, the heavy silence around them stilling their tongues.

It was too quiet in the kitchens. It had been for two days.

The rebellion had attacked again.

This time, there had been casualties.

One of the lords, some baron or such, had tried to fight back. He'd been a mage, with the power to turn invisible.

He'd been killed in the front lawn of his townhouse.

The council had supposedly been in an uproar. Many of them had arrived at the palace in black, standing in solidarity with their fallen peer as they attended the funeral that morning. Laurel hadn't seen the ceremony, but she'd watched as they'd come to the palace after. She'd been helping Cook pick rosemary in the kitchen herb garden when she saw the carriages stream in. She couldn't have imagined a more somber parade if she tried.

Laurel placed the bowl she'd used to season chickpeas in

the wash basin next to Jeannie. The girl didn't even look up, simply grabbing the bowl and slipping it into the sudsy water. She sniffed and wiped at her eyes.

The screech of a chair split the silence.

Galen stood, his hands clenched at his sides. "Oh, stop your blubbering, Jeannie! You didn't even know Lord Roland."

Cook turned around and whacked his arm with her wooden spoon. "You don't get to decide how people feel, Galen!" She took a deep breath, setting her hands to her hips. "Now listen here. I know this rebellion is a bit of a fright for all of us, but there's no reason for us all to lose our heads just yet. Our king is relying on us. There have been more wars won with a belly full of food rather than an empty one. We're supporting our kingdom the best way we know how— by feeding and caring for those whose job it is to watch over our kingdom and fight for those of us that weren't built to wield a sword or the law."

"But someone died!" Jeannie wailed. "How are we supposed to just move on from that? How are we supposed to just sit here and wait for The Cartographer to get us next?"

"That's just fear taking hold of you, girl." Cook shook her head. "We can't let what-ifs and could-bes rule over us. This palace is a fortress, built by the fae and has withstood hundreds of years' worth of war. She will not fall if there are people within her walls with hope in their hearts and the Goddess's name on their lips."

Laurel met Aspen's eyes over Cook's head. For all Cook's talk about not being able to fight in battles, she could certainly instill bravery in the hearts of even the weakest men.

Cook turned back to Galen. "We're all on the same side, the same team. It's time to start acting like it."

She turned back around, but Galen didn't watch her march back to the stove.

He kept his eyes trained on Laurel.

Laurel tugged Aspen back around the corner and waited. The sound of footfalls found their way down the servant's corridor. She crouched low, bringing Aspen down with her. Laurel held her breath as a scullery maid passed right by them, not seeing them even as the light of her candle brushed over them.

Once the sound of her steps faded away, Laurel stood.

"I can see how you stayed alive in this place for so long," Aspen whispered. The black fabric concealing the bottom half of her face muffled her words, but Laurel heard them well enough.

Laurel didn't reply. Keeping up a steady stream of conversation while they were sneaking about a very high-strung palace wasn't wise, even if Laurel understood Aspen's desire to hear something besides her own thoughts as she had the past two days.

But they needed to get this job done without any hitches.

They crept down the hall, and Laurel stopped at one of the many doors. It was unlocked, just as she expected, and she slipped through quickly.

Aspen slipped in behind her but stopped just inside the door. "The Underworld meets in a storage closet?"

Laurel shook her head and led Aspen farther into the room. At the back of the room hung a large tapestry. She moved it aside to reveal a door.

Aspen chuckled. "This palace is just full of surprises."

Aspen pushed through the door first and Laurel closed it silently behind them. She'd found the door earlier on in her palace reconnaissance, back before Lord MacGregor had stuck his nose into her business. She'd remembered Adira Durant's warnings about the youngest prince, however, so she'd avoided using them, figuring the prince would notice a random person in his secret tunnels more than he would if she just used more public avenues. It had made the job a little more difficult, but she hadn't run into the prince.

However, with the prince gone, Laurel had had plenty of time to scurry around the secret tunnels. She'd been preparing since Luc had given her the drawing of the magic box. This was the first time Aspen had joined her, however. Aspen's nights had been filled with whatever secret mission she was working on.

But Laurel's smile tonight matched hers.

They stopped at an intersection and Laurel peeked around the corner. This was the riskiest part. While the operatives of the Underworld were far fewer than those of Stellatus Hall, they were an organized unit. There were operatives in these offices at all times of the day.

With no one up ahead, Laurel crept forward, staying on the balls of her feet. She drew one of her daggers from the sheath at her hip. Aspen had brought enough steel to share, and Laurel had been able to refill her sheaths after her fights with Lord MacGregor.

Why did she keep thinking of him tonight?

She swept through the hallways, Aspen her shadow. They stepped into a training room just before a pair of spies came around a corner, one of them the size of a horse. Possibly as large as Sir Heff. By the Goddess, what was in Olympia's water? They crept back out after the pair passed by.

Aspen took doors on the left side of the hallway and Laurel took the right. They systematically swept through each room, avoiding ones with people in them. Laurel's ears nearly rang with the quiet she was searching through.

Aspen stopped at a door at the end of the hall, signaling to Laurel that it was locked.

Laurel pulled out the pouch of lockpicks she had in her jacket and set to work while Aspen watched the hall. While everyone in Stellatus Hall could pick a simple lock in less than thirty seconds, Laurel had the types of locks memorized and remembered the sequences.

She had the lock open in ten.

They swept into the room. An office by the looks of it. The room stood in perfect order. Bottles sat in neat rows in their shelves, books lined up straight on the bookcase. Even the maps on the walls hung perfectly level.

Someone took great care with their surroundings.

"Do you think it's in here?" Aspen asked.

Laurel locked the door and slid the cloth covering her face down around her neck. "Might as well look around."

Aspen went to the desk while Laurel perused the cabinets and shelves. *Feverfew, foxglove, galena, goldenrod, hyssop...* She could name every herb and mineral on the shelves. They'd even been alphabetized. She peeked behind the cabinet, looking for seams or hinges that could lead to a hidden door. She also opened all the drawers and found nothing.

"Desk is clean," Aspen reported. She moved on to the bookcases by the desk.

Laurel blew out a breath. "Same with the cabinets." She turned and rifled through the cases of rolled maps next. Still no enchanted box.

The maps on the wall caught her attention. There was a map for the city, marked with notes in a neat, straight script likely belonging to a man. Next to it was the kingdom, then the island, then the world. Laurel brushed a hand over where the isle stood in the middle of an ocean, the Continent the next closest land mass. It was a lovely map. Laurel would have had it framed rather than nailed to the wall. The nail at the top left corner had even worn down the thick paper.

Something niggled at the back of her mind, and she tugged at the nail. It came away from the mortar in the wall easily, as if done many times before. The paper rustled as it curled away from the wall.

"Find something?" Aspen asked.

The niggling in her mind grew and she pulled the paper down to reveal a safe tucked into the wall.

Lord MacGregor's drunken words came back to her.

The box is in the safe behind the map.

She took a step back, looking to Aspen over her shoulder. "How long has it been since you took a class from Master Horace?"

Aspen approached the safe, grabbing a small funnel off the shelf of jars Laurel had looked through earlier. "It hasn't been that long."

Laurel moved one of the chairs in the room closer and Aspen stepped up on it. Pressing the funnel's wide mouth to the safe and the small end to her ear, she waved at Laurel.

"Go stand on the other side of the room so I don't mistake your breathing for a click."

After ten minutes, Aspen finally stepped away. "Got it." She turned the handle.

"Wait!" Laurel hissed, but it was too late.

Aspen opened the safe, setting off a magic ward.

"*RISSA!*" a voice roared. "*STAY OUT OF MY OFFICE!*"

Laurel clamped her hands over her ears. Aspen mirrored her. The booming voice ceased a moment later, but the damage had been done.

"Quick!" Laurel charged forward, pulling boxes and files out of the safe. It really was too bad. She was certain this safe held a wealth of knowledge that could come in handy later on.

At the very back, she found the small wooden box engraved with a rowan tree on the top. She snatched the box, not caring if it had been charmed against thieves. When nothing happened, she sent a silent thank you to the Goddess and pulled her mask back up to her nose.

Aspen burst out into the hallway, her mask in place and Laurel following right on her heels.

"Stop!" a voice called from down the hall.

Laurel looked up and met the gaze of Lady Delmar.

Curses.

"Move!" she shoved Aspen forward as Lady Delmar came barreling down the hall toward them.

"*Stop!*" Lady Delmar's voice echoed behind them, this time, making the mark on Laurel's spine burn.

Aspen grunted ahead of her, likely feeling the same sensation in the back of her leg where her charm was tattooed. Her steps faltered for a second before Laurel pushed her forward.

This was one of the biggest reasons Laurel preferred to do jobs alone. She didn't have to worry about anyone else if she had to run for her life.

"Here," she thrust the box into Aspen's hands. "Get this to Luc. I'll lose them."

Aspen nodded and raced ahead, taking a turn at the next intersection in the passageway.

Laurel continued to run, slowing her steps only slightly to give time for Lady Delmar to see her go a different way. At the first sign of the lady's red hair, Laurel took a turn in the opposite direction.

The siren took the bait.

Praise the Goddess Laurel had traversed the tunnels prior to that night. She would have been trapped in the maze of the secret halls.

Lady Delmar's steady gait behind her grew louder as Laurel

continued to take sharp turns, trying to keep the lady's eyes focused on her and not on the fact that Aspen had disappeared.

Laurel passed by secret door after secret door, the small corks in the walls allowing small beams of light through whatever rooms had magelights lit as she passed by. If her internal compass was correct, she was in the walls of the guard barracks.

"You will stop right this instant!" Lady Rissa called from behind her.

Laurel shook off the inkling of desire to listen to the siren voice and kept running. It wasn't long before Lady Delmar's voice faded far enough behind her for Laurel to change tactics.

They'd reached the residential wing.

She stopped at one of the doors leading into a room and popped the cork from the wall to peer through.

A bedroom stood on the other side, the curtains drawn tight over the windows, though Laurel heard the quiet hush of deep breaths. She replaced the cork and pushed the thin door open. Laurel pressed her ear to the edge of the door and heard the faint tap of Lady Delmar's boots on the wooden planks on the other side.

Laurel pulled away, silently stepping toward the bed, her eyes trained on the hidden door.

Hands came around her waist and her mouth.

In a blink, she was hauled onto the mattress, her back pressed up against a warm chest, the large hand clamped on her lips.

She stayed still as she heard the almost silent brush of the hidden door opening.

Her heart pounded in her chest, the urge to jump from the bed and run burning through her limbs.

The arm around her waist tightened.

The door snicked closed.

She remained still for a count of two hundred. Then, she tapped the fingers at her lips.

They dropped away.

"Thank you," she whispered.

The arm around her waist tightened as if in a hug. "You don't need to thank me. I told you from the start. You can trust me, Laurel."

She spun to face him.

Lord MacGregor's eyes were hidden in the darkness of the room, but she knew the forget-me-not blue stared back at her.

"Even still, I thank you, my lord."

"I've accosted you in a darkened hallway and you've sneaked into my room in the middle of the night." His grin pierced through the dark. "I think it's high time you start calling me Paulo."

39
AN UNFORTUNATE FAREWELL

Prince Evan will arrive at the Aigean Citadel, the merfolk about him buzzing. He will approach a large room filled with all types of water folk, from mer to sea hag to selkie. The mer queen with her crown of coral and sea glass, sits at the far end, pointing a wicked spear at the prince.

PAULO STOOD IN THE PROCESSIONAL LINE BETWEEN PETER AND DIANA, Oliver on the other side of his father. Many of the people around them still sported black armbands in solidarity with the death of Lord Roland. Lady Roland stood in a corner of the room with red-rimmed eyes, having already paid her respects to the king and his brother.

King Dion had decided to have a small gathering to bid Prince Evan good luck and attempt to liven the spirits of the court. The prince's journey brought hope to those around the room. He would go and bring back help from their allies. They would be saved from the rebellion crawling out from the shadows where it belonged.

Their hopes would only feed the nightmares already haunting them.

Diana nudged Paulo, and he looked up to see it was their turn to approach the dais. The king stood in front of his throne, the queen's empty.

Word around the palace said she was visiting her mother in Speculo and hadn't been able to make the journey to bid her brother-in-law farewell in time.

Paulo knew different.

Prince Evan stood beside his brother, his blue eyes sparkling as he received the last compliments of Lady Discordia and her daughter Clarice.

When Paulo reached the top step of the dais, he bowed. "I pray you have safe travels, Your Highness. May you return victorious in your endeavors."

The prince smiled. *Thank you, cousin.*

Paulo stepped aside to allow the rest of his family to offer their well-wishes and approached the king. "I hope the queen's trip hasn't been too much for her?"

King Dion's eyes flicked over the faces around them, and he lowered his voice. "I've been assured she's in fine health, if not a bit fatigued. She hopes to rejoin us here at the palace in a fortnight or so."

"Wonderful." Paulo offered a bow in farewell as the rest of his family caught up to him.

Diana sidled up next to him as they stepped back down to join the rest of the crowd. "What were you and the king talking about?"

He smiled at Lady Nikitas as she offered him a nod in greeting. "Nothing of great importance," he answered.

Diana didn't speak until he met her narrowed eyes.

"My twin sense is pinging. Something's up."

His gaze flicked about. "Can we discuss it in a more private setting?"

She nodded, but her expression said she would hold him to his word.

"Lord MacGregor?" Paulo turned to see Lord Hermen approaching. The man smiled and gave a bow to both him and Diana. "A pleasure to see you both."

"Can I help you, my lord?" Paulo asked.

Lord Hermen drew closer. "I was wondering if you've had word of Lady Barclay recently."

Paulo's brows pulled together. "I can't say I have. Why? Is something wrong?" He knew she was still on the hunt for Penny, checking under every nook and cranny. She'd departed from the palace a few weeks ago, though Paulo's visions hadn't kept him apprised of every stop she made. The last he'd seen of her, she had been headed south, down to Discordia.

"I received word two weeks ago that she made it to my home. Patricia has done her best to help her, but there hasn't been a trace of Lady Penny anywhere. My family has slowly grown more concerned about Lady Barclay's state."

"Is there cause for such concern?" Diana asked.

"I believe so. In fact, she abandoned my home not four days ago, according to my wife's most recent letter. Sneaked out on her own before the household woke and Patricia found her room empty."

Lord Hermen met Paulo's gaze. "Do you know anything about where Penny is?"

Paulo quirked a brow. "Do you?"

Lord Hermen's lips split into a shining smile. "No, I can't say that I do."

With a smile of his own, Paulo bid the minister a good day and pulled Diana forward.

"I feel as if I just watched a conversation happen that didn't match the words being said." Diana leaned closer to him. "Is Dominique all right?"

"She's just fine, Diana."

At least, she would be.

Hopefully.

How Paulo found himself hovering in the doorway of the kitchens that night, he couldn't say.

Prince Evan and the Aigean delegation— Adam, Caspian, and everyone else— had already left, taking advantage of the high tide. Diana had been a bit clingy, likely looking for someone to hold her attention now that Caspian was gone. Paulo had sparred with her for a few hours that afternoon, but it did little to relieve the gnawing in his belly or the ache behind his eyes.

The visions kept coming.

He couldn't do anything to silence them. He wouldn't go to Donnie again, even if the thought of forgetting for a few minutes made his hands shake with desire. He couldn't afford to be anything but alert. To be ready.

But that didn't mean it was easy.

That didn't mean he didn't want to seek out comfort where he could find it.

Cook stood at the stove, using a metal brush to scrub off the flat top. Laurel stood across the room, wetting a rag with oil and setting to work polishing the cupboards. With supper having finished a few hours ago, it looked as if only the two women were left.

Laurel must have felt his presence, as she looked about

until she found him in the shadowy doorway. Her head tilted to the side, but she didn't expose him.

He stepped into the light of the kitchens, revealing himself to the rest of the room.

Laurel stood from her crouch. "Good evening, my lord."

Cook spun around. "Oh, Lord MacGregor. Lovely to see you as always."

"You're too kind." Paulo took a seat at the large table where the taster usually brooded. The man wasn't there tonight, likely abed or waiting on the king for any late-night snacking.

"Something we can help you with, my lord?" Cook asked.

He trailed a finger over the wood grain of the table. There were marks and dents all over its surface, telling stories of stray knives and heavy loads. Splotches of discoloration painted the surface as well, likely from colorful foods long since eaten and forgotten.

Would this be what the kingdom eventually became? Merely another place marked by time, only remembering the lives it had sustained by the scars they left behind. Or would this table be thrown into the fire and a new table brought in? A history thrown away and forgotten completely to make room for something newer.

"Lord MacGregor?"

Paulo looked up and met Laurel's gaze.

Her dark brows pulled together. "Are you all right?"

A breathy sound passed over his lips, but whether it was a sigh or a laugh, he couldn't rightly say. "It seems not even a marquess is immune to the woes of the kingdom."

Cook nodded. "And we'd all be right worried if you were, my lord. Being in a position of leadership without a heart is as worthless as trying to use a colander to carry a bowl of soup. Can't hold anything together for very long."

Paulo smiled at the metaphor. "Yet, we see it happen time

and time again, don't we? Those without heart or empathy climbing the ladder until they're at the top and trying to rule over the rest of us."

Cook settled her hip against the table. "But how long do those leaders really last? They might win through brutality and cruelty, through power and strength, rather than courage and mercy. They might win, but those that are good in their hearts will rise up against them eventually."

"How would you encourage them to rise up, Cook?" Paulo asked. "How would you feed that fire in them, help them overcome the darkness around them and see the light?"

"Well, it's a team effort, you see? We as mortals can only do so much. We have our limitations— not to say that we can't accomplish marvelous things on our own. But to change a heart takes more love than one person can give."

"Are you talking about family?" Laurel asked.

"I'm talking about faith. We have the opportunity in this kingdom to know about a divine creator. While there are few who might know without a doubt that the Goddess is real, the majority of us believe in a celestial being who cares about Her creations and Her children. If we can remind those in darkness that there's someone who's continually shining light around them, who has power to overcome the darkness and that there are others who are there to help and support, then those without hope, those that can accomplish marvelous things, can find it in themselves to do so."

Laurel gave Cook a soft smile. "And how can you be so sure of the Goddess's goodness? I can admit that I was raised to know we have a creator, but I have little to suggest She still cares about those She abandoned to this world."

The back of Paulo's throat went a bit tight. He had never once believed the Goddess abandoned them. Were the teachings about the Goddess so different on the Continent than they were here? From what Paulo remembered, much of their understanding of the Gaia's relationship with mankind came from what humans from the Continent knew. Even the name they worshipped Her with came from the Continent. How much did those people across the sea not know about Her?

Cook snorted. "You're looking at Her very gifts to us right now, child." She pointed at Paulo. "Why would an absentee goddess give her children the gift to see into the future, to prevent calamity from striking and to offer us a better future by the power she has given us."

Laurel turned to Paulo. "Can you do that, Lord MacGregor? Can you save us all from the calamity you've seen?"

Her words were daggers, slicing again and again into an already gaping wound.

"I'm sorry, but I can't say that I get to pick which calamities I save others from."

"So, perhaps your Goddess doesn't care as much as you think She does, if She can't save you from the choices of others."

Cook's brows rose. "I think that's a very narrowminded way of looking at it."

"How so?"

"You can only see one step of the recipe at a time." She walked over and reached up, grabbing one of the cookbooks off the shelf. She opened it up to a single page. "Now, look at this first step in the recipe for *magiritsa*. The pot is boiling with lamb organs. It's violent, and tasteless. If we were telling ourselves that we only had this one step, this one moment, it would look like a calamity."

"But what about the rest of the recipe? It's obvious we would take the lamb from the water and do something with it."

"You're right. There's a thousand different ways we could

dress the lamb, but only one good way to make perfect *magir-itsa*. Eventually, we might be able to figure it out on our own, though it would take much trial and error. But the Goddess, She knows the recipe by heart. She can quote this cookbook front to back and even show you new ways to enhance flavors. How much better off are we if we simply go to the one who knows the recipes? Who understands how the flavors work?"

She gestured to Paulo once again. "We've also been given those who come with the next step or even a new ingredient to add. All these things, the boiling, the chopping, the sweat and tears and feeling like we just can't get it, are all part of making a culinary masterpiece just as they are part of the trials of life."

"While I might see how this metaphor could translate," Laurel said, "what does it have to do with this rebellion? They also claim to be creating a masterpiece. How do you know they're wrong?"

Cook tapped her nose. "A nose never lies. You can usually sniff out a bad egg before you take a bite. We have those instincts, often nudged by the Goddess even, to show us which meal will taste the best and it's usually the one at Her table."

"But if you don't know what She looks like, how do you know where she is?"

Paulo sat there for a moment, pondering. He'd always understood his relationship with the Goddess but hadn't ever thought about what it would be like not to truly know what She had in store for him. He'd had Father to lead him by example. He'd had Mater show him the goodness of his creator even when he doubted.

Who did Laurel have? Who had taught her about her creator? About her goddess?

Cook took one of Laurel's hands. "I think the Goddess is always the one who invites instead of commands. Yes, She is a goddess of order, but She doesn't make you do anything you truly don't wish to, while those who sit at the other tables are doing everything in their power to chain you to a chair."

Paulo smiled. "I can agree with that."

Laurel looked between them. "You're both very sure about all of this."

Cook shrugged. "When you know, you just know. There's no what-ifs about it. I might not be able to say I've sat down and had a cup of tea with our Creator, but I know She's out there. I've lived too long and seen too many things to say otherwise."

Laurel turned to Paulo. "What's your reason, my lord?"

"Perhaps I'm only behind Cook by a year or two"— Cook snorted— "but Gaia has been a part of my life since I was very young. She might be a bit more insistent in Her invitations She sends to me, but it's because She knows better than to be gentle with me. I can be a stubborn lout when I feel like it, but the world needs me— as egotistical as that sounds."

"You? Egotistical?"

Cook swatted at Laurel's quip, but Paulo chuckled.

"I have a mission here, Laurel. A mighty one. Even if I were to stray from the Goddess's path, I know She would still accomplish Her will in spite of me. Sweet Gaia, She still does! I'm an imperfect man who continually goes against what She says in order to get what I think I want, believing that I know better."

"And how has that worked out for you, my lord?" Cook asked.

He barked a real laugh. "I'll let you know when I've grown past it."

Trying to keep his feelings from surfacing in his eyes, he looked at Laurel. "There are still things I'm trying to fight Her on. Things I hope I can change Her mind about."

40
THE RIOT

LAUREL WHIPPED AROUND, HAND ON HER BLADE, WHEN THE BEDROOM door opened.

Aspen swept into their tiny room, her wavy hair in disarray and her cloak tucked close under her chin.

"By the Goddess, it's *freezing* outside."

Laurel straightened. "Where on Gaia's green earth have you been? We're supposed to be at the meeting spot in thirty minutes and you aren't even wearing gear."

Aspen shrugged out of the cloak. "It's fine. Luc will wait for us."

Laurel balked. "I wouldn't. Everything about tonight has an order to it and if he waits for us, he could unravel all his plans— which you would know if you had attended the meeting you were invited to before the first riot or were around enough for me to properly explain what was going on."

"Sweet Gaia, Laurel! There's no need to squawk at me like a hen." She stripped out of her dress and slid into her more tactical clothing that Laurel had retrieved for her earlier.

Laurel watched her carefully. "What are you doing, Aspen?"

Aspen tucked her hair down the back of her hood. "I'm getting ready for this blasted riot, like you wanted." She went to walk to the door, but Laurel grabbed her arm.

"Do we have a problem?"

Aspen rolled her eyes. "Maybe Teagan was right about you. Do you have to act like you're better than everyone else all the time? Aren't you exhausted yet?"

Laurel yanked her hand back. "Excuse me?"

Aspen shook her head. "Never mind."

"You can't just say something like that and drop it, Aspen. You know better than to listen to Teagan. What's going on with you?"

"We're going to be late, Laurel." She strode for the door again.

Laurel grabbed the small pack off her bed. She'd gathered a few supplies— rope, magelights, etc.— that she thought might be useful that evening.

She crept after Aspen, watching the back of her head. Had she really just quoted Teagan? At Laurel's face? Something was decidedly off, but what, Laurel didn't know.

But she would find out.

Once this riot was over and they took the capital, Laurel would sit down with Aspen and get this sorted.

They crept out of the palace. The guards on the walls had increased, cutting off their route through the cave tunnels, but the rebels seemed to be in more places than Laurel had thought. A pair of them had been guards for years, their loyalty to The Cartographer bought over their tenure. How many others in the palace claimed the same? It was only natural that there should be some members of the rebellion in the palace.

Not everyone could be loyal to their monarch. But would the siege actually be more peaceful than Laurel had first believed?

Aspen walked past the guards, Laurel quick on her heels.

Darting a glance at one guard's face, she noticed the large scar running across his nose.

These men knew violence. Were led by violence.

The siege would not leave anyone unscathed.

Laurel took lead once they were out of sight of the palace. Even if Aspen was bitter about her taking charge, she hadn't been there to meet with Luc, so she couldn't have known where to go anyway. She would just have to deal with it.

The streets were empty that night, shutters shut against the cold. While the sky was clear now, it hadn't been earlier, and a fresh layer of snow coated the ground. The streets had been cleared earlier in the day, but there were mounds of the stuff everywhere else. The crisp crunch of it under Laurel's boots had her flinching at every step. It was worse than sneaking through sand and her boot sank into the snow more than once, making her have to trudge through it.

They found Luc right where he said he'd be, in an alleyway a few blocks from the watchtower they were supposed to take down that evening. His shoulders visibly relaxed when he saw Aspen and a smile stretched across his cheeks. "Long time no see," he said.

Aspen sent him a small smile. "Sorry, it's been a busy few weeks."

Luc nodded, as if that explanation were enough. It wasn't, at least for Laurel. But she wouldn't bring it up again. Not when there were other ears and they needed to focus on the task at hand.

"Right," Luc began. "We're to hit the western watchtower. We'll split into two groups." He pulled out the map and laid it down over a barrel someone had left out to collect snow.

Laurel watched the faces around her as Luc continued to go over the plan one more time. There were three others that had been added to their group. Two men and a woman who had a scarf pulled up over her face and a hat pulled down over her forehead. In the lighting, Laurel couldn't make out her features, but none of them wanted anyone to be able to say what the others looked like should any of them be taken.

The thought didn't stop the hairs on the back of her neck from standing on end though.

Luc turned to Laurel. "You and I will take the lead. As the two with the most experience, I would feel better about us taking the brunt of the attack and smashing our way through the tower to the top, where we'll use their fire signals ourselves."

Laurel gave a nod, ignoring Aspen's pointed glare.

He turned to Aspen next. "I want you to take rear. We need someone to keep an eye out and take care of any backup that might show up."

There was wisdom in his decision. As the third most experienced, Aspen would be able to take care of herself and help the team.

Not that Laurel liked the sound of that.

From the narrowing of her eyes, Aspen didn't either, but she knew better than to complain in front of the rebels around them.

Luc then explained their formation. Luc and Laurel would go first, hitting the lower level hard. The trio of rebels would file in one by one, taking down any watchmen that didn't go down under Luc and Laurel's quick attack. Aspen would arrive last, her eyes peeled as she helped take care of the watchmen left. They were to subdue as many watchmen as they could but would use whatever force necessary to take the tower and hold it until the rebels came with their signal.

He rolled the map back up. "Any questions?"

"When is the signal supposed to go up?" one of the men asked.

Luc shook his head. "That depends on the other teams, but hopefully they'll be ready for us after we take the tower.

Without further questions, they got into formation.

Laurel drew her dagger, bouncing on her toes. Her limbs buzzed with energy, and she ran through her breathing exercises, doing her best to keep the adrenaline running through her body at bay. While it was a useful function of her biology, it could lead to sloppy work if she wasn't careful. The rebels settled in behind her, each of the men on either side of the girl.

Luc started forward and Laurel stayed in his shadow. While they were only two blocks away, the pace felt slow even to Laurel. Luc continued to check his watch, making sure their timing was just right. When they reached the street where the watchtower stood, he stopped and turned back to them.

"Last chance to back out." He seemed to say this particularly to the girl in the middle.

No one said a word.

Luc smiled. "Let's go."

Laurel trailed him, no longer worried about keeping pace for the others. The lights from within the watchtower flickered. Two guards stood at the base of the tower, each scanning the street to either side, then turning.

Luc hit the first before he could turn to look at him. Laurel took down the other just as quickly. She clamped a hand over his mouth so he couldn't yell and ran her blade over his throat to steal his voice permanently.

Luc burst through the door ahead of her.

A couple of shouts went up, but Laurel was there a moment later.

Four men stood in the center of the room, their swords drawn.

Luc kicked out at one, snatching the blade from the man's hand and knocking him in the head with it before engaging with the next watchman.

Laurel drew the other dagger from her waist to mirror the one already in her hand and spun them. A watchmen rushed her.

She dodged both of their blades, sliding down and slashing at the backs of their ankles. While their leather boots were thick, her blades cut through them like butter, slicing the tendons there. Both men fell into a heap, not able to hold their weight with their injured legs. Laurel left them for the others to tie up and followed Luc up the stairs. The tower was a small fortress, the stairs running clockwise from the base up to the top. Most architects created fortresses that way, discouraging opposing forces from taking the towers since the curve of the stairs would hinder right-handed swings.

Stellatus Hall trained all of their operatives to be ambidextrous with a weapon.

Three watchmen stomped down the stone steps and Luc met them. He was able to throw one over his shoulder and Laurel took him down.

Luc finished with the other two as another pair came around the corner, stopping when they saw their comrades on the stairs. They raced back up and Laurel heard a door slam.

"Come on," Luc whispered. He took the steps two at a time.

Laurel followed a little slower, keeping distance to prevent herself from being bowled over should he fall or throw someone over his shoulder once again.

She made it to the top of the stairs right as Luc kicked the door in.

He took down two of the four guards before she made it into the room.

She engaged with one as Luc took the other. The guard's short sword came at her stomach, and she twirled, letting the blow sweep past her. She dropped one of her daggers at her feet and snatched the watchman's wrist as he jabbed at her with his sword. With a twist, she snapped the man's small wrist bone and he howled. His sword fell and she shoved him back. As he staggered, she swung her fist at his jaw, knocking him out.

Luc ran for the ladder that would lead to the signal pyre at the top of the tower.

Laurel took a step in that direction, but something told her to stop.

Lord MacGregor's words from weeks ago came back to her.

The watchtower has a man behind the door.

She turned right as a knife came spinning toward her face.

Instinct had her plucking the blade from the air. The watchman couldn't throw as fast as Aspen.

She sent the knife spinning back toward him.

He couldn't even blink before it sank into his chest. He crumpled to the ground.

Laurel stared down at him, her breaths heaving.

Lord MacGregor had seen this.

He'd seen her in this watchtower.

Seen her kill and maim these men.

Yet, he'd warned her.

Why?

Why did he keep protecting her?

More of his words came to her.

I'm sorry, but I can't say that I get to pick which calamities I save others from.

He had saved her from this calamity. He had warned her.

Why?

Luc came back down from the top of the tower. "Threw the last two off the roof. We should head down and check with the others."

Laurel tucked her daggers back into her sheaths and followed him down the stairs.

Aspen stood at the bottom of the steps beside the girl as the men stood watch over the other watchmen. Someone had pinned pieces of paper with crudely drawn compasses to each of their chests.

"We're clear," Luc announced.

Aspen skipped over to them, patting Luc on the shoulder. "Good work, commander! I had full faith in you."

Luc smiled down at her and threw his arm over her shoulders, directing her toward the door. "I appreciate that."

They walked toward the door and the rest of them followed. The rebels fell into step behind Luc and Aspen and Laurel was left with the girl.

Brown eyes met Laurel's and cold rushed down her spine.

Delilah.

Before Laurel could say anything, they'd crossed through the door and the old undercook ran off.

By the Goddess, Delilah was part of the rebellion. For how long? Laurel reached up and made sure her half mask was still in place. Had the girl recognized her? What else did she know about the rebels plans for the future?

Luc and Aspen stopped on the other side of the street where a small group waited. She joined them, coming up beside Luc.

When she looked down, she nearly gasped.

Lying on the ground at their feet was a small child, a boy with hair as brown as Aspen's eyes. His breaths were labored as he lay at her feet, chains clamped around his arms and legs. He had burn marks everywhere the metal touched him.

"Thank you for your assistance," said one of the men. "The Cartographer greatly appreciates it."

They hauled the boy up and he didn't even whimper. His eyes were glazed as they looked up and past Laurel.

Something in her soul fractured the tiniest bit.

41

AN UNFORTUNATE RAMIFICATION

PAULO STARED OUT THE WINDOW OF THE PALACE SITTING ROOM.

He could still see the smoke.

The Cartographer's men had burned down every single watchtower in the city the night before. Reports continued to stream in. Some of the watchmen on duty were injured in the attacks. Most killed. Many of the buildings around the watchtowers had been damaged. There had been businesses known to support King Dion's reign smeared in red paint, crude images of compasses marring their storefronts.

What have I done?

A knock sounded on the door, but he didn't turn. No one could pull him from this window. This tightness in his chest and the pain in the back of his throat.

Jenkins stepped between him and the window, his entire face drawn down in a frown.

"Lord MacGregor?"

Paulo sighed, running his hands through his freshly done hair. "Yes?"

The valet didn't even flinch at Paulo's now ruined hair.

"There is a messenger at the door, my lord. The Council has been gathered."

Paulo's lungs finally took in what had to be the first full breath he'd had all morning. "Thank you, Jenkins. I'll be on my way presently."

Jenkins waited a beat, his eyes flicking over Paulo's face. The man was a worrier through and through. Paulo didn't know what he saw to make him hesitate. Was it the heaviness he felt in his shoulders? The dark circles of sleepless nights under his eyes? Paulo was sure there wasn't a single particle of him that didn't scream his guilt at the world around him.

Jenkins shook himself and stepped away, off to tell the messenger Paulo would be on his way.

What Paulo wouldn't give to stay at that window and not have to confront the dozens of faces in that council room.

But when his king called, he answered.

Jenkins helped him straighten his neckcloth and put on his jacket. The gold paisley did little to brighten his mood.

He met Peter in the hallway, his cousin's face drawn.

"Do you think they'll enact a curfew?" he asked when Paulo took up step beside him.

Paulo nodded. "I don't think they have any other choice. Do you?"

Peter blew out a breath. "Unfortunately, no. I was hoping you would have a solution for all this."

"If I had seen something that ensured the future of this kingdom, don't you think I would be screaming it from the palace turrets?"

Peter grave him a knowing look. "I'm not just talking about your gift, Paulo. I know you. If you knew how to fix all of this, or how to prevent the worst from happening, you would have. You don't need to allow guilt to dog you when there's nothing you could have done to stop what's happened from happening."

The lump in Paulo's throat nearly choked him. As the doors to the council room came into view, the words fell from his lips unbidden. "Cousin, do you have any plans to leave the palace soon?"

"No." Peter frowned. "Should I?"

"It might be for the best. You and Oliver should go to Iatrus Castle. I know Mater will appreciate having you there. Send for your wife as well. Plan to come stay for a few months. Bring your sword."

Peter's eyes went wide. "Paulo, what are you saying?"

But the doors to the council room opened, the roar of angry voices stealing any chance of Paulo blurting everything to his cousin. He stepped through, leaving Peter to either follow or run for the hills. It didn't matter which.

Half of the council was on their feet, yelling over top of one another. Demanding justice. Demanding order. Demanding blood.

Paulo found an empty chair near the head of the table, where the king sat, his face empty of emotion as the nobles around him raged. There wasn't even the usual spark in his eyes. His shoulders bent, his hands limp in his lap. He was breaking. A man on the brink of losing everything he'd worked his whole life for.

Paulo understood the feeling.

"Quiet all of you!" Lord Hermen shouted over the crowd. When the voices settled slightly, he looked up at the king. "The riots aren't the only thing we're here to discuss."

King Dion took a long breath, as if filling his lungs with enough courage simply to hold him up straight. "Thank you, Lord Hermen. Yes, we have much to talk about."

The others settled into their chairs.

He held up a green sheet of parchment. The thick paper shook slightly in the king's hands.

"We've received a ransom note."

"The fae finally reached out?" Lord Discordia asked.

"No, this ransom note is not for my youngest brother, but for Prince Evan."

The room remained silent.

The king set the letter down. "The Isles of Aigean have asked us to surrender the palace to The Cartographer and her rebellion in exchange for Prince Evan. They ask that we treat with them in one week."

The room exploded in a cacophony of outrage.

But Paulo heard none of it.

He watched his king.

He watched as a single tear fell from the corner of the man's eye and was swiped away before anyone else could see.

Paulo sat on the edge of a cliff, watching the churning of the ocean below him. He could hear the crash as the water slammed into the beach, even from a hundred feet above the sand. He could see where the waves had eaten away at the snow-covered rocks below, where the sea had reached its highest tide earlier in the day. The weather really had been cold that year, as he'd told Lady Barclay months ago. Sweet Gaia, had it only been months since he had visited Penny after her abduction by the rebels? When all this truly started?

He should have told someone. Should have confided more in Mater or the king or even Lady Barclay. Perhaps if he had, he wouldn't be sitting on the top of a cliff watching for yet another event he couldn't stop from happening. Another tragedy he allowed because it would save the one thing he cared about in this world.

"What are you doing?"

As if summoned by his thoughts, Paulo looked up to see Laurel standing just behind him, fully dressed in her assassin gear.

Her eyes narrowed. "Are you drunk again?"

"No." He tried to push the word out, but it slipped past his lips in more of a whisper.

She craned her neck, looking down the cliff. "You know if you jump, you won't even hit the bottom. There's a ledge about fifteen feet below you. You'll probably break your legs, but death would be a long time coming."

Paulo startled. "I wasn't going to jump."

"Good." She settled down beside him. "What are you doing down here?"

He sighed. "Did you hear about the curfew?"

"Why do you think I'm back here before midnight?" She grabbed a small chunk of snow and tossed it off the side of the cliff.

The clump of white broke on the ledge fifteen feet below them, as if to prove her point about him jumping.

"I can see into the future, love. Not read people's minds."

She looked up at him. "Is there a mage that can do that?"

"Several. It's not as uncommon as one would wish it to be, though many of them don't like to be out in public."

"Too loud, I imagine."

"Quite, though most learn to control it early on."

They sat in companionable silence for a moment.

"Is there a particular reason you're sitting out here in the toe-eating cold or are you just that crazy?"

Paulo tugged his gloves to cover his wrists. "I was pretty sure I saw something happen tonight. I just wanted to make sure it did before I say anything to anyone."

"What? You don't just automatically know when things happen?"

He shook his head. "Sometimes, I can tell, but it's only because of the things that I see after. Like, I could see Lady Alvis eat a slice of cheese in a vision but won't know if it happened until I see her wrapping an arm around her stomach because it aches. Sometimes, I don't even see that much. I just get to pray what was supposed to happen did."

"That's frustrating."

"You have no idea."

"So, what's happening tonight?"

He looked back out over the water. "There's going to be a large tidal wave. I don't know if we'll see it from the beach, but I wanted to look just in case."

Laurel straightened. "Where? Is it going to hit the coast?"

"Not our coast."

Her posture eased a fraction. "So, you're interested in oceanography?"

"It's oceanology."

"Um, I'm pretty sure you're wrong."

"I guess it wouldn't be the first time."

When she didn't come back at him with another quip, he looked over at her.

She stared out at the sea, her brows pulled together. He watched as her dark eyes soaked in the stars above them, creating their own constellations in her irises. By the Goddess, she was lovely. Radiant. Beautiful.

"Were all the things you told me when you were drunk true? Were they all visions of the future? All warnings?"

He turned his body toward her. "I don't remember much from that day. What did I say to you?"

She looked down at her hands. "My name. A lot, but in between there were other things. You told me not to trust him, though I don't know who you were talking about. You said the box was in the safe behind the map."

"Did you find it?" Paulo didn't know what the box was, but he felt it had been important to her.

She nodded. "Then, you talked about the man behind the watchtower door." She looked up at him, her eyes searching. "Paulo, you saved my life last night. If you hadn't told me that, I wouldn't have even thought to turn around when the man was throwing a knife at my back."

He closed his eyes. The sound of his name on her lips clashed against the knowledge that she'd been in danger. After everything he'd done to make sure she wouldn't die.

"Did I say anything else?"

"There were a few more. 'They'll come after the grinning taster' was one. I imagine you were referring to Galen. I can't imagine who would go after him, no matter how annoying he may be. You said 'she's been poisoned,' though I don't know who you were referring to. Then you told me to choose the knife and to go with you. What does all that mean?"

Paulo might have been referring to the queen about the poisoning. However, after their conversation in the king's study, he didn't know if it was actually poison that killed the queen. Enough women died in childbirth when complications arose.

He swallowed. "Sometimes, there are things I see that I'm permitted to share. That I can see if I don't share, those things will most definitely happen. Then, there are other things I see that if I were to tell anyone about them, they will also happen or in diverting the bad from happening, something even worse will take place. And then there's the third. Those are terrible things that happen, those awful, hard things that I see happen that the Goddess forbids me from speaking about."

"Why would she show them to you then?"

"Because She also shows me the ripples that will take place if those things don't come to pass. There is often more bad for our benefit than good. There is fire in the forest so there can be new life after."

"But why must you be the one to carry that burden?"

He shrugged. "I can't say that I could even guess. Maybe it's that the Goddess is a hilarious prankster or that She is punishing me for the sins of my ancestors."

"I don't think Cook would agree with any of that."

He dug a small stone out from the under the snow. "You're probably right." He tossed the stone down, hitting the ledge below. "I always liked the reason my mother gave. That I was one of few She could trust with such a gift. That She knows me and gave this to me because She could trust me to use it."

"That's a lot of responsibility."

"I don't see how it's any different from other gifts. You remember everything. I don't think I'd want to dwell on my past mistakes or recall in perfect detail every horrible moment I've had to live through."

"I suppose we all have our thing, huh?"

"I think so."

Silence descended on them again, but it was the comfortable kind. Paulo liked that he could talk to Laurel. That she saw through his masks and his ridiculousness. That he could say things that scared most people, and she didn't even blink. That she understood him to some degree instead of dismissing his deeper thoughts as folly or brushing him off for lighter topics. She met him wit for wit, thought for thought.

She pointed a finger out to the waves. "There it is."

Paulo followed her gaze and saw the dark hill of water roll over the waves on the horizon. They watched it until it disappeared to the north of them.

He sighed. "So, it begins."

42
THE TRUTH

Laurel will meet the smiling taster's eyes. They'll have a sort of staring contest, Laurel not willing to give the man whatever victory he thinks he's won. The garnet color will flash with triumph, and he'll turn to the door. Three guards will burst into the room from the outside. Laurel will leap in the direction of the dining hall but will be cut off there as well. Galen will come at her with a large pan. She will cut off his arms. She will fight all six of the guards at once, taking out five when more arrive from the outside. She finally goes down with a sword in her back.

"Cook, have you seen Aspen anywhere?" Laurel asked, coming into the kitchen. Only Cook and Dan stood in the room, the other kitchen staff regularly arriving a quarter hour or so after Cook and the undercooks did. Laurel grabbed her apron off her hook and slid the loop over her head. One of the laundry girls had washed it last night, praise the Goddess.

"I can't say I have, dear." Cook flipped the couple of *pita* breads in the oven over. "I know she swapped half-days with Dan here to have this morning off, but I didn't see her head out. She must have snuck past me."

She hadn't mentioned trading her half-day when they'd gone to bed the night before, especially after they'd asked for the same day off that week to go into the city. Laurel looked to the door as if Aspen would simply appear there, blond hair framing her face and brown eyes sparkling.

But she didn't.

"I'm sure she'll be back in time for the luncheon rush. Praise the Goddess most of the nobles have finally left for their own homes. I imagine the attacks have spooked them. Though, I hope we can rally and take back our city soon."

After the last riot and news of Prince Evan's capture, the nobles had begun leaving the palace in droves, racing home to get their own lands fortified or simply to avoid the conflict they could feel coming. The air practically screamed with apprehension.

But that might have just been for Laurel. She pulled a false smile on her face and grabbed the knife from the block to start chopping up the spinach Cook would need for her *spanakopita*. "As do I."

Cook, Laurel, and Dan fell into rhythm around each other as they normally did. When the rest of the kitchen staff arrived, Cook barked out orders, sending everyone in the kitchen scurrying about as she always did. It was the first piece of normalcy Laurel had felt for days.

After finding Paulo on the cliffs only two nights ago, something in her gut had twisted.

No, that wasn't right either. It had started the night of the riot. First, the words Aspen had said. *Maybe Teagan was right about you. Do you have to act like you're better than everyone else all the time?* They kept echoing over and over in Laurel's mind. She still hadn't been able to talk to Aspen about what had sparked such contention between them. It had started to fester in Laurel's chest, making it hard for her to stay focused.

Then, there had been the little fae boy.

Paulo had been right. Sometimes, it was difficult to remember everything so clearly.

The little boy's emaciated frame laying in the snow was burned into the backs of Laurel's eyelids. He couldn't have been older than ten, his dark hair matted in tufts around his head. The harm of children was one thing Laurel didn't tolerate. It was one of the biggest reasons she wished to leave the Order. No child should have their lives sold out from under them. No child should ever fear anything from her. She didn't harm expectant mothers for the same reason. No babe should have to face retribution for the choices of others. She'd fought tooth and nail on multiple occasions to not take jobs on children. The first few she absolutely said no to she'd been severely punished for. Teagan had had her flogged. He'd even stuck her in an isolated chamber for two weeks, barely feeding her.

But she hadn't broken, and it had cost him more not to have his favorite pet available. So, he'd learned to give those jobs to others. She didn't pay attention to who got them, but it wasn't hard to guess. She didn't associate with those assassins either.

If Adira Durant was using children to win her war, Laurel would certainly be avoiding any other geases with the woman's name attached to them.

A squeak of a chair announced Galen's arrival.

"Good morning, Galen," Cook greeted him. "I'll have breakfast for His Majesty ready in ten minutes."

"No rush at all," Galen said. "I'm more than happy to wait."

Laurel looked over her shoulder at him.

His garnet eyes glittered with glee as he looked back at her. His generally grouchy demeanor had disappeared. A large smile stretched across his face.

How he could grin like a maniac at that moment, she had no idea. The man had been absolutely curmudgeonly for the past few months.

It happened again, that niggling in her mind. Laurel's entire body stiffened.

They'll come after the grinning taster.

Her ears caught the sound of boot falls and the chink of metal.

She bolted for the door.

Three guards slammed it open, cutting her off.

She leapt, using both feet to kick the one in front back into his comrades. They all tumbled back, but that doorway was cut off.

Spinning the other way, she raced across the kitchen, hurdling over the large table.

"Laurel!" Cook shouted.

Laurel didn't even look at her. More guards streamed through the doorway leading to the dining room. She ducked under the sword of one, landing a blow with her knife to the back of his unprotected knee. He yelped and went down. Laurel grabbed his sword and used it to fight off the next guard. He lost several of his fingers on his sword hand. The next one came, then the next. She laid them all flat, blood smearing the apron around her waist.

Her heart thumped hard against her ribcage. So, Lord MacGregor had finally called in the cavalry. Or Delilah had. Someone had exposed her and now her position in the palace was void.

More guards arrived through the doorway leading outside and Laurel grabbed a second sword off the ground. She spun toward the door, ready to fight her way out of the cursed palace once and for all.

She didn't see Galen coming at her until he swung the cast iron pan right into her face.

Darkness took over before she hit the floor.

Consciousness came, though Laurel wished it hadn't. Her head spun. She tried blinking, but only saw swirls. She also couldn't move her hands. Or legs. She tried to breathe evenly. By the Goddess, her head *hurt*. She closed her eyes again, waiting for the vertigo to pass.

For being such a layabout, Galen had a swing.

Keeping her eyes closed, Laurel prodded her teeth with her tongue. None had cracked, praise the Goddess, but she could feel the swelling grow on her cheek. If he'd fractured her jaw, she probably wouldn't know until the swelling went down a bit. She licked at her lips and found a split on the bottom one.

Once the initial dizziness had somewhat faded, she squinted her eyes open. She'd lost consciousness long enough for the guards to bring her to some sort of cell. She was strapped to a metal chair in the middle of a room. The chair was bolted to the ground, unfortunately. A drain sat a few inches from the toe of her left boot.

That was all she could see.

Carefully, she looked up.

The magelight above her head shone down in a perfect circle, isolating her in the room but also making it difficult to see anything not in the circle of light around her chair. Laurel recognized an intimidation tactic when she saw one. The light was crafted to make her feel like she was completely alone when she wasn't.

Her fingers tingled and she wiggled them. None of them seemed to be broken, though all of them boasted bloody knuckles that were still scabbing over. They really had gotten her into this room quickly, which meant she was still in the palace. She twisted her wrists and ankles in the bindings. The blasted things were probably half an inch thick.

"It was Laurel, right?"

A fog crept into Laurel's mind and her head snapped up. A burn started up between her shoulder blades, clearing the mental attack.

Lady Delmar stepped out from the shadows.

Ah. They were in the Underworld part of the palace.

Laurel sat back in her chair. "Good morning, Lady Delmar."

The lady's eyes narrowed. "So, I was right. I remember you, standing on my doorstep. If I'd thought we would find ourselves in this situation only a couple months later, I would have done things a little differently that day."

Laurel bobbed her head. "I can understand that."

Lady Delmar reached into the shadows and pulled another chair across from Laurel. "Do you know why you're here, Laurel?"

"Do *you* know why I'm here?"

Lady Delmar primly settled her skirts around her. "You're here because we received a tip that you were seen colluding with known members of the rebellion. You were witnessed killing multiple watchmen the night of the last riot and seen meeting with known rebel sympathizers."

Of course someone had turned her in. But who?

Delilah's shining eyes flashed in her memory. The old undercook would have loved to get this kind of revenge on Laurel, but how had she exposed her without showing her own hand? And who would trust her word after what happened with the king?

But then, Lord MacGregor had known about the guards coming. Had it finally come time for him to betray her? He knew she was supposed to assist Aspen and Luc with the siege. Had he simply bided his time until they were days away to finally expose all of them. Where was Aspen? Did they have Luc too?

"That's a lot of work for a kitchen girl."

Lady Delmar smirked. "If you're just a kitchen girl, I'm just a knight's wife."

She studied the siren across from her. The woman was staring at her, waiting for her answer. At least they wouldn't be hemming and hawing throughout the conversation. Laurel's respect for the lady went up a notch.

"What are you getting at, my lady?" she asked.

Lady Delmar pursed her lips. "You were exposed this morning and instead of coming quietly, you attacked royal guards, severely injuring six and killing two. When the king hears the report from the captain of the Guard, he'll sentence you to death."

"Yes, that's generally the consequence of killing people."

Lady Delmar leaned forward. "Give me a reason to convince the king otherwise."

Laurel chuckled darkly. "I don't think so." She wouldn't talk and she wouldn't expose Aspen. If the Underworld went digging deep enough, they would find their connection.

I am watchful. I am focused. I am silent.

"Why not?" Lady Delmar asked.

"Because it wouldn't matter in the end anyway. I stay or I go, the result is the same." She'd been made. Teagan would leave her to rot on this island if she took the deal or she would hang. Death was still death.

"Is your allegiance so tied to The Cartographer?"

That earned the lady a real laugh. "I have no allegiance to the rebellion or their crazy leader." And it didn't matter either way. She wouldn't be able to act in contradiction to the geas. Lady Delmar wouldn't be able to get any valuable information from her.

Lady Delmar tilted her head to the side, exposing a bit of her neck. Three lines marred her skin. Siren gills.

"Who does hold your allegiances?"

Laurel shrugged. "Why does it matter? You and I are still on very opposite sides of this war, no matter how much you offer to pay or how many times you threaten to wrap a noose around my throat."

"I really would hate for that to happen."

"As would I, but we don't get to pick and choose when we die."

"Oh, you are too much fun." Lady Delmar crossed a leg over her knee. "Where are you from, Laurel?"

"Not from somewhere as interesting as you, I'm sure. Did your kingdom's betrayal and capture of Prince Evan come as any shock to you?"

"If I'm being totally honest? No, it didn't. What I am shocked about is the fact that it was Adira Durant who was able to turn them against King Dion. Even if she was only known as the wife of the spymaster, the name *Durant* is not one that goes hand in hand with trust in any form."

The siren was trying to catch her in a trap now. "Who's Adira Durant?"

Lady Delmar tsked. "Please don't embarrass us both by pretending you don't know."

Laurel shook her head. "I'm not the wealth of knowledge you think I am. I'm no one."

"Are you sure?" The lady's lips curled up at the corners.

"I've worked in this palace for nine months. I know how to cook fish a hundred different ways, yet you're saying I'm some great mastermind in this rebellion. How can you be so sure I am someone important?"

She uncrossed her legs and leaned forward once more. "Because I'm pretty sure I'm looking at a Daughter of Stellatus, one with a charmed tattoo somewhere on her body that keeps her from being influenced by magic. I think I'm looking at an assassin who has been paid by Adira Durant to help dismantle our monarchy so she can enact revenge on those that she has it in her deranged head wronged her. I think you've come to make sure the throne is all cleaned off for when she returns from Faerie on the bloodied backs of fae slaves."

All of Laurel's good humor fled.

Lady Delmar smiled. "Did I miss anything?"

43
AN UNFORTUNATE GOODBYE

Diana will follow Paulo through the palace as he escorts the king and queen through the halls. When they reach the royal sitting room, she will stop at the door. Paulo won't be able to convince her to come inside with them. She will say she is the last line of defense. For the queen. She will shut the door between them. Paulo will never see her again.

PAULO GRABBED WHAT HAD TO HAVE BEEN THE FIFTIETH KNIFE HE'D found scattered around Diana's room and threw it into the nearly overflowing trunk on the bed.

"Why do I surround myself with women with a propensity for pointy objects?"

"Why do you feel it necessary to invoke your own death by touching said pointy objects without permission from one of the women you surround yourself with?"

Paulo whirled and found Diana leaning in the doorway, a hunting knife spinning in her hand.

He swallowed. "Jenkins said you were scouting."

"I'm back from scouting." She sheathed the blade and took a predatory step into the room. "What are you doing, Paulo?"

He turned back to the bed and went to the trunk. "I'm helping you pack." He tried to shut the lid, but one of Diana's many furs had stuck in the hinge.

"I didn't realize I was going anywhere."

Paulo got the lid on without damaging anything, but he couldn't get it to shut enough for the latches to close.

Diana grabbed the trunk's handle and pulled it across the bed, out of reach. Her blue eyes flashed. "What's going on?"

"I need you to head back to Delphine." He reached for the trunk and pulled it back.

Diana stopped the trunk halfway. "Why would I do that? Laurel is in the dungeon, the queen is sick, and I know the rebels aren't done attacking yet. Why would I leave when everyone needs me?"

Paulo yanked the trunk toward him. "Because you need to go to Delphine where you'll be safest."

Diana yanked it back toward her. "I just told you that I'm needed here. Whether I'm safe or not, I'm not going to leave behind those that I care about."

"Don't be obstinate, Diana." Paulo tried to pull the trunk back towards himself, but Diana held firm.

"I'm not the one being obstinate. You're the one who won't stop bossing me around long enough to sit down and tell me what's going on inside that gigantic head of yours."

"What's going on is that our kingdom is under attack and like the rest of the nobility we need to be fortifying our lands and our assets against invasion. You need to be in Delphine, so you aren't underfoot, and I don't have to worry about you."

She snorted. "When have you ever had to worry about me?"

"Only every cursed day of my life." He pulled the trunk back toward him. "Now be a good girl and help me get the rest of your things packed."

Diana grabbed the trunk and threw it off the bed, scattering its contents all over the floor. Daggers landed point down in the carpet and packages busted open and sent dozens of arrowheads all over the floor. The trunk hit the wall with a *thunk*.

"Stop it!" Paulo snapped. "You're being a spoiled brat."

"And you're being a child with a superiority complex. You don't just get to come into my room and tell me I have to leave just because you say so."

"Yes, in fact, I do."

"How do you figure?"

"Because I'm the *cursed marquess!*" Paulo hollered. "That's why! My job is to make orders, and, as a woman in my household, you're supposed to follow them. That's the blasted way it's supposed to work!"

Diana's blue eyes turned dark. She stared at him for what felt like an eternity, not breaking his gaze. A wolf come up against an opponent. Her chest fell in slow, calm motions, but the roiling fury in her eyes told Paulo she was ready to go to blows, to the Goddess with what he said.

There had been few times over the years when Paulo had seen that look.

When she'd been ten and someone had commented on how she would be forced to wear dresses within the year. She'd taken the few dresses she did have and set them on fire in the front drive.

She'd been fifteen and Lord Angus had come asking for her hand, telling her that no other man would take her. That time, she'd grabbed the scrawny man and threw him out the second story window of Iatrus Castle's parlor before Paulo could stop her— not that he tried very hard.

Then, last year, one of Delphine's local hunters had reported poachers in the forest north of the castle. The poachers had nearly killed an entire lodge of otters Diana had been working for years to repopulate. She'd gone off for a few days and Paulo hadn't heard any more about poachers, though he didn't look too closely at why.

And now, she gave him that look.

It had never been directed at him.

He nearly caved, right there and then.

But he ducked his chin, not breaking eye contact. He needed her to go home. He couldn't risk her being there. She was too impulsive. If she truly knew what the next few days would be like, she would make it even worse by trying to help.

And he would have the guards drag her to the carriage kicking and screaming if he needed to.

Her jaw clenched and she came around the bed.

Paulo stood his ground. "Diana—"

She punched him square in the eye.

He fell to the floor. By the Goddess, when had she gotten so *strong*?

Before he could push himself to his feet, Diana grabbed the front of his shirt and pulled him up.

If Father hadn't pounded it into his head not to disrespect the women in his family, let alone *any* woman, he might have hit her back.

That predatory gaze remained as she brought her nose within an inch of his.

"I'll go, brother, but when all this is over, you'd best not forget what happened in this room. Because I won't, and I'll have at least several days to mull over what kind of revenge I'll enact for this." She shoved him away and he barely caught himself before he fell again. "Get out of my room."

He strode toward the door and opened it, but before he could close the door behind him, he stopped. "I'll have Jenkins accompany you. To make sure you get to Iatrus Castle."

She grabbed one of the daggers from the floor. "Get out!"

He closed the door and heard the dagger sink into the wood on the other side.

Again, he asked himself why he had to be surrounded by such difficult women.

He followed the guard down rows of cells. There were several men and women in the dungeon cells. More than Paulo thought there would be. The Underworld seemed to do a good job at rounding up the rabble— a characteristic that would serve them well in the coming months.

The guard stopped at an iron door that stood guarded at the end of the hall.

"What's this?" he asked.

"Another cell, sir, though this one is charmed."

Paulo frowned. "But she can't do magic."

"It's also the most secure cell in this section. She's already attacked four guards."

Yes, Paulo had seen that. After her first altercation in the kitchens with the guards, they'd thrown her in here and after two days she had tried her best to escape. Paulo hadn't seen much, the future shifting so rapidly he didn't know which future had become the past.

He took in a deep breath. "Can I still see her?"

The guard grabbed a handle in the door and slid a small

section of the door open. There was just enough room to shove a bowl of gruel through. Two such bowls sat on the ground, still full.

He couldn't see Laurel anywhere.

Paulo looked to the guards. "Can I speak with her in private?"

The guards exchanged a glance. "Our captain has made it clear we aren't to leave anyone alone with her."

He waved a hand. "Then walk away far enough to let us speak but keep an eye on things. I can assure you, she isn't going to pull a knife on me."

The guards hesitated for only a moment before deciding it would probably be fine. They walked halfway back down the row of cells, their eyes never straying from Paulo.

"Are you sure I won't pull a knife on you?"

Paulo's gaze returned to the little window, but he still couldn't see Laurel.

"While we have a past history of sharp things pointed where they shouldn't be, I thought we'd moved past that."

Her brown eyes filled the small window. Ah, she'd been standing just to the side, keeping out of view. A bruise crawled up her cheek and flakes of blood speckled her forehead. He couldn't tell if it was her blood, though he guessed it wasn't.

The expression on her face was guarded. Blank. "Then you had to go and expose me. I knew it would happen, though I thought we'd moved past that."

She didn't spit or growl her words. They were cold and matter of fact. Like she was only talking about the weather or which of Prince Evan's prize stallions would win the race that summer.

But a small fissure of hurt sat in her eyes. Paulo stared at it for a long time.

"I didn't turn you in, Laurel."

Her eyes narrowed. "How else would the palace guards have known who I was? You were the only one who knew I was here to try to assassinate the king."

Paulo leaned his head against the top of the little window. "I never told anyone, I swear. I told you I was trustworthy. Why would I turn you in when I've been working so hard to gain your trust?"

"If it wasn't you, then it was Delilah." She let out a heavy breath. "That's why Galen was smiling. It was him. He must still be talking to her."

"How did she even know?"

Laurel scrubbed her face with her hands, the knuckles of each finger scabbed over. "Don't you already know, oh mighty seer? She's part of the rebellion. She was there at the riot. She recognized me, I know she did. This is her ultimate revenge— or what she thinks is her revenge. I won't be in here long."

Paulo grabbed the edge of the window. "Laurel, the king is going to put you to death for this."

Her brown eyes squinted at him. "Before tomorrow night?"

"I've seen..." His words were swept up in a vision, this one taking complete hold of his mind.

Laurel will stand on the other side of the door, watching the rows of cells as someone unlocks her door. When they finish, they look up at her, the silver of their mask gleaming in the firelight.

He jerked back from the cell door.

"What?" Laurel asked. "Paulo, what did you see?"

He blinked at her. "There's more of you here." While Laurel had told him there wasn't any other masked assassins in Olympia, it couldn't be true. Someone with a mask was poisoning the queen and would possibly help Laurel out of the cell.

"What are you talking about? What did you see?"

"Laurel," he reached for the cell again, laying his fingers over hers, "you have to stop this. You have to stop whoever else is here from killing anyone. There's too much at stake."

She ripped her hands from his. "You can't tell me to stop. This is exactly what I was sent here to do. This is my job. This is how I'm going to free myself."

"Don't you get it?" he hissed. "This is the freest you've ever been! You can let go of this life, this terrible honor you've been holding onto. Why can't you understand that there's nothing keeping you from coming with me? From becoming everything you were meant to become?"

"You aren't the author of my destiny, Lord MacGregor," she snapped back. "You don't get to decide who I am. You don't get to decide how I feel or what I want. You're *nothing* to me."

Paulo reared back, the words a knife in his chest. Of course he was nothing to her. She'd made that clear from the start. They were too different. Too deep in the trenches on opposite sides of a war. She was an assassin sent to kill his king. He was a marquess with a superiority complex, just as Diana had said.

He blew out a breath. "Do you even know what you want, Laurel? What you truly want? Or are you so mired by the skewed sense of honor that you can't let yourself take what you want?"

Laurel kicked the door enough to rattle it. "You know what I want, *my lord*? I want you to leave. You and I have nothing else to say to each other."

Paulo's heart sank. "You're so much better than all of this, Laurel. You can be so much more than what those around you think. You said I'm not the author of your destiny. You're right. But neither is your sister or your mother or your master. Don't let them hold you back either."

"I'm not," she ground out.

Paulo looked over his shoulder. The guards were walking toward them now. He turned back to her one last time.

"I desperately hope not."

44

THE LIES

LAUREL WATCHED PAULO'S RETREATING FORM UNTIL THE UGLY GUARD slid the window cover into place and took most of the light back out of the room.

Who was Paulo to tell her who she was? Why did he constantly have to assert himself into her life? They had no history. They had no relationship. Honestly, she was more likely to kill the man than kiss him.

Though she hadn't killed him.

And she had kissed him.

"Blast it all," she hissed. She stayed near the door until her eyes readjusted to the low light in the cell. It wouldn't do to go romping around without being able to at least make out where the walls were. She had enough bumps and bruises from the last several days.

When she could finally make out the lines of lighter mortar between the dark stones of the cell, she stepped forward. Hopefully, Paulo hadn't been able to see the sad state of her temporary home. The guards had stripped the cell of every-thing but a chamber pot, which hadn't been emptied since she'd arrived. Not that she blamed the guards. She'd bloodied too many of their comrades' faces. But it was still disgusting.

She stepped over the crusty mush the guards had been trying to get her to eat. She'd eaten the first day, only to find the meal laced with poison, enough to knock her senseless if not kill her. She'd recognized the rebel guard from when she and Aspen had gone to help Luc. She had seen the frustration in his eyes when she had set the bowl down. Apparently, the rebellion didn't do well with loose strings. When he reached into the cell for the bowl, she'd grabbed him, pulling him against the bars, breaking a few of his teeth and nearly getting her hands on a few keys before the other guards on duty got involved. All of them had left a bit more banged up than they'd been when they'd arrived that morning.

On the other side of her mush, she laid down on the ground, trying to stay near the slivers of light coming through the crack between the door and the floor. There wasn't much, but it was enough. She set her fingers behind her head and brought her knees up. She began another set of sit ups, the only thing keeping her sane in the tiny room. Well, crunches, pushups, sit ups, and a number of other exercises. It wouldn't do to let her body atrophy while she sat in this dank cell.

But exercise on an empty stomach could only go for so long.

Her belly cramped furiously as she did her last set of sit ups. If all went according to plan, she would be out of here in two more days.

Two more days without food or water.

She would have to eat some of the next meals they brought. Luckily, she'd built up a tolerance to most poisons over the years, so while she could still die, it had to be by a much higher dose than what would normally be appropriate for someone of her weight. Not that that would really be an issue, considering whatever untrained idiot they sent in here to kill her could simply dump a handful of belladonna in her breakfast and get the job done.

Poisoning to kill didn't take as much finesse as it did simply to sicken someone.

Laurel sat up and scooted toward the side of the cell. The stones were cold under her hands, but the exercise would also help her stay warm. The weather outside had been growing warmer, but the cells stayed at a cold, dank temperature that made her shiver herself to sleep and had her waking up with leg cramps.

She rested her head against the wall. As the night grew quieter, the voices in her head— mainly Paulo's— grew louder.

Why had he come to see her? Didn't that cause people to ask questions? Or was the cursed marquess simply above such reproach? If that was the case, the kingdom of Olympia needed to open their eyes. The man was playing all of them even better than he played his stupid lyre.

And why would he even want Laurel to be on his side? He didn't even really know her. Yes, she was an assassin and having her on their side would keep her from killing the king, but with Paulo in the king's pocket, they didn't need to get her to ally herself with them. He could counter any attack the kingdom faced.

She sat up. Really, why hadn't he been the one to turn her in? He'd already mentioned Teagan. He must have known about Aspen and Luc. Why hadn't he turned them all in? He had everything he needed to implicate them. She'd asked herself the question before, but her confusion around it only grew.

If Paulo MacGregor was so loyal to his king, why wouldn't

he do everything in his power to stop her? Or was it something else?

Where did his true allegiances lie?

Something on the other side of her door clicked and she jumped to her feet. The door opened enough to let someone in and then shut immediately after.

"Laurel?" Aspen whispered.

Laurel grabbed her, burying her face in her shoulder.

"Where the curses have you been?" Laurel said. "How did you get in here?"

"Don't worry about that." Aspen pulled back. "After you were taken, they interrogated the entire kitchen staff, me most thoroughly. Honestly, Laurel, you shouldn't have gotten caught."

"I know that." Laurel took a step away. She still couldn't see Aspen's face, but just having her close eased some of the hurt in her chest, if only a fraction. "I've been in here for days without a word from you, and I didn't even really see you before then. What's going on?"

Aspen moved about, grabbing something out of a bag tied to her waist. "You need to eat." She stuffed the bundle in Laurel's hands.

Inside, two *pita* breads and what felt like some kind of cured meat sat at the bottom.

"Bless you," Laurel whispered. She grabbed the bread and took a big bite. A moan worked her way up her throat. There was just something special about food that hadn't been poisoned.

"You're welcome," Aspen said. "Now, you don't need to fret about what's going on outside of this cell. I've got everything under control."

Laurel swallowed the bread. "So, the plan is to leave me in here until the siege?"

"Unfortunately. We don't want anyone running off to go find you. We have everyone right where we want them. But part of the original plan was to free the rebels in the cells anyway. You were just added to the list."

"What's the rest of the plan?" She took a bite of the meat, a mixture of lamb and beef that melted on her tongue.

Aspen laid it out. First, they would take the guard barracks. There were plenty of rebels who would be able to overpower all the guards stationed there, especially as they would strike right at nightfall, when the guards were getting ready to switch for patrol after supper and most of the palace would be distracted getting everything ready for the night. That was also when they would be letting the prisoners out of the cells. All of them, much to Laurel's distaste. She knew there were several within the dungeon that had committed serious crimes, not just working for the rebellion.

They would hit the servant's section right after that. There were several members of the rebellion already sitting in high-ranking service positions. They would be taking control of the servant quarters and locking up anyone they didn't know were directly involved with the rebellion.

After those had mostly been finished, they would strike at the residential wing. Without anyone to stand in the way, the nobility still in the palace would be sitting ducks. The rebellion would take the dining hall, blocking off any exits and taking the nobility there.

"What about the queen?" Laurel asked.

Aspen shook her head. "We don't need to worry about her."

Laurel's stomach twisted. "Is she all right?"

"Why does it matter? We're going to kill her anyway."

Laurel chewed on the inside of her cheek. Of course they were. They would have to if they were going to truly take

Olympia for the rebellion. Her and King Dion couldn't be kept alive, not if they wanted true control. She knew that.

Why did it make her chest tighten?

"And what are you going to do about Paulo?"

Aspen's head tilted, though Laurel still couldn't see her expression. "Who?"

"Lord MacGregor. The seer?"

"Oh, right. We actually don't have any particular plans for him."

Laurel's jaw fell open, and her teeth clicked when she closed it again. "What do you mean you don't have a plan for him? He's the most dangerous man in the palace."

"I think you're giving that man way too much credit. If anything, he's a charming lordling who can perform party tricks."

"You're kidding." Paulo was fooling everyone around him with his games. Even Aspen. Laurel reached out and grabbed her arm. "Aspen, the man can see the future. He knows we're coming and there's no telling what he's going to do about it."

Aspen tugged her arm away. "I think someone fell for a handsome face and didn't want this job in the first place."

Laurel froze. "Is that really what you think? That I let myself get distracted and was slacking on the job?"

Aspen shrugged. "All I know is that you weren't able to get a very easy job done. You're not infallible, Laurel. You can have feelings. Desires. It's all right to admit that you want to enjoy yourself before you finish a job. Everyone does it."

"What?" Laurel couldn't even grasp the words coming out of Aspen's mouth. "Are you saying I'm not doing my job because I'm falling in love?"

"Sweet Gaia, Laurel. You don't have to keep up your pious act. I'm not a child. Teagan has told me enough of the things he's heard you do on your missions."

"*What?*" Laurel snapped. "What the curses does Teagan even know? He doesn't have any access to my missions." And why on Gaia's green earth was Aspen even talking to Teagan? The man was a snake on even the best days. Why would Aspen believe anything that came out of his mouth?

"Just stop." Her voice grew quiet. "You don't need to make excuses. I get how easy it is to get distracted, but I'm here to help you. The king will be easy to take care of. Honestly, the only reason he's even still an issue is that I'm trying to let you make the kill so we can all go home after this."

"If you think Lord MacGregor would let you anywhere near the king, you're insane."

"Why can't you just be grateful that I'm helping you?" Aspen took a deep breath. "It doesn't matter. Lord MacGregor doesn't matter. The only thing that *does* matter is getting this mission done."

Laurel bit back the torrent of angry words. Aspen didn't think Laurel was grateful? That she didn't understand where Aspen was coming from? Everything Laurel had ever done was for her sister. For their future. She'd done heinous things in the name of letting her sister have some sense of normalcy growing up. She'd sacrificed her happiness, her future, her life so that Aspen wouldn't have to do the things she did. So she could help her sister have options Laurel never had. Laurel had been sitting in a prison cell for days, keeping Aspen safe as she was interrogated and poisoned. She'd come to this cursed kingdom to win Aspen's blasted contract.

Where was Aspen's cursed gratitude?

Aspen stepped toward the door. "I'll come get you in two days. Be ready."

"Aspen, wait. We need to—"

The door shut and the click of a key in the lock sealed the silence between them.

Laurel threw the bag with the half-eaten food against the wall of her cell. Her breaths came out in hot, angry gasps.

What just happened?

Laurel had believed they understood one another. That they were a team. That they were working toward the same things. That even though Laurel had to be gone so often, that even if she wasn't around as much, they were both on the same page. They both wanted the same future.

She swiped at a tear running down her cheek.

It was fine. They could talk about it after all this was over. They would get back on the same page.

Only two more days and Laurel would fix all of it. Just like she always did.

45
AN UNFORTUNATE VICTIM

PAULO KNOCKED ON THE DOOR TO THE KING'S STUDY BEFORE STICKING his head into the room. "Good morning, Your Majesty."

The king looked up, and Paulo got his first real look at his face. Dark circles bruised the skin under his eyes. Hairs had fallen from his signature queue at the nape of his neck, catching on the overgrown stubble shadowing his jaw. His amethyst eyes stared back at Paulo, dull and exhausted.

Paulo stopped halfway across the room. "Forgive my impertinence, My King, but are you all right?"

King Dion barked a laugh, though there was not even an inkling of humor in it. "If you were king of a kingdom that you had barely been coronated to and not four months later it was all falling apart in your hands because you killed your father for being a tyrannical ruler and saved your people, would you be all right?"

Paulo leaned against the back of one of the chairs across from the king. "No, I can't say I would be."

"No, I don't imagine many people would. Especially not with everything else."

"Your Majesty?"

King Dion clawed at his scalp with the tips of his fingers, freeing more of his hair from his queue. "It's not just rebels, is it? Denny is gone, taken only the Goddess knows where. Ev is in some Aigean prison somewhere, likely fuming and cursing every mer that crosses by his cell. He's going to get himself killed. Shaunie is feeling absolutely wretched, not even able to leave her bed. I haven't seen her all week, one of the midwives telling me she doesn't want to see me. What am I to do?"

Paulo came around the chair and sat. "How can I help?" He swallowed back the lump in his throat. It was alarming to see his king in such a state. To see the mighty man crumbling right in front of him.

"I need you to tell me the future. I need you to tell me if my kingdom is going to be taken by these blasted rebels or not. I need to know when they're going to attack. I need to know how to reach Denny and free Ev and help my wife have our child. I need to know the next step."

Nausea swirled in Paulo's gut, and he had to breathe for a few seconds before he could talk again. "I'm sorry. It doesn't work like that."

"Then make it work like that!" the king snapped. "You have a duty to this kingdom, cousin. You're Olympia's sole seer. What use are you if you can't keep tragedy from happening or even tell me what I need to do next. Sometimes, I wonder if the MacGregor gift actually died with your father."

Paulo rubbed at the warmth spreading up the back of his neck. "I'm sorry to be a disappointment, Sire."

"Then don't be." King Dion stood. "Get off the seat of your fancy pants and find me some cursed answers."

Paulo sat alone in the blue sitting room, his eyes focused on the small fissure he'd found on the ceiling. Some of the paper hadn't been glued properly when they'd decorated the room, and he could just see where the seam had come apart.

He didn't know how long he'd been sitting there.

It could have been hours or days.

No one came looking for him.

No one in the palace likely cared where he was.

Well, that wasn't completely accurate.

The king would come looking for him eventually, demanding something. Paulo couldn't even blame the man. Everything was falling to pieces, and Paulo wouldn't change it. Not for anything.

So, what was he to do? What could he give the king that would satisfy him? Just for a couple days more. Just long enough for Laurel to get out of that cell.

The king had ordered her trial next week, not wishing to deal with anything at the moment. He might even push it back again, wanting to get things settled before he went into something so serious. While King Dion could be emotional, he'd learned not to allow his emotions to make him a bad ruler. They'd had enough of those for generations.

But there was only so much a man could take.

Paulo closed his eyes, reaching for the strings of Fate once again.

He glided through them, not really touching any and simply letting his mind wander through Fate and Time. They really felt like two separate things sometimes. Both entities influencing the world, working together to weave experiences and a path forward for every person. He brushed against the strings of amber and green. Colors whirled around him, fabrics and faces blending together in a miasma of color and noise. A ball, from the looks of it, though Paulo had never seen anyone dance in such chaotic ways. He let go of that line and brushed the crimson one he found. Prince Evan paced in a cell. At least, it looked like pacing. His cerulean tail whipped back and forth angrily as he swam from one side of his cell to the other.

Paulo sighed, though if his body actually went through the motion, he didn't know. He was too far into the magic to know what was happening around him.

He pushed out of Prince Evan's string and moved on toward the peacock blue. He scanned the other colors, searching for it. There were so many strings that sometimes they got all mixed up. It also didn't help that he knew he was avoiding it. After seeing her death, after letting Donnie talk him into too many drinks, he'd avoided the queen's fate.

Light flickered to his left, and he turned his attention that way. A strand of fate flickered, going from white to peacock blue.

No, that wasn't right. The queen's fate had been sealed. He'd seen it. He'd seen her die.

Paulo hastily grabbed it, just before the place where it turned white.

The queen curls over her coverlet, her hands to her stomach.

"Your Majesty, you really should take this. It will make you feel better."

Paulo shot up from his chair.

He raced out of the room and sprinted for the king's study.

By the Goddess, the queen was getting poisoned.

But it had never been Laurel who would do it.

Sweet Gaia, why had he avoided looking deeper? He'd thought her death had been natural, but of course not. Of course, all the strings had been crossing. He'd been such a cursed idiot.

His boots slid on the polished hardwood as he skidded around the corner toward the king's study. Night was coming quickly to Olympia, the last vestiges of light coloring the sky before the sun finally left. Supper would likely come in less than an hour.

He stopped at the door to the study and knocked. He waited for half a second before realizing there weren't even guards outside the door.

The king wasn't in his study.

He was probably down in the dining hall.

Curses.

Paulo continued sprinting through the halls of the palace. Thankfully, no one barred his way, most of the palace likely having found their way to their own supper tables. When he got to the stairs, he flew down them, nearly twisting his ankle and breaking his neck. He slowed down, but only a bit. He needed to get to the king, but killing himself before he got there would gain them nothing.

He paused when he reached the bottom of the stairs. Guards stood at the doors to the royal dining room. The public dining hall sat on the floor beneath them. His Majesty must have wanted a semblance of privacy that evening. Paulo wouldn't look too far into why the king was avoiding his people. It benefited both of them that he had avoided it.

Approaching the doors, he nodded at the guards.

One of them turned to him. "The king is not to be disturbed."

Paulo froze. "Apologies, but this isn't something that can wait."

The guard stepped between him and the door. "The king has requested he not be bothered while he sups."

"See, that's not going to work." Paulo allowed his magic to layer the world around him. He grabbed the guard's blue surcoat and pulled him forward.

The guard twisted out of Paulo's grip and his companion reached for them.

Paulo used both of their momentums to duck and hook his foot on one of their ankles. As that man toppled, he took the other with him. They both rolled back to their feet, but Paulo had already accomplished his aim. He darted through the door.

The king looked up from his empty plate. "Polly?"

The guards crashed through the door after him. "Apologies, Your Majesty. We'll get rid of him."

King Dion raised a hand. "No, he can stay."

The guards exchanged a glance but filed out of the room.

"You could have been skewered," the king said as the door closed behind them.

"It was a risk worth taking." Paulo hastened to the end of the table. "I need you to come with me, Your Majesty."

King Dion frowned. "What's happened?"

"It's about the queen."

The king was out of his chair in a fraction of a heartbeat, his hands on his cane. His hair rose from his shoulders slightly, the first spark of emotion Paulo had seen from him in days. "What about the queen? Is she all right?"

Paulo took a deep breath and a step back. "No, Your Majesty, and if we don't get to her quickly, I don't know if she will be."

They rushed to the door.

No guards stood in the corridor.

Something in Paulo's gut sank, but the king was already racing toward the stairs. The man probably had a hundred pounds on Paulo, but he moved like a blasted deer through the palace. Paulo had to push himself to keep up, though not too close. Small sparks of electricity bounced off the king's hair and it was probably uncomfortable to be touched by one.

They reached the royal wing, and King Dion opened the top of his cane and touched the small rod sticking out of the top. His hair fell back around his shoulders as the energy of his magic was subverted into the cane.

"What am I walking into here, Polly?" he asked

"I'm not totally sure yet, Your Majesty. My vision led me to believe someone is poisoning the queen. For how long, I don't know, but I pray we aren't too late."

King Dion nodded. The top of his cane shut with a small click that echoed around the hallway.

Paulo looked about the hallway. *Where was everyone?*

They approached the queen's suite and the king knocked on the door.

"Shaunie? Are you in there?"

No one responded.

King Dion tried for the handle and found it locked. He reached into his tunic and cursed.

"Stand back," the king ordered.

Paulo took a very large step away from the door.

Electricity coalesced around the king, making the air around them heavy. His amethyst eyes glowed and his hair stuck out straight from his head. He lifted his hand, aiming toward the doorknob. A bolt of lightning flew from his palm, making a loud crack as the light hit the space between the door and the door jam. The door swung open a tiny bit, the door frame burnt in one section.

The king didn't wait. He pushed his magic into his cane once again and strode into the room.

Paulo debated following him in but decided not to leave his king unguarded. He allowed his magic to overlay his sight again and walked in.

King Dion had already made it to the queen's bedroom. Paulo strode through the suite, stopping in the now open doorway.

The king was on his knees on the side of the bed, his hand around the queen's.

The queen lay much in the same position that Paulo had seen in his vision. Her hair fanned about her. The blood on her gown.

The only thing that was different was the rise and fall of her chest.

"We need to get her out of here." Paulo grabbed a blanket off one of the chairs scattered around the room.

"Just leave me," the queen whispered. "I'm not going to last much longer anyway. Not after—" Her voice broke, and a keening cry wracked her body.

How long had she been like this? Where was her midwife? Her maid?

The king took the blanket from Paulo and wrapped it around his wife. "I am not going to leave you here." He wrapped an arm around her shoulders and one around her knees and hoisted her from the bed.

He turned to Paulo. "We need to get to the family sitting room."

46
THE SIEGE

Laurel will be sitting in the isolated cell when they come. Shadows will flicker under her door. A key will jingle on the other side. The door will burst open, and a flood of armored men will swoop in. One by one, guards will march her out. She will not go quietly. She will rip the wire from the lining of her trousers, and many of the guards will fall by her hands. They will have locked the cellblock. She finds a key.

LAUREL STARED AT THE LINE OF LIGHT UNDER THE DOOR.

If her mind calculated it correctly, supper would have started within the last hour. How long would Aspen wait to come get her? Would she even come?

The question stopped Laurel short. Of course, Aspen would come. They might be having a little tiff between them, but this mission was bigger than the both of them. Bigger than lies Teagan had been hissing in Aspen's ear. Bigger than whatever she was doing. Because as Laurel had mulled over their conversation over the past two days, she'd realized that something had been going on with Aspen. That the truth between them had grown sour with lies.

Laurel had to get to the bottom of it. Nine months was a long time to be away from someone. She'd grown in that time. So had Aspen. But had they grown up or apart?

The light under the door flickered just a bit.

Laurel got to her feet, rushing to stand against the wall next to the door. It would swing outward, but from where she was standing, someone would have to stick their head all the way into the room to see her.

The jingle of keys in the lock set her pulse thumping.

Aspen had come.

Well, probably. It could be a guard, but she doubted it. That didn't mean that she moved from her somewhat strategic position by the door though.

The light blossomed and a person that was surely not Aspen stepped through.

"Laurel?"

Her shoulders sagged at the sound of Luc's voice. She stepped into the light and his head snapped in her direction.

"Where's Aspen?" she asked

Luc stepped to the side, allowing her room to come more fully into the light. "By the Goddess, Laurel, you are rank!"

Laurel rolled her eyes. "Yes, that happens when you've been sitting in a dungeon for nearly five days. You didn't answer my question."

Luc shrugged. "She said she had something to do. She tossed me the keys with an order to let you out and set off."

Shaking her head, Laurel finally stepped out of the cell. While the air was exactly the same as it had been on the other side of the door, it felt lighter. The other prisoners watched her with serious envy, a few of them reaching out toward Luc who had the set of keys.

At the end of the row, two other men stood waiting, both with red fabric around their upper arms, white compasses embroidered there.

Luc tossed the keys to the men. "Let them out."

The roar behind Laurel was almost deafening.

Luc guided her out of the dungeon, coming up into the guard barracks. All was quiet in the corridor, though Laurel guessed that wouldn't last long.

"Where are we headed?" she asked.

"The rebels will start on the kitchens any minute. I recommend you sneak over there and get your gear then meet me in the grand hall. If Aspen hasn't arrived by then, you and I will help the rebels take the public dining hall before we attack the king."

"Isn't the king with the rest of the nobility?" He'd eaten in the main dining room since Prince Evan left. Probably seeking company while those closest to him disappeared one by one.

"No, he took supper in the royal dining room for some reason."

There was obviously something else going on. Laurel frowned. She just couldn't put her finger on it.

Ever since Aspen had bailed on going with Laurel to meet with Luc at the inn to talk about the riot, she'd been distant and aloof. She'd disappeared many of the nights, saying she was working on another project for the siege. What was it? Was she working on it even now?

Luc stopped at the fork between the main part of the palace and the rest of the servants' corridors. "Get your gear. I'll meet you in five minutes." He raced down the hall to the right.

Laurel took the one to the left. She did her best to do a

quick check at every corner, but no one crossed her path. Even during the slowest supper hours, there had always been servants bustling about. The empty halls felt like a tomb.

Even when she reached the servants' quarters, she heard nothing. She crept past silent doors until she reached the room she shared with Aspen. A small part of her hoped to find Aspen waiting for her, but the room was cold and empty when she opened the door.

Closing it behind her, she raced over to her bed where someone had laid out her gear. Her schola mask was still hidden in the cave tunnels on the cliffs, so she pulled her half mask on around her neck and clipped it to her hood. Next went her knives, a dozen in all. Two long daggers on the outside of either thigh. Four small throwing knives went into sheaths wrapped around her abdomen. She put two short daggers in the sheaths of her boots. Then the two smallest ones at the cuffs of her jacket. The last two went into a sheath at the small of her back which would be covered by her jacket.

She slipped the mask over her nose and strode out of the room. Hopefully, she would never have to look at the poor excuse for a room ever again. She turned a corner, reaching the corridor to the kitchens, and found her first semblance of life. Voices rang out from the kitchens. Voices she recognized.

When she reached the entrance, she had to stop.

Delilah stood in the middle of the kitchen, her hands on her hips as she looked over at Cook and Esther, both standing against the far wall, their chins high as they watched rebels move the other servants out of the palace.

There were others lingering on the edges of the room. Dan stood next to Galen near the counter and Jeannie cowered under her sink.

Delilah was speaking, her high-pitched voice ringing over the ruckus. "All of this is your fault," she said, thrusting a finger at Cook and Esther. "Firing me was a big mistake. Now, neither of you will leave this kitchen. I'll be the one in charge from here on out. You'll both report to me."

"Delilah!" Galen snapped. "What's wrong with you?"

Delilah whirled on him. "Oh, so now you're going to get all up on your high horse? You're as much to blame for this as they are. You helped me find the rebellion and then helped me get rid of Laurel."

By the Goddess, the woman really was drunk on her own power.

He shook his head. "I helped you find a job in that inn. I never wanted you to do something like this."

"Well, it's too late!" she fired at him. "Now, all of you will be doing my bidding."

Laurel had had quite enough from the little witch.

"All of you will be under my—"

The pommel of Laurel's dagger cracked against her temple and the girl fell like a sack of potatoes.

Galen gaped at her as she stepped over Delilah's prone form. She walked up to where Cook and Esther stood.

"Go," she ordered.

Neither woman questioned her, though Cook gave her arm a parting squeeze as she passed. Maybe Laurel's half mask wasn't as useful as she thought it was.

"How dare you!"

Laurel spun, watching as Galen leapt at her, a filet knife in hand.

Without thought, she drew her long dagger.

But Galen stopped, his mouth wide with shock. He dropped to his knees, revealing quiet Dan standing behind him, a bloodied butcher knife in hand.

Dan met her eyes. "For The Cartographer."

By the Goddess, the man had been part of the rebellion the

entire time? Laurel nearly gaped, but she gave him a swift nod and raced out the other door. There was a small hallway that subverted from the dining hall, coming out in the grand hall instead. She stopped, frozen as she took in the scene in front of her.

What had to be two or three dozen fae stood in the grand hall, each leashed to one another by iron chains. Men, women, children. There was no fae free from the iron that burned their skin and locked their magic. They were all in a state of anguish. The children's cheeks dirty and hollow. The women's hair cut away from their ears in jagged lines, their arms bruised. The men stood with open wounds, some still slowly dripping onto the floor.

By the Goddess, this was what she was fighting for?

"Laurel!"

She turned to find Luc coming toward her.

"You're late."

She couldn't even mumble an apology. Her eyes strayed to the fae being ushered out of the grand hall.

"Impressive, isn't it?"

Laurel couldn't even lie. She diverted the conversation instead. "Where's Aspen?"

"Here! I'm here!" Aspen came barreling through the door behind Laurel, blond hair stuck to her cheeks.

"Where have you been?" Laurel asked.

Aspen beamed and wiggled her fingers in front of her face dramatically. "All will be revealed in time."

Luc chuckled but Laurel didn't find it funny in the least. She shook her head. "What's our objective?"

Luc straightened. "We've set the rebels to taking out the public dining room. The guards have barricaded the door, but it won't be long before the rebels are able to get through."

"In the meantime," Aspen said, "we're going after the king."

"Where is he?" Laurel asked.

Aspen huffed a breath. "The silly man was in the royal dining room, but once I'd gotten rid of his guards, he'd disappeared. I figure he'll lock himself up in the royal sitting room before too long and we can simply take him there."

Luc nodded. "And the queen?"

Aspen smirked. "Taken care of already."

Laurel's gut twisted. "What does that mean?"

But Aspen ignored the question. "We need to get going."

Laurel grabbed her arm. "What happened to the queen?"

Aspen ripped her arm from Laurel's grip. "We don't have time for Saint Laurel right now."

"Then answer the question. There are several people in the queen's suite that don't deserve to be harmed." Queen Carnation's ladies-in-waiting. The maids. The young girls that always walked around the palace with bundles of dried lavender for the laundry. There were so many that could have stood in the way of Aspen and the queen.

"Sweet Gaia, no I didn't hurt anyone innocent! Can we go now?"

"Swear to me, Aspen."

"Great Goddess, I swear, all right. Now, do you know where the door to the royal sitting room is or not?"

Laurel watched Aspen's face. Her perturbation felt overly dramatic. Was she hiding something? Sweet Gaia, of course she was. She'd been hiding things from Laurel for weeks. But what?

Luc gave a little cough, and Laurel shook herself from her muddled thoughts. "It's actually on the far side of the palace. It'll be difficult to get into."

Aspen reached into the pocket of her jacket and pulled out

the box with the rowan tree. "That's what this little darling is for."

"Do we even know how to use it?" Laurel asked.

"Luc gave it back to me a few days ago and I've been practicing," Aspen said. "All we have to do it pop it open and the enchantment goes active. No magic within a hundred-foot radius works as long as the box is open."

"Great!" Luc chirped. "Lead the way, Laurel."

Laurel shook her head. "What's the plan once we get there? What if we encounter guards on the way? I know there are at least two stationed in the royal sitting room at all times along with another man, though I have no idea what role he plays. I've only seen him once in all the time I've been in the palace."

"We can cross that bridge when we get there." Luc grabbed Aspen's hand. "Let's go!"

Aspen giggled as she followed behind him, their steps practically bouncing as they ran toward the residential wing of the palace.

Laurel was slower to leave, her eyes scanning the faces of the fae being led away.

She spotted a head of matted brown hair being shoved through a door.

By the Goddess, it was the little fae boy she'd seen the night of the raid. Where were his parents? His family?

"Laurel?" Aspen asked. "What are you doing?"

She shook her head and turned away. "Nothing."

47

AN UNFORTUNATE COLLISION

Paulo set his hand on the king's shoulder. "Wait," he whispered.

The king paused before going around the corner. "What?"

Paulo pushed ahead of him, crouching as he approached the intersection in the hallway. When he peeked around the corner, he saw what his magic had revealed to him. Two rebels stood at the end of the hallway, blocking the door to the royal sitting room. At their feet lay a body.

Oh, poor Dexter.

While the man was a complete and utter blackguard, Paulo wouldn't have wished him dead. Not like this, at least.

He crept back to where the king waited, watching their backs. "Your Majesty, I need to make you aware of another situation."

"Spit it out, Polly."

Paulo sucked in a large breath. "The rebels are attempting to take the palace. There are two at the end of the hall, guarding the doors to the royal sitting room. If you allow me, I can take care of the guards to allow you and the queen through."

King Dion's amethyst eyes narrowed. "There are rebels in my blasted palace?"

Paulo couldn't meet his eyes as he nodded.

"And you've known all along, haven't you?" The king scoffed. "While I'm most hesitant to even allow you to remain standing there, I need you to take the queen."

"Sire?"

King Dion pressed forward, gently setting the queen in Paulo's arms. Her face had grown ashen. She'd lost consciousness on the way, but she still breathed. *For now.* He looked into the queen's fate, but it was so muddled with possibilities his head started spinning.

The king kissed her temple. He pointed at the floor. "You will stand right here. If you move even an inch before I say, you will regret it."

Without waiting for a response, the king walked forward, his cane bouncing against his back as he strode toward the intersection and disappeared around the corner. A shout went up.

Blue light crackled along the wall, filling the hallway.

The shouts turned into screams.

There was a loud popping sound.

The light disappeared as quickly as it had come. Even the magelights that had lit the corridor had gone out.

The king came back around the corner, the strands of his hair back around his shoulders, though tendrils of smoke curled from their ends. He held out his hands and Paulo gently eased the unconscious queen back into her husband's arms. Paulo's chest ached as he saw the king's expression crack the smallest bit. Even for all his infidelity, the man loved his wife.

Those amethyst eyes moved to Paulo. "Clear the hallway."

Paulo gave a sharp nod and strode toward the intersection. When he came around the corner, he found Dexter's body a few feet closer to the intersection. The rebels, however, were gone except for the mangled remains of their swords on the ground and scorch marks on the floor.

Sweet Gaia.

"It's clear," he called back to the king. He stopped at the door to the royal sitting room and stared at the blank door. When the king got close, he gestured at the knob-less door. "Where's the handle?"

The king adjusted the queen in his arms and brushed his arm over the wood of the door. It opened and he pushed through.

Paulo slipped in right behind him, closing the door quickly and waiting to hear it lock. He didn't hear anything, but the king spoke.

"No one but the royal family can get in without express permission. The only one who has that is the royal seneschal and the healer."

"Your father was quite the paranoid king."

King Dion stopped at a fainting couch set against one wall. "My grandfather was the one who had it built, though he died only a few weeks before its completion." He set the queen down and knelt at her side.

The king brushed strands of her hair away from her face then got to his feet. He strode across the room, shedding his fine blue jacket and rolling up his shirtsleeves. He banged on a piece of wall next to the fireplace. Three hits. Then four. Then one.

Before Paulo could speak, a hidden door opened near the fireplace. Two guards and another man stepped through. The guards wore the regular garb of palace guards, though each of them boasted the brooch of an oak tree on their uniforms. The man, though, had no such regalia. He was a simple man, middle-aged, with kind gray eyes. Eyes that scanned the room quickly, flicking from the king to the queen to Paulo.

The king didn't even look up at the new arrivals as he returned to Queen Carnation's side. "Ashton, I need you to care for the queen."

The man stepped past the guards, eyeing Paulo as he did. "What's happened, Your Majesty?"

"Polly," the king called. "Explain."

Paulo stepped forward, facing the man. "I believe the queen has been being poisoned, sir. I receive visions, you see—"

"You don't need to explain every cursed detail, Polly. Just tell the man what he needs to know so he can help her."

"I saw a bottle of poison." He stuttered as he tried to recall all the details he could think of. "Uh, dark blue. I know someone from the Continent had access to the queen. I know the, uh, the queen might have started being poisoned any time after the solstice until now. I imagine with the pregnancy, it's heightened the effects of the poison."

"The Continent you say?" Ashton asked. "I know a great many poisons from that region of the world, but only one with that color. Stellataen Arrow is not a poison to be taken lightly, and it is only used by the assassins of Stellatus Hall."

The king turned. "Are you saying this isn't simply some poisoning by the rebels, but that an infamous assassin guild from another country has set their sights on killing my wife?"

Ashton knelt beside the king. "I can't say for certain, Your Majesty, but most questions are often answered by the simplest means." He laid a hand on the queen's fingers draped over her stomach. He closed his eyes as golden tendrils of magic, almost like the strings of Fate Paulo saw with his own gift, worked their way over the queen's body.

Ashton sucked in a breath. "I'm glad you got her to me quickly. The poison had almost reached her heart." All the golden strands coalesced over the queen's chest.

"Can you heal her?" the king asked.

Ashton opened his eyes, rubbing the heel of his hand against his chest. "It isn't only the poison that is killing her. The loss of the child in her womb in addition to the poison is causing her organs to shut down. She's on the precipice of death, Your Majesty, and my job at all costs is to ensure the royal bloodline continues."

"She is my wife!" the king roared. "She is the royal bloodline."

Ashton laid a hand on the king's shoulder. "You're right, but that doesn't mean I can risk using my gifts on her at this moment. I've stopped the poison for a couple hours, and I swear I will finish my work once she's safe. Let's get both of you out of the palace."

The king let out a shaky breath and stood. "We'll use the portal."

"The portal?" Paulo parroted, feeling very out of the loop—which was not normal for him.

Ashton gathered the queen in his arms. He gently cradled her head against his chest with his chin and hoisted her off the couch. He was stronger than Paulo had given him credit for, as he easily brought the queen to where King Dion stood beside a tapestry.

The king grabbed the fabric and pulled it from the wall. The hooks broke from the mortar and the heavy tapestry fell to the ground, revealing a swirling, black hole in the wall. The king turned to the guards.

"One of you is to go through the portal first to assess the situation on the other side. If you do not return to the palace in two minutes, we'll break the magic of the portal and find another way out."

One of the guards stepped forward and bowed. "I'll go, Your Majesty."

King Dion nodded, and the man stepped through.

Paulo joined the group of them. "How are you proposing we escape the palace if the rebels have taken it?"

The king's nostrils flared. "As someone who didn't even know there would be rebels in the palace this evening, I propose that someone who *did* know make the first suggestion. Hint, Polly, that's you."

Paulo bowed low. "Your Majesty, I—"

"Save your apologies for when I actually require them. Right now, I need to know the best way to get my wife out of danger and somewhere safe where she can recover from the poison that's even now trying to kill her."

The guard arrived back through the portal. "The safe house is clear, Your Majesty."

King Dion pointed to the guards. "You will act as frontline and as rearguard. We'll proceed in a line as follows: Ani first, then Ashton and the queen, myself, Lord MacGregor, then Alex. When you clear the portal, make sure to take several steps away to allow the next person to pass through unimpeded."

The guards saluted the king and lined up in position. The first guard passed through, then Ashton carrying the queen.

Magic flared across Paulo's vision.

"Wait!" He pulled Dion back, who had just barely stuck his arm through.

The next second, the portal blinked out of existence.

"*What the devil are you playing at?*" the king roared.

The door behind them swung open.

Aspen stepped into the room, an open box in her hands. "Hello there."

The king straightened. "Aspen?" His amethyst eyes narrowed. "You are a bold one."

Aspen chuckled. "That's a compliment coming from you." She stepped more fully through the door. "This is a lovely room."

Two more shadows swept in behind her.

Paulo watched the second one, her wide brown eyes meeting his before flicking between Aspen and the king.

The king pulled his cane back over his head. "I imagine you three are the assassins from the Continent I've heard so much about. Tell me, is the weather just so terrible you had to come look for a new home? Or was The Cartographer paying you a small fortune to take a palace that no one really cares about."

Aspen's expression remained smug, but Paulo saw the small flare of surprise in her eyes.

"We've come to take more than just your palace," the man next to Aspen said. "We've come to take your head as well."

48

THE KING

Laurel will march forward, Aspen right behind her. Without his magic, the king will be defenseless. Paulo will attempt to reason with her, but reason does not break through her cold exterior. Laurel fights against the king as Aspen holds Paulo back. It is over within seconds. The king is dead.

FINALLY.

Finally, Laurel was in the same room as the king. She was actually going to be able to complete this mission and get off this cursed island. She could forget about fae slave children and the war and the contention between her and Aspen. She could go home, get both their contracts, and sail far from this cursed life.

But the king wasn't going to go down easy.

And neither was Paulo.

The nobleman stood beside his king, his expression pensive but stalwart. He always had to come between her and the king, didn't he? Why couldn't he have run like all the other nobles? Why did he have to be in her way every time?

Luc took another step forward, but Aspen stopped him, eyeing the guard that had also taken a step between them and the king. "There will be plenty of time for that in a moment. I want to make sure our king understands exactly what's happening here." She set the small box down on the table. "See this? It's an enchanted relic—"

"I know what it is," the king snapped. "It's how you got it out of my brother's office that I have questions about."

"Oh, I've got quite the knack for breaking into things I'm not supposed to."

The king's eyes narrowed to dangerous slits. "Yes, like an enemy king's bed, right?"

Luc sucked in a breath from beside Aspen, but he kept quiet.

Laurel couldn't even breathe.

But Aspen wasn't phased. "It was just *so easy*. I knew I could do it the moment the little undercook showed up at the inn I was staying in, talking all about her precious king and how he loved her above all the other women he snuck around with. About how much he hated the woman he actually ended up marrying. See, I knew it would be so easy to get close to you because you are an absolute failure as a king with no regard for his kingdom. You go through life like you go through women, without thought or care. It is your fault that all this is happening."

She turned and gave Laurel a smile that looked twisted on her face. "I did my job, now it's time to do yours."

Laurel stared at her. She'd seduced the king? Aspen? The girl who had painted the walls of their bedroom in different colors and wrote her favorite quotes from songs all over them. The girl who had only ever been devoted to Luc since she was fourteen. Who hated eating *pastitsio* because she didn't like tomato sauce. Who had snuck into Laurel's bed more times than Laurel could count simply because she liked being with her.

The girl standing in front of Laurel looked like her sister, but she couldn't be.

What else had Aspen done?

"Oh, don't give me that look, Laurel. You needed the king, so I made sure I could get him. This way, you can keep up your little farce that you're the perfect little assassin. You'll have to thank me later."

Laurel blinked and looked up at the king. His amethyst eyes narrowed on her.

"Laurel? The undercook my wife took such a liking to?" He barked a laugh. "Wow. Adira Durant really knows how to pick the most deceiving people on the planet."

She couldn't say why, but the king's words struck Laurel in a way she didn't like. There was a tightness in her chest. In her throat. She ignored the sensation and drew her dagger.

Paulo stepped between everyone. "Listen here, all of you. This rebellion isn't what you think it is." He met her eyes. "Adira Durant is a murderess and a liar. Whatever promises she's made, she's made with the intention of breaking them. She doesn't do anything for anyone else, only what will help her get where she wants to go."

"Whatever she's paying you," the king said, "I can double it."

Aspen laughed. "The two of you really don't get how this works."

"I know exactly how it works," Paulo said, taking a step toward Laurel. "I know there's good in your Order, in the way you operate. There's honor. Where is the honor in following a woman that killed other women who fell for a man she wanted for herself? What honor is there in helping someone who steals children from their beds and wraps them in chains? This war is only going to end in blood and anguish."

She could see it in his eyes. The things he'd seen. Those visions he couldn't speak about. War was bloody. It was always bloody.

"Unfortunately, story time is going to have to be cut short." Aspen sighed. "Your little parlor trick visions will have to wait."

Paulo's blue eyes narrowed dangerously. "You really don't understand what is going on here, but you will. You'll realize the mistakes you're making. The honor you've blatantly spit on has teeth, and when it bites, it takes more than just a chunk of flesh with it. Not even the silver mask you wear will hide you."

"Laurel, please shut him up, will you?"

But Laurel didn't move. She stared at Aspen instead. "What mask, Aspen?"

Aspen groaned. "Of course, your little lordling had to go and ruin the surprise. I was going to tell you I'd been sworn into the scholae eventually, but I wanted it to be the right time, you know? I didn't want to worry about making you jealous or anything. I know I'm progressing faster than you, and I didn't want to make you mad."

"You think I was going to be mad that you were a schola?" Laurel seriously didn't understand how everything had devolved so quickly. That her sister had somehow gotten her hands on a schola mask and didn't know Laurel already had one. Of course, Laurel hadn't told Aspen, trying to protect her from the things the scholae did. How had everything— all the trials and stress and little white lies— simply meant nothing? To anyone?

"Of course, I thought you'd be mad. I know you think I'm some kid, but I've worked hard to get here. Teagan even told me I'm one of the youngest members. I didn't want you to feel like I'm surpassing you or anything."

"Why would I think that?"

Luc stepped between them. "Is this really the time for the two of you to deal with your family issues?"

Aspen shook her head. "Sorry. You're absolutely right." She let out a breath. "Now, Lord MacGregor, if you stay right in that corner, I can promise that no harm will come to you. You aren't the one we're here for, and I know Laurel would be somewhat sad that I had to kill you— though, she does understand her duty, so I can't promise she'll be sad for very long."

Paulo straightened. "As someone who actually understands your sister and knows what she's been through, I know that she would eventually move past me and fight for what she really wants."

Aspen flicked her hair over her shoulder. "Kill the king, Laurel, and we can all go home."

Laurel met Paulo's gaze.

She'd seen that look in his eyes. That knowing. He knew exactly how this war ended. He knew every step all of them took. He could see the outcome and he'd seen the rebellion lose.

That was why he was doing all of this.

He'd already seen their downfall.

Those blue eyes spoke to her. She knew he'd seen her in all of it. He'd said so himself, hadn't he? He'd been telling her this entire time that she could trust him. But she'd thought it was only a matter of trust that he would have her best interest at heart. While that might have been a part of it, it wasn't all of it. Not in the least.

He was the puppet master. The man who controlled everything, even the fierce king standing behind him. Even The Cartographer.

But what was the endgame?

"Laurel," Paulo said. He looked over her shoulder.

She spun, finding Luc standing right behind her.

He tilted his head to the side, his face scrunched in empathy. "Sorry, old friend, but I can't let you take out the king."

His fist whipped toward her face.

Laurel hadn't sparred with Luc in several months, but the man had always been more strength than speed.

"Luc!" Aspen shouted.

Laurel's body took over before her mind could. She ducked low, grabbing his arm as it soared over her head. Without thought, she spun him around, twisting his arm until his shoulder popped out of its socket.

Aspen gasped. "Laurel! Both of you, knock it off!"

The pain caught up to Luc and he hissed. He grunted and popped his joint back into place, but his focus remained on Laurel. He drew a knife, sending it spiraling toward the king.

By the Goddess, Luc was meant to be her replacement. Teagan had made true on his promise. If Laurel couldn't get the job done, he would send someone else.

Luckily, the king had a brain in his head, and he leapt to the side, hiding behind a couch. His guard engaged Aspen then, swinging his sword. Aspen used her long dagger to counter the attack.

But Laurel couldn't watch her sister anymore. Luc recovered from his miss and drew his long dagger, headed in the direction of the king.

Laurel hooked her foot around his ankle, taking them both to the ground.

Luc roared as he landed on his now severely injured shoulder and flipped around to get to his feet. Laurel used his momentum to bring him back down and positioned herself on top of him.

He tried to grab for her hands, but she punched him in the nose.

"How much did he offer you?"

Luc laughed. "You think you're the only one who cares about Aspen? He promised me her cursed contract, and I'm going to get it so she doesn't have to go with you. So that she can stay and make her own decisions."

She punched him again. "If you think that place deserves Aspen, you're as cracked as Teagan."

"She definitely doesn't deserve to have you drag her from the people she loves. That's why I also signed to drag you back to Stellatus Hall, free of charge." Luc shoved his hips up, making Laurel catch herself. He grabbed one of her arms, pinning her to him and rolled.

Laurel kept her legs locked around him as he stood. She curled herself up, grabbing his head in her hands and headbutting him in the face.

He staggered back and she dropped. However, she wasn't prepared when he grabbed the low table next to them and smashed it into her side. She fell to the floor, the left side of her body screaming.

Aspen cursed and Laurel looked her way. Blood bloomed along her arm. The guard came up with another swing of his sword, but she caught it in the cross guard of her dagger.

"I really don't like you," she spat in his face. She dropped her hold on the long dagger. The guard stumbled forward, and she spun, drawing another knife. This, she slammed into the side of the guard's neck

"Alex!" the king cried out. He grabbed one of the other canes lining the wall, wielding one in each hand as his guard went down.

Laurel got to her feet. Luc was three strides ahead of her.

"Stop!" Aspen hollered.

Laurel looked up and saw Paulo making his way across the room, going straight for the box.

But Luc jumped in the direction of the king. The two of them locked weapons.

Laurel took one step in their direction.

"I said stop!" Aspen screamed, her blue eyes narrowed on Paulo. The man was only a few steps away from where the box sat on the table but he didn't stop.

Aspen drew one of her throwing knives.

And she threw it.

49
AN UNFORTUNATE CHOICE

PAULO CLOSED HIS EYES.

Without his magic, he couldn't see how to dodge the blade.

He'd been so close to getting his magic back.

He couldn't see what making that move would look like or what repercussions it would have.

If he dodged it, would it ricochet off the wall behind him and hit Laurel? The king? Would Laurel pause before she could stop Luc from hurting the king?

There were too many variables. Too many ways it could go.

Without his magic, he was a sitting duck.

He heard the knife hit.

Odd.

He didn't feel it.

It must be the shock.

He opened his eyes, finding the tip of the knife hovering not an inch from his eye.

Blood dripped off the edge.

"Paulo?"

He blinked and looked up. Laurel stood next to him, her face turned toward her sister and the knife in her hand.

He looked over at Aspen, her arm still extended from the throw.

"I'd gotten faster!" she raged.

"You have." Laurel straightened and flicked her wrist. The bloody knife dug into the floorboards next to Paulo's knee. "But I've always been the one who took the risks. I was the one who was willing to stay up late with the masters. I was the one who focused on my training. I was the one who became the one to beat and remained unbeatable. You say you're one of the youngest scholae. Well, I'm the one you didn't beat. You think you're on track to be the best, but Aspen, you've always been the talent. The girl who could throw knives without training and was praised by every master you came across. But I was the skill. I was the one who you were never going to beat because I was always one step ahead of you, even if it looked like I wasn't."

Aspen gaped. "You're a schola?"

"No, I'm *the* schola. Why Teagan decided he could give you a mask when he has absolutely no authority over my sect or my mask maker, I will certainly be discussing with him when I return."

She flicked her hand, and another dagger went sailing across the room, hitting Luc in the back of the leg.

The assassin stumbled, allowing the king to get his hands on him.

King Dion met Paulo's eye. "The box!"

Paulo turned back and snapped the lid closed on the box.

Visions slammed into him.

Laurel battling Aspen, stabbing her in the chest with the guard's sword.

Luc grabbing the knife from his leg and slamming it into the king's throat.

Blinding white light.

Paulo pulling Laurel through the portal.

Paulo cradling her still form in his arms, her neck at a wrong angle.

Both of them lying side by side, blood pooling around them.

He snapped out of the visions, allowing his magic to overlay the room around him. Without another thought, he clicked the clasp shut on the box and threw it at Luc. It knocked into the assassin's hand, which was attempting to pull out the blade. The box landed next to King Dion's feet.

Luc roared in pain.

But it gave the king just enough time.

Paulo leaped forward, tackling Laurel to the ground before she got halfway to her sister. He tucked her under him, and light exploded over the room.

Aspen screamed.

But not as loud as Luc did.

Then his screams cut off.

Every hair on Paulo's body stood at attention and it felt like the very sun itself had burst into the room. He kept his eyes closed, but it didn't help. The light still burned his eyes no matter how hard he clenched them shut.

Laurel's hand grabbed his where he'd wrapped them around her waist, but she didn't shove him away. She held him there, as if she wanted him to stay there.

And he would. For as long as she would let him.

The crackling in the room stopped abruptly, the light going with it. It couldn't have lasted more than a few seconds, but it had felt like an eternity. The pressure in the room decreased and Paulo's ears popped.

He rolled off Laurel, allowing her to get to her feet. Hopefully, he had shielded her from the worst of it and she would recover the fastest.

He opened his eyes, but he could barely make out anything in the room. He attempted to blink away the black spots.

A keening cry pierced the air.

"LUC!"

Paulo looked in the direction of the sound and found Laurel prowling toward her sister.

"Kill him, Laurel! Kill him right now, or by the Goddess, I will!"

Paulo pushed himself to his feet. He found where the king stood, his breaths heaving as he stared down at a spot on the ground.

The stones under the floorboards glowed white. Even the enchanted box that had laid near the king's feet had been incinerated.

He raced toward the king and grabbed him, pulling him in the direction of the portal. Praise the Goddess he had dispelled the energy in his body before Paulo did. There would have been one more victim to the king's wrath.

He stopped close to the portal, which was once again swirling. Ani, the other guard, came through, sword drawn.

Paulo pushed the king in the guard's direction. "Go. Now."

The king shook his head, grabbing Paulo's forearm. "You need to leave too."

Paulo pulled away. "I can't leave her." He turned away from the king, trusting the guard to do his duty and get his king to safety.

"Laurel! He's getting away! KILL HIM!"

Laurel sank into a crouch in front of Aspen, who was crawling toward the portal.

Aspen finally stilled, looking up at her sister.

Paulo took a step forward. The visions he saw could still

come to pass. He wouldn't leave her here, though. He would face whatever came at Laurel's side.

But her hand shot out, telling him to stay where he was.

Aspen's face twisted in unhinged ferocity. "You're letting him get away."

Laurel shook her head, a quick back and forth once. "No, I'm letting you go."

Aspen shot to her feet, her hand on the knife at her waist. "Excuse me?"

Laurel didn't even stand, but simply looked up at her. "You have acted abominably, Aspen. The scholae are an order of directness. Of honor— the only cursed sect in Stellatus Hall to do so. *I am watchful. I am focused. I am silent.* You have proven yourself to be none of those things."

"*How dare you!*"

"How dare I? You broke every code the scholae live by, even going so far as to impersonate one."

"Teagan *gave* me that mask. I *earned*—"

"You earned *nothing*! Teagan is a lying snake who will twist the truth any which way he wants in order to convince others to do what he wants." Laurel finally stood. "He has no control over the scholae. I do. I am Master Schola, and I am the only one who decides who wears a mask. You are not a schola."

"Even now, even after I have the mask, you can't see that I deserve this!" Aspen drew her knife.

Paulo allowed his magic to flood the room once again, watching. Waiting.

Aspen's chest heaved. "Why didn't you even tell me? I figure you would have thrown this thing in my face just like everything else. No matter what I do, you always have to be one step ahead. You always have to be the favorite."

Laurel's gloves creaked as she clenched her fingers. "Even if it wasn't a rule of the scholae, I wouldn't have told you. You were never supposed to know."

"So, you stand there and judge me because I did my cursed job— because I did it in a way that's different than Saint Laurel's way— and yet you've been the liar all along? You've been the one who's been sneaking around and keeping secrets? I knew you were a phony, but I didn't realize what an absolute hypocrite you were." She shook her head. "I can't believe I ever thought you cared about me."

Laurel took a step closer. "I do care—"

Aspen raised her knife.

Paulo was already there, pulling Laurel back a step.

Aspen's brown eyes flicked over to him. "At least she was right about you. You're far more dangerous than I gave you credit for."

"Aspen—"

Aspen's eyes flicked back to Laurel, cutting off her words with a glare. "You need to leave."

Laurel shook her arm free of Paulo's grip. "I'm not leaving. I love you and I'm here for you."

Paulo pulled her back again as Aspen's knife slashed between them.

"I HATE YOU!" she screamed. "I hate you so much it's tearing a hole in my chest. You're a *liar*. You're not here for me at all! If you were, you would have killed the blasted king and come back to Stellatus Hall. You would have never hurt Luc. You would have let me become a schola because you love me. But you *don't*. No, all you want is to run away from our life, from everything that we've built together. You want to abandon *everyone* for some silly fairytale. Well fine! Go! If you don't leave, I'm going to kill you and your precious marquess and everyone in this cursed palace!"

Paulo's magic flared.

Laurel, lying on the ground at Aspen's feet.

Paulo grabbed her arm again. "Laurel."

She turned to him, her eyes wide with a mixture of fear and sadness and fury. "Knock it off, Paulo."

He let the future play out again before his eyes before he pulled her away. "We need to go."

Laurel's whole body stilled. She saw the truth in his expression.

She wouldn't kill her sister, but right now, Aspen would stop at nothing to kill her.

Laurel turned back, meeting Aspen's darkening expression. "Get. Out."

Paulo yanked her toward the portal. By the Goddess, if she fought him, he would throw her over his shoulder and deal with her anger about it after.

But Laurel didn't fight him this time.

She let him pull her along.

"I'll be waiting for you, Aspen. I'll still be here when you're ready for the truth."

With a scream, Aspen threw another knife.

Paulo saw it happen three seconds before Aspen drew her arm back.

He pulled Laurel and twisted at the same time. He caught the knife before it sailed through the portal and hit the king on the other side, as he'd seen.

Not even a scratch marred his fingers.

He tossed it onto the ground between them.

"Your sister might not be willing to kill you, but if you ever attack her again, I won't hesitate to."

Before anyone else could say a word, he swept Laurel through the portal.

50
THE BETRAYAL

Laurel will come through the portal, knives out.

LAUREL'S HEAD CRACKED AGAINST THE ROUGH BRICKS OF THE WALL AS she was shoved against it.

"Close the portal!" the king snapped, his amethyst eyes not leaving her face as he made the order.

The guards set to work, scrubbing a marking from the wall beside it.

"There's not time!" Paulo snapped. He grabbed one of the guard's swords and slashed through the marking.

The portal flashed once, then disappeared.

Laurel closed her eyes and leaned her head back against the wall.

The king shook her. "Don't ignore me, assassin. I can fry you to dust in a heartbeat like I did your comrade back there."

Laurel opened her eyes, but kept her mouth shut. Luc hadn't been her comrade in the end, had he? She couldn't believe he'd betrayed her like that. That he hadn't at least given her the common decency to know they were in competition. They'd been friends for years. For what felt like lifetimes.

And in a blink of an eye, he was gone.

Laurel snapped.

She headbutted the king, sending him staggering back. He'd killed one of the only people on this earth that had treated her like family. Yes, he'd betrayed her, but could she blame him? What he'd done, he'd done for Aspen. No matter how misguided it was.

The king growled, blood dripping from his nose. "You dare strike a king?"

She drew a blade from the sheaths at her back. "You're not my king."

"Stop. Stop. Stop." Paulo came between them. "Fighting is going to get us nowhere."

The king shoved at him. "Don't get in the way, Polly. The girl is an assassin sent to bring my kingdom to ruin."

Paulo tried to get between them again, but this time it was Laurel who shoved him back.

"Let him attack me. I can kill him before he can zap me. Then, I can leave this blasted island and never see any of your faces again."

The king growled.

Another voice spoke. "Both of you need to pull your heads out of your rear ends and come up with a plan to get us all out of here before we all die."

Paulo and the king turned to look behind them.

Laurel met the eyes of the queen. Her face was sallow, though her blue eyes sparked with tired defiance.

The king visibly sagged. "Shaunie." He stumbled to her, taking her face in his hands.

The queen closed her eyes, allowing the king to hold her for one blissful moment.

Laurel felt like she should look away, but she couldn't. Had she ever seen such adoration? Such relief? By the Goddess, how much the two of them must trust each other was astounding.

The queen pulled away first. "There will be time for this later. We aren't out of danger yet." She situated the blanket on her lap, though only by just a little. She looked as frail as a bird.

A jolt went through Laurel.

She'd been poisoned.

Laurel recognized the signs. The yellow tinge to her skin from liver failure. The dark circles under her eyes. The sick sag of her skin from weight lost too fast.

The queen had been poisoned and Stellataen Arrow had done it.

How was she still alive?

"Paulo," the king said, turning to him, "the time for play is over. Your deception has gone too far, and your kingdom needs you to be serious now."

Paulo bowed. "I'm your humble servant, Your Majesty."

Laurel had never seen the man so solemn. She watched him as he approached the royal couple, shoulders straight and gait sure. How had she mistaken him for a fool for so long?

She recalled his words to Aspen as they left.

Your sister might not be willing to kill you, but if you ever attack her again, I won't hesitate to.

While the thought of Paulo attacking Aspen twisted her stomach, something in her chest, something deep within her, felt at ease. How long had it been since someone had thought about her as something to protect? While he might have threatened Aspen, he acknowledged Laurel's wishes first.

He trusted her.

That feeling in her chest grew.

Could she actually trust him in return?

Paulo kneeled down by the queen. "What would you have me do?"

Queen Carnation's face grew more serious, her blue eyes calculating. "We need help. Who do we go to that we can trust? We all need to recover, and while I would suggest we all go to Delphine, I believe the rebels will attack there first, considering they know you helped us."

"You are wise, my queen. It's smart for us to split up anyway. I will take Laurel to Delphine for now and keep an eye on her." Paulo looked up to her. Was he asking for her approval? Even now? After everything? She gave a slow nod, just one dip of her chin. He reciprocated and his eyes turned the pearlescent color as he turned back to the queen. "It's likely best that you go to the Hermen's."

"And you're sure they won't betray us?" King Dion asked.

Paulo's lips turned up slightly. "I know they won't betray you. Not to ruin anything, but your youngest brother recruited them to work for the Underworld ages ago."

The king slapped his leg. "Sweet Gaia, I should have known. Lord Hermen always knew way more than he should have."

The queen looked at her husband. "You didn't know?"

"Of course I didn't know! I can't keep track of all the people my brother bamboozles into working for him. Stone Hermen. Blast it all."

Paulo blinked away the magic in his eyes, returning to his normal blue. "Yes, the Hermens are your best shot. They'll be a resource to you and in a few short months, you will be a resource to them as well."

"Don't go back to being vague, Polly," the king growled.

Laurel took a step forward, but the guard gave her a very firm shake of his head. She stilled. While she would go to Paulo's defense, she didn't need to start a fight where there wasn't one. Not when she was trying to prove she was on their side. Sort of.

She still needed to kill the king if she wanted to get off this island.

But how would she accomplish that now that so many people knew?

And did she really want to?

Paulo brushed a hand through his hair. "Apologies. Old habits. If you go to the Hermens, Lady Delmar will find you quicker, as she works closely with Lord Hermen. You'll also be some of the first to hear about what's going on in Faerie, as Angelica Elie will reach out to her family at the first possible moment. While the Hermens are situated near the Black River in Eleusia, due to the nature of their business, they have fortifications in place to guard against invasion that not many other estates do."

The Hermens sounded like a regular warlord family.

"I think you're right," the queen said. She looked to the king. "What does the safehouse have that can help us?"

"Where even are we?" Laurel asked.

The king sent her a scathing look. "I don't think assassins get to speak right now."

She raised her hands, taking a step back.

Paulo stood. "We're in the mountains guarding Olympia, right?"

The king nodded. "If you walk up the path behind the cabin, you'll see the city."

"Come, Laurel." Paulo carefully grabbed her arm, pulling her toward the door. "Let's go get an idea of where we are."

Laurel looked back to the king and queen again as they watched her. Their faces were haggard, hair wild and eyes hollow. She'd done that. Well, she'd helped do that. Would they have a moments rest from then on? Would they ever see her as more than the assassin that tried to kill them?

She shook her head. "Let's go."

She let Paulo pull her out of the room and into a hallway. The house might not have been a palace, but it wasn't a hut either. The floor was solid under her boots and paintings hung on the wall. The hallway ended at a small landing that gave a view of the floor below. She marched slowly down the stairs, watching her step in the cold darkness that had seized the house. Obviously, no one had made it through to light any fires, not that they would. It might be best for them to hide their presence there.

Paulo stilled at the bottom of the stairs for a moment before he turned. "The path starts at the back of the house."

"How do you know?"

He shrugged. "Trial and error. I watched us find it by going around the house, but now we can cut out that time and just go that way instead."

"Your magic is frightening sometimes."

"But it's also efficient."

They walked out the back door of the house. The cold mountain air seized her the moment they stepped outside, sending goosebumps pebbling all over her skin.

Paulo dropped her arm and pointed ahead. "There's a rise just there."

Laurel walked that way, slowing her steps. If it was to keep pace with Paulo or to avoid finding out what they would see when they got to the top, she couldn't decide.

But they made it to the top.

And Laurel gasped.

The entire city spread out before them, alight with fire and magic. The rebels weren't just taking the palace, but the entire city. Buildings were awash in flames. Colors of magic clashed in the streets.

But the palace drew her eye.

A large dome glittered over the whole of it, only allowing its tallest turrets to peek through the top. A shield. The rebels had put a magic shield over the palace.

How were they to take it back?

How would she ever get Aspen back?

"I'm sorry, Laurel."

She turned to him. "What?"

He blew out a breath. "I'm sorry for everything that's happened."

"You can't apologize for the actions of others."

"I could have warned you."

"But you did." She stopped in the middle of the path. "When you came to me, drunker than a cursed skunk, you told me. You warned me not to trust Luc. You told me the queen was being poisoned. You told me to choose the knife instead of going after Luc. You have been warning me at every turn. Why? Why are you trying to help me? Why do I matter so much to you?"

Paulo sucked in a large breath. "I told you before. I saw you. I've seen you for years."

"That doesn't—"

He raised a hand, silencing her. "Let me finish."

She clamped her mouth shut.

"I was eight the first time I saw you, but I didn't see you as a seven-year-old. I saw you about the age you are now. I saw you fighting on the side of the rebellion. I saw you kill the king."

"So, you stopped me?"

"No. I stopped what came after." He took a deep breath. "You killed the king, but Teagan was still working with The

Cartographer. He asked you to help him with a couple of things. You refused, but he had already asked Aspen and the two of you had to wait for her geases to be met before she could leave with you. So, you stayed."

"Of course I did."

"But then you realized what was wrong with the rebellion. You saw what they were doing. You saw how they were torturing the fae and you realized it was wrong. One night, you decided to sneak into the palace and free some of the slaves there."

Laurel's stomach sank. "I betrayed them?" Of course she did. She'd only scratched the surface on what the rebellion was doing. By the Goddess, she'd already thought that they were in the wrong. She wouldn't have been able to help herself.

"You freed slaves, Laurel, but eventually you were caught." He ran a hand through his unruly curls. "Over the years, it shifted. How you went about trying to save the slaves changed, but every time, you were found out."

"What happened, Paulo?"

He took a shaky breath, something Laurel felt in her core. "You died, Laurel. Every single time, you died."

"So, you decided to get involved? To keep me from dying?"

"Yes, Laurel. Every move I've made, every future I've altered has been to save you."

She turned to him fully. "Why? I'm no one to you."

"See, I've been trying to tell you this whole time." He wiped a hand down his face. "You are *everything* to me."

Laurel's chest tightened. "I don't understand, Paulo."

"I know, but I hope to help you see, to help you trust me enough to truly show you." He held out his hand. "Come to Delphine with me. Give me a chance. Let me help you find your freedom. Let me help you seize your future and fight your fate."

She stared at his proffered hand.

Could she? Could she go with this man who had deceived so many? Who switched masks like he changed clothes? Who had always had the upper hand in every way? Her instincts screamed at her to run. To leave all this behind and lay low until she could figure out how to get to Aspen and how to cancel the geas.

But her hand betrayed her.

She settled it in Paulo's warm palm.

And the doubts in her mind went silent.

EPILOGUE
AN UNFORTUNATE FUTURE

PAULO LOOKED UP AT THE WINDOW ONCE AGAIN, THE STARS ABOVE HIM sparkling with laughter. Of course they should laugh. All of this was his fault. His lies. His wants. His desires. All of it.

He sighed and looked down at the pages he'd written. Those months in the palace. The visions. All of it glared up at him, condemning him for every sin he'd ever committed. He could feel the words freshly tattooed on his heart, raw and bleeding.

> *And so, you see, none of it matters. Nothing I did changed the future that I saw. Fate had decided and it was futile to ever think I could beat Her at Her own game. That I could change anything.*

A single tear hit the back of his hand, and he pushed himself away from the desk, keeping his emotion from marring the paper. He couldn't write that again. Every word was a cut to his soul. His shame ran deep.

I know you'll believe what I did was out of love for you. But every push I gave you, every time I told you something, it was never for your own benefit. Even though you've received the greatest of joys, none of this was for you. All of it was for her and her alone.

His fingers clawed at his breast pocket. He was almost surprised to find it wasn't wet with blood from the gaping hole left in his chest. It felt like it should be. Mater had said the grief would lessen, that it would transform from this ugly thing into something beautiful. She told him there was joy in such pain, because it meant that the love he felt had truly meant something. That it wasn't a figment of his imagination like Laurel had thought it was in the beginning.

But it didn't mean anything. If it had, he wouldn't be sitting here, writing this cursed letter as one last hope to make it all better. This one last chance.

He set the pen to the bottom of the page, his words coming out as jagged as he felt.

None of what I did mattered, because I still lost her. She still died in my arms and there wasn't anything I could do to save her.

AUTHOR'S NOTE

Paulo's story has been something I've thought about since I finished writing *The Spring Maiden* over three years ago. When I was researching Apollo, I couldn't help but be moved by the tragedies he and Artemis faced throughout their lives. From being born in the middle of nowhere to facing monsters at young ages then overcoming tragedy after tragedy as they grew, my thoughts were with them often as I wrote Paulo and Diana's characters. Zeus and Leto's twins were loved, but with the adoration of many came fierce scorn from others.

So, I started sewing in tiny pieces of Paulo's story from the very beginning of The Cartographer's War. I saw where his story intertwined so much with Penny's, and I knew I had to tell it. From the moment he appeared in Barclay Manor, I knew he had a story worth telling.

And I knew Laurel had a place in it too.

Her character came to me while I was writing *The Unwanted Queen*. I knew Paulo would need someone that could keep up with him, someone who would see right through him. While I was writing this book, I discovered how absolutely incredible Laurel actually is. Because of her, I had to rewrite the first half of this book. She isn't a girl driven by emotion or one who runs from things she doesn't understand. She has a quick mind and a deep heart and doing her justice was very important to me. I can't tell you how many times I hit the Backspace muttering, "Freaking Laurel." It became somewhat of a tagline with my writers' group.

Both Paulo and Laurel have a big role to play in the coming collision between the rebellion and the Kingdom of Olympia. This battle is about far more than just a mad woman trying to take over a kingdom. It's about people who love each other and how that love can change even the darkest of fates.

I really can't wait for you to see what happens next.

ACKNOWLEDGMENTS

This particular list of acknowledgements is going to start a little differently than my other books and it's all Kate Ward's fault.

Thank you, Kate, for telling Tanya Anne Crosby about this story while you guys were in that meeting. I totally lied. I didn't have any intentions about actually pitching her these books until I had finished the other series, but I think you were right, and this piece of the story needed to be told now. I also discovered that I can write a 120k-word book in two months, so I guess I should also thank you for the huge boost to my already inflated ego. And thank you, Tanya, for listening to Kate's insane idea and for being such a champion of this book. It obviously wouldn't have come into existence without your excitement about it.

I also want to thank my family. Thank you for putting up with writer-goblin-mom for two straight months while we were supposed to be on summer break. Thank you, Eric, for making sure the biohazardous waste in the kitchen sink was regularly washed out. And a huge thank you to my kiddos who didn't burn the house down while I was working. Seriously, your patience with me was saintly and I really couldn't do any of this without you.

I would also like to give a big shout out to Chris and Martin Kratt for filming twenty-two seasons of *Wild Kratts* for my kids to watch while I wrote this beast of a book. I'm so glad that my kids now know so much about Pileated Woodpeckers and Sockeye Salmon. I couldn't have written this book without your help.

I need to thank my writers' groups as well. Thank you to my first group, OSAWG, and our glorious members— Dad (yes, this book is also your fault), Ben Bailey, Aimee Hall, Jared Jensen, Tracy Tyler, Marci Johnson, and Robbie Stufflebeam. I know I didn't go to any of the meetings while I was bleeding out on my keyboard, but I'm so grateful for your support and for your check-in texts. I promise to be a little more present in our future Zoom calls. I also want to thank my Third Thursday group— HR Boyd, Bonnie Jo Pierson, Kayla Tillotson, Tarry Perry, Amber Marcusen, Nat Kraus, KayLynn Flanders, and an extra special thank you Kelsey Larson and Lindsay Hiller who told me I actually could write this book even though it was scary and hard and who also said I really did need to rewrite that first half. And I could never forget Sally O'Keef. Seriously, her and her magic editing machete have saved my books three times over.

And as tradition must continue, Tyleah Merino will likely get her own paragraph in every single one of my books. Thank you for always reading my stories at their worst and telling me they're better than the last. Thank you for crying at the end of this book and for taking all my ridiculous phone calls when I'm trying to get a story figured out. You're seriously my favorite.

I would also like to thank Jeff Wheeler. People tell you not to meet your heroes, but I did, and I couldn't be more grateful. I know I was meant to find your books all those years ago and I thank my lucky stars every day that I did. I wouldn't be where I am now without your continued support of me and these books.

And thank you, Cauldron Press Designs, for another

gorgeous cover. It seriously turned out beautifully. I can't believe you did it again.

Last, but certainly not least, I need to thank my Heavenly Father. I said a lot of prayers while writing this book and You answered every single one of them.

While the rebellion has taken Olympia's capital, the story is far from over.

Continue reading for a snippet of the first chapter of
The Unwanted Queen
The Cartographer's War Book 5
Coming January 2025

CHAPTER ONE
AGONY AND FORTITUDE

Pain ripped through Penny— a living, breathing monster raging inside of her. The magic scraped its scorching claws through Penny's body, and she screamed.

Or at least she thought she screamed. There wasn't noise wherever she was. Only pain.

Always pain.

She bucked against it, hoping, praying, begging the Goddess to make the magic let go of her. It only sunk in its roots. The well of plant magic within her broke apart, drowned in the burning, clawing, ravaging monster beating down her defenses. Devouring everything inside of her.

But all of this had to be worth it. Something deeply buried underneath the pain and the magic held her resolve. There was a purpose to this pain, this agony.

A flash of amber streaked through the waves of green and hurt.

There was a reason she had subjected herself to this seemingly endless torment. If only she could remember what it was...

"By the Goddess, I tried to get back to you. I had dreamed up so many adventures..."

"Do you want to know something funny? There hasn't been a day since we met when I didn't think of you. Did you..."

"I need you to be all right."

"Please, Penelope."

"Just open your eyes."

ALSO BY ALLISON ANDERSON

Children of Ash

Children of Ash

Son of Steel

The Cartographer's War

The Spring Maiden

The Shadow Lord

The Unseen King

The Unwanted Queen

The Cartographer's War: A Necessary Tragedy

The Seer's Assassin

The Fated Mage

ABOUT THE AUTHOR

Allison Anderson lives her best life as a wife, a mom, a dedicated member of The Church of Jesus Christ of Latter-Day Saints, and a fantasy writer. As a lifelong fantasy nerd, she finds it natural to create stories of her own and you can often find her jotting down new story ideas or talking about dragons. She's spent most of her life across the southwestern United States.

https://www.allisonandersonauthor.com/

    X